Andie Newton is the *USA Today* bestselling author of *A Child for the Reich*, *The Girls from the Beach*, *The Girl from Vichy*, and *The Girl I Left Behind*. She lives in the beautiful Pacific Northwest with her family. When she's not writing gritty war stories about women, you can usually find her trail-running in the desert and stopping to pet every Yellow Lab or Golden Retriever that crosses her path. Andie is actively involved with the reading and writing community on social media.

X x.com/AndieNewton
f facebook.com/AndieNewtonAuthorPage
O instagram.com/andienewtonauthor
BB bookbub.com/authors/Andie-Newton

Also by Andie Newton

A Child for the Reich

THE SECRET PIANIST

ANDIE NEWTON

One More Chapter
a division of HarperCollins*Publishers*
1 London Bridge Street
London SE1 9GF
www.harpercollins.co.uk
HarperCollins*Publishers*
Macken House, 39/40 Mayor Street Upper,
Dublin 1, D01 C9W8, Ireland

This paperback edition 2024
First published in Great Britain in ebook format
by HarperCollins*Publishers* 2024

1

A catalogue record of this book is available from the British Library

ISBN: 978-0-00-854199-6

Printed and bound in the UK using 100% Renewable Electricity
by CPI Group (UK) Ltd

For Matt, Zane, and Drew

Prologue

Somewhere over France

The pilot had been trained to fly his RAF Whitley over enemy territory at night, memorizing the bends of the French coastline, the railways, and the location of the villages, while trying to avoid German emplacements. He was prepared for almost everything that night except for a change in the weather. Thick clouds blanketed the moon, dangerously concealing the cliffs along the shore and threatening not only the crew's lives but the fifty special agents he was ordered to drop over Belgium.

It didn't take long before the pilot had flown off course, lost above enemy territory with only a vague idea of where they were when anti-aircraft fire popped against the fuselage. *Tink, tink, tink, tink...*

As the pilot struggled to keep his crew alive and the aircraft steady in the air, he got annoyed with himself for even flying at all. Why was he taking such risks for pigeons?

Pigeons indeed.

He'd had quite the discussion with his supervisor about the birds before he'd taken off from the airfield at Newmarket. Nobody at the Air Ministry thought messenger pigeons would win the war. Nobody. He'd heard the few pigeons that survived previous missions had flown back with hand-drawn cartoons and personal messages to family, but no hard, usable intelligence. Definitely not information that was worth his life or his crew's, he'd decided.

He shouted to one of the crewmen in the back. "Dump the cargo!"

"But we don't know where we are, sir!" he answered.

"We're turning around," the pilot said, hands white as chalk gripping the yoke, "and I'm not taking those birds back up again! Dump the bloody things!" A barrage of enemy bullets punched holes in the wing. "Now!" he barked.

The crewman pushed the pigeons out of the plane as the enemy fired—all fifty of them, individually packaged in tiny bird boxes with parachutes like agents of war.

"Rest in peace, you poor little buggers," he said as they spiraled toward their doom.

Northern France

April 1944

Chapter One

Every step I took down the rickety old stairs sounded like knuckles cracking in the silence of the night. I winced, wondering if my neighbors could hear across the road, but it was freezing and the warmest shawl I had was downstairs. I tried to walk a little softer, squeezing behind my piano and pulling the shawl by the collar from the back of the chair.

I often wished for an electric heater on these cold coastal nights, but we couldn't afford electricity for heat every night, especially in April.

I slipped the shawl over my shoulders, trying to remember when I'd bought it new—that corner shop in Paris on Boul'Mich. I felt a small thread of comfort remembering the life that once was, running my hands up and down my arms for warmth and feeling the cottony yarn when the front door snapped open and closed.

My eyes sprung open. Outside air breezed over the black lumps of furniture, prickling my cheeks. My heart sped up, hearing the soft pad of footsteps move across the shadowy parquet floor and down the old cellar stairs.

My sister Simone was asleep upstairs, and Martine would never be so delicate—she didn't know how to tiptoe—and that's what scared me. We'd had intruders before; bad French who knew there wasn't a man in the house must have come back to steal whatever jewels the Germans had yet to take.

That's what everyone called the collaborators—bad French. The good French kept to themselves and would never do business with a German.

I lit a candle, walking the few steps through the main salon to the cellar.

A crash under the floor shook me with a gasp—glass and falling crates. I followed the noise with my eyes, knowing whoever it was had walked the length of the house to the coal chute before stomping back over to the stairs, making their way up. *Thump, thump, thump…*

I set the candle down, reaching for Martine's beloved porcelain vase, the only thing big enough to crack a skull. She'd be angry when she found out that's what I used, and as I lifted the vase, I regretted not having enough time to search for something else.

Six steps left—five, four, three, two…

I grunted, flinging my arms over my head to get enough momentum as Martine threw open the cellar door, screaming at the sight of me. "Ack!" She covered her head with her arms. "What are you doing?"

I collapsed against the wall, nearly dropping the vase. "Me?" I asked. "What are *you* doing? I thought you were an intruder."

"I asked you first." Martine watched me struggle against

the wall, trying to breathe after the scare, before noticing what was in my hands. "And my vase?" She took it gingerly from my fingers to carefully set it back on the side table. "Gaby, how could you?"

"I'm sorry. It was the only thing—" I stood straight, noticing her dirty fingernails in a flick of light, and a smear of dirt on her cheek. "What are you up to?" I glanced once at the cellar door, then back to Martine. "What's down there?"

"No, don't!" she said when I reached for the doorknob, and if there was one thing I knew about my little sister, it was that when she asked me not to do something, it usually meant she was hiding something.

"What are you up to?"

She crossed her arms. "Nothing."

"Something," I said, reaching for the doorknob again, but she threw her back up against the door. "You've been at the cliffs again, haven't you?"

She chewed her thumbnail.

"Are you hiding a boy?" My eyes narrowed, and she shook her head, but I didn't believe her, not with how vigorously she was chewing on that thumbnail. "You know what the penalty is for keeping a boy from the factories?"

"It's not that." She pulled her thumb from her teeth. "And nobody saw me," she added, making my stomach swirl like a pot of cold soup. She *had* done something, and I was immediately reminded of when we'd fled from Paris and why. I covered my mouth. "Don't do that, Gaby. Don't make that face."

A lorry rumbled down our road, and we both turned toward the front door. In the dark, in the night, in occupied France, we'd been trained to know the difference between a

7

lost lorry and a German one on a mission. The engine glugged instead of hummed, and the speed was recklessly fast followed by a lurching stop. Doors opened and closed and mounting footsteps walked the pavement in heavy boots.

"Two," she breathed, and I shushed her. "Three…"

"Four," I said, before pulling back the curtains. "They're speaking with Antoinette." I saw shadows and our neighbor holding a candle as she stepped out into the night, lighting up her face and her fast-moving lips. After a brief conversation with her shaking her head, she pointed an accusing finger at our home. I gasped, turning around, the curtains fluttering closed behind me. "She's sending them here."

Martine squinted. "*That* woman. I swear she—"

"Martine!" I said, my heart racing with the sound of their jackboots headed to my front door. "What did you do? Tell me." But she refused to answer, and instead chewed her thumbnail again and watched the door.

Knock! Knock!

"You're the best at talking to them, Gaby," she said, and I glared. "Just don't let them go into the cellar."

"I might never forgive you for this."

"You will," she said. "One day." She dusted the traces of dirt away from her face with hurried swipes. "Go on. Answer it."

I closed my eyes briefly, gripping the doorknob. "Coming," I said a moment before answering the door.

Three Germans in double-breasted coats and pointy hats stood before me, and while I wondered how I could have gotten the number wrong—four when there were only three—the last German appeared from behind. The others parted, making way for him, and I understood that meant he was in charge.

"Gabriella Cotillard?" he asked, and I shivered, hearing my full name read aloud by a German.

"Yes." I examined his strange uniform. They weren't SS, soldiers, or the police, and that was even more troubling. "Who are you?" I rewrapped my shawl, standing in the chilly open doorway with the faint flick of candlelight dancing over his shiny buttons.

"Pardon us this evening," he said in French, but I knew not to trust him despite his politeness, his smile, and the smooth way he spoke our language. I wouldn't dare tell him I understood German. "However, we believe you have something that belongs to us."

"We have nothing that belongs to you," I said.

"Yes, of course." He motioned with his head for the others to walk in and they pushed past us both, forcing me and Martine to stand flush against the wall.

"We did nothing wrong!" Martine piped. "What gives you the right—"

"Martine," I said to quiet her, and she pressed her lips together.

"Excuse my sister's outburst," I said, trying to sound civil amidst the wailing alarms going off inside of me, a warning of what I already knew: the enemy was in our home. I felt my chest.

"Turn the lights on," he said.

"But it's almost ten," I said. "We'll get fined."

"Turn them on," he said, motioning with a curl of his fingers.

I flipped the light switch, and Martine and I instantly

covered our eyes from the brightness of the salon lit up in yellow, not accustomed to using electric light at night. "I have a right to know why you're here, do I not?" I asked, squinting, as the others looked behind chairs and opened my kitchen cupboards. "If my neighbor sent you, told you something, I'll have you know she's known to make false claims."

"Is that right?" he asked.

"It is right," I said.

"Your documents," he said, holding his hand out.

I heard the Germans circling my piano while my back was turned, the clunk of their boots against my floor feeling like hands grabbing at my limbs. I pulled our documents from our handbags.

"Who plays the piano?" He'd given back Martine's documents after a quick glance but was now examining mine, tilting my photo in the light. "Is it you?" His eyes flicked up when I didn't answer. "The piano?"

"I don't play anymore."

"And you two are sisters?" he questioned, studying the stark difference between me and Martine, her light hair on a petite frame, cut bluntly near her shoulders, compared to mine, which was brown and wavy and pulled delicately back with a few silver clips—we couldn't look more different. Aunt Blanche said we might have different fathers, but our mother died of fever when we were children and we had nobody else to ask.

"Yes, we are sisters," I said, and he finally handed me my documents.

The Germans sat down at my piano, opening the lid and plunking a few keys. My neck turned warm—forced to watch and forced to listen. They had no idea what kind of instrument they were dealing with. It was the piano I learned on with my aunt as my teacher, right up to the day I was accepted into the Paris Conservatory.

"God, enough! You're awful," he said to his men, and the brief wave of relief I felt as they abandoned the piano was replaced by utter panic when they became interested in the cellar door.

Martine batted my hand to act, to say something. We'd fashioned it to look like a closet, complete with a wardrobe of hanging jackets. They'd only know about the stairs behind if they crawled through the jackets.

"Well!" I said, throwing my hands up in the air before swinging open the door. "Want to see our closet, too?" I asked, pointing a finger inside. "Better yet, want to buy a jacket?" I motioned to the old jackets we had hanging on the dowel. "We run a seamstress shop in the village and use the extra fabric for altering clothes because of the rations."

Martine smiled, chest puffed from a sudden intake of air, knowing I had outwitted them by opening the door first as the officer scanned the empty top shelf and the space below the jackets. Nothing to see but the floorboards.

"Seamstress shop? Is it near the harbor?" He had a questioning look on his face, probably trying to place us among the black ribbon shops. "And you have a ribbon?"

"No," I said, yet he seemed unaffected by this and motioned for his men to leave. A black ribbon was the unofficial sign that a shop welcomed, if not catered specifically, to the Germans.

I followed him out, but he stopped to touch the wall that separated the main salon from my aunt's private apartment. He gave it a press, testing the wall's strength.

"Odd to have a division here, isn't it?" His eyes skirted over the wall.

"I... Ah..." I straightened, trying to recapture the upper hand I had seconds ago when they were on their way out, but it slipped effortlessly away. If he'd gone around the back, he'd see the apartment had its own entrance too, but I wasn't about to admit the truth—that our home had been completely split in two from when it was a boarding school, and my aunt had been dead for six months. Vacant apartments were supposed to be declared. It was a wonder Antoinette had never found out. She'd reported on us for just about everything except the truth.

"And you are the only two who live here?" he asked, looking at me over his shoulder. "In this large home? Detached, too, when there are so many row houses on this street."

Simone burst through the front door before I could reply, startling me more than anyone else because I thought she was asleep upstairs. My mouth gaped open when I saw her dancing shoes, and I moved to block her from the Germans, keep their eyes on her face and not those shoes peeking out from under her long coat. She tucked a blonde curl behind her ear.

"Another sister?" the officer asked, and I nodded, waiting for him to question us further about the private apartment, but instead he motioned for his men to leave for good this time.

"Now, I believe you wanted to know who we were?" He patted his pockets from his breast to his trousers, pulling out a simple white card with his name on it. "Commandant Streicher. German Abwehr."

"Abwehr?" I took the card with a furrowed brow. I'd never heard of the Abwehr before. "Who—"

"We hunt spies." He took one glancing look at my sisters standing behind me before walking out the door and into the dead of night.

"Spies?" I turned off the lights and shut the door. "At our house?"

Martine paced the foyer with the candlelight flickering over her shirt and women's trousers. "The nerve of that woman next door. One day she'll get what's coming to her." She pointed in the air. "One day!"

"Who's in the cellar, Martine?" I asked, which drew a gasp from Simone.

"Someone's in the cellar?"

Martine stopped pacing. "It's not a who," she said. "It's a what."

I stepped toward her. "What do you mean?" *Another scheme*, I thought. Another one of her ridiculous plans that would never get off the ground, ending with one of us getting caught. In Paris, she had an idea to stuff rags into the Reich's tailpipes, and when that didn't work, she'd hatched a bad plan to poison their gin at the brasseries. "Why do I have a feeling this is another one of your dangerous ideas?"

It was true, we were already breaking the law by keeping our aunt's death a secret, but it was necessary in order to give Mme. Leroux our aunt's ration coupons for her sick boy. At most, I thought we'd pay a fine when they found out, which was what I told my sisters and what made them agree; it was definitely not a crime that should warrant a search by Germans looking for spies.

Martine paced again, and Simone and I reached for the doorknob at the same time—whatever she had down there was going to cost us more than a fine.

"Don't," Martine said, blocking us. "Let me tell you the story first." Martine swiped her fringe back, and Simone and I gave up the door to listen. "I was at the sea cliffs."

"So, you *were* at the cliffs," I said. "Nothing good has ever happened at those cliffs, and we've talked about the danger. The German patrols, the bunkers... the... the..."

"Let me finish!" Martine closed her eyes briefly. "I was at the sea cliffs, as I said, and there's a cave there, you know the one. It's where I—" She coughed into her fist.

"You met a boy there, didn't you?" Simone asked, and Martine stomped her foot.

"Can I finish, please? Would you rather we talk about your shoes and where you've been?"

Simone shook her head. Dancing was forbidden—only the *résistants* and the communists didn't seem to care—and she'd have to explain herself, but now was not the time.

"I thought so." Martine pushed her sleeves up. "As I said *twice* already, I was at the sea cliffs, minding my own business, and I heard this plane. It was flying low and I knew it wasn't a German plane because I know these things." I rolled my eyes because Martine thought she knew everything. "It flew off, and the next thing I heard was this popping noise—*puh, puh, puh.*"

"What was it?" I asked.

Martine threw a finger at Antoinette's house. "She sent those Germans here. They didn't come because they saw me. I believe it. And we can do something with this. Something extraordinary. Something..." She took a deep breath through her nose before opening the cellar door. "Stay here." She pushed the jackets aside and disappeared into the cellar.

I rubbed the back of my neck. "If she's brought a boy back

14

here destined for a factory, I'll... I'll..." I let out a heavy breath and Simone reached for me.

"She wouldn't," she said, delicately, then our eyes met.

"She would," we both said, and we peered through the open door, and down into the cellar where it was pitch black.

Martine came back up with her hands behind her back.

"Now," Martine said. "Don't scream." She moved her hands out, showing us a plump little bird in her palms.

I blinked once.

"Well?" Martine pushed him at us, and his wings flapped wildly, scaring us both into screams too loud for the night.

"Shh!" Martine rasped. "What's wrong with you two? It's a bird. He's nice. Here, pet him." She pushed him at us again, and Simone leaned in.

"I didn't expect a bird." Simone stroked the bird's head after some coaxing from Martine, sliding her hand down the back of his smooth neck. "I bet his skin will crisp right up like a chicken's."

"No!" Martine said, pulling the bird away, and a poof of feathers floated up between us. "We're not frying him!"

"We can stew him," Simone said, which made my mouth water. "I have a bottle of wine under my bed, and there's just enough left to add to his juices and make a nice brown sauce." She clutched at her stomach over her coat.

"Mmm..." we both said, and Martine looked horrified, face stretching.

"He's not to eat," Martine said. "This is the spy the Germans were looking for."

I scoffed. "The pigeon's the spy?"

She nodded incessantly. "You've heard the stories. The secret pigeons from Britain."

"Those stories aren't real," I said. "They're made up."

"This is a messenger pigeon," she said. "He came in a box with a parachute, all very English in how he was packaged, including instructions for care."

"A parachute?" I laughed and Martine's face turned the color of a tomato with the candlelight flickering on her cheeks. She marched back downstairs into the dark with the bird. "Wait! Martine," I said, but she'd already stuffed the bird back into the coal chute where she'd evidently made him a nest and was pounding her way back up.

"You didn't have to laugh," Martine said. "I wasn't even going to show you until tomorrow. That... That..."—she flicked her chin toward Antoinette's house—"miserable neighbor of ours ruined it." She let out an angry huff, then looked us up and down, waiting for us to say something. "Well, are we going to do it?"

"Do what?" we both asked.

She couldn't be thinking what I thought she was thinking, but then again this *was* Martine.

"Spy on the Germans of course," she said.

"Keep your voice down!" I tossed up the curtains, making sure our neighbors were in their homes. Everything appeared to be normal. "Do you want to get us arrested?"

"Fate brought this pigeon to us," Martine said. "It's a way to get back at the Germans. A way to help!"

"You're mad, Martine. Fate—a way to get back," I said. "A way to get killed, you mean."

"This isn't like my other ideas," Martine said. "Besides, I know we can outsmart them."

"Outsmart the Reich?" I said, not sure if I should laugh or cry. "Listen to yourself."

"Gaby!" Her mouth hung open for a moment. "You opened the cellar door and they couldn't see the stairs beyond the jackets. They're like turkeys in the rain."

I shook my head.

"You always think my schemes are impractical, that they'd never work," Martine said. "I'll admit that stuffing rags into their tailpipes wasn't thought out, but this pigeon has physically flown into our lives—sent from the British—it must work!"

I folded my arms. "But it's so risky." I knew Martine needed this. She craved revenge daily, and I'd always been able to talk her out of it, pointing out that her schemes were sure to fail against the Germans and their resources. "I need some time to think before I can agree."

"Well, what does Simone think?" Martine asked and Simone's eyes shifted to mine.

"I'd rather eat him," she said, but when Martine pressed her lips, Simone quickly added, "but it depends on what Gaby decides."

Martine slapped her thighs with frustration but she'd have to wait for my decision. It had been our pact since we fled Paris. All three or none.

There was a knock on our door, and we peeped through the curtains to see Antoinette.

"What's she doing here?" I whispered, though I shouldn't have been surprised, not after she'd sent the Abwehr to our doorstep. She'd want to know about their visit—figure out what new fact she could exploit—and she still had a few minutes to do it before curfew.

"Don't answer it," Martine hissed, but how could I not? She knew we were home, and it would look suspicious if I didn't.

"I have to," I said, and Martine huffed.

Antoinette turned Martine in to the police once, saying she was a man dressed as a woman since she liked to wear trousers. Only the police didn't believe Martine's documents, and she was forced to prove she was a female in some other way. She never told us how, and she never forgave Antoinette.

"Be civil," I said, as if she would be.

I patted my hair back, tucking in all the strays, before answering the door. "Hallo, Antoinette," I said. "Is there something wrong? It's late." I had smiled, but purposely changed my face to look more concerned as she shivered in her blue housecoat on my doorstep.

"I thought I'd check on you." She stood on her tiptoes to look over my shoulder, trying to get a good look inside, scrunching her nose. "I worry about you girls."

"We're ladies to you," Martine shouted from behind me, and Antoinette's feet fell flat. "Go home, Marie Antoinette."

"What did she call me?" Antoinette questioned, eyes squinting, and I shook my head as if I didn't know, though it was Martine's favorite nickname to call her. "I saw the Germans on your doorstep."

"I saw them on yours first," I said, which drew a giggle from Martine.

Antoinette threw her voice over my shoulder. "I wouldn't laugh about a visit from the Abwehr."

"I wasn't laughing at the Abwehr," Martine said back.

Antoinette's mouth hung open before shivering again from the coastal sea breeze, but I wasn't about to ask her in.

I smiled, and she cleared her throat.

"Did the Germans tell you why they were on our road?" she asked.

"No," I said. "Did they tell you?"

She handed me a folded piece of paper from her pocket, a plea from the Germans to turn over any pigeons in exchange for a reward. Martine leaned in, reading over my shoulder.

"Pigeons?" I asked, playing dumb.

"Oh, they are a nuisance—droppings, disease, and pillaged gardens," she said, her lips pruning, "but even more so when they carry information to the British."

Martine and I exchanged a shift of eyes. *Bad French*. As if we needed confirmation—Antoinette was one of them. If only her soldier husband was alive to see her now; fought his heart out defending the Maginot Line was the rumor.

I handed her back the paper. "It's late, Antoinette." I moved to close the door when she poked her head in.

"Do give my regards to your aunt. I haven't seen her in months. Is Blanche feeling well?" Her eyes roved over my foyer.

"Why would you ask?"

"Why wouldn't I ask?" she countered. "She's my neighbor."

With that, Simone took a step toward the door, and Martine too. There were only so many questions from Antoinette we'd allow.

She turned to leave but then spoke back up. "Oh, I should tell you one more thing. I'm doing some remodeling in my garden, adding a chicken coop so I can have eggs of my own. I've got a fine hen coming to me, maybe two. I hope she won't cause you any issues."

"Only if you give us some eggs," Martine said.

Antoinette smirked, and I closed the door, resting my back up against it.

"She knows something," Simone said, just as I thought the same.

"She doesn't know anything," Martine said.

I glanced around the room in the flickering candlelight, looking at all the things the Germans had disturbed. My piano with the bench pulled out and the lid still flipped up, displaying the keys they'd had their dirty fingers on. "I want to go back, before the Germans—"

"We can never go back," Martine said, turning on her heel and walking upstairs.

Chapter Two

I woke before the sun broke and padded downstairs in my socks, thinking the entire evening before had been a dream, before coldly eyeing the piano where the German's fingers had been. I held my stomach, pausing with that thought, and then did something I swore I'd never do since returning to Boulogne-sur-Mer.

I turned on my heel for the bureau and deliberately pulled my sheet music from a drawer.

God… I smelled the crackling pages, inhaling the papery, dusty scent from being left untouched in a drawer for months. It was what remained of my first and only composition, written with heart and sweat and passion in our tiny apartment when I was enrolled at the Paris Conservatory. Professor Caron told me it would transform the way we thought about music, and that pianists would study my methods for years to come. "It is," the professor had said when I first played it, "a masterpiece."

"Gaby!" Martine said, and I fell into the upholstered chair

behind me, shocked breathless and holding the sheet music to my chest. She stole a pointed look at the music.

"Ah… I didn't hear you," I said, scrambling to shove it back into the bottom drawer and pretending I hadn't reached in to begin with. I swiped my hands together after turning around as if I'd just tidied up. "Good morning. How'd you sleep?"

She watched me pour a cup of hot water from the kettle, and she was still watching me when I sat down at the kitchen table, stuffing sprigs of dried tarragon into the tea strainer.

"Well?" She slid into a kitchen chair, slamming her elbows on the table and making me jump with a spill of my tea. "What did you decide?"

I blotted the tea up with a rag.

"About what?" I asked.

She let out a breathy sigh. "About the pigeon."

"Martine, I…" I started to say, and she immediately slumped forward from my tone and look. "Why can't we cook it? We could all use some extra meat, and Simone's always hungry."

She collapsed on the table, arms spread, and groaning.

"I know this means a lot to you, but we don't have any secret information to pass on," I said, the tea strainer skimming the side of my cup as I swirled it around, waiting for the water to turn. "We're seamstresses in a seaside village."

Her head popped up. "Near a secret German U-boat pen," she said.

I let go of the tea strainer.

"I told you this scheme was different."

She got up to pour her own cup of tea, and toast a slice of bread, leaving me to think about what she'd said. Our shop had a direct view of the German U-boat pen next to the harbor, hidden under bushes and shrubs. Only a few small vessels served as obstacles from our vantage point, but they were usually out at sea.

Martine spread lard on her toast, scraping her knife back and forth over the burnt bits. "I'm sure the British would like to know what's hiding under those shrubs. And what about the Reich's oil facility? If they knew about it the RAF would have bombed it already." She sat down with her plate. "Admit it, Gaby. This scheme could work."

I turned away at first, but she was right. This scheme was different than all her others. "I admit it." She slapped the table, clinking and clanging the dishes, and causing me to spill my tea again. "Stop doing that."

"You won't regret it! I've been thinking of this for so many months, how to get back at them, what to do—I can't wait." She squinted, fist clenching. "They deserve it for what they've done to us."

"Wait a minute, Martine. I haven't said yes."

"What do you mean, you haven't said yes?" She sat board-straight in her chair. "I heard you."

"I only admitted that this scheme was different," I said.

Her shoulders dropped.

"Martine, what if they dismiss what we have to say, think it's a German message meant to fool them? We'd be risking our lives if someone saw us, and they could be tossing the message in the bin."

"What's the matter with you?" she asked. "After all you've lost."

"Others have lost more," I said, realizing I'd opened the door for such a conversation when she saw me with my music.

"Martine, why can't you understand I need more than one night to think about this? The risks are too great. This is different than giving rations away." It looked like she'd finally accepted that I needed more time, then I wondered how much time I could take. "Did you feed the bird? How long do we have?"

"I fed it," she said. "And from what the instructions say, we have a few days until the bird forgets where he's from. But not many."

"*What* did you feed it?" I asked, hoping she didn't give the bird any of our bread, which was still fresh from the bakery and Simone hadn't even had her slice yet.

Martine dug her hand in her pocket, pulling out some seed. "There was a packet of feed in his box." Seed slipped through her fingers and landed on the kitchen floor.

"Martine!" I said, looking around as if the Germans were watching. "See. Mistakes like that can cost you your life! Simone's too, and mine. You put us all in danger." I patted my forehead where I'd broken out in a cold sweat, and she picked up the seed, licking her fingertip and pressing it to each little individual seed on the floor.

"But if you'd just trust me—"

"Not now, Martine."

"But Gaby…"

A lorry barreled up our road at a distance, leaving our words hanging in the air. Martine reached for my hand. When it lurched to a stop outside, I stood up.

"Is it the Germans?" Martine whispered.

"I don't know," I said, but if it wasn't the Germans, it was most definitely bad news—a lorry that sat idle in the road with its engine rumbling only brought bad news. The scuff of boots preceded a tap on my door. I ripped off my apron and fixed my hair, smoothing back the strays before walking to the front door and catching their first words. *Germans.*

I nodded back to Martine, and she held on to the wall.

I opened the door. "Yes?"

These Germans were administrative, with medals and stiff black jackets from having retired from active duty. "Gabriella Cotillard?" he asked, reading my name off a piece of paper, causing me to shiver for the second time in a row at hearing my full name spoken by a German.

"That's me."

"We've come to survey the vacant apartment next door."

"What?" I breathed, though I should have known to expect a visit after last night. Martine had joined me in the foyer, and Simone rushed down the stairs wearing her pink peignoir over her thick nightgown. She promptly reached for her coat to cover herself even more when she saw they were Germans.

"I was left the entire house in a will. It's not separate. I can prove it."

He tucked the paper into his lapel pocket. "Is that so?"

"It is so," I said.

He'd already motioned his men forward. "This is all very standard. It is by law we must record the residence. Entrance is in the back?" he asked, and all I could do was nod. "And you have a key?"

I retrieved the key from a drawer, and they walked around the side of the house to my aunt's private entrance in the back. Martine hung on my arm as we listened to them stomp through our aunt's salon on the other side of the wall, down the hallway, and around her kitchen, opening and closing her cupboards—*bang, bang, bang, bang*—like clapboard during a storm, while Simone repeated what they'd said. "It's standard. They're just making a record."

Another knock sounded on my front door. Martine moved to answer it, but I wouldn't let her in case it was Antoinette, so I did.

Commandant Streicher.

"Good morning," he said, but he hardly sounded pleasant. "You remember me from last night, no?" I smelled the stark cut of his cologne against the salty sea breeze. He flicked his chin to something behind me. "Have you taught children?"

I looked at him strangely. "What?" I asked, and he motioned with his chin again. "The piano. Have you taught children to play?"

I turned, looking at the piano behind me, then fumbling for the word. "N-No," I finally said. "I haven't. Why?"

"My new wife has a child. A girl," he said. "I want you to teach her how to play."

My mouth gaped open, and he smiled from ear to ear, almost laughing. "I can't. I told you last night I don't play anymore."

He remained on my doorstep longer than he should have, his gaze skirting to my piano and all those shiny black and white keys, before pivoting to leave and joining the others who were climbing back into the lorry.

Antoinette had come out in her blue housecoat, getting an eyeful before Martine had shut the door. We listened to the lorry drive away.

"Gaby, we can use the pigeon. They deserve it—"

"I told you, not now, Martine." I marched over to the piano and slammed the lid down, sending a jarring pang through the salon.

We walked to the sewing shop together, arriving just as the French trawlers motored out to sea under German guard. Situated at the highest point above the harbor, our seamstress shop was part of a row of shops that lined both sides of the cobblestone street, with foot traffic that mainly flowed downhill toward the fish market. Someone was always walking by, but it didn't bother Martine that she looked suspicious with her nose to the glass that morning, making bets with herself on how many French boats would meet a mine that had strayed from its mooring.

"Get away from that window," I said. "Rumors will start."

Martine placed her hands flat against the glass. "Well, I wouldn't have believed it if I didn't see it."

Simone and I looked up. "What is it?" I asked.

"Pigeons," she said, and we rushed to the window to see, clamoring for the best view next to Martine like three nosey neighbors. The Germans had set up a station for pigeon collection and to hand out rewards, grabbing the birds by their wings, giving them a fling in the air then chucking them into a basket, necks broken and dead. Reward followed in the form of a few paper notes.

"The Germans are going to eat well tonight," Simone whispered.

"Like they always do," I said, followed by a pause when I saw that Madame Roche's curtains were closed on her lock shop. "Madame Roche isn't going to be pleased when she sees the Germans set up their station outside her shop."

"No, she won't," Martine said. A pregnant woman got in line holding her bird. She was wearing a new green hat and a coat that hardly fit. "Is that Francine from down the way?" Good French heckled and pointed as she stood in line while she pretended she couldn't see or hear them. "What was she thinking, lying with a German?"

"You don't know her story, Martine," Simone said. "What if it's her husband's? Women are getting pregnant by Frenchmen too."

"But he's at a factory," Martine said. "Somewhere in Germany, I thought."

"Maybe he's in hiding or maybe—" An old man shouted "traitor" while shaking his finger in Francine's face, and forcing her to step into the gutter. Simone turned away, unable to look. "But I guess it doesn't matter. She'll get treated as if she's a collaborator, won't she?"

"I pray it is her husband's," I said, though Francine's husband had been sent away more than a year ago and we'd heard nothing to believe he'd escaped the factory and was in hiding. "For her sake, and the baby's."

"Me too," Martine said. "God have mercy."

Our door opened and the sharp clang of the bells turned us all three around.

Rémy—one of Martine's cliff boys.

He stood in the doorway with his hat in his hands, fingers blindly searching the brim. He'd just turned eighteen and was about to be sent off to a munitions factory for forced labor. Martine hated it when the boys came to the shop. Though when Rémy came to the shop, she hated it because he reminded her of what she was missing, and made her question all that she believed about love.

"Hallo, Martine." A dark swatch of hair fell over his eyes.

Martine rushed over to him, whispering. "What are you

doing here?" Simone and I exchanged looks after she refused to let him brush an eyelash from her cheek. "Stop it," she said, moving her face away. "I told you already. You'll go off to the factory and that's that. There's no future for us."

"You don't believe that, do you?"

Martine didn't answer because lying again after being pressed would be the final goodbye.

Rémy's gaze lifted over Martine's shoulder to me and Simone, probably thinking how odd it was that we were staring, but what else could we do? The shop was small and nearly empty, and we couldn't look away.

"You can send for me, write a letter that my mother is dying."

Martine scoffed. "Your mother's been dead for years."

"Yes," he said. "But the Germans don't know that, and I heard the French laborers in Stettin are let out for funerals—a roundtrip train ticket. Only I wouldn't go back. I'd stay here for you, if you asked."

"But I'm not asking." Martine folded her arms when he kissed her forehead. "Is that where you're going? Poland?"

"I don't know yet," he said. "You still have the vase I gave you, don't you, Martine?" His eyes lit up, a slight flicker at the prospect that she'd kept his gift.

She'd never told us how she got the vase, though I'd always had my suspicions, especially because of how she treated it, always wiping it with a clean rag, situating it carefully on the side table with fresh flowers, when we had fresh flowers to put inside.

"Yes." Martine turned, glancing at us only to see us still staring.

"You have to go." She pushed him outside, but I'd seen the

way she held onto his hand, wanting him to go, but also wanting him to stay, a lingering touch to remember and savor. It was how she protected herself, denying him before he had a chance to deny her.

"That poor boy," Simone said. "He loves you and you've broken his heart."

Martine turned her attention back to the window once Rémy was gone.

"He'll recover."

"Yes, but will you? He's the only boy you've ever loved," Simone said, which drew a pointed look from Martine for being put on the spot. Neither of us expected her to answer, and she didn't, but Simone was in a mood after witnessing Rémy and her together and wasn't about to stop. "And he said he'd come home if you sent for him, risk being arrested, or worse. That's romantic. Something you read about in books."

"It's all promises. No man would risk that, once it came down to it."

Simone shook her head after snipping thread from a spool. "He would," she said just above a whisper. "Because he loves you."

Martine let out a huff that lifted her fringe.

"Shame on me for saying the word *love*, Martine." Simone looked up from her needle and thread. "Love is what makes life worth living—it's what gives us hope."

"Is that so?" Martine asked.

"It is."

Martine braced the window ledge, watching passersby, the Germans, and the bad French. "Well, so does revenge."

After a while, Martine's staring became obvious, and I knew she wasn't just watching people, but whatever she could glimpse at the harbor—she hadn't given up on using that pigeon and was waiting for the right time to bring the subject back up.

"Martine, get away from that window," I said, but she'd pressed her nose to the glass.

"Boche," Martine called out.

"Shh!" I said.

She turned around. "They can't hear me."

"But what if they could?" I asked. "You get comfortable saying Boche inside, you'll get comfortable saying it outside, and it's illegal."

"You worry too much, Gaby," Martine said.

"It's my job to worry," I said. "I'm worried about the Germans, and why they were in our aunt's apartment this morning—what they're going to do."

"And Commandant Streicher," Simone said, looking up from her needle and thread.

I nodded. "Him too."

Martine moved away from the window once Mme. Leroux and her young son arrived for their ration coupons, pretending to be busy while I went to the back office.

I heard her tell her son it would only be a minute as I tore off the coupons. A protein, a dairy, and a grain. I stuffed the coupons into my apron pocket before returning to the front. "Here we are—" My voice got caught in my throat. A messenger had walked in and stood in the open doorway.

Mme. Leroux pulled her son closer by the hand, his feet stumbling over each other, while Simone and Martine stared at the messenger as if he were a leper. I wondered how I missed the bells, then thought he might have snuck into the shop behind Mme. Leroux on purpose.

"Greetings," he said, looking at his clipboard. "Gabriella Cotillard?" he questioned, and normally I would have shivered hearing my full name read from a list, but this was the third time I'd heard it. He handed me an envelope after I nodded. "This is for you."

He stole a look at Mme. Leroux standing hand in hand with her son before walking out—he was a messenger, but it was a French secret never to underestimate the power of a messenger.

I pulled the coupons from my pocket and gave them to Mme. Leroux, who quickly concealed them in her handbag. "How can children survive off a half liter of milk?" she asked. Her son looked up at her with hollowing gray eyes. I knew he needed that protein ration the most for the iron. "I heard we lost two fishing boats this week to mines, which means less fish to purchase too. How long will this cruelty last?"

"I don't know." I felt the envelope in my hands, wondering what news the messenger had brought, but I wouldn't dare open it in front of her, the news that the rations would stop was bad enough. "But I'm afraid these might be the last of the ration coupons. The Germans know my aunt is dead."

She gasped. "You said not to worry!"

"They only know that she's dead," I said. "Not that we've been giving them to you."

She'd covered her mouth, and her weak son lost his balance without her support.

"Martine can see what's available on the black market," I said, "and I'll do my best to see what can be spared."

She looked to the street before taking her son's frail hand. "I better go." His legs bowed just a hair more as they walked away.

"The children," I said as we watched them through the window. "Look what they've done to our youth."

"It's time to get back at them, Gaby." Martine braced the window ledge again. "You only have to say yes—"

"Passing war information to the British... Do you know that crime carries a death sentence?"

"It's a risk I'm willing to take," she said. "And remember, it's one pigeon. That's all."

"I don't want a box with your things sent to me from prison," I rasped. "We have enough to worry about as it is."

I went back to feeling the envelope, fingertips following sharp edges. Posts delivered by messengers were like lorries in the night. Nothing good ever came of them. I tore off a corner, running my finger the length of the envelope, and was surprised to see it wasn't a plain paper letter, but someone's personal butter-yellow stationary.

I covered my mouth after reading it. "Oh no," I said, feeling a stab of pain behind my eyes. "He can't. He just can't!"

Martine rushed over, snatching the letter away before Simone could reach for it.

"*Mon Dieu*, Gaby," she said after reading. "What are we going to do?"

"What does it say?" Simone asked. "You're frightening me."

"I've been summoned," I said.

"Summoned?" Simone asked. "Summoned where?"

I gulped. "To Commandant Streicher's home. To teach piano to his new wife's daughter." I hung my head. "I should have known—that look he gave me this morning and his request that wasn't a request."

Simone gripped my hands. "You must tell him no."

Martine paced the floor in a circle. "The Germans never stop. They take our family, take our lives. Ruin us slowly and make us watch." She stopped abruptly, facing me. "How much more are you going to take, Gaby?"

I closed my eyes.

"How much more?" she repeated.

Teaching his wife's daughter piano—we'd lose our customers. We'd lose our friends. And what little money we had saved would be gone in a matter of weeks after the grocer refused to sell to us. We'd have to buy the bulk of our food on the black market and we'd be destitute in order to eat.

"There'll be a black ribbon on our door," Simone said. "As soon as someone finds out, as soon as someone knows."

I felt faint and weak in the knees, but then thought of his face when he stood at my door this morning, that sly smile, and his voice—condescending and bone-shivering—and found my strength instead, heating up behind my neck and straightening my spine.

He can't make me play. I was a grown woman of twenty-five, and there wasn't a law that said I had to teach anybody anything.

I took off my apron, wadding it up and tossing it on the counter, exchanging it for my coat and handbag.

Martine looked alarmed. "Where are you going?"

"To see the German," I said, and I threw open the door and left under a clang of doorbells.

Chapter Three

I walked defiantly up the street, past the bad French turning in their pigeons, and straight up the hill toward the German neighborhood before gathering my wits and taking the long way to avoid peeping eyes, which took a bit of my steam.

I stood on the pavement looking up at the big peach house with white dormers, wondering if I had the right address, when a child yelled behind a closed window followed by a brutal clash of piano keys. I closed my eyes.

This is the house.

I stepped up to the door, knocking forcefully despite my cold fingers. "She's here!" the child squealed, opening the upstairs window and getting a look at me, head hanging out with her blonde hair shaking like a mop in the breeze.

The housekeeper answered the door. "Hallo," I said before she could. "I'm here to see Commandant Streicher. I'm—"

"You're the piano teacher," she said.

I blinked.

"We've been expecting you."

"Yes, but I'm not—" I felt the warmth of a burning fire when I stepped inside, catching me off guard and losing all my thoughts. The buttery-scented pastries baking in the kitchen didn't help. She motioned to take my coat, and I shoved my fists into my cold pockets. "I'm not staying to teach."

Her eyebrows rose into her forehead as if she didn't believe me. "You can wait in the study."

I hiked my handbag over my shoulder and followed her through an opened set of French doors into a cozy office area with pink and white striped fabric-covered walls, and dark wood beams and wallpaper on the ceiling. I was reminded of the swanky cafes off Boul'Mich with rooms for rent. But this wasn't a cafe or a hotel. This was a home, a Frenchwoman's home who'd married a German and given him a place to do his dirty work.

The fire crackled from a fresh log the housekeeper had thrown into the flames. "He'll be in shortly, mademoiselle."

I waited, taking a seat near his fabric walls, sandwiched between Limoges miniatures on glass shelves and a tall metal filing cabinet with the bulkiest padlock I'd ever seen. I slipped off my coat to keep from sweating.

A crying fit gave way to more fists on the piano keys above. I winced, wondering how much more that poor piano could take as the mistress shouted for the girl to put her doll down, which I assumed was being used as a tool after her fists gave out.

"Mademoiselle is waiting in your study," I heard the housekeeper say, and I sat up stiffly, listening to them talk in the hall with my heart thrashing violently against my ribs.

"I see you got my note," Commandant Streicher said, snapping the doors closed behind him.

I stood, watching him walk the length of the room to his desk and set a pile of folders down.

"Well?" he asked, before looking at me.

My mouth hung open with words to be said, but my voice had disappeared. He was a commandant in the Reich, and what was I going to say? I pulled my collar away from my neck, swallowing dryly.

"I can't teach piano," I blurted.

He walked the few steps to his file cabinet, paused with the lock in his hands as if deciding whether or not I'd had my hands on it, then turned toward me with his arms folded. I reached for my coat, sparing no time to slip my arms back into it.

"Why not?" he asked.

"I don't play," I said. "There are plenty of other people you can ask. I'm sure you can find someone—"

"But you have played. You admitted this to me. And it's just one child. I'm not asking you to compose anything." He laughed from his belly, as if the thought of a woman composing a piece of music was the most absurd thing he'd ever heard.

My jaw clenched. He was the type of man who didn't think women had anything valuable to contribute, something I was well versed in from my early years at the Conservatory. Part of me wanted to tell him about my secret life as a pianist, and while he pondered such knowledge and skill with a dumbfounded look drawn on his sharp face, I'd tell him I knew multiple languages, including his own. "You'll have to find someone else." I turned to walk away.

"Do you know the penalty for using a dead woman's rations?" he asked, and I froze, two steps from the French doors. "I'm sure it's a steep fine."

"I'll pay it," I said, my back still to him.

"And what about the Lerouxs?" he asked.

I whipped around.

"I wonder what the penalty is for *stealing* someone's rations? She is not family, so that must be what's happened. And since you had a secret to hide, with the vacant room you didn't declare, you couldn't alert the authorities. Pity." He ticked his tongue. "Her child will go to an orphanage. Might not last too long there. I have eyes everywhere, you must know, and I heard he looked rather sickly in your shop this morning." He made a disgusted look. "Gaunt face, skin and bones…"

"I gave them to her," I said, not willing to let Mme. Leroux get punished for something I did, but he shook his head.

"No," he said. "It's whatever story I tell, you see? She stole them. And now that we found out about your aunt, you turned her in. That's the story she'll hear just before we take her away."

The child ran downstairs asking the housekeeper where I was. Moments later she burst into the room like a terror, stomping her feet and pushing back her unkempt hair.

"When are we going to start?" She folded her arms, lips pursing.

Her mistress ran in behind her, apologizing for letting the child run wild and loose. The commandant seemed to understand, which surprised me, and waved them both out. The mistress dragged the child from the room by her elbow and up the stairs against her will with her feet scraping the floors.

"I believe you have a lesson to get to."

"But… but…" I didn't know what else to do but drop to my knees, throwing myself to the floor. "You know what will happen to me, don't you?" I asked near his feet. "Please. I'll lose customers, and my neighbors will turn on me. My sisters, they'll be shunned and ridiculed when people find out. Heckled in the street!"

"Mademoiselle Cotillard, get a hold of yourself, will you? Such despair and hopelessness." He adjusted his cufflinks, studying me on the floor. "I must admit, this isn't what I expected from you. Not after the way you presented yourself last night and this morning." He pulled a few gold coins from his pocket, clinking them in his hands. "I will pay you."

I hung my head. Now we'd be called whores.

"You're teaching a child. A French child. I did mention she's my wife's daughter, didn't I? How bad could it be?" He flipped one of the gold coins in the air before sliding them all back into his pocket. "Stand up."

I reluctantly stood as the child beat on the piano keys upstairs, a waterfall of notes from left to right and right to left —she must be using her doll, running its whole body along the keys. I closed my eyes, and the commandant walked out, brushing my shoulder.

"Mademoiselle?" the housekeeper said behind me, and I turned around, gripping my handbag and sweating with my coat on and the fire roaring up behind me. "This way?" she questioned as if unsure if I'd make do with my promise to leave.

"Yes, Madame," I said, following her upstairs.

The child turned sharply around from the piano bench when I entered her playroom. I noticed her cheeks first, still pink from being upset earlier.

"This is Mademoiselle—"

"Cotillard," I said, cutting the housekeeper off and trying to hold onto any kind of control I thought I might have had. The housekeeper left, leaving me in the room with the child and her mistress, who seemed more than relieved I'd come upstairs.

"I'm so..." The mistress took a deep breath. "Glad you're here."

The child took her doll by the legs and pounded its porcelain head on the piano keys. I instinctively reached for it, stopping her from the assault.

"Don't do that," I said.

She looked up at me, pulling her doll in close.

"That's better." I walked to the window instead of sitting on the bench next to her and stared outside, feeling stuck in a bad dream and not knowing how to snap out of it. The child asked her mistress what I was doing, and when the mistress herself repeated the question, I closed my eyes.

"I haven't taught in a while," I said, which was true, though I'd never taught a child. I turned around, smiling the best I could. "Just gathering my thoughts."

I took a seat before I caused any more suspicions, sliding onto the cold side of the piano bench. Her mistress slipped out of the room.

"Can I play now?" she asked, tucking a swath of hair behind her ear before placing her fingers lightly on the keys.

"What's your name?" I asked, and she huffed, hands falling on the keys. *Clang, clang, clang...*

"Do you want me to make up a name?" I asked. Spoiled little French girl with a bad French mother was my best guess.

"Lauren," she said. "I'm nine! Now, let's play!" She repositioned herself on the bench with her hands poised.

"Well, nine-year-old Lauren," I said, and I began to tell her about the piano, the keys, and why she should be gentler. "Never beat the keys with your fists. You'll ruin your piano." I made a sour face. "It'll make everything you play sound like an old woman's cackle."

She laughed.

I took her doll from the top of the piano, petting her hair away from her cracked face. "And your poor dolly! What did she do for such a punishment?"

Lauren raced to set the doll back on the shelf, one out of a hundred she had to choose from, only the doll flopped over to one side and she had to go back and fix her. Lauren slid next to me on the bench once she was done, out of breath and anxious to start.

"Where's your mother?" I asked, looking over my shoulder as if she'd be walking in soon.

"Gone," she said, hands poised over the keys.

"Gone?" I questioned, and she hung her head this time. I didn't want to lose her moment of good behavior, so I didn't press how I wanted to meet her—the woman who sold herself to the devil. "We can begin."

She sat up tall, setting her hands gently on the keys, and I automatically did the same as if it hadn't been more than a year since I'd done so. I pulled back sharply, shoving my hands in my lap.

"Something wrong?" she asked.

"Why don't you show me what you already know."

"A performance?" she asked, and I nodded.

"Yes, give me a performance. I don't want to spend time teaching you something you know," I said, but from what I'd already heard, I understood she knew absolutely nothing about the piano. I pointed to the doll she had used earlier. "And I don't think your doll wants to tell me."

She giggled then played a few keys here and there, a song she'd made up using only her index fingers. "Aren't you going to take off your coat?" Her hands fell onto the keys again, sending a shudder over my body from the sound.

"Just keep playing." I moved away from the bench feeling light-headed and faint, and walked around, looking interested and pleased, but all I thought about was leaving, and how many more minutes I had to stay. I tried hard not to wince, hearing the disjointed clatter of a child tapping indiscriminately on the keys, when out of nowhere, in between the tap, tap, tap of her index fingers, she played a chord progression.

I spun around with my mouth hanging open, and she withdrew her hands. "What was that you just played?"

"This?" She tapped the keys randomly, and I shook my head.

"No, those chords you played. Can you do it again?"

"What's a chord?" She blinked, making me think I'd imagined it.

The door burst open, and I forgot all about the chords. "Sounds lovely in here!" her mistress said, carrying in a tray of biscuits and herbal tea. "Time for a break?"

Lauren shot up from the bench to reach for a biscuit, then a small argument followed over some secret, better-tasting biscuits in the kitchen, which the mistress denied.

"I'm Irma. Sorry for not introducing myself earlier. Sugar?" She'd poured me a steaming cup of tea from a silver teapot, offering me a lump of sugar from her serving tongs while Lauren stewed about being served the wrong biscuits.

"No sugar," I said, even though my mouth watered for it— to feel the grainy grit of it between my teeth.

Irma shrugged, dropping the sugar back into the bowl. "This is from Commandant Streicher." She slipped an envelope in between the teapot and the sugar bowl. "Lauren has never liked her past teachers. She's destroyed three dolls, yet she hasn't destroyed one with you, and you've had a full lesson."

I peeked into the envelope, spreading it open with two fingers. It was more money than we'd make all week at the sewing shop. I couldn't take it. If I did, that meant I was in collaboration with a German. I officially worked for him. I pulled my hand back and left it on the tray.

"Something wrong?" Irma asked.

"No." I gulped my tea so I could leave. "Have a good day."

I made my way to the door while Lauren started up the biscuit argument again with Irma, and I thought I could escape unnoticed, only Irma dashed across the room with the envelope in her hand, shaking it in the air.

"Don't forget this!" She pressed the envelope into my palm, and before I could say anything, she was gone and the door had closed between us.

Martine and Simone had already closed the shop and were in the kitchen by the time I'd made it back home. They'd brought the pigeon up from the cellar and had him on the table, feeding him seeds. "What did Streicher say when you refused?" Simone asked, and when I hung my head, both of them stood.

"You stayed at his house? You worked for him?" Martine asked, and I nodded.

"Where else do you think I've been?"

"Gaby, how could you?" Martine asked. "We'll be crucified! The good French will never forgive us."

"They'll call us whores!" Simone said, and I knew that was Simone's worst fear besides finding a black ribbon on our door.

I sat heavily at the kitchen table with my sisters peering down at me, and told them about the commandant's threats, how he'd make up stories about Mme. Leroux, arrest her, and send her son to an orphanage.

"What a dirty—"

"Boche—blockhead bastard," Martine said, fists tightening, and I closed my eyes.

"Martine, shh…"

"I'm not going to shush. It was that messenger," she said. "He saw Mme. Leroux in the shop and he must have told." She shook her head, and I thought she was thinking up a punishment, a scheme to make the bad French messenger pay.

"Did you take the long way to his house?" Simone asked. "Maybe nobody will find out. Maybe nobody saw!"

I pulled the envelope from my coat pocket and set it on the table. "Only there's this too."

"Nom de Dieu!" Martine said. "He paid you?"

"We don't have to spend it," I said.

"How can we not spend it?" Simone asked. "Now that it's here and in our home. I'm not that strong. Are you?"

Martine sat back down and so did Simone, slumped over the table as the pigeon pecked at the seed scattered about.

"We can hide it away for an emergency," I said. "If asked, we can say it was Aunt Blanche's." I pulled the money from the envelope and flipped through the notes, when I found a folded piece of yellow stationery stuck in the middle.

"Oh no," Martine said, while Simone covered her mouth. "He wrote you a note."

I unfolded the stationary, trying to hold my composure, but inside I was panicking. "Mademoiselle Cotillard," I read aloud. "You are to report to my home for lessons two times a week and promptly at nine in the morning. Not a minute earlier or later. Marked improvement must be evident, otherwise penalties will be imposed as discussed."

I closed my eyes tightly and tried desperately to think of all the things I could do to get out of teaching. I was sick. My hand went lame. But nothing sounded plausible, which made me feel even more hopeless than I was.

"I hate the Germans," I said. "I hate him, making me go to his house, teach that girl." I pounded my fist on the table, sending the pigeon flying into the air, wings outstretched with a few puffs of feathers.

"Coo, coo, coo…"

It was quiet as he walked the edge of the table, head jutting and tilting, looking at us, then to the table, then into the air. He gave his leg a shake where the messenger capsule had been fastened.

"Gaby?" Martine sat up in her chair. "Let's use the bird."

"No, Gaby," Simone said. "I'm hungry. Let's eat him."

They looked at me, but I was still looking at the bird, thinking seriously for the first time about Martine's proposition. There was just one thing I couldn't get past. "But the risks, Martine. I said it before, what if the British think we're Germans trying to fool them? Then we'd be endangering our lives for nothing."

"I have an idea." Martine walked across the room, and although it didn't concern me at first, I was definitely concerned when she pulled my sheet music from the bureau's bottom drawer, but not just a few sheets here and there – she had what remained of my life's work in her hands.

My heart rate instantly picked up. "What are you doing?"

She walked toward me with the sheets crackling in her hands.

"Give me those," I said, reaching, but she pulled away.

"What if I told you I have a way for the British to know who we are, with certainty, without saying who we are."

"How?" I asked, worrying that her scheme was taking a sharp turn into the unknown.

"I thought of it today after I saw you with your music." She paused, almost waiting to see if I'd deny handling it. "There's only one person who knows this music better than you. And they're in England, *and* a visiting professor at the big school there."

"Give me those," I said, taking another grab, finally able to snatch my music away from her.

"It's true, isn't it?" Martine asked. "Professor Caron escaped to London?"

I nodded. "That was the professor's plan. Royal College of Music."

"This is how, Gaby!" Martine beamed. "We can write our

messages on the back side where it's blank, and we can lead the British to check with the professor for verification. Say something about the visiting professor at the Royal College of Music."

"But I'd never see it again, all that music, all those hours it took for me to compose, and I can't make a duplicate. That would be suicide if the Germans intercepted the pigeon."

"You left half in Paris already," she said, and my mouth hung open.

"And whose fault is that?" I snapped.

"The Germans deserve to be punished for everything they've taken from us. You never play anymore, not even a few notes, and you can't blame that on me," she said. "The Germans did that to you. Maybe not directly, but that's what happened, and now they're going to take Mme. Leroux's son if you don't teach that girl how to play."

She took me by the shoulders, but I pushed her away to stand by the window.

"Gaby, many years from now, what will be more meaningful, the remnants of the composition you stuffed away, or the composition you used to smuggle information to Britain?"

Martine had always been the brash one. Never mixing eloquent speech with the cold hard truth. But this time they were one and the same. Aunt Blanche talked about hard decisions before she died, and this one was no exception.

"Simone?" I asked.

Her eyes lifted, big and blue. "I still want to eat him, but I know how much this means to Martine."

Once Simone agreed, I knew what my answer would be. Though it wasn't easy and breathing felt like a struggle. I dipped my eyes for a yes, and Martine flung her arms around my neck, nearly choking me.

"This is going to work, Gaby. You'll see. This is how we get back, and how we make a difference. Your life's work will not be for nothing!" She reached for the kitchen shears.

"Wait!" I said.

Martine blinked and blinked.

"This has to be done carefully, and with some planning. We should wait a few days. The villagers are probably on the lookout for pigeons flying out of windows. I don't want to be turned in." I stopped short of saying I also needed some time to digest the idea of destroying my music. "This has to be done carefully," I repeated. "Or not at all."

Simone nodded, but Martine was still blinking.

I walked over to the bureau, tucking my composition back into its hiding spot. "Promise me, Martine. You'll wait?"

She moved her hands behind her back, hiding the shears. "Yes. Of course," Martine said, but she had a strange look in her eye and my gut told me not to trust her. "I'll wait." Her eyes darted to the bureau's bottom drawer. "I promise."

"Martine, if you don't keep your word—"

"She said she'd wait, Gaby," Simone said, but now Martine was biting her nails.

Chapter Four

G uy Burton sat back in his office chair, unconsciously twisting his wedding band while waiting for his damn phone to ring. When it did, it sounded like a fire alarm had gone off in his basement office, scaring him half to death. He leapt to his feet. "Yes?" he said into the receiver, eyes shooting to the clock. He swiftly added up how long it had been since the pigeons left the airfield at Newmarket—plenty enough time for one to fly back. "Who is it?"

He held his breath.

"Is this Guy Burton?" a man asked, but he didn't wait for a response and kept talking. "Yes, well…" A buzz of static drowned out the rest of the words, and Guy shook the receiver before giving it a slam against his metal desk.

"What?" Guy shouted. "Sorry, I couldn't hear you. Can you repeat that?" He pressed the receiver to his ear, causing a little pain.

"This is Arthur Ripley. We have a pigeon here—"

"I'll send someone right away," Guy said, cutting him off. "Don't move!" He hung up the phone, and what followed was a frantic phone call to services on the ground floor with explicit instructions: retrieve the pigeon from Ripley in Ipswich and deliver him to the War Office, now.

Operation Columba and his messenger pigeons were on thin ice with the Air Ministry as it was, even before the last drop, which he'd heard was a bit of a cock-up with birds dropped willy-nilly somewhere over France. He needed this bird. More so, he needed this bird to provide tangible intelligence.

By late afternoon, Guy was a ball of nerves waiting for the pigeon to arrive and snapped at everyone who came into his office. He paced, rubbing the back of his neck as minutes stretched into hours, until he heard the messenger's distinct clippety-clop in the corridor.

"Bring it here!" Guy motioned for the messenger even though he was hurrying as fast as he could. Hearing the commotion, a few others in the basement at MI6 headquarters had come out of their offices to see what was going on, but only Clive, the colleague who shared his office, asked questions.

Guy examined the bird closely. He looked a little weathered, with a few feathers missing from his breast and tail —an ordinary pigeon at the park—which Guy thought was impressive since he'd been dropped from a plane into enemy territory.

"And what of the falcons?" Clive asked.

Guy signed for the delivery and sent the messenger on his

way. "What falcons?" he asked jokingly because what was even more impressive was that this pigeon managed to make it past the death squad of German falcons they'd been hearing so much about in northern France—falcons that had been trained to seek and destroy his beloved winged messengers—and he was amazed.

Guy took the bird into his office, as was policy, and unlatched the canister around the pigeon's leg. He delicately pulled the scroll out and was surprised to find it wasn't the rice paper the pigeons had been supplied with, but nearly an entire sheet of paper that had been folded and rolled up tight like a thin cigarette.

He flattened it out on his desk, his heart pounding, knowing the future of his secret pigeon service depended on what information the scroll revealed. He didn't want to say it out loud, but he was hopeful—extremely hopeful—that this bird had brought back something special.

Only instead of a message, Guy had unraveled a sheet of music.

He threw his hands up. "I'm finished!" The music fell to the floor where it folded and rolled back up into itself. "Columba's over." Guy stormed off while Clive picked the message up and gave it a look.

"Nah, there's a message written in French on the other side," he said, and Guy rushed back to his desk, pulling his desk lamp close.

"Blimey," Guy said, looking more hopeful. There was a message, and a map! He pulled his magnifying glass from his top desk drawer to read the text, hoping it wasn't a personal message to family.

"Well?" Clive asked. "What does it say?"

Guy thought he'd stopped breathing. The intelligence was even better than he imagined. More than he could have asked for. An expertly drawn map showing a secret U-boat pen in northern France, an oil facility, and a number of secret German emplacements hidden in the cliffs near Boulogne-sur-Mer. The bottom portion had the smallest text and he had to squint even with his magnifying glass. *The sender of this message is the composer of this work. Please refer to the visiting professor with white hair at the Royal College of Music…*

Guy looked up, barely able to keep himself in check. "You know I can't tell you," he said, as was policy, but he wanted to tell the entire basement floor.

"It's good?" Clive asked.

"It's good," he said, smiling. "But if you ask me more about it, I might think you're a spy."

"Well, I wouldn't want you to think that now, would I?" Clive shook Guy's hand and congratulated him; a job well done. "Are you taking it up to the second floor?"

The second floor. It was where his supervisor, Rex Smith, had his office. From there, and in a matter of hours, a report would be passed up and down Whitehall before landing on Churchill's desk. There would be no going back once it reached Churchill. No, he needed to verify who the sender was first before he showed it to his supervisor. It was within reason to think the message was a ruse to draw the RAF in for an ambush, and if that was so, the loss of the pigeon service would be the least of his worries.

Guy put on his hat and coat. "Not just yet." He placed the message between the pages of a hardback book for safekeeping and obscurity, then slipped it into his messenger bag for a visit to the Royal College of Music, to find that professor the sender had written about. "Wish me luck!"

Clive shouted out the door as Guy took off, "Hey, what do I do with this bird?" The pigeon flew into the corridor, running circles around agents as they left for the night.

"Keep him safe!" Guy said just before he rounded the basement corner.

It was raining when he left Whitehall, which made the drive across London to the Royal College of Music a wet and slow one. Thankfully, the front doors were still open even though it was late.

He pulled open the frosted glass door to the main office. "We're closing," a secretary said, her back turned to him.

He cleared his throat. "Hello, madam," he said, "I'd like to talk to the visiting professor here. I understand he might be French, perhaps new in the last year?" he asked, repeating what little information he had about the professor from the message.

The secretary turned around. "Who?" Her brow furrowed, and Guy's stomach took a tumble—she didn't know the professor, he didn't exist!

"A visiting professor from France. Is he here?"

"Right." She folded her arms before elaborating. "Professor Caron?"

"So, he is here?" Guy felt a twinge of relief, but remained guarded because her arms were still folded, and her lips appeared to be sealed beyond admitting he worked there. "Please, madam, it's an urgent matter. Where might I find him?"

She pointed down the corridor. "Down there," she said, before reaching for her handbag and turning off the lights. "Room six."

"Room six," he repeated. "Thank you, madam!"

Guy found room six but was even more relieved to see the door ajar and a light on. He hadn't left yet.

Guy took a second to tidy himself, using a sliver of door glass as a mirror. His jacket was damp after running up the pavement in the rain, but he could do little about that now.

He knocked twice on the doorframe. "Professor—" He took a step inside, expecting to see the professor at his desk, or even at his piano, but instead found a woman pulling papers from a filing cabinet.

"Can I help you?" She stuck a pencil behind her ear where her hair was tucked under her beret.

"Oh!" He took his hat off and smoothed back a lock of sandy blond hair. "I'm sorry, madam," he said. "I'm looking for Professor Caron. Is he in?" Her eyes were brown like his mother's, which made him think she had brown hair under her beret, but unlike his mum, she looked as distrusting of him as the secretary down the corridor had.

She fingered her collar, playing with the top button closest to her neck. "Who are you and what do you want? You're too old to be a student." She adjusted her glasses, her eyes narrowing.

Guy was wary of saying too much before knowing who she was, and before meeting the professor. "That's a private matter between me and the professor."

She pulled her shoulders back, and Guy saw how thin and wiry she was. "The professor isn't in." She went back to her papers, shoving them into a file and closing the heavy metal drawer with a locking clink. "That's your cue to leave, sir."

It was then Guy heard an accent. It was very light, and only detectable when she said "sir," but he had noted it. "Are you… Professor Caron?" He was embarrassed that he'd presumed the professor was a man.

She glanced up while reaching for her briefcase, but it was only the slightest of hesitations.

"Please, if you're the professor, I humbly ask for just a moment of your time."

She clicked both locks on her briefcase. "And I asked you who you were."

"My name's Guy Burton. I'm with the War Office."

"The War Office?" She adjusted her glasses again, but now she didn't look as suspicious as she had. "I am Professor Caron." She pulled the beret from her head, where a wave of gray hair that looked almost white fell over her shoulders. "Though I'm rather puzzled. What do you want with me?" She took a seat at her bench, tapping her fingers on the piano lid.

He reached into his messenger bag. "Can you identify this?" He showed her the sheet music he pulled from between the pages of his book.

The professor leaned in, getting a good look, first seeming intrigued, then looking concerned and snatching it away. "Where did you get this?" She stood up, taking the sheet music with her toward the door as if she was about to walk away with it. "Did something happen to her?"

"Happen to who?" Guy held his breath.

"Gabriella Cotillard, of course." She pointed to a set of notes on the sheet just above where it had been sheared of its

ANDIE NEWTON

last bar, as if it was the sender's signature, though it was just notes. "The composer of this work."

His jaw dropped. "You *can* identify it."

"Why exactly are you here?" The professor pursed her lips.

Guy decided she could be trusted and told her what was necessary about Columba and his secret pigeons. He was very aware of the hand-drawn map on the back, which she hadn't looked at yet. He put his hand out, asking for the sheet back, and she reluctantly gave it to him, but only after he'd finished telling her why this particular piece of sheet music was in London.

"So, you see, I'm only trying to find out…"

"Mademoiselle Cotillard was my most promising student," Professor Caron said. "She played with dignity. She played with passion. A rare gem among rare gems."

"Can I trust her?" he asked.

She had a special look on her face that was neither a smile nor a frown. "That sheet there is part of a larger composition. Some of it was lost in Paris through no fault of her own. I can only imagine she has a few sheets left, and what remains is her pride and joy, her most guarded treasure. Now, I ask *you*… Can you trust a woman who is willing to cut up the last of her life's work and send it across the sea, presumably never to see it again?"

"Yes?"

She nodded. "Yes, Mr. Burton."

Guy had his answer, yet he was still in Professor Caron's studio, holding the sheet music. He wanted to know everything about Gabriella Cotillard and was searching for a delicate way to ask because she seemed like the kind of

56

woman who would get irritated fast. He'd already made the mistake of assuming she was a man.

"Is that all?" She adjusted her glasses as Guy looked at the sheet music.

"You pointed to something in the notes after you recognized it."

The professor smiled, then motioned at the sheet. "She hid her name in the music. Look here." She pointed to some notes that made no sense to Guy. "It's a musical cipher, something I teach when studying Schumann." She paused, and Guy blinked. "Gaby." She pointed again to some notes. "It says right here, see?"

"Gaby?"

"That's her nickname." She smirked. "Perhaps in this pigeon program they don't teach you about musical ciphers? Why don't you tell the agents at the War Office to come to one of my lectures? Maybe they'll learn something." She asked for the music back. "I'll play it for you."

The professor took a seat at her piano and after adjusting her glasses, set her hands on the keys. Guy wasn't sure what to expect—a joyous melody, perhaps, or something somber like what he'd heard in church when he was a child—but he couldn't have prepared himself for what the professor began to play. It was haunting in the way images from your dreams haunt your waking day. His fingers tingled, and he felt something stirring inside, though he had no idea what it was, or that music could make you feel anything. Before it was over, he found himself sitting underneath a photo collage she had pinned to the wall, and having no memory of finding a chair.

"Her style is all her own, though it does remind one of Debussy's *La Mer* with its harmonic shifts, denoting movement," she explained, but Guy missed half of what the professor said. "Then the muscle of it grabbing for your heart, which is very Wagnerian, though you didn't get to hear any of that."

He looked up with a gulp, finally coming out of his daze. "It was so short."

She handed him back the sheet music. "Well, there's only one sheet, and the last bar is cut off. I did reprise some of it for you, so you could get a feel of the theme. The Heroines will always be my favorite."

"The Heroines?"

"It's what she named it while the piece was still in development. The Heroines."

"Sounds like the title of a novel," he said, and the professor just nodded.

"Well, every composition tells a story. She would have given it a generic name eventually if she'd stayed in Paris." The professor's voice took a cynical turn. "Her youngest sister Martine is responsible for why she fled, and her boyfriend Beau, well, he's another story. One joined the resistance and died, and the other thinks she *is* the resistance." She hesitated. "Are you asking me?"

"If you're willing to tell."

"I don't know all the details, but what came out of it was an agreement—a pact—between her and her two sisters. They won't do anything without the other's permission. It's meant to keep them safe." She handed him back the music. "So, if she sent her music to you, it was all three of them sending it."

"Is the piece known publicly?" The thought of Gaby being a famous pianist crossed his mind, which would definitely complicate things.

"No, no," she said, shaking her head, "and aside from myself, I'd be hard-pressed to imagine more than a few pianists in her cohort would have known the title when she was in Paris. She's in northern France now, Boulogne-sur-Mer, where she runs a seamstress shop with her sisters— bequeathed by their aunt who raised them. Or, at least that was where she was when I last visited her, before I managed to escape and board a clandestine boat to England."

Guy smiled. It was the extra bit of validation he needed, since the U-boat pen was in the same location. He got up from his seat, accidentally knocking a few of her photos loose, which she quickly pinned back to the wall.

"Thank you for your time, Professor Caron. If I have any more questions, can I call on you again?"

"Certainly," she said.

"I'm sure you understand, but what we discussed here today is between me and you. Talk to nobody else." He handed her a card with only a phone number on it. "If anyone asks about me or Miss Cotillard, or anything to do with what we talked about just now, call that number. It's my direct line."

After studying the card, she shook his hand. "Good evening, Mr. Burton."

Guy left to find his supervisor Rex Smith, but it was late, and he knew he'd left the War Office for home, so he drove out to Hampstead in the rain to reach him at his residence because he didn't think he could wait until the morning.

Guy rapped on his front door, and Smith answered with a surprised look on his face and a napkin tucked in his collar. "Sir, I have news!"

Smith ushered him inside, where it smelled of beef stew

and freshly baked bread. Three little children looked up from the kitchen table.

"Oh, I'm terribly sorry." Guy nodded his apologies to Mrs. Smith for interrupting their dinner as she tried to quiet the children.

"I'm afraid you caught me on the hop," Smith said, pulling the napkin from his collar. "Here, come into my study."

Once inside Smith's private study, Guy could barely contain himself. He pushed the message at him, talking fast, yet with detail. He knew at times the information seemed too good to be true—a clandestine U-boat pen in northern France, and the best part, it was left unguarded, protected only by a village ahead of the cliffs where the emplacements were noted. "And look at this secret oil facility." Guy tapped the map.

It was the most significant and detailed message they'd ever received from one of their pigeons, and by the look on Smith's face, he recognized its significance too at first glance.

"Can we trust it?" Smith asked. "How do we know this wasn't sent by a German? An ambush, trying to lure us to this location? I'm sure I don't have to remind you about the other pigeons we've received with phony messages."

"You don't, sir," Guy said. "The sender gave us a contact to verify their identity, and it checks out. All of it checks out." When asked who Gaby was, Guy said that she lived in Boulogne-sur-Mer with her sisters.

"This *is* news!" Smith turned on his lamp to give the map a better look, pulling out his magnifying glass like Guy had done already back in his office. "Extraordinary detail, and she's asked for more pigeons, which means she has more to tell." He looked up. "This is truly a find. Does anyone else know?"

"Nobody knows the contents but me, and now you, sir."

Smith copied a translated version of the message into a ledger and logged it with a number, as was policy, before locking the copy in a box behind his desk. The map would need to go up to Imaging tomorrow. "I'll write up a report and see this gets dispatched to the brass without delay," he said. "After I get the go-ahead from the top, you can ring up Bertie at the BBC, get a coded message dispatched on the Radio Londres broadcast, and tell the sisters we received the message."

A message to their French agents on Radio Londres was exciting for the Secret Intelligence Service, and also for the French—a slice of notoriety, albeit anonymous and coded.

"I'd like to get another drop in the diary as soon as possible, sir."

"I'll let you know what they say, fair enough?" Smith said, but Guy had no reason to believe another drop wouldn't be approved now, not after this, and quite possibly larger than before. A hundred pigeons, he expected. "Keep that original message safe. Lock it up."

"Yes, sir."

Back in the front room, Mrs. Smith tried to persuade Guy to stay for a bite, insisting that since he'd driven all the way out to Hampstead at night he should at least stay for dinner.

"Thank you, Mrs. Smith, but I must be off," Guy said.

"Oh yes, I imagine your wife is expecting you at home now, isn't she?" she asked, and Guy immediately shoved his hand into his pocket to hide his wedding band, though clearly, she'd already seen it. "Another time?" She gave her husband a kiss on the cheek, welcoming him back.

"Ah…" Guy swallowed hard. "Yes. Another time."

Smith gave Guy a sympathetic look as his wife cuddled up

next to him. He was one of the few people who knew that Guy's wife Jennie had died three years earlier.

"I'll show you out." Smith patted Guy on the back and walked him to the door. "Oh, and Guy…" he said. Guy was hoping he wouldn't bring up what his wife had said, because he just wanted to sweep it under the rug. "Nice work with the pigeon."

Guy stood in the pattering rain even after Smith closed the door, catching a glimpse of him returning to the dinner table to be with his wife and children. "Thank you, sir," he said into the cold night air.

He returned home to the dark and empty flat he rented above his sister Madge's house. After putting his keys on the side table, he found a note she'd left him, and a casserole. He flicked on a lamp just long enough to read the text.

Must be working late again, I see. I'll nip back up for the pan tomorrow. Enjoy. And don't work so hard. Damn the Germans. I worry about you. Jennie wouldn't want you to live like this, just so you know.

Love, your sis.

Guy popped open a bottle of beer, then had a seat at the table meant for two by the window to drink his ale alone. The rain had dissipated with a thinning of clouds, and twinkling stars sparkled above the smokestacks. Guy wasn't someone who normally looked at the stars, but in this case, he wondered if Gaby the composer was looking at the same stars.

They had never met, and he found it incredibly interesting that an unknown composer from northern France just might have saved his career, and the entire secret pigeon service.

He played with his wedding band, twisting it at first and then sliding it up his finger, before knocking back the rest of his beer. "The Heroines," he said to himself, thinking of the professor and the tune she'd played, a melody that had been in his head since he left Hampstead, and hoped not to forget.

He pulled the sheet music from between the pages of his book, gazing at it in the soft moonlight that was gleaming through the windowpane, studying the notes and trying to find where Gaby had hidden her name, but it was a mystery.

Chapter Five

I sat bolt upright after a night of tossing and turning, breathing heavily, with perspiration soaking through my nightgown from a nightmare. I threw back the covers and pulled Beau's jacket from my oak chest, sitting with it near the window where my lace curtains hung to the floor. I slipped my arms into the sleeves, feeling the satiny lining against my skin, and the heaviness of the wool as I pulled it over my shoulders. The cologne coming from the fabric was a heartbreaking reminder that he was gone, and I sniffed and sniffed, trying to find where the scent was the strongest, but the more I tried to find it, the harder it was to locate, fading, fading...

The lorry arrived after breakfast, rumbling in a way that didn't sound German but private, with clanging chains and grating metal. Simone rushed down the stairs along with Martine to stand in the foyer with Aunt Blanche by the door. We reached for each other's hands to hold onto.

Aunt Blanche's face took on a grave appearance after looking out the window. "Oh, my dear Gabriella."

My stomach sank.

"What is it?" Simone asked. "Who is it?"

Martine went to the window and peeped through the curtains herself. "It's a delivery."

"I told you to leave it alone, Gaby," Aunt Blanche said. "Nothing ever comes of this but pain…"

"What did you do?" Martine asked.

I wrung my hands. "I sent word to my friend in the city, along with some money, to find out anything they could about Beau. I expected a note, a message in the post." I swallowed. "She'd only send something if…"

Aunt Blanche opened the door, and the delivery man walked a few feet into the house before dropping a hefty box on the floor near our feet. When he began to talk about what was inside the box, what had been shipped, she shushed him. He handed her a note. "Thank you, monsieur," she said, showing him out.

Martine demanded to know what was in the box, but it was Aunt Blanche who answered because I couldn't find the words. "It's what remains, ma chèrie."

I hoped to see something that didn't belong to Beau—my friend was mistaken—but I saw his jacket lying inside when I lifted the lid. Only the dead left their clothes behind. His smell saturated the fabric —cigars from the café and ale from brasseries on Boul'Mich.

I burst into a wrenching cry.

Aunt Blanche paced the carpets with the note the delivery man had given her. When I asked what it was, she folded it up and tucked it in the jacket's pocket. "When you're ready, Gaby. And not a moment sooner."

I pulled the note from the pocket, staring at the scrunched ball of paper in my palm and wondering if I was strong enough to read it, when a knock on my door startled me.

I stuffed the note back in, wiping my nose and my watering eyes. "Yes?" I ripped off the jacket and slung it over the back of the chair because the chest was too far away, but that was too obvious, so I hid it under a blanket instead.

Simone opened the door a crack. "Can I come in?" she whispered.

I adjusted my nightgown over my bare knees, nodding.

As she headed to the window, I prayed she wouldn't mention his jacket, though it appeared she didn't even notice the lump under the blanket. She placed her fingertips to the glass, looking longingly over the rooftops.

I sensed something was wrong. "Simone?"

She turned, dressed in her satiny peignoir with layers and layers of nightgown underneath to keep warm. "I've been keeping a secret."

We already knew about the dances, and I figured she was aware, even though we didn't ask her outright. "Simone, we already know—"

"It's not about the dances." She rushed toward me sitting on the bed, taking my hands. "If I tell you, you must promise not to tell Martine."

I swallowed. "Why?"

"Because she won't understand. She'd never understand. You know how she feels about love." She'd looked up after dipping her eyes. "I've been seeing a man."

"You have?" I was surprised—she'd never kept her affairs secret before, which filled me with dread. "Is he..." I could barely say the word. "Simone, is he German?"

"God no," she said. "How could you think that?"

The relief was only slight—he wasn't German.

She pulled away to look out the window again, where the

morning sun had risen over Antoinette's roof and shone on her face through the glass.

"Simone." I gulped. "Is he a résistant?"

She whipped around when she heard my tone. "Please, hear me out."

"Simone…" I put my hand to my forehead. "What were you thinking? After what happened to us in Paris." I pressed my lips together. "If we're forced to leave Boulogne-sur-Mer because of this, we'll have nowhere to go."

"I know, I know," she said. "I'm sorry. I've been successful in keeping things between us discreet. But I knew you'd probably have questions after seeing me come in late the other night, and I didn't want to hide it from you any longer."

"You'll have to break it off," I said. "It's an added risk, now that we've agreed to use the pigeon. Last thing we need is for someone to get suspicious of you, dressed up, meeting a man in the shadows of the village and underground at dances. What if Antoinette sees you come home after curfew?" I folded my arms. "You'll break it off. Tell your lover he'll have to wait until the war is over."

"No, I can't," she said, shaking her head. "I won't."

"Why not?" I asked. "You've had lovers before and this shouldn't be any different."

"This is different." She pulled her shoulders back. "I love him, Gaby. He fills my heart with hope—hope for a free France, and hope for companionship that lasts a lifetime."

I scoffed. "Love with a résistant is your death, maybe not physically but when he gets caught, and one day he will," I said, waving my finger in the air, "nothing alive will remain including the hope you talk about."

It was I who turned away this time, realizing I was talking about myself. My hands shook from speaking up.

"You regret it?"

"Regret what?" I asked.

"That you didn't say yes to Beau."

I turned back to her, words on the tip of my tongue, wanting to tell her I didn't regret it, but I did. Beau and I had been together for months, meeting every morning for breakfast at a little cafe on Boul'Mich. Our time together was special, despite the Germans. Then one Tuesday morning, while I was poring over my sheet music and dissecting every little note, Beau reached across the table and asked for my hand in marriage.

I sat frozen with my hand in his, wanting to say yes, but couldn't—not right then—not with my unfinished work strewn out on the breakfast table. I would have had to quit my studies at the Conservatory, give up my dreams, and I wasn't prepared to give up anything, including Beau, but he was making me choose.

He gazed at me with those smoldering brown eyes of his before nodding once—my silence was enough. He stood from his chair to throw his arms around me, but I was paralyzed. I felt him shaking, my cheek against his warm chest.

He said something about difficult choices, and knowing when to let go, then he left just as our toast and jam arrived, stepping over a steaming sewer drain and into the street, leaving me stunned and still.

If I'd said yes, his life might have turned out differently. He'd still be alive, and maybe hope wouldn't be a memory sketched faintly in my heart, though I'd never admitted this out loud before.

"It would be nice to share breakfast with someone again," I said, lifting my chin, and a sad look drew over her face, which I could hardly bear watching. It was the simple things that I missed. The intimate moments we shared over breakfast and music together, holding hands, and being in love.

"I'll keep your secret from Martine for the time being," I said. "Only because I feel you must be the one to tell her yourself. But if she asks me, I won't lie. Promise me you'll be careful." I reached for her hands. "If anything happens to you—"

"I'll be careful," she said, and when she moved to leave, I pulled her back, closing my eyes with my face hidden in her hair where she smelled like Chantilly, half of me praying that she knew what she was doing with this lover of hers and the other half praying they'd break up.

We walked downstairs for breakfast to find Martine setting the table, complete with Aunt Blanche's special china that we only used on holidays. "What's all this?" I asked.

"I traded for some strawberry preserve on the black market," she said. "Thought we could use the china this morning."

"What did you trade?" Simone asked, and I knew she thought the same thing. Martine had traded kisses.

She popped the lid on the preserve, her nose to the jar, inhaling. "Does it matter? I got it and we're eating well this morning."

She passed the jar to me. It was a small jar, and just enough for one large spoonful each, but I scraped the inside with my spoon, licking every last jellied drop. "We should talk about the pigeon and what we're going to do," I said. "It's been a few days and the commotion in the village has settled. I think it's safe to let him go. What do you think?"

"Oh yes," Martine said. "We should talk about the pigeon."

Martine pulled a quart of milk from the icebox and as soon as I saw it, my spoon slipped from my hand and clanged on the floor—we'd already drunk our ration of milk, and to get extra on the black market was more of a feat than getting the strawberry preserve. Martine had paid well, and not with kisses. She'd paid using one of Aunt Blanche's silver spoons, and there was only one reason she'd trade one of the spoons without asking. She had a secret to spill, one she knew Simone and I wouldn't like.

She set the milk on the table.

"Martine," I breathed, staring at the milk, chilled and frothy with a nice layer of cream at the top. "What did you do?" I glared.

She sat up properly and poured herself a glass. "Stop looking at me like that, Gaby," she said, but then slumped forward and confessed. "All right. There's something I need to tell you—it's something I did."

"What?" I folded my arms, and she closed her eyes, holding her breath, and all I kept thinking about was how she'd better not have let that pigeon go, and how could I have trusted her?

Her eyes popped open. "I let the pigeon go."

Simone gasped.

"*Mon Dieu*, Martine! You said you'd wait!" I held onto the table, shaking the milk and clinking the china, which made Martine wince. "When? Where?"

"A few days ago," Martine said.

"A few days ago?" I shouted.

I looked back at the cellar, then at Martine, because this whole time I thought the bird was in the coal chute.

"What if someone saw?" Simone asked. "What if someone tells?"

"Nobody saw, so nobody can tell," she said. "I was discreet. Out the window with his capsule he went, flapping into the night. Only he had more information about German U-boats and emplacements in northern France than Hitler himself—"

I dashed to the bureau, pulling open the bottom drawer, seeing the first page of my composition missing, except for its last bar. "My music! You cut my music up without me."

"You said we could use it," she said.

I closed my eyes.

Simone chastised Martine while my back was turned, telling her that it wasn't right what she did, especially after what happened in Paris, as if she had to be reminded. "It's Gaby's work, not yours," Simone ended, pointedly.

I tucked the remaining sheets away and took my seat again at the table, taking a deep breath through my nose. There was no going back now, and no need to linger. I had agreed, after all, though it still didn't excuse her timing, and how she'd promised to wait.

"Gaby?" Martine said, and I looked up. "I'm sorry. I know you trusted me, but I just couldn't wait. I was too excited."

I'd felt uncertainty in my gut when she'd promised, and I blamed myself because I should have known. Martine rarely held herself back when she seized upon an idea. "I know you were excited, but you'd promised."

"Please forgive me. Tell me you do. He must be in London by now."

I reached for the milk to have a gulp, then something

changed inside me I hadn't anticipated. It was done, and a piece of my music was most likely in England now, like she said, and that slight bit of exposure felt like I'd done something useful—that the heart of my composition lived on, even if it was dead in my drawer. I probably wouldn't have been able to go through with it, in the end, so perhaps it was for the best that she'd let him go while we slept.

I nodded.

"Can we turn on the radio?" Martine asked, though we had agreed it was too dangerous to turn it on in the past because radios were illegal. We hid it in the cellar, a place where nobody would find it, not even a burglar.

"We should," Simone said. "They'll mention our pigeon on Radio Londres if he made it back. It's quite the acknowledgment for a résistant to be mentioned."

Martine shifted in her seat, looking at me.

I knew about the evening broadcasts, though I'd never listened to one live, only heard about them secondhandedly from the good French. By the sound of Simone, it appeared as if she had listened, and with her résistant lover no doubt.

"Please, Gaby?" Martine asked as I chewed on my thumbnail.

I wanted to know the fate of our pigeon too, especially after what we'd sacrificed to send him. "Go and get it," I said.

No sooner had I said the words than Martine was racing down the cellar stairs and bringing it back up. "Where should we plug it in?" She struggled with it in her hands.

A lorry drove up our road, grumbling louder and louder with chains rattling, much louder than the Abwehr's vehicle. We listened to the engine, praying it would keep on driving, but it came to a stop just outside our home.

"Hide that radio," I hissed.

Martine bobbed on her feet cradling the radio in both hands. "But where?" she asked in a shouted whisper, knowing there wasn't enough time to stash it back in the cellar.

I looked frantically around the salon, before settling on my piano. "In here." I took the radio away from her and hid it amongst the strings. "Get behind me."

I walked to the front door, after adjusting my morning robe and tucking back my hair.

"We stay calm like the last time and the time before that. We are used to their visits now," I said, but saying it out loud didn't make it any easier.

Jackboots pounded up the walk. I put my hand on the doorknob. "One," I whispered, just as Simone and Martine whispered the same.

Knock! Knock!

I manufactured a smile, opening the door. "Yes?" My smile vanished.

A man stood at my door while others unloaded furniture from the lorry along with some boxes. "Gabriella Cotillard?" he asked. "Here." He handed me a piece of paper, but I was now looking over his shoulder.

"I'm here to inform you that we're commandeering the apartment next door."

"What?"

"You have a spare apartment and we need accommodation for one of our own." He pointed to the paper in my hands. "A requisition of property notice. It's there in the fine print."

I looked up after reading. One of our worst fears had come true. I just didn't expect it to happen so soon. They assured me the other day that their visit was for their records, but when did I ever trust what a German had to say?

"As you can read from the notice, he's a retired naval captain. Highly revered. Don't knock on his door or call on him for help." His eyes shifted to my sisters. "I know how women need help with the simplest things."

I prayed Martine wouldn't pipe up after that comment as she breathed noisily through her mouth behind me.

"And what's the tenant's name?" I asked.

"Not a tenant." He laughed. "A tenant implies you will get paid. Captain Weber is a guest. Free of charge. This is the meaning of commandeering, no?" He smiled. "A guest that can see and hear almost everything."

He turned on his heel, walking back toward the lorry where the bulk of the captain's furniture was being pulled from the back and hauled around the side to my aunt's private entrance. Antoinette walked out of her house, trying to talk to the men unloading furniture to find out what was going on.

I swiftly closed the door, slamming my back up against it. The commandant never mentioned hosting a guest when I was at his house teaching Lauren. He'd done this on purpose. A surprise, to keep me guessing.

"I'll bet you two German fingers that witch Marie Antoinette had something to do with this. She has empty bedrooms in her house too," Martine said.

"No," I said. "This is Commandant Streicher's work." I sat heavily on one of our cushioned chairs, exhausted from the day – and it wasn't even nine in the morning yet.

Martine pulled back the window curtain when we heard something clanging in the road. "Gaby…"

"I don't want to watch."

"But there's something you should see."

Simone rushed to the window to have a peek. "Gaby doesn't need to see this."

They had a short argument, which made me sit up. "What is it?"

Simone turned. "It's nothing. An old man's things. Nothing to worry about."

"It's hardly nothing," Martine said.

I saw something big and black being hauled out of the lorry through the curtain split, and got up from my chair, swiping the curtain to the side.

A piano.

My lips pursed, watching them haul a nice-looking Steinway—if I trusted my eyes at this distance—out of the lorry and around the back, but after the initial shock had worn off, I thought maybe I could use this to my advantage. A German captain who plays the piano would be the logical choice to teach bratty little Lauren. And while I entertained that thought, another one pulsed through my brain. Only a disciplined pianist would move his piano from Germany to France during a war. He played. And he played often.

"It's bad enough to have a German living next door, but now I have to listen to him play?" I shivered all over.

"Sorry, Gaby," Simone said, touching my shoulder.

"How are we supposed to listen to the broadcasts now?" Martine whispered. "With a German living next to us."

It was quiet while we let that thought sink in—piercingly quiet despite the movers next door.

"We'll take it to the shop," Simone said. "Smuggle it in a garment bag and listen to it there." Martine nodded feverishly, and they both waited for me to agree. "Gaby?"

Martine was right to be concerned. It wasn't safe to listen to the broadcast now, here in our own home with the German sharing our wall. We'd have to move it to the shop.

"Fine," I said.

Martine reached for a garment bag after taking the radio out of the piano. She added in a wad of jackets we used for scrap, but the radio was a bulky thing and made the bag look bottom-heavy and odd.

"We'll have to use the rolling cart. The one we use when we move sewing machines."

Martine lifted the bag onto the cart, which she had retrieved from one of the back rooms. "I hope this works," she said, in a way that made me think she had doubts.

My face fell. "Martine—"

"I mean it will work." She nodded to herself. "It will."

Chapter Six

We walked up to the shop a little later than normal and closer to lunch time, with shopkeepers already busy with their sandwich boards out. Cawing seagulls flew overhead, which startled Martine when normally it never would. "Why is everyone staring?" she asked.

"They're staring at you because you're staring at them," Simone hissed.

"She's right," I said to Martine. "Act normal." I waved to Madame Roche at the lock shop, whose curtains were open today, while Martine huffed along, lugging the cart behind her as if it indeed had a radio on it.

"Wait for me," she said, giving the cart a pull, but it had gotten hung up on the curb. "Gaby!" Her plead for help attracted some attention.

I walked briskly back, taking the cart by the handle and helping her maneuver it across the street.

"What has gotten into you?" I asked under my breath. "I said to act normal."

I unlocked the front door, and we slipped inside under the slight ting of bells. Martine immediately lugged the radio to the back to plug it in and I had to stop her. "What are you doing?"

"The broadcast," she said.

"We can't listen *here* in the daytime," I said. "What if a customer comes in and overhears or gets suspicious, wondering why we are in the back and not minding the shop? What are the chances they'd mention something early, anyway? We'll have to wait until the end of the day."

Martine slumped forward, nearly dropping the radio she'd picked up.

"There," I said, pointing. "Put it under the counter with the other garment bags."

She swiped her fringe from her forehead while balancing the radio. "But—"

I shook my head. "When we're closed. I can't agree to anything else now."

Simone gave her a look. She was on my side with this one.

"Fine." Martine slid the radio under the counter.

We worked in silence, with very few customers coming in for mending and services, which normally would have caused concern, but I rather liked the shop being quiet today. Martine wouldn't do much of anything except look out the window, watching passersby and jotting down anything suspicious.

"The reward station is back." Martine whistled. "And Madame Roche is *not* pleased about it, not in the least." Simone and I dashed over to see, and sure enough, Madame Roche paced the cobblestones in front of the German receiving table, arms folded, only to throw them into the air every time a

French person tried to collect on a reward when they could have eaten the bird.

"She reminds me of you," I said to Martine, who gave me a side-eye. She hated it when I compared them.

"Here she comes!" We scuttled away from the window, pretending we hadn't been looking, and took up our usual spots with Simone behind the counter and me sitting on a stool.

Madame threw open the door, panting like a dog in the doorway and tousling her gray fringe. "Those damn Huns," she said. "One day they'll pay. It's because of them I sell locks and not herring. It's because of them we lost our boat. It's because of them I lost my husband." Her eyes went to the ceiling, talking to God. "You know I'm right."

"Hallo, Madame," Martine said, closing the door.

She blustered into the shop and took a seat by the window. "Hallo."

Monsieur Roche was a proud man who led a delegation during the first war on horseback, but what he always talked about, what he was most proud of, was when he marched alongside his remaining troops through the streets of Paris during the Paris Peace Conference. In return, he was the first veteran targeted by the invaders upon their return. *General Roche*, the Germans called through the streets, *you can't hide*!

And he couldn't. Not that he would.

Aunt Blanche said he marched through the old town in full regalia after the Battle of Boulogne with all his medals and stood at attention when they took him away—a prison somewhere is what everyone hoped for. Then one day not long after we arrived home from Paris, a lorry pulled up to Madame's home, delivering a box with his clothes.

Madame sat with her legs crossed tightly at the ankle, lips pinched, scraping flecks of blue paint from her thumb before looking up.

"I might have some cleaner that can get that paint off," I said, and she dug her hands into her lap.

"It's not paint."

I heard she'd been a painter, mostly seascapes and the herring stand she and her husband once owned, but those were rumors—nobody had seen her paintings since the Germans came.

"Madame Roche, do you know how many pigeons have been turned in?" Martine asked.

"A lot. I heard one of the Huns say they found two parachute boxes crushed and burned, and remnants of two others. All the birds that have been returned have boxes. That means at least four of them must still be out there." Her eyes went to the ceiling again. "I hope someone uses those birds to inflict pain and suffering on these Boches."

"Shh... Madame, you know the walls have ears," I said, even though the businesses on either side of us had shuddered.

"I don't care who hears me," Madame said. "My husband is dead, and I'm too old." She pointed a shaking finger toward the window. "Leave, you occupiers. Leave!"

She took a deep breath after Simone touched her shoulder, which broke her temper. "I'm sorry, girls," she said. "Sorry to get worked up in your shop. I'm putting you in danger, aren't I?"

"No," I said, though she probably was. The Germans knew of her feelings, and they made no secret of how much they hated her. It was a wonder she still had a shop to keep, with the fines they imposed on her, but everyone needed a lock shop, especially during a war.

She handed me something wrapped in foil from her pocket. "I saved this for you girls." She smiled, watching me unwrap it.

"Chocolate?" I asked. Martine and Simone wasted no time reaching in to snap a square from the bar. "Where did you get this?" Chocolate was harder to find than coffee on the black market. "This must have cost you a lock or two, or maybe even a spoon."

"I can't reveal my source," she said. "And don't worry about how many locks it cost me. It's my treat." She smiled. "It's good, isn't it?"

Martine ate hers in one chomp, while Simone savored hers, letting it melt on her tongue.

"Thank you, Madame," Simone said. "I've been so hungry, and this tastes so good. It's…" She closed her eyes briefly. "It's a forgotten taste, and it brings back so many memories."

Aunt Blanche used to bring us chocolate on holidays. The entire boarding school was given a hunk the size of her palm.

"Thank you, Madame," I said.

She pulled a tin of herring from her pocket next. "Thought I'd give you the chocolate first. Hard to get excited over herring now, isn't it?" She set the can on the counter.

Madame was right about not getting excited about herring, though we were glad to have the extra portion. We never asked, but we thought she might have enough canned herring to feed the village from before the Germans seized her drifter, not that she'd tell us. A secret like that was worth keeping, even from your friends.

"I'm sorry about your aunt," Madame added. "Blanche.

She was a friend to me once, when I needed her."

I straightened. "You heard?"

"I had a feeling," she said. "I really did. But I wasn't going to say a peep about it. I heard the Germans talking about a captain taking up residence somewhere in your neighborhood. I had a sinking feeling it was your aunt's apartment. Then Antoinette was in early this morning, just before I saw you—"

"I despise her," Martine said.

"Martine!" I snapped, though I didn't have a problem with her despising our neighbor. I had a problem with her saying it so loud.

"Don't be sorry," Madame Roche said. "She knows everything. A German sow she is."

Martine folded her arms, nodding and looking at me along with Madame Roche, and I thought I was looking at Martine's future self. Madame Roche, thirty years her senior, *was* a dead ringer for Martine at twenty—with her hair lopped off at her shoulders, gray and coarse, with her fringe in her eyes, just like Martine, only hers was dark blonde. I wasn't sure why my sister couldn't see it, especially with the same look in their eyes as they cocked their heads.

"Have you met him?" Madame asked.

"No. They were still unloading his things when we left. Does anyone else know about our *guest*?" Word had already spread faster than I thought it would. I shuddered to know who else knew.

"I don't know. Oh girls," she said, taking a deep breath, "I worry about you three. I do. How are you? I heard poor Hélène from down the street weeping last night over her brother Rémy. I hope he's all right."

"She was crying?" Martine asked, and when Madame

Roche nodded, she looked a little sad—the boy who loved her *had* left for the factory just as she commanded him to.

"We're doing as well as we can," I said.

"My best advice is to stay away from all Germans. Don't talk to them, sew for them, work for them—" Her gaze shifted to Simone after she'd slunk across the room like a cat on a wire, picking up a thread box. "And whatever you do, don't walk like that around a German." Madame pulled Simone's coat lapels tightly around her, wrapping her up like a package and covering all but her blonde head of curls. "Save that kind of walk for after the war. Not during."

"Yes, Madame," was all Simone could say.

"Why would we work for them?" I asked, to see if she knew something about the piano lesson, but she shrugged. My sisters shot me strange glances.

"Oh, I know you wouldn't." Germans looking through her shop windows startled her. "Get away!" she shouted as if they could hear her, then she left like a gust of wind, returning to her shop.

"Why'd you ask her that?" Simone asked.

"Because I wanted to see if she knew. Madame Roche knows everything – as much as Antoinette – and if she doesn't know about Lauren, then there's a good chance our neighborhood doesn't either."

"Believe me, Gaby," Simone said. "When she finds out, we won't need to ask."

Martine looked back out the window, gazing up and down the street with her nose pressed against the windowpane, while Simone and I did busywork the rest of the day, waiting for time to pass.

"Let's close up. We've had hardly any customers and it's

getting late now." Martine pointed to Madame Roche as she flipped her closed sign over. "The lock shop is closed."

"The lock shop always closes at four-thirty. It's normal. But for us it would look suspicious because our regular time is five o'clock," I said.

"But the streets are nearly empty. A chilly and damp April evening near the sea. Nobody's out now. The day is over," she said.

Simone looked over from the counter, and Martine waited for me to give word. Rain clouds had rolled in, adding to the darkened sky, with a kick of sea wind scraping the glass.

"In the back," I whispered, and each of us scrambled, pulling down window shades and locking the door. Martine lugged the radio into the back, situating it on the floor where Simone had lit a candle instead of using the lights.

We sat awkwardly around it after I'd plugged the cord into the electrical socket, my hands twisting as Martine spun the dial through the static and fuzz before finding a station. "I think I found it…"

It was a Frenchwoman with a distinct cut to her voice that sent a chill down my spine, addressing the Germans far and away, telling them that their women were lying with others back at home. "Nobody hates the Germans more than me," she said.

"Who is this?" Martine breathed, and I swear she had hearts in her eyes.

Simone sat up. "Oh, I know! I heard about her at the—" She caught her tongue with a hard swallow. "They call her The She Wolf. Nobody knows who she is, though the Germans are trying desperately to find out. Turn the dial some more," she said, and Martine turned the dial.

I held Simone's gaze—more information she'd learned from her lover, I was sure. I wondered if Martine would catch on, notice Simone knew a lot about a subject we'd never talked about, and when she looked up, I thought the reckoning had come.

Simone blinked and blinked, but Martine was still too mesmerized by The She Wolf's broadcast to care.

"Well, she's wrong," Martine said. "Nobody hates the Germans more than *me*, Martine Cotillard."

I patted her knee. "Spin the dial."

Martine found the BBC station without too much interference. French words, English words, and after a long speech about patriotism and staying the course, they played "Le Chant des Partisans"—the song of the resistance.

"It's past five o'clock. When's the broadcast going to start?" Martine asked, but of course, neither of us knew.

"What did you expect?" I asked. "To turn on the radio and hear something straightaway?" I stood up on my knees, looking serious and stern. "To the French women in Boulogne-sur-Mer, thank you for the U-boat details…"

Martine rolled her eyes. "Sit down."

"You know what Aunt Blanche used to say," I said. "Ask for patience and God sends you the opposite." I pulled a bottle of gin out from behind our storage boxes and gave it to Martine because it was her favorite. "She'd also tell you to drink her gin."

Martine gasped, snatching the bottle away even though I had freely held it out for her to take. "I didn't know we still had this." She wiped her mouth with a snarl after she swallowed. "Ah, and it tastes like cleaner—that first sip." She took another sip to wash the first one away. "The second sip is always better." She passed it to Simone, who took one sniff and passed it to me.

"It turns my stomach," Simone said.

"More for us, then," Martine said.

I took a sip, feeling the burn in my belly, which fooled me into thinking I had something of substance in my stomach other than tea and toast. "The herring!" I retrieved the tin Madame had brought us, and we shared forkfuls of herring and sips of gin as the music played.

"Herring from a tin reminds me of beach picnics in the sun with Aunt Blanche, our loungers in the sand, sitting under striped umbrellas, and eating our ice-cream cones," I said. "We can't even spend a day on the beach now, not with the Germans controlling the best parts of it and banning us from the rest."

"I remember the buoy bells jingling in the water—not the German ones, but the colorful French ones, and the local fishing boats. Not a slip to be had before the invasion," Martine said.

"Forget about before. I want to talk about the future," Simone said, shifting on the floor in her coat while Martine guzzled the gin. "What are your hopes and dreams for after the war?"

Martine wiped her mouth. "I want to see the Germans running away. Not retreating. I want to see them run. That's my dream, my wish. And of course, a big celebration in the street, and Rémy—" She stopped herself, and I thought she might actually admit something out loud to us about the man she loved, but she'd looked away. "That's all. A celebration in the street."

Simone pulled her coat up, folding her arms. "Gaby?"

"My dream for after the war?" I didn't want to be alone. That's what my dream was. To have someone sit beside me as the sun rose—someone I could play for. Someone to share breakfast with. But those seemed like impossible dreams, dreams not worth repeating. "I don't know. What about you?"

"Love," Simone said. "My dream is for my sisters to find love."

Love. The space between us turned awkward and silent.

"Hmm," I said, followed by Martine. Static crackled from the speaker, with me looking at my hands in my lap.

"It's almost time to walk back home," Martine said, changing the subject. "What if there's not a broadcast at all tonight?"

"There always is," Simone said, and not even a second later the first notes of Beethoven's Fifth Symphony beat through the speaker. Martine hit my knee repeatedly, holding the gin bottle to her chest.

"This is it!"

"Shh!" I said. "For God's sake, Martine."

We all three leaned in.

Bom, bom, bom, bom… Bom, bom, bom, bom…

"This is London calling. Before we begin, please listen to some messages to our friends…" Then what followed was a series of odd statements that made no sense. "The wine is warm, and storms are on Saturday. Tell your uncle hello, and to The She Wolf, we are forever indebted to your spirited arrangement of words. Thank you. Take Courage. We will not forget you."

The station went back to playing "Le Chant des Partisans" over and over.

"That's it?" Martine asked.

Now it was me reaching for the gin, taking a swig.

"But there has to be more," Martine said, shaking the radio, but that did nothing. She pushed it away, sliding it slightly across the floor, before folding her arms. "Bastards. The She Wolf gets a mention but nothing about us?"

Simone felt her forehead. "Maybe our pigeon was caught by the Germans?"

"And maybe it wasn't," Martine said.

"Maybe they're still verifying the information," I said. "They'll have to find Professor Caron first, and I'm sure that will take some time and it's only been a few days." I nodded, believing my own story. "That's it. We just have to wait. Listen again tomorrow."

I closed my eyes. Listening again came with risks.

"This scheme will work, Gaby," Martine said. "It will. Have faith in it, and me."

I nodded to appease her, and we got up off the floor to leave.

"What do we do with the radio?" Martine asked. "Keep it here?"

"We can't," Simone said. "We've been burgled once already. What if someone finds it and turns us in?"

"They didn't find the gin," Martine said.

Part of me didn't like keeping the radio so far away, left to burglars to find or bad French who wanted to intimidate us, but hauling it daily to and from the shop was riskier than keeping it here. "We have to leave it."

We searched for a place to stash it for the night, but there wasn't a place hidden well enough. We decided to keep it in a cabinet by the door, accessible to anyone, but hidden in plain sight. "What was that you said about the Germans, Martine?" I asked.

"Stupid as turkeys in the rain," she said.

The cabinet doors were thin with a rusty latch. A bump in the night could burst them open.

"Let's hope they really are that stupid," Simone said.

"Come on," I said, while Martine tucked the bottle of gin in her coat pocket, and Simone locked the door.

The house was dark, as expected, but not empty. We stared up at our aunt's old bedroom window from the pavement, where the curtains were drawn.

"He's in there," Simone whispered. "Isn't he?"

"Of course, he is," Martine said. "Boche—soulless German, steals a woman's house and calls it his own."

"Shh!" I said. "Someone will hear." Antoinette's curtains were drawn for the night, but I wouldn't put it past her to be watching us through a slit, studying us from the shadows, wondering why we came home so late when it wasn't like us to push it so close to curfew.

I opened the front door to a dark salon and an even darker staircase. I put my finger to my lips for the girls to be quiet after softly closing the door, and we followed each other up the rickety old stairs to our bedrooms without a candle.

"Damn that Marie Antoinette," Martine whispered. "None of this would have happened if it wasn't for her."

"Shh!" I said through my teeth, and we continued walking upstairs, one, two, three steps more, creaking, creaking...

Creak!

Chapter Seven

I woke with a start, and lay staring up at the ceiling with my blanket pulled tightly up to my neck. I felt the German's presence in our home, even though we were separated by a wall. I imagined him thinking of us, and wondering what we looked like, as we thought of him.

I threw off the blanket and padded to my doorway, looking blankly to the end of the hallway. Simone stepped out of her bedroom next, her pink peignoir draping her body in folds with layers of nightgown underneath, followed by Martine, hair a muss and pressed to one side of her head.

Martine jabbed the air. "He's in there listening," she said.

"Shh..." I whispered, before waving for them to come into my room, where we could talk without fear of being heard. Martine tiptoed the best she could without making a sound, while Simone took giant floating steps through my door, her peignoir tossing up with her feet.

I closed the door softly.

"What are we going to do?" Martine asked. "We can't whisper all the time. Can we?"

"No," I said. "We can't."

Simone twisted her hands. "I didn't think about it before, really think about it, but now it feels so real. Scary. A German living in Aunt Blanche's apartment."

"I know, I know," I said, pacing my room in my bare feet, before facing them as they sat on my bed. "We'll carry on like normal. It would look suspicious otherwise." I lowered my voice. "Only no talking about the pigeon out loud, the radio, or anything about rations, and God knows what else we've gotten ourselves into."

"Espionage," Martine said. "That's what we've gotten ourselves into."

I sat heavily on my bed next to Martine. "I'm glad you found only one pigeon." I lowered my voice even more. "I don't think we're meant to be spies."

"I can find another," she whispered back. "What about the missing pigeons? The Germans are still looking for four others. One of those was ours, so where are the other three?"

"We've done our part, even if our bird died or was caught," I said. "Be glad with what we did, or tried to do. There's only so much we can control, Martine. The rest is up to God."

Martine turned to Simone for a reaction but she was staring at her hands.

"Did you hear me?"

"I heard you." Martine moved to the window. "So today is an average day. Except I'd like to leave early. The less time I'm at home with the German next door the better."

"Yes, let's leave early for the shop," I said, but then closed my eyes with a heavy sigh. "But I can't. I have lessons with Lauren this morning."

"Why don't you tell the commandant our German guest should teach her," Martine said. "He plays the piano."

"I plan to." The last thing I wanted to do was visit the commandant's house again and teach that bratty Lauren how to play the piano. No French child should behave that way. Shame on her mother. "Do me a favor and remind me when the war is over…"

"Remind you of what?" Simone asked, and my eyes popped open.

"To visit Lauren's mother," I said.

"Why?" Martine asked.

"To tell her what a spoiled brat she raised," I said, "and the only reason I agreed to teach her daughter piano was because her husband had threatened a mother and child. She needs to know. And I want to be the one to tell her."

Antoinette's voice lifted from her garden and we got up to look out the window, pulling the curtain back. "I'll remind you," Martine said as we squished in together, faces to the glass. "As long as you remind me to visit our miserable neighbor."

"What are you going to do?" I asked.

We watched Antoinette chase her chickens around her garden, laughing with a basket full of brown eggs hooked on her arm before traipsing back inside into her warm home, complete with smoke billowing from her chimney from a morning fire. Extra wood was expensive on the black market. Only the bad French who received rewards or the Germans could afford to keep a constant fire and their homes impeccably warm.

"You don't want to know," Martine answered.

Although we shouldn't be acting any differently, we still tiptoed through the house and mouthed or whispered our words. I put my coat on near the front door, getting ready to go to the commandant's house. "I'll be a few hours," I said, my voice booming through the quiet house like a horn, causing Martine to bolt from her chair in the kitchen and Simone to spill her tea down the front of her peignoir.

"Stop yelling," Martine mouthed, but I motioned for one of them to hurry up and answer back, like a normal conversation. Her lips pinched before she realized what I meant.

"See you in a few hours," she finally said back. I kept motioning for more words, something that sounded ordinary, when she added, "Have a good day!"

I rolled my eyes—in our attempt to sound normal, we sounded suspicious.

Simone scooted from her chair. "Don't forget your scarf." She snagged a scarf from the rack only to pull it back because I already had mine on, and besides, he couldn't see us, so why bother giving it to me? She shrugged, hanging it back up. "Since you'll be that way, can you pick up our bread? I heard the fresh loaves are pulled out nearer to noon."

"I'll pick up the bread," I said, projecting my voice.

Outside, I took a moment to button my coat, wondering how much more time would pass before we'd be able to act like ourselves again without the threat of someone hearing us, informing on us, or treating us badly. I felt the captain watching me from the window, but when I turned around it was Martine.

"What are you doing?" she mouthed through the glass.

I walked away, looking over my shoulder and checking for

neighbors, before looking at Antoinette's house and her closed curtains where the slightest ripple of movement could be seen.

———

Smoke curled out from tall chimneys in the German neighborhood, and I felt the warmth of all those morning fires in my lungs when I breathed. I walked up to the commandant's big peach house and raised my hand to knock, but the housekeeper opened the door before I had a chance, giving me a fright. "Oh..." I said, pulling my hand back. "Good morning."

She grinned, smooth-lipped and big-eyed, holding the door open, and I thought I should introduce myself even though I'd met her once already.

"I'm—"

"Mademoiselle Cotillard." She made way for me to walk through the door. "It's nine o'clock and you're right on time. We've been looking forward to it."

I'd just stepped into the house when I heard Lauren yell upstairs. "I want my teacher!"

"We've *all* been looking forward to it," the housekeeper said.

I waited for instructions, standing awkwardly in the foyer and not sure if I should go on up without first being told to.

"Today the commandant will be expecting improvement. Do you understand?" She pointed for me to go upstairs, but now I was stunned and couldn't move even if I wanted to.

"But it's the second lesson," I said.

"Still, he is expecting it." She pointed upstairs again for me to move along, then walked away herself, leaving me in the foyer listening to Lauren yell for her teacher upstairs.

I padded up the carpeted steps to where Lauren was running rampant around the piano in her playroom, waving ribbons above her head while her mistress Irma chased after her.

I cleared my throat in the doorway, and Lauren made a sudden stop, the ribbons dithering in the air behind her. "I didn't think you'd come back!"

I smiled politely, resisting the urge to tell her I was forced to. "Of course I came back."

Her mistress slipped out of the room and I pointed to her piano, which had its lid pulled up and her blanket slung over the bench. Ragged dolls lay halfway off the top with their hair dangling toward the floor. "Have you been practicing?" I asked.

She tilted her head. "You didn't tell me to practice."

She was right, I didn't tell her to practice. I'd left thinking it was the last time I'd ever have to see her. "Oh, I thought I did," I lied. "My mistake." I motioned to the bench to have a seat. "Shall we?"

She skipped over to the piano, throwing her blanket off to the side and swiping all the dolls from the top to the floor. I sat next to her while she got seated, staring at the piano keys with my hands in my lap, wondering how I was going to achieve marked improvement by the end of our lesson.

"What do you want me to do?" she asked, but I was still staring at the keys. "Teacher?"

I forced a smile. "Let's start with your hands."

She set her hands brashly on the keys, and I winced—it might as well have been her fists. "Not like that." I positioned her hands in the form of a loose "c" and she was eager to know why and if she was doing it right, looking over my hands as I maneuvered her fingers, which I thought was a good sign.

I showed her a few basic chords, pointing out how they look on the staff, and moved her fingers into position. I remembered what Aunt Blanche had said when I was Lauren's age. That everyone learns differently, and some will need to do it themselves, and others learn by watching others do it. I lifted my hands, wondering if she'd learned anything.

"Like this?" She bent her hands backward, cracking all ten of her fingers before wiggling them in the air and placing them back on the keys, and failing miserably with a clang, clang, clang.

"No," I said with a sigh. "Not like that." I got up and walked around the piano, noticing the time and how I was running out of it. Holding her hands properly and perfecting her posture were all important elements to know when playing the piano, but I was sure that wasn't the kind of improvement the commandant was expecting.

"I'll try it again." She plunked a few keys with her index fingers, followed by a chord progression that slowly turned into a melody, and then, shockingly, a song—one that sounded remarkably similar to the beginnings of Debussy's *Reverie*.

I turned around, my mouth hanging open as she continued to play.

"Lauren," I breathed, and she pulled her hands away. It wasn't a slip of her fingers or beginner's luck. "You already know how to play."

She stood from the bench, hands twisting.

Neither of us said a word, but I saw it in her eyes, and she saw it in mine—I knew her secret.

"Did you like it?" she asked. "Was it good?"

I could only stare at her, my eyes large and dry from not blinking, while she looked up at me, pleading for a response.

"Did you like it, mademoiselle?"

Her mistress burst in, causing Lauren to freeze in the middle of the carpet and me to clutch my chest as if I'd been caught doing something wrong. But she was only coming in with the mid-morning tea.

I smelled the mint and honey. "Sounds lovely in here…" Irma said, head down, arranging the linens, teacups, and saucers. "I brought you different biscuits this time, Lauren, as requested." She pointed to what looked like a sugary brown biscuit on a tiny plate, before scooting out the door.

I followed Lauren to the divan, sitting next to her and looking up at the dolls displayed on the shelf as we drank our tea.

"Are you going to tell?" she finally asked.

"Do you promise to show improvement when the commandant asks?" I asked, and she nodded, saying she would. "Then I won't tell. But why, Lauren?"

Lauren set her tea down and whispered in my ear, her breath warm and minty and sugary from the biscuit. "Because if nobody comes, I'd be alone." She pulled away, her little hand cupping her mouth and looking into my eyes, and my heart nearly broke into two. As bratty as she had been, she was a child, in the end.

"Yes," I said.

"Yes, what?"

"You asked me if I liked what you played. Yes."

She smiled after closing her eyes briefly, and it was that reaction that stayed with me while we sipped our tea, separately yet together, and I understood her more than I ever thought I would. Pretending to be a novice when she was obviously advanced wasn't easy to do. Especially for a child. I admired her for it. At such a young age, this little French girl had taught herself how to survive the occupation, and it had nothing to do with her mother. It had everything to do with her will to survive in a world that was bent on destroying itself and the light that burned inside of her.

"But, why me?" I asked. "Your mistress said you'd had other teachers, and you didn't like any of them."

"The others were German," she said. "You're the only French woman who has come."

A bedroom door opened and closed in the hallway, followed by the commandant's voice. He called for Irma and they talked on the other side of the door about Lauren, about her lesson and how much she'd improved. I stood sharply when it sounded like they were coming in. Lauren dashed to the piano and placed her hands on the keys.

"Don't worry, mademoiselle," she said, but I did worry and held my breath.

The door opened with a swoosh of air, and the commandant stood in the doorway, his broad shoulders nearly touching both sides of the doorframe while Lauren played a simple chord progression like an amateur, even missing a few notes and frowning to get it right.

He looked at me and then turned to Lauren.

"Do you like it, Papa?" She set her hands in her lap once she was finished. "She's so much better than those other teachers."

Irma came in behind him and confirmed how much Lauren

had changed since I'd arrived, and he looked pleased, genuinely pleased.

"You are content?" he asked Lauren, and she nodded.

"I knew I chose right," he said. "See, Gabriella Cotillard. You didn't want to teach, yet you did. Look what I made you do." He chuckled with that, his voice bumping across my limbs like a knife to the bone.

It was on the tip of my tongue to mention that our German guest played a Steinway, and how perhaps he could be Lauren's teacher, but when I looked at her little face, I couldn't do it, not after what I knew about her now. I patted her head when she smiled up at me.

"Is there something you want to say?" the commandant asked.

I shook my head.

"Very well." He talked to Irma quietly in the hallway, nodding and looking in our direction before turning on his heel and going downstairs.

Irma pulled an envelope from her pocket. "For you," she said, pressing it warmly in my palm. "The commandant has stepped out, but will be back at the top of the hour for a meeting, and you must be gone at that time." She leaned in to whisper. "I wish you could stay longer. She's different when you're here and she's rather mean when you're not."

It was then I heard a very distinct German accent that hadn't been there before. Lauren's eyes lifted from the piano keys, and she smiled slyly to herself behind her mistress's back.

"Understand?" Irma asked. "Top of the hour, and not a second after."

"I understand," I said.

"Mademoiselle, sit," Lauren said once we were alone again, patting the empty space next to her on the bench. I thought she'd play for me, but Lauren wanted to talk. She told me how she didn't like the dolls, even pointing out which one she hated the most, but that the commandant bought them for her because he thinks all little girls want them. She handed me one with a checkered black skirt only to replace it with a doll wearing a lacy blue one.

"Where do you live?" she asked. "Do you have children?"

"No children," I said, still holding her doll, "but I have two sisters. Martine is the youngest at twenty and Simone is twenty-three. I'm the oldest."

"I've always wanted a sister," she said. "Do they play the piano too?"

Martine would only play the piano if she knew some sort of revenge could come of it, and Simone would rather listen. "I'm the only one. My aunt taught me. She was a brilliant pianist and raised us after our mother died when we were little."

"Do you have a husband?" she asked, but I'd answered enough questions about myself, and felt her doll's chipped hands, thinking about the number of times her porcelain head had met the piano keys.

"Lauren, why does the commandant serve you so?"

She turned away before taking the doll from my hands and setting it back on the shelf. "Because he'll do whatever my mother wishes. No matter how badly I behave."

"Where is your mother?"

Her back was still to me. "In his bed."

I stood, wanting to reach out for her, but before I could, she'd whipped around, latching onto my waist, hugging me tightly. There was nothing more to ask, as I understood perfectly. I hugged her back.

"Don't go," she said at the top of the hour.

"I have to. Irma insisted."

Voices lifted from the commandant's study, and I felt a slight panic in my chest. His meeting was starting two minutes early, and I was still in the house. But why did they sound like they were in the room with us? Even from one floor up. I looked at the carpet, lifting my feet as if I was standing on them.

"It's because of the hole in the floor," she explained. "It's wallpapered over now in the study, but I hear everything. Day and night and sometimes in between."

"A hole?"

"My real papa and I used to play a game. A telephone game with a copper hose and an old oil funnel. It was fun for us, but he's dead, and now I have this new papa." Her lips pinched. "But he's *not* my papa."

I threw my coat up into the air like a cape, shoving my arms into the sleeves.

"You will come back, won't you, mademoiselle?" she asked. "What I mean is, you'll come back because you want to?"

I lifted her head by the chin, nodding, and her eyes lit up.

Chapter Eight

I walked head down out of the German neighborhood into the village, cutting across the street to the bakery to pick up our ration of bread. "All out," I was told. Only day-old remnants of white bread that had turned gray and hard were available, and the portions were already tiny, palm-sized versions of what a loaf used to be before the war.

Simone would be disappointed, but it was the best they had.

"Do you want the remnant?" the baker asked as I was deciding, when another woman offered to take it if I didn't, holding out her ration coupon and telling the baker I was taking too long and to just give it to her.

"I want it," I said, digging out my coupon.

He leaned forward over the counter. "Aren't you Simone's sister?" he asked with a smile, and I nodded. "Give her my regards." He passed the bread over and I realized he had given me a softer one from under the counter.

I stared at him, a little shocked and not sure what to say.

He'd never passed on a message for her before or had given me a better loaf free of charge. I tucked the bread under my arm before the woman behind me made a fuss. "Thank you, I will."

Martine burst through the door. "Gaby!" She pushed past the others in line to get to me, causing quite a stir, and took my arm. "Pardon us…"

She led me out of the bakery and far enough away where nobody could hear. I worried something bad had happened. Simone was arrested even though the dances were at night. Or maybe the Abwehr found our radio.

"What is it?" I asked.

"I'm so glad I found you. I have news!" Martine's face was a mix of emotions and I couldn't tell if she was excited or frightened. "The pigeon made it."

"What?" I asked, and she smiled. "How do you know?"

"Come on. I'll tell you at the shop."

We raced to the shop as quickly as we could without causing alarm, but startled Simone behind the counter with her needle and thread when I threw open the door.

"Did you hear?" she whispered once our door had closed.

I nodded, sloughing off my coat after setting down the bread. "But how do you know?" I looked at both of them. "Well…" My heart thumped.

"We turned the radio on while we were closed for lunch, and you said it was all right when we were closed," Martine said.

I crossed my arms; that is what I said. "And…"

"The broadcaster said he had news from a special visitor that had just flown in, and his name—"

"Emile," Martine said breathlessly. "His name is Emile." I

gave her a confused look, and she motioned with her hands for me to understand. "Emile is the pigeon, you see? Remember the comic Aunt Blanche used to read in the paper?"

My face changed. Aunt Blanche did read a comic about a pigeon named Emile, but that was so long ago. I hadn't seen or heard about that comic for years. "And you heard this just now?" I bit my lip, holding back my enthusiasm.

"Yes," Martine said. "And we would have heard more but our miserable neighbor Marie Antoinette came by and knocked and knocked and knocked even though our closed sign was up. Now we're just waiting until five o'clock so we can listen again."

"She's never called on us here before," I said. "You didn't let her in, did you?"

"Why would I let her in?" Martine asked.

"She probably wanted to know about our guest," Simone said. "You know how she is."

"This is good news about Emile, right?" Martine held my hands. "You're not mad at us for listening, are you?"

"Not since you closed the shop to do it, and especially not if that message was for us." I looked at the clock, feeling my pulse race, but now we had to wait. Martine took a seat by the window like she normally did and Simone went back to sewing behind the counter. I went over the bookkeeping, but I could hardly work. None of us said a word, waiting in agony for five o'clock to strike.

Rain had started to spit on the pavements, keeping the customers away, while I penciled in our meager take from that week's alterations and went over the figures from weeks past, looking for an error in our favor, a little more money to spend, but I had always been good with math. We still had the money from my last lesson and today's, but it wasn't money we could spend without consequences. I reached down and felt the envelope in my pocket, listening to the thready pull of Simone's needle over the tap of rain, and Martine's heavy breathing, watching the hour hand's slow tick to the top of the hour.

"It's five!" Martine announced, and I snapped my book closed.

"Get the door," I said.

After Martine pulled down the window shade, she locked the door, flipping the closed sign over. Simone reached for the radio, sliding it across the floor still dressed in her thick wool coat, and all the way into the backroom.

"Shh, shh, shh…" I said as Martine flipped on the switch and adjusted the dial. A burst of static replaced the silence. Then words in French and English. Words about resistance. Hearts and bravery. Words we've heard a thousand times in Paris when all we wanted to know was if they received our message. The longer the announcer rambled on, the more I started to think there was added information the girls missed after Emile was mentioned, and now Radio Londres had moved on.

"Maybe we already missed it?" I asked.

"It's all that Marie Antoinette's fault if we did." Martine had stood up from the floor to pace, shaking her head and folding her arms, saying words about Antoinette only a sailor would repeat. "I loathe that woman. Loathe!" She pulled her collar away from her neck where she'd started to perspire, while Simone folded her arms over her coat.

"Aren't you warm?" Martine asked, but Simone shook her head. "I'm burning up."

"Antoinette always makes you hot under the collar," Simone said.

"Keep it down," I said, though I had to admit, Antoinette was becoming more than an annoyance with her intrusions, starting with her visit after the Abwehr. "I don't like her coming to our place of business."

"Who does?" Martine asked.

Bom, bom, bom, bom... Bom, bom, bom, bom...

Martine dropped to the floor from hearing Beethoven's Fifth Symphony boom over the radio. "It's starting!" She adjusted the volume and we huddled close next to her.

"This is London calling. Before we begin, please listen to some messages to our friends..." We held hands, knuckles white, waiting, waiting, and waiting for news about us. "We thank our new friends across the Channel. We tracked down the adviser. May The Heroines be remembered for generations."

I let go of their hands to cover my mouth.

"Did he just mention The Heroines?" Martine asked, pointing to the radio, nodding, answering her own question as if she couldn't trust her ears. "He said it. I heard it!"

I thought my heart had stopped. Thinking about something that I had spent so much time trying to bury—a story silenced in the music, now heard kilometers away across the sea—had stirred up an array of emotions. I wasn't sure if I wanted to laugh, fall to my knees and cry, or collapse into my sister's arms. I felt my music all over again, tingling my skin. I felt the story. Professor Caron had shared a little bit of my soul with at least one person in London, and I knew that feeling would stay with me for many days.

I held my chest, eyes closed.

"Gaby?" Martine said, but I was deep in my own mind, now wondering who she had shared my music with, exactly, and what he thought of the motif because surely the professor had played it for him. "Gaby!"

"What?" My eyes popped open, and Martine threw her arms around my neck.

"Thank you," she whispered, and we embraced without words, yet understanding what this success meant to each other. So many schemes, and so many failures. She kissed both my cheeks, and I squeezed her a little tighter.

"Girls…" Simone had stood up from the floor, looking toward the front of the shop, but we were lost in our own triumphs and in our heads. "Girls!" She yanked on my arm to break us up, and we pulled away. "Someone's here," she rasped, and when her eyes searched the air, my stomach sank.

Knock! Knock!

"Hide the radio!" I shouted in a whisper, and Simone slid it across the floor to the wall under a pile of outstanding orders, tossing a robe, a gentleman's jacket, and an old apron on top. I turned to Martine, but she'd stomped off to the front of the shop.

"I've had it with Antoinette," Martine blustered.

"Martine," I said, only she kept walking amidst more knocking, much more forceful than Antoinette had ever sounded when she knocked on our door at home. "Wait!" I said, running in from the back to stop her, but she was too quick for me and flung the door open.

"What do you think—" The door slipped from her hand

when she saw who it was, hitting the wall with a gust of wind and spitting rain.

"Hallo, Fraulein."

It wasn't Antoinette. It wasn't even Madame Roche.

It was a German officer of the Reich.

He stood in our doorway, rain dripping off his hat and pooling around his black jackboots while Martine stood like a pole, unmoving.

My mind ran wild with explanations of what brought him to our door. We'd kept the radio down. How could he have known?

I gulped.

He looked right over Martine's head to me and Simone standing behind the counter, then took a step inside, carefully taking off his hat. "I have a button that needs mending." He pointed to a lost button on his feldgrau jacket.

Still, none of us moved, not even Martine, who was dwarfed by his size and standing behind him with the door still open.

"We're closed, officer," I finally said.

"You are Gabriella Cotillard, no?" he asked, and I blinked hard.

"Yes."

Martine shut the door, and the shop turned stuffy and warm even with the chill of the coastal breeze that had blown in with him.

"Commandant Streicher said to come here," he said, and my stomach sank even further.

"I see."

He turned his head slowly, taking in every detail of the shop, from the bare walls and tacky wallpaper to the blackboard above our counter with our rates for alterations and services. I smelled his musty cologne, like a thumbprint hovering over us.

"Though I wasn't sure..." He pointed over his shoulder to our door where a black ribbon would have been tied around the knob if we catered to Germans. "You will sew?"

He slipped off his jacket, shaking it like a tablecloth in front of him before offering it to me to fix. All I could do was stare at the jacket hanging from his strong hand as I thought about what to do.

I could hide the lessons I gave Lauren from most people, I was sure of it, but this—this was different. The commandant sent him here specifically. If I didn't take the jacket, he'd report back, and Mme. Leroux would be arrested and her son taken away. If I did take it...

I flashed a smile. "Yes, of course." I handed the jacket immediately to Simone, closing my eyes. I had no choice. In the end, I knew I didn't.

"One last customer, sister," I said, feeling the pain of each spoken word. "And do hurry. I'm sure the officer has somewhere to be." Simone had yet to move, save for her eyes over my shoulder, fixed upon the officer. "Now!"

Simone sprang to life, throwing open her needle kit and reaching for her thimble and thread.

I turned back around, hands clasped in front of me while listening to Simone search for a button out of a hundred to choose from, whereupon he handed her the missing button from his pocket. "It will be ready shortly," I said to him.

He nodded before making himself at home in the comfortable cushioned chair by the door.

Martine scooted next to me, both of us listening to Simone's needle whip through the buttonhole beneath the tap of rain and counting the passing seconds.

"Done!" Simone held the jacket up. It was the fastest I'd ever seen her sew in my life. A record for anyone. He got a good look at himself in the mirror with his jacket on, feeling the button with his fingertip before eyeing Simone in the reflection.

She pulled her coat inward by the lapels.

"Is it satisfactory?" I asked, and his eyes moved to mine through the mirror. "Your jacket," I said to clarify, making sure he knew I wasn't offering him my sister. "You are satisfied with the work?"

"Yes," he said. "Very nice. A clean, tight stitch." He gave his button one more feel before putting his hat back on, fitting it to his head. "Good evening." When he took a step toward the door, I was glad he forgot to pay us.

"Oh!" He turned around and dug into his front pocket. "Almost forgot." The coins jingled and clanged. "Payment, and a little extra."

He dropped a few coins in my reluctant hand, then left without much ado, and like any ordinary customer. Martine threw her back up against the closed door like a wet rag while Simone smelled her palms in disgust where his musty scent had transferred from his jacket to her skin.

I was still holding the German's coins in my open palm, staring at the space where he'd stood, and at that moment, I thought of the series of events that had transpired over the last few days, one spiraling into the other. I never wanted us to be in this position.

Simone handed us our coats to leave.

"I had no choice," I said.

"We never seem to have a choice anymore, do we?" Simone asked.

We followed each other outside where we hooked arms. Shop lights cast a yellowy glow on the wet pavements all the way down the street with the tick and tack of rain still falling in small pools, but the harbor was dark with bells chiming from the roll of waves against the buoys. I popped open my umbrella.

"How many people do you think saw?" Simone clenched my arm a little tighter.

"We're about to find out," Martine said.

"Hold your head up, girls," I said, and we took our first step. Madame Roche had kept her light on, then one shop here and another there went dark as we passed—a sign of contempt —the owners looking through the windows, obscured by a pull of their shade or curtain.

"Stupid turkeys in the rain, can't even sew on a button," Martine grumbled, and both Simone and I stopped on the slick pavement. We were used to her calling the Germans turkeys, but the sewing comment was new. "What?" she questioned, looking at us both, and we couldn't help but laugh.

"You're right, Martine," I said. "They can't even sew on a button. God help them if all the seamstresses go on strike. Maybe that's how we win the war?"

We laughed again and it was good to laugh, especially at the Germans' expense, but the moment of levity was lost the second we turned onto our road and saw all the lights on in my aunt's old apartment with people mingling behind the half-drawn curtains.

We stood still as statues. The captain was having a party.

"How can he do that?" Martine asked, pointing her finger

as if we couldn't see for ourselves. "The fines."

The rain had dissipated, and I folded up my umbrella as the clouds swept past us from the sea.

"He's German, Martine. He can do anything." His guests sipped cocktails between bantering laughs, cocktails from my aunt's special glasses no doubt.

I pulled them both to walk. "Come on."

Antoinette called us from the dark, and Martine froze, looking toward her house, but she was coming from the opposite direction.

"Over there," I whispered, and when Martine twisted around and saw Antoinette, her jaw nearly hit the ground. Not only was she leaving the captain's party, but she was also leaving with a man.

A tall, well-dressed man with a tie.

"Antoinette," I said, though it wasn't a greeting.

"Girls." She winced. "I mean ladies." She sauntered past us on the pavement, talking to her date about the evening sky, and what evenings were like in Berlin, where he had just visited, before pausing with a glance over her shoulder. "Sorry about your aunt. She was such a lovely woman."

"Don't come to our shop again, Antoinette," Martine said, but she'd already turned away with her date and walked into the night. Probably to her house. Maybe to his. "Whore," she added, and I jerked on her arm. "Bad French bastards—"

"Let's go," I said, unlocking our door.

We walked stoically into the dark salon, plopping our handbags on the table with heavy hands. Simone lit a candle as we listened to the din of the party next door. Germans and bad French sitting in our aunt's salon and enjoying the space gave us a sickening feeling that contrasted with the aroma of seasoned pork wafting through the vent.

The only blessing about the party was that with all that clatter, we didn't have to whisper and we didn't have to make up conversations for his benefit.

Simone took a deep breath through her nose. "Do you smell that?" She exhaled with a moan. "Pork crackling and butter."

Martine hung up her coat. "You can't smell the butter."

"I can smell the butter. I love butter so I can smell it." Simone took another deep breath, but this time she closed her eyes. "Is this what it's going to be like, Gaby? We have to smell his food, listen to his parties?"

I hung up my coat. "I don't know."

"I wonder what he looks like," Martine said.

"He looks like what he eats," I said. "A pig."

Candlelight flickered over the faded patches on the wall where Aunt Blanche had once displayed our photographs. We took them down at her request when Germany invaded. "We mustn't give the Germans more information than they need," she had said.

But now, with the photographs gone, and a German living under our roof and another visiting our shop, it felt as if we were strangers in our own home and that we'd failed. I placed my palm on the wall, feeling the cold wallpaper beneath my hand, when a man from the party belly laughed about France's defeat. "Weak and dumb but know how to run," he said, and a roar of chuckles pulsed through the wall and over my skin like a bristly brush.

"I'm going to bed," Martine announced as she turned for the stairs, but I had an idea.

"Wait," I said.

They watched me walk away into the darkness of the house only to emerge seconds later with a hatbox full of old photos I'd pulled from the bureau. "Remember our photos?" I lifted the lid.

Martine and Simone reached into the box, thumbing through the countless photos Aunt Blanche took of us as children all the way up until we left for Paris.

"All the things she was proud of, our milestones." I pressed a photo to the wall, the one of me during my first piano lesson, then added the one of Martine on her eighteenth birthday just two years ago, and Simone with the first garment she sewed herself. "Right here, in photos."

Martine tossed the handful of photos she'd been thumbing through into the box. "Do we have to do this now?" She gave me a strange look—a look that normally came from me after she'd pitched one of her schemes.

"In Professor Caron's class, she'd pin photos to the wall of her students who received perfect exam scores. It was an honor. Soon enough she'd made an entire collage on the wall in her classroom. It was her way of seeing the results, and it was a way for us to be proud of ourselves."

I dug into the box, finding one of us three, smiling on a parkside bench by the sea when we were adolescents. "I know that German officer set us back—I didn't like staying open for him any more than you two—but after that broadcast tonight," I held the photo to the wall, centering it in a rectangle of faded wallpaper, "we deserve our photo on a wall."

Candlelight flickered between us. Another laugh came from the party, only this time a thud against the wall knocked the photo from my grasp. "This is our house," I said, reclaiming the photo from the floor. "Our home." I pinned it in place this time. "And the next thing you know, we'll have a collage of our own."

"What are you saying, Gaby?" Martine asked.

"I don't understand either," Simone said, folding her arms over her coat.

I smiled. "We need another pigeon," I whispered.

Martine yanked me by the arm, dragging me into the dark kitchen where we could talk without fear of being heard, despite the party noise. "What do you mean, we need another pigeon?" She bit her lip.

"Why stop now?" I asked.

"I can't believe you're saying this." Both hands moved to her head, sliding down her face to her cheeks in disbelief.

Simone, who had been standing at the candlelit edge of the room, came closer and whispered. "We agreed it was just the one time. Besides, we don't have another pigeon. Unless they drop more from the sky."

Martine turned toward the window, looking into the night where the rain had stopped and a glimmer of moonlight shone eerily through the clouds. "They'll send more," Martine said.

"How do you know they'll drop more?" Simone asked.

"Because I asked for more in the message," Martine said, which got a glare from Simone.

"But also, we just gave them ten German fingers worth of information." Martine put her hands on her hips, smiling. "They won't stop now. I'm sure of it! Ten. German. Fingers."

"We did. Ten German fingers worth," I said, then turned to Martine. "For once I'm glad you acted without telling me, but from here on out, we have to be a team and work from a plan. Agreed?"

"Agreed," Martine said.

I put my hand out, followed by Martine's on top. We waited for Simone. "All three or none," I said, but Simone hesitated, chewing on her fingernail as if she wasn't sure. Martine beamed, motioning with her chin for Simone to add her hand.

She sighed heavily. "All right," Simone said, finally adding her hand. "But only if one drops from the sky into our hands. That's all I'll agree to."

Chapter Nine

London

Guy Burton sat by the wireless with his colleague, Clive, waiting to hear the message he'd dispatched to Bertie at the BBC to announce on the Radio Londres broadcast. He'd worked hours on it at the Secret Intelligence Service's request, selecting precise language to convey the right meaning. All this while he'd been humming Gaby's piano piece. He thought he'd finally got the melody out of his head when the broadcast cut in to play Beethoven's Fifth Symphony.

He turned up the radio, leaning in, while Clive jotted down some notes. Afterward, Guy waited for a response from Clive, but he appeared to be thinking, tapping the end of his pencil on the table.

"The message you wrote was too easy," Clive finally said.

"Have a go at it, then." Guy challenged him because he knew his message was spot on with its encryption, even for an MI6 agent like Clive.

"Well, for starters, the 'heroine' term you used must mean it's a man. And using the word 'adviser' could mean he's a solicitor? 'Across the Channel' obviously means Belgium because you wouldn't lead the Germans exactly to where he was, in Calais or northern France."

Guy smiled. He'd composed the right message.

"I was right?"

"Well, you're an MI6 agent. You're trained for these things," Guy said because he wasn't about to tell him he was wrong.

"And I am up for promotion too, so I must be doing something right," Clive said, and Guy shrugged. "But what I didn't understand was the mention of Emile earlier in the day."

"Ah, yes. Emile." Guy laughed to himself about that one. It was a comic he'd come across when he was in France before the war. He knew the Germans would figure it out eventually, but hoped it would at least take them a few days.

"You think your heroines knew the meaning?"

Guy would have bet a pound to a penny that The Heroines knew exactly who Emile was. "I think so."

Clip-clops echoed down the corridor, and Guy leapt to his feet. There was only one person who made echoing clip-clops like that, and it was his supervisor, Rex Smith.

Guy's heart sped up. Before he wrote the message for Radio Londres, he'd worked out a possible location for another pigeon drop—a place where the German emplacements couldn't shoot the aircraft, or get to his precious pigeon cargo. It was also a place Guy had been before marrying Jennie, landing his Whitley there when he was in the RAF. He was waiting for word from Smith, who was waiting for word from the top.

Just before his office door opened, Guy realized his clothes were crumpled from sitting at his desk for hours, and tried to straighten his jacket, but what he couldn't do anything about was his beard stubble where he'd forgotten to shave.

"I have some good news—" Smith looked startled by Guy's appearance and gave him a look over from the doorway. "Meet me in my office in ten minutes."

Guy nodded, trying to keep his excitement in check. Still hearing Gaby's music in his head didn't help. *Second floor.* The War Office must want to act on the intelligence, and that meant upstairs had renewed faith in Columba after years of misleading information coming from German pigeons in disguise. Word to dispatch more English pigeons to northern France would surely follow now.

Smith turned on his heel, but not without giving Guy another once-over. "You look like you've been working day and night."

Guy was suddenly very aware of the stark difference between himself and Clive, who was clean-shaven with pomade-slicked hair. "I have, sir."

"Well, you don't have to look like it. Have a shot of whiskey, if you have to, and make it a healthy pour." Smith left, clip-clopping back down the corridor.

"Second floor..." Clive sat back in his chair, whistling. "It's no surprise. That broadcast essentially said more pigeons were arriving in France."

Guy pulled a flask of whiskey from his bottom desk drawer to have a slug before looking at his watch. "Ah, it's late!" He'd told his sister to expect him that night for dinner. "Do me a favor, will you? Phone the ground floor and have them call my sister." Guy took the book with the original message tucked inside from his cabinet drawer and shoved it into his bag. "Tell her I'll be late again." He slung his bag over his shoulder. "Wish me luck."

"Good luck!" Clive shouted from his desk, but Guy was already halfway down the corridor.

Guy was feeling pretty confident in the lift, but things took a turn when Smith's secretary, Daisy, told him the meeting had been moved.

"Where to?" he asked.

She looked over the top of her glasses. "You don't have much time, Mr. Burton." She ushered Guy into the corridor just as Smith came out of his office. "And straighten your jacket."

He gave it another tug before following Smith down the corridor.

"Where are we going, sir?" he asked, trying to keep pace.

Smith turned, taking a puffing breath. "The War Rooms."

Guy's heart raced from this information, though it wasn't nerves. It was excitement—this was more important than a second-floor meeting. They took the lift and another set of stairs to a part of the War Office where he'd never been, which felt even lower than the basement. Another secretary met them in the corridor, leading them all the way to the end and to a single steel door.

"You ready for the top brass?" she asked, then knocked twice on the door and left.

Guy thought he'd done his best to look sharp, tugging his jacket into place one more time, but then regretted he didn't try a little harder after the door opened and he saw the Prime Minister seated at the table, waiting for them both behind a cloud of cigar smoke.

"Good afternoon, Mr. Chur— Prime Minister, sir," Guy

said, cringing silently for messing up his name, and stood at attention, with his heart knocking in his chest, waiting to be told what to do. Four advisers, some in uniforms, some in suits, looked up from under bright lights—the Churchill war ministry, or The Five as they were known around the War Office.

Guy gulped. Every agent at the War Office dreamed of being summoned to a meeting with The Five; it meant their intelligence was not only worthy but integral to the war effort.

"Have a seat," one of them said, but Smith had taken the seat off to the side, which left only the vacant seat directly in front of Churchill.

Guy sat down, pulling his messenger bag from his shoulder, and while Churchill inspected him inch by inch with his lit cigar tucked in his mouth, he wondered if anyone, Churchill especially, could tell he was having a heart attack.

"MI14 came up trumps this time, I hear," one of the advisers said, which meant Guy and his supervisor since they were the only ones who made up the tiny MI14 crew inside the MI6. "Appears a pigeon delivered solid intelligence?"

"Yes, sir. He delivered," Guy said.

"I trust you've been briefed with a translated version of the message?" Smith asked.

Above Churchill's head, Guy saw a full-size copy of The Heroines' map pinned to the corkboard with x's near Boulogne-sur-Mer and topography notes.

"Yes, we read it," the adviser said.

Churchill coughed like a lion, startling Guy but nobody else at the table.

"But can you tell us a little more about how you verified who the sender was?" The adviser shifted to look at the rest of

The Five before continuing. "And who exactly *are* The Heroines?"

Smith directed Guy to answer, and he pulled the book from his bag and searched for the original message between the pages. "As you know from the text, the sender left a clue to their identity by providing a source—Professor Caron. I've visited her and have confirmed without a doubt who the sender is—senders are, I should say. The Heroines." Guy plucked the original message from between the pages of his book, and held it up, music side facing. "The Heroines is the name of this secret composition. Composed by the sender of the message and known only to one other person, Professor Caron." Guy was still holding the music in the air, turning his body so that everyone could get a glimpse.

"A composer in northern France?" the adviser questioned. "His work must be known to the Germans."

Guy told The Five all he knew about Gaby and her sisters, including where they lived in France and what they did for money. He expected a comment after learning they were women, but they only stared at him—all five of them.

Guy pulled his collar from his neck where he felt a little constricted, wondering if Churchill was going to talk, when finally, he did, but only after a roaring, harsh cough to clear his throat.

"Why should we trust this particular woman?" Churchill pointed his cigar at Guy, leaning forward, elbow to the table. "This... Gabriella Cotillard."

"Because she's an ordinary person, Prime Minister, and this is exactly what the secret pigeon service set out to do with Operation Columba. Reach the citizenry." He moved to the edge of his seat with a pounding heart; talking about the program always got him excited. "There's no special training, no policy to follow, no right way to send a message. She also has everything to lose, sir, with no promise of gain, and she's eager to share what she knows. Miss Cotillard is one of the bravest agents I've ever had." He paused after talking about Gaby's bravery because not only had she risked her life but, like the professor had said, she'd parted with the one thing dearest to her heart—her music—and that took an incredible amount of courage. "All three of the sisters are, as they do everything together. This message is proof of the spirit that burns inside the hearts of Frenchmen—"

Churchill and his advisers huddled in whispers with some jerking a thumb toward the map behind them on the wall, which effectively silenced Guy.

He looked to Smith for what to do.

"We can get another crew in the air immediately," Smith said while The Five continued their private discussion, which was only slightly awkward. "You have some reports, Guy?" Smith snapped his fingers.

"Yes!" Guy said, digging into his messenger bag for his notes. "I've been comparing flight reports with the map they sent, and I have a firm idea of where the next drop should be to reach The Heroines. I'll notify the Air Ministry at once and get a flight in the diary."

"That won't be necessary," one of the advisers said, before going back to whispering with Churchill and the others.

Guy looked at Smith, who appeared just as shocked that there wouldn't be another drop.

"You are surprised?" the adviser questioned.

"I am surprised, sir," Guy said. "Not only was the intelligence the best we've ever had, The Heroines asked for more, and after that shining Radio Londres announcement, mentioning the name of her composition over the airwaves, Miss Cotillard and her sisters will be emboldened, sure to be gathering more information and anxious for a drop."

Churchill pulled away from the group. "Will they be emboldened?" he asked, though it wasn't a question and he looked rather pleased about that—which was even more confusing, because what use was an emboldened agent without the means to dispatch their message?

The adviser stood, showing Guy and Smith the door. "The meeting has been adjourned."

The next thing Guy knew, he and Smith were standing in the corridor while The Five continued talking about Gabriella Cotillard behind closed doors. "I don't understand, sir," Guy said to Smith. "Is there something I'm missing?"

"I don't know," Smith said. "It doesn't make sense. None of it. But I'll do my best to find out."

Guy went back to his office, feeling empty-handed and still confused. Clive was just slipping on his coat to leave for the night.

"Hey, so how'd your meeting go?" he asked, but Guy was looking at the plate of food on his desk, all wrapped up with a bow and a note from his sister.

Guy picked up the note.

It's not as good as Jennie's, God rest her soul, but I did try. I never see you. Stop by tonight, will you?

Love, your sis.

"She visited the ground floor, said she hasn't seen you in a while, and wanted to make sure you're still alive. Her words, not mine."

"What?" Guy looked up after reading Madge's note, having not caught what he'd said.

Clive reached for his hat, but hesitated to leave. "You're welcome to come to my house tonight, visit with me and my wife," he said as Guy's eyes trailed to the photos of Clive and his wife, proudly displayed on a shelf. One of her at the beach, and another in the city where they were both holding hands. "I didn't know your wife—"

"I have plans." The offer caught Guy by surprise since he'd never told Clive that his wife had died, then he realized he must have read the note, and he wasn't sure if he was angry about that or just annoyed. Guy pointed to his desk as if he had a mountain of work still left to do, but his desk was cleared with only a pencil cup on it.

"Sure, I understand." Clive nodded once. "See you tomorrow?"

"Yes. See you tomorrow."

Guy filed the music away in his cabinet, then sat down in his desk chair, replaying every word of that meeting in his head, looking for clues as to what went wrong, but he couldn't put his finger on it because he was sure he'd done everything right.

Gaby's music was still in his heart, a thrumming feeling that had stayed with him, yet it was becoming harder to recall now—harder to imagine and hear the right notes. He tried to capture it, like a butterfly just out of his grasp, then thought it was more like fingers under his skin and an itch he couldn't scratch, which he knew would drive him mad. "Ah, bloody hell," he said to himself, and he reached for his coat after unlocking his file cabinet to take back his book.

Guy drove to the Royal College of Music in hopes of catching the professor, even though it was well past closing time. He thought he'd explain to her that he needed to hear the piece again for intelligence reasons. Guy shook his head at how daft that sounded. It sounded even worse when he said it out loud.

He ran up to the building's front doors. Most of the lights had been turned off, shrouding the corridor in grayness, but he reached for the handle anyway and was pleasantly surprised when the door opened.

He heard a piano playing from room six, and followed the melody all the way down the stairs to her opened studio door where the music poured into the corridor and filled his ears. He wasn't about to interrupt her, but she must have sensed him because her hands lifted abruptly from the keyboard.

"Yes?" she called out.

Guy winced, then walked in gingerly. "Professor Caron?"

She pulled her eyeglasses from her face. "Mr. Burton. I've been expecting you." She gathered her sheet music from the stand and stood.

"You have?" He took his hat off and gripped the brim.

"As I said before, Gabriella Cotillard was my most promising student." She walked to the far wall and tucked her music into a folder. "Her composition settled into your bones, I see. Haunted you during the day, and now you can't quite place the melody and want me to play it again. A thirst to be quenched. Or maybe it's a needling that needs to be soothed."

"How..." Guy swallowed dryly. "How did you know?"

"Because Gaby's music will do that to a person. I only wish she was here to witness the effect her music had on you." She motioned for the sheet music, and he reached into his messenger bag. "I'll reprise it for you again, make it last a little longer." She paused, looking over the sheet after putting her glasses back on. "Maybe you should have a seat before I start. I wouldn't want you to stumble backward like you did last time," she added, but once she began to play, he did stumble backward and plummeted into the chair. It was everything he remembered but couldn't quite place. Then it was done. Over. And he sat, wishing for more.

He looked at his hands where he thought he felt the music pulsating.

Professor Caron watched him from her piano bench, sliding her glasses up her nose before handing him back the music. "Maybe one day you'll hear the rest of it. Such an inspiring story."

Guy rubbed his hands together, looking up. "Story?"

She nodded. "The Heroines is a composition, yes, but it also tells a story. I mentioned this before, but you probably forgot."

"What's it about?" he asked.

"It's about a group of women," she said. "Warrior women who don't know they are warriors. Women who feel helpless at home while their men are off at war, then take matters into their own hands, though of course nobody expects women to help win the war, which is to their benefit."

"It's a war story?"

"It is. They come together, each lending their unique traits and talents to fight back, with no guarantee of triumph, only the strength of their hearts." She tapped her chest.

"Oh," he said, yet still he didn't move from the chair.

"If you ever have the chance to hear the entire composition, you'd understand. Like I said before, it's Wagnerian in the way its dramatic ending pulls you to the edge of a cliff by the heart, leaving you breathless and changed. It's impossible not to fall in love with it. You might just fall in love with Gabriella Cotillard too. She's as brave as her music."

Guy reached for his chest without realizing why, which drew her eyes to his wedding band. "Fall in love?"

"Oh, I'm sorry, Mr. Burton," she said. "I was out of line. I didn't know you were married."

Guy's instant reaction was to shove his hand in his pocket, but for whatever reason he found himself holding his hand out and looking at his ring.

The professor took off her glasses again but this time to rub her eyes. "No disrespect to your wife. Gaby is a talented woman, that's all I meant."

Guy pulled his shoulders back. "My wife died in The Blitz," he blurted, which shook him a little since he'd never said the words out loud before. "May, in forty-one."

Professor Caron looked even more embarrassed than she did when she thought his wife was alive. "My condolences, Mr. Burton. I'm very sorry."

"It's been three years now, hasn't it? I don't know why I haven't taken my ring off. Habit, I suppose." He took a deep breath through his mouth because Guy knew exactly why he hadn't taken it off. The ring made him feel as if she'd still come home, that she was just out for the day, but Jennie was lost to him, and she'd been lost to him for quite some time. He swallowed, realizing he might have said more than she would care to hear. "Thank you for your time." He turned toward the door.

"Wait!"

Guy stopped.

The professor pulled a photo from her collage wall. "This is Gaby. You should know what she looks like. What bravery looks like." She folded her arms and watched Guy look over the photo.

He thought she was beautiful, with her hair pinned delicately back and wisps cupping her face.

"You gave Gaby a voice with her music, Mr. Burton. One that had been dead for many months. That was some Radio Londres announcement. I can only imagine she's preparing her next sheet of music for you. She must feel incredibly emboldened."

Guy looked up, not sure what to say to Professor Caron, given what had happened in the War Rooms earlier.

"You can keep that photo for your files," she said, and Guy thanked her. "Would you like to know how to read her name in the notes too?"

She showed him the technique of reading her name, which felt like codebreaking with the use of math. It took him a moment to see it, then he found himself looking at Gaby's photo again.

Chapter Ten

May

I woke in the middle of the night to the buzzing roar of planes flying over our rooftop, loud and heavy, vibrating in the windowpanes and the walls. My hands flew to my ears and I stumbled out of bed to my door, where Martine was trying to make her way in, yelling at me that it was a raid.

"Simone!" I pounded on her door, and she burst from her bedroom to follow us downstairs into the cellar.

We grabbed onto each other in the dark, the floor above shuddering like a house of cards over our heads and about to collapse as the planes passed. Explosions sent us to the ground.

Boom! Boom! Boom!

I pulled my sisters in even closer. "Keep your head down!" I yelled as dust and debris sprinkled from the shaking rafters. Martine screamed, and Simone held on even tighter until the blast of the bombs faded along with the vibration of the house.

Then all was quiet.

"Is it over?" I asked. We looked up one by one. The cellar door was open but it was just as dark upstairs as it was down.

Martine broke away first, walking cautiously up the cellar stairs with deliberately placed steps. She handed me a candle from the top and told us to wait while she looked outside.

"Be careful," I called up.

"I will."

I turned away with my candle, standing with Simone in the cellar's deep dark bottom where it smelled like moss and mildew, shivering in my bare feet and thin nightgown, but Simone looked warm in her coat.

"Were you out dancing?" I asked, even though it was clear she had been. Simone didn't put her coat on while running downstairs, she'd had it on because she'd just come home. "But things are different now." I held my tongue about our German guest and our renewed efforts with pigeons, figuring she'd know what I was talking about. "You must know they're different."

"I know they are."

"Then why did you go out?" I asked, but she looked away. "Simone," I said, reaching out for her, and even though she tried to step away from me, I caught her lapel, pulling her coat off and exposing her round little belly in her tight dress.

"Gaby, don't." She hiked her coat back up, but I'd already seen. It was one of those things you don't notice until you notice, and with her wearing her coat every day and even in the house sometimes, she'd managed to conceal it.

"Oh no, Simone," I said, hand to my mouth. "You're pregnant."

Martine came back into the house and shouted down the

cellar stairs, "Come up! They're gone." She'd lit another candle and waved us up, but I couldn't move. I just stared at Simone, not sure what else to say or how to react, especially with Martine watching us from above.

"Simone," I breathed, and she pushed past me to go upstairs, ignoring Martine near the door and going up to her bedroom. I chased after her, but Martine held me back with conversation as I tried to get around her in the foyer.

"That was frightening and exciting at the same time," Martine said, oblivious to Simone's rush upstairs to her bedroom. "Look at my hands." They were shaking even though it had been several minutes since the planes had flown off.

"Yes, yes, I see them." I finally got around her and darted upstairs after Simone, but Martine followed, pounding up the creaking stairs behind me and still talking about the bombs.

"And now we're supposed to go back to sleep after that?" Martine laughed. "Welcome to northern France, Captain Weber!" she said loud enough for him to hear through the shared wall, before closing her bedroom door.

I lingered in the hallway with my candle, wanting to talk to Simone, but also wanting to leave her alone. I tapped lightly. "Simone," I said, followed by a pause when the door opened enough for me to see inside. "Do you want to talk?"

She blew out her candle and rolled over in bed.

I lay in my bed for another hour or so, thinking only of Simone. What were we going to do now? I curled up with Beau's jacket under the covers, but still, I felt alone. The village was going to crucify us, and I was scared, not only for Simone and the baby, but for all of us. I tossed and turned, and my stomach hurt. I only sat up when I heard Antoinette call for her chickens outside in the breaking sunlight.

Martine knocked on my door, and I sloughed off Beau's jacket in a hurry. "Yes?" I'd thrown the blanket over it and smoothed down the lump before she walked in.

"Can you hear that?" she asked. "Doesn't she know none of us have slept a wink since the bombing?"

"She doesn't care," I said, giving the blanket a tug one last time when she wasn't looking. My sisters probably knew I slept with his jacket on occasion, but I wasn't ready to talk about it.

Martine watched Antoinette from the window. "She treats those chickens like pets." She pointed and I had a look. "She blows kisses to them when they give her eggs. Who in their right mind does that? Blows kisses to chickens..."

Antoinette traipsed around her garden in her housecoat, one hand poised in the air for balance and the other, indeed, blowing kisses to her hens for the eggs they left her, presumably for her and her lover's breakfast.

"She'd better watch those hens," Martine said. "Never know who is hungry around here."

I cracked open the window to eavesdrop after she walked to her fence to chat with a neighbor. "An oil facility and a U-boat pen," I heard him say to Antoinette. Martine stepped away from the window, cupping her mouth.

"Did he say 'U-boat pen'?" she asked, and I shushed her, trying to hear more, leaning out the window, the salty sea air nipping at my ears.

"It's as if they had a map!" he said in disgust.

I gasped, letting go of the curtain.

Martine's hands shook again like they did when we were bombed, her eyes shocked wide open. "Gaby, a map," she said. "It didn't even cross my mind when the bombing happened. It was my map!"

I didn't know what to say. I could only smile and think.

Martine took a deep breath, holding her chest. "I need to get to the shop! What if there's a special lunchtime broadcast again? I don't want to miss it." She let out a squeal before bolting for her room to change, and I went to wake Simone up, but she was already in the hall buttoning her coat.

"I'm going to the shop too," she said.

"Did you hear the neighbor?" I asked.

Simone nodded, taking a step toward the stairs to avoid me.

"Wait," I said, and she turned just slightly. "We need to talk," I whispered, because we weren't protected by our bedroom walls anymore and the captain might be listening.

She shook her head and continued downstairs. Martine flew out of her bedroom chasing after her. "Wait for me!" Martine said.

I threw on my own clothes and tried to catch them, running into the road where Antoinette was still talking to her neighbor. The sun shone in my eyes, breaking through the clouds.

"Simone…" I reached for her hand, and I thought she'd pull away, but instead, she turned toward me, closing the gap between us for privacy.

"Don't tell Martine," she said before I could talk. "She wouldn't understand."

"But, Simone—"

"It's a great day for her," she said, and my eyes shifted over her shoulder to Martine, who was nearly bouncing on her feet. "You don't want to spoil it for her, do you? It's her day of revenge, everything she's dreamt about. Let me tell her, when I'm ready."

"But what are we going to do? The neighbors. The village. They'll think it's—" I gulped. *German.*

"We're in love, Gaby." She took me warmly in her arms, and I smelled the rose of Chantilly in her hair. "We've made plans to marry as soon as it's safe to do so. Everything will be all right." She tapped her heart. "I feel it in here."

"But aren't you worried and scared?" I asked.

"Terrified," she said, smiling breathlessly, and that's what struck me. She was terrified, yet elated and full of hope and love.

She walked on after Martine, leaving me in the road with the rest of the neighborhood who'd come out to talk about the bombing. And as I watched my sisters walk away, I thought maybe it would be all right, just like Simone had said.

I walked back inside our home, and instead of hiding in my bedroom or in the kitchen with my diluted tarragon tea, I sat down at my piano and played Rachmaninoff, the first chord speaking to me like a forgotten friend, and healing a bit of the past.

I reached up and wrote my last note, completing my first composition, an undertaking that spanned months. "There!" I celebrated with a sip of red wine, before playing the first few sheets one last time to make sure it was right—make sure it was perfect—when our building's concierge burst into the apartment we three shared on Boul'Mich.

"Girls!"

My fingers slipped violently from my piano keys. "Madame Basset—"

"There's a raid!" *Madame rushed toward me, taking me by the shoulders after I stood and giving me a shake. Martine got up from the lounge, cigarette falling from her mouth to the floor, and Simone ran in from her bedroom.*

A siren wailed outside, followed by an explosion. We dashed to the window, hands gripping the ledge, watching a ball of fire engulf a car and light up the buildings. Madame closed the curtains on us.

"They're arresting the Communists," *she said, just as pounding footsteps traveled up the staircase to the apartments one floor up.*

Most of the tenants in the building were students, and most of the students were Communists, holding secret meetings in the basement, and defying German orders and laws. One of Simone's lovers was a Communist, a poet she'd recently met at a nightclub on Boul'Mich, and she'd gone to a meeting because he invited her. Martine also had attended once, but it was for research after she'd enrolled at the Sorbonne.

"You must all run! They're throwing women into Black Marias —sending them to prison—and killing the men."

"No!" *Simone shrieked, wanting to run out of the apartment for the street, find her lover before the Germans did, and give him a last kiss, but Madame told her she'd be a fool and would only lead the Germans to him.*

"But they only lecture in the basement," *I said.* "They haven't bombed a police station or a train station like others have done. And my sisters have only attended once." *I turned to Martine, who knew what groups did what, and when, because of her studies, and would certainly know what had been going on in the basement even if she'd only attended once.* "Isn't that right?"

Martine's eyes shifted to Madame's.

"Martine? You only went once? Right?"

She hung her head. "No, Gaby. It's more than lectures, and I've been many times."

I covered my mouth.

"Ma petite," Madame said to me. "They've been planning reprisals for weeks after the arrests in the cafés. Last night they hurled a grenade into a German patrol lorry as it traveled down Rue de Courcelles."

I gasped. "Martine!"

Doors burst open upstairs, followed by shrieks and more stomping. We gazed at the ceiling, listening to the Germans trampling from one side of the building to the other.

"They're working their way from top to bottom," Madame said. "They'll be looking for Martine first when they come to your floor, then Simone."

"And what about you?" Madame was the concierge—she was in charge—and had allowed the student Communists to have their meetings in the basement. If the Germans were coming for my sisters, they'd be coming for her too.

"I'm too old to run." A glimmer shone in her eyes. She'd been waiting for this day. She'd prepared.

"Madame Basset," a German yelled for her through the ceiling. "Where are you?"

"Leave," she said, running from our apartment. "My arrest will give you time." She looked over her shoulder in the doorway. "Go!"

We three stood with our backs to the wall, reaching for each other's fingers. "We can catch the evening train."

"And go where?" Simone asked.

"Back home," I said. "Back to Aunt Blanche."

"I'm sorry, Gaby," Martine said, and I knew she was. My life was in Paris now. My career, which I'd chosen over Beau. "But don't blame me, it's the Germans."

Once the decision had been made, there was a mad dash to collect our valuables. "Grab your things!" I pulled back the rug where we kept our money, taking every last franc I had stashed away for safekeeping. Simone stuffed what jewelry she hadn't sold on the black market into her handbag. The last piece was a locket her lover had given her, which she placed on the top of my piano after pressing it to her lips for a kiss, thanking him for their sweet time together, even though it was short, and wishing him safety.

We were on our way out when I ran back to my piano.

"What are you doing?" Martine cried as I reached for my sheet music.

"I'm not leaving this!" I haphazardly shoved the crackling papers into my handbag and a few sheets floated to the floor, escaping my grasp. Martine took my hand, pulling me into the corridor before I had a chance to gather them. "Wait! My music…"

"They're coming!" Martine said, pulling me away with a tug of all tugs.

We rushed downstairs and out into the street, ahead of the Germans who'd yet to find us, leaving pieces of my dream scattered on the floor and taking the others as crumpled memories in my bag, feeling as if I'd never play again.

I lifted my hands from the keys and waited for the quiet to return, with the vibration of the last chord fading softly. I was a bit surprised that I was all right. I didn't sink into the earth or contort on the ground with debilitating pain after having played. On the contrary, I felt rather good.

I started the kettle, only to stumble forward, spilling water all over the floor when piano music thrummed through our shared wall. Copying me note for note.

"No," I said, running to the wall because I was sure the neighbors could hear, and I'd just played. They'd think we were playing a duet—*Mon Dieu!*—they'd think we were friends. "Shh!" I put my finger to my lips as if he could see me. "Shh!"

A banging knock at my front door silenced him. "Hallo," I said, lunging for the door.

Antoinette.

I tried to collect myself but my heart was thumping painfully in my chest and I knew I looked flustered. "What do you want?"

"Good morning," She looked in, over my shoulder, and to each side. "Are your sisters home?" She smiled, showing all of her teeth.

"You saw them leave, Antoinette."

She paused before sucking in a mouthful of air, as if she'd just remembered. "Oh yes, that's right. I did see them leave. I'm sure you heard the bombing. Did you hear the dreadful news about the harbor?"

"No." I swallowed dryly. "No, I did not. Is that what was bombed?" I closed my eyes, wishing she'd just leave but she talked some more, and I couldn't tell you what she said. All I was thinking about was the captain and if he was going to start playing again, and how she must have heard.

"Gaby?" she said, and my eyes popped open. "Did you hear me? I said your duet with the captain was beautiful. I could hear it from the road."

"There was no duet," I said, shaking my head. "Just me." I smiled. "It was me all along."

She made a face, eyes narrowing.

"Goodbye, Antoinette." I grabbed my coat from the hook before locking up our house and pushing past her on the step.

Chapter Eleven

I arrived for Lauren's lesson earlier than I was supposed to. I took a moment to collect myself near the front door with the nip of the coastal breeze biting at all my exposed skin. I was just a few minutes early, and if the commandant was gone, maybe nobody would notice. I certainly wasn't going to stay at home any longer.

I rapped on the door.

The housekeeper answered, and I thought I was safe because she let me in. The commandant's study was dark. "Go on up," she said.

I padded upstairs as usual to Lauren, who was jumping up and down near the baluster. "You're back!" Her mistress tried to forcibly keep her still, which made Lauren stick her tongue out at her.

"Of course I'm back. Have you been practicing this time?" I asked, and she nodded.

"You're early," she said. "Did you get permission?"

I brushed the comment off, turning to her mistress and giving a little laugh, before walking into the playroom and closing the door.

I unbuttoned my coat, glad I'd escaped questioning and all was well.

"Did you hear the bombs?" she asked. "Is that why you're here? You were scared?"

I looked up, seeing her wondering face. "Yes, that's right. The bombs. I was scared. Were you?"

"Yes." She took my hand, walking me toward the piano. "My mother screamed, and I haven't heard her scream since my first papa died. Then the commandant rushed downstairs half-dressed, opening and closing all his file cabinet drawers, looking for someone's name, and cursing! Words I'm not supposed to hear, even in German." She covered her mouth, laughing with her shoulders in her ears. "I offered him one of my dolls to throw, but he said it wouldn't reach his spy in London." She looked up. "What's MI6?"

I blinked, wondering about this spy she mentioned. "I don't know what MI6 is."

"Can I start?" She hopped on the bench, getting into position before playing a nice tune, but changed to one finger —*tap, tap, tap*—before her hands fell on the keyboard, noticing my mind was somewhere else. "What's wrong?" She swiped her fringe from her forehead.

I smiled. "Nothing's wrong," I said, finally taking the seat next to her. "Now, play how you want to and I'll tell everyone it was me, if they ask." I put a finger to my mouth. "Our secret."

She inhaled deeply with a satisfied smile, before setting her hands on the keys, fingertips at the ready. "There's this one…" she said as she began to play.

It was beautiful and smooth with a crescendo of notes. I wished I could take credit for her skill, but it was quite apparent someone else had that honor. "Who taught you?" I asked, and her eyes shifted to mine.

"I did," she said.

"No," I said. "Who was your teacher before?" I motioned with my hand. "Before the commandant married your mother."

"Me." She began playing again, this time a little stiffly, and I could tell she was irritated with my question. "My real papa said I was playing the piano before I could talk."

"And your mother doesn't know?" I asked, and she shrugged, but surely she had to know, and for some reason didn't bother telling the commandant about her skill.

I encouraged Lauren to continue playing, but she had questions about intervals and tempo. I set my hands on the keyboard to show her.

"It's like this," I said, but I didn't stop at a few chords and played several bars of the sheet music. "Now your turn again." I flipped the sheet over for her as she stared at me, mouth open.

"That's the first time I've heard you play," she said.

"I've played for you," I said, and she shook her head.

"I must have," I said, knowing full well I hadn't, and she was still shaking her head.

"Well, I'll make sure to play more from now on. Go ahead and play," I said, urging her to continue and forget her question, and she moved on, playing well and with refinement.

"Lauren!" we heard down the hallway, and the music stopped abruptly, her hands frozen over the keys. I looked at the door after she did.

"My mother," she breathed.

"I'd like to meet your mother."

She shook her head again, but this time she looked alarmed.

The door flew open with a bang, jolting Lauren from the bench. Her mother stood in the doorway dressed in a silky red peignoir that pooled on the floor around her white, manicured feet. Gold bangles clinked around her wrists.

"Lauren," she said from her chest. "You haven't introduced me to your teacher." The door swung back and she lost her balance, flinging her hand out and clawing at the doorframe.

Lauren hung her head, refusing to look.

"Hallo. I'm—"

"I know who you are." She slunk toward me, giving me a shake with a limp and cold hand. "We just haven't met."

"Lauren is such a lovely child," I said.

She leaned against the piano while playing with a tassel on her peignoir. "Is she?"

"Yes, absolutely."

"Do you know how many teachers she's had?"

She stooped down to reach Lauren, who stood still as a rabbit. "Mama loves you…" She tried to kiss her cheek but smooched the air instead after Lauren turned away. "Lauren."

Lauren reluctantly moved her face back so her mother could give her a peck.

"Good morning, Mama," Lauren said.

"Yes, good morning," she said back.

She smelled of flowery perfume, the expensive kind that

transferred to my hand and felt heavy in my lungs. "I'm Madame Streicher." She straightened. "But you can call me Danielle."

I thought that would be the end of it—she'd leave or have a seat—only her eyes welled with tears.

"I'm glad you're here. Lauren is very fond of you." She turned away, taking a few short steps to the window where she gazed outside, tugging on a locket she drew from her peignoir.

Lauren watched her mother like a deer caught in headlamps.

"I'm glad too," I said.

There was an uncomfortable silence as she stared out the window, Lauren and I still standing near the piano. I wasn't sure if I should resume our lesson or continue the conversation.

"I only wanted to meet you." She placed her palm to the glass when the commandant's car motored up to the curb. "I'll leave you to your lesson now." She rewrapped her peignoir even though it was already securely tied around her waist, her bangles clinking as she wrestled with the tie. "Good day," she said, lifting her head and walking out like an unruly wind, tossing the skirt of her silky peignoir to each side to make way for her feet, and closing the door.

I swallowed, staring at the closed door.

"Shall we play?" Lauren flipped the sheet music over, cracking her knuckles in front of her and taking a stretch as if nothing had happened, and it was perfectly normal for her mother to be walking around dressed for a sultry day of lovemaking.

My hands twisted. I didn't know what to say, but felt I had to say something. "Lauren, I—"

Lauren played on with zest, pounding on the keys and cutting me off. "Do you think the RAF will save us?" she said, her eyes lifting from the music, but still playing. "They dropped the bombs, but what if they stopped, loaded us up, and flew us away? Far away where it's sunny and warm and there was candy." Her fingers still thumped on the keys. "Do you think it could happen?" She stopped suddenly, closing her eyes tightly.

"I would love it if that happened," I said, and she opened her eyes to look at me. "In here, we are rescued. In here—" I whirled my finger around her playroom "—we are safe."

She surprised me with a hug, throwing her arms around my neck. "Can you live here and be my mistress?"

"Oh, Lauren," I said, smoothing her hair away from her eyes. "I can't. I have a home of my own and a business to run with my sisters."

"Soon Irma will be in with the tea. She'll say it sounds lovely in here like she's done the last two times, and then you'll be gone. But you'll come back again, right? Because you want to."

"Yes, I will," I said.

Not a second later, Irma swooped into the room with her silver tea tray and biscuits. "Sounds lovely in here."

Lauren and I shared a look and a smirk before Irma moved to the rug to unload her tray on the table and set out the cups.

"What kind of biscuits did you bring?" Lauren asked, but Irma made her way to the door and left before Lauren could make a fuss.

Lauren took a bite, only to promptly spit it out. She pulled a different biscuit from her pocket, one with white icing. "I stole this biscuit from the kitchen. She keeps them from me, and she's not supposed to."

I drank my tea by the fireplace, watching her play on the carpet with some miniature dolls she'd taken from the shelf. She had a boy doll in one hand and a girl in the other, tapping them on the floor to mimic walking and whispering their words. "Be my wife, yes. Be my wife, no," she kept saying, before ramming them together and letting them fall to the floor, one after the other.

Doors slammed closed in the study below, followed by the commandant's voice booming through the floor. I pulled a corner of the rug back and found the hole Lauren mentioned—the hole that had been wallpapered over in the study.

I heard the phone ring and Commandant Streicher pick it up, talking to whoever it was on the other end in perfect English, which Lauren didn't understand and I supposed neither did the staff. "The performance at the Monsigny Theater is still on," he said, and my ear tilted to the floor, following my eyes. "Yes, that's right. May twenty-ninth. My team will be firmly in place for the Führer."

I put a hand over my mouth. *The Führer?*

"Mademoiselle?" Lauren said.

"Yes?" I looked up, feeling for my chest, but my heart pounded in my ears.

He'd hung up the receiver and was yelling for the housekeeper. "My key! Where's the key to my filing cabinet? I put it right there and now it's gone!"

"It's where you left it, Commandant," the housekeeper said. Even through the floor I could tell she was about to cry, her voice half weepy, half frightened. She yelped when the file cabinet clattered and clanged, as if he'd hit it with his fist.

"He's so angry," I said.

Lauren petted her doll's head. "Nobody is allowed to touch his file cabinet. Mama will calm him. She *always* calms him."

A sweep of crashes came next which made us both wince even though we were safe upstairs. Photo frames? Or maybe those Limoges figurines I had seen displayed on glass shelves? I set my tea down, motioning to the piano, and Lauren started to get up, but then sat down again, her bottom on the rug, when we heard Irma calling for Danielle in the hall.

"He's breaking everything!" Irma's voice was shrill and Danielle's was equally frantic.

"Stay away from him," I heard Danielle say, a moment before she called for the commandant on her way downstairs: "Streicher... Streicher..." I imagined she was still dressed in her satin peignoir and rushing as fast as she could because what I heard next were the study's French doors opening and then closing.

Then there was silence.

"I know what they're doing in there," Lauren said, and with the hole in the floor, I wondered how long before I knew for certain too.

"Come here, Lauren," I said, but I didn't wait for her to take a seat, and played the music that she'd left on the stand, louder and louder, with pomp and sloppy chords for extra clang, trying to drown out their lovemaking until Lauren placed her hand on mine, stopping me.

"They're done."

Her mistress came into the playroom tapping her watch. "Mademoiselle, it is past your time," she said, but I was just glad I couldn't hear a peep from down below.

Lauren looked sorrowfully up at me. "Stay."

"You must get going," Irma said.

Lauren latched onto me as I tried to leave. "Stay! Please, mademoiselle," she begged.

I patted her head, acting like it was normal for a child to cling to me, but her strength surprised me. "I'll come back, Lauren. I said I would."

Irma somehow managed to pry Lauren from me, who moped back to the rug to pick up her dolls. "Leave down the servant stairs, through the kitchen." Irma was still panting from the wrestle with Lauren, looking particularly perturbed.

I nodded once, grabbing my coat on the way out and walking down the stairs into the kitchen, only to find the commandant waiting for me.

"Fraulein."

He smoked casually against the wall wearing day clothes. His hair was only the slightest bit mussed. I tried passing him, reaching for the door, but he took a sliding step in front of me. I caught a heavy dose of Danielle's perfume from his collar.

"You were here early today." My stomach sank at his tone, which was accusing and suspicious. "Well, do you have something to say about that?"

I shook my head.

"I don't like surprises." Smoke billowed between us, floating up from his cigarette but also from his nose. "If you arrive early again, I'll have to let you go, and I don't think Mme. Leroux will be very pleased once she finds out about her crimes and where she's going, where her son will go."

Air escaped from my mouth. "Why are you doing this?" I asked. "Over some extra rations…"

"Would you have come willingly?" He pushed a thick envelope toward me on the counter, thicker than either of the two he'd given me before. "This is yours. Another day's pay." He walked away. "Tomorrow there will be more."

"Tomorrow?" I asked because that seemed soon.

He looked over his shoulder on his way out, holding the door. "You are too good, Fraulein. Lauren is like a different child when you're around. The staff know it, and all have asked for you to be permanent. Four days a week."

"Four days?" My mouth hung open.

"It is in my interest to keep her content. I will not let you go now. Have a good day." He left, flipping a gold coin in the air, but I'd already run out the back door.

A smoky haze hung over the harbor from the explosions and filtered into the streets. I pulled my scarf from my pocket to cover my mouth, coughing, looking over my shoulder, checking to see if anyone was watching, if anyone had seen from what direction I'd come. Madame Roche stood at her front window, watching passersby, and I stopped in the street to wave like I'd been doing since we'd come home to Boulogne-sur-Mer, only she seemed more startled than pleased to see me.

A man threw his shoulder into mine, sending me flying backward with a yelp. "Collaborator," he grumbled, and I looked up to Madame Roche again, but she was nowhere to be seen. An eerie feeling passed over me. An unwelcome feeling. I ran to our shop, reaching for the doorknob only to gasp.

A black ribbon.

I yanked it away, ducking inside under a clang of doorbells and immediately turning for a peep between the curtains. Simone stood up from behind the desk. Martine demanded to know what was wrong with me. I turned around, opening my palm, the ribbon entwined in my fingers.

Martine hit the desk with her fist. "Bastards! When did that happen? Who did it?"

"I... I don't know," I said, exhausted from the encounter in the street and the thought that all the shopkeepers knew about our visitor last night, instead of just the few that had turned off their lights. I tossed the ribbon on a pile of clothes and Martine went to the window, hands on her hips, looking up and down the street. I rubbed the back of my neck where it ached. "A man in the street called me a collaborator."

Simone's hands flew to her mouth. "What's going to happen when they find out about your employment?"

"What am I supposed to do?" I asked. "Mme. Leroux and her son."

"Speaking of her." Martine pointed out the window. "Here she comes."

Mme. Leroux arched her shoulders back before stepping inside, leaving her son on the pavement. Her face was stern and unforgiving. "Is it true?"

Martine stepped forward as if she was about to give her a talking-to, but I put my hand out to stop her.

"Of all the people," Mme. Leroux said. "God rest your aunt's soul." She folded her arms tightly, looking over Martine and her shocked face, and Simone, who stood helplessly by the counter. "I came to collect my clothing. I won't be doing business here anymore."

"I... Ah..." I motioned for Simone to retrieve her things from the back, and not to forget the pants we'd mended for her son, using our old jackets for material we couldn't buy because of the rations.

Her lips pursed while she watched Simone carry her garments in from the back. "It's bad enough you've become a black ribbon shop, but allowing a German civilian to live in your aunt's apartment, free of charge? Blanche would be disgusted." She snatched her things from Simone, nearly scratching my sister's arms.

"Watch it," Martine said. "You don't know what—"

"Martine!" I said. "Leave Madame alone. If she doesn't want to do business with us, that is fine."

Mme. Leroux took her things in her arms and gave us a look of contempt. "I hope you go to hell. All of you." She threw open the door and stormed out.

"Why didn't you tell her?" Martine pointed to Madame Leroux as she dragged her son to the other side of the street, her clothing bundled under one arm, never looking back, not even a glance. "Gaby! She needs to know what you're doing for her. What those rations have cost us."

I held my face. "I can't," I said. "It's not fair to burden her."

Martine turned back toward the window to stew, while Simone walked to the opposite side of the shop, her dress plainly exposing her swelling belly, before slipping on her coat to cover herself up.

"At least they haven't found out about your lessons," Simone said.

I felt the envelope in my pocket and the lump of money the commandant had given me. It was only a matter of time now: no matter how many backstreets I took, the fact that I walked to the German district every day would be discovered eventually. I closed my eyes tightly. I should have told Streicher the piano wasn't mine.

"Sisters," I said, eyes opening. "I... I..." Martine stepped away from the window as I fumbled my words, and Simone's mouth hung open as she watched me pull the envelope from my pocket and set it on the counter. "I have some more bad news."

Chapter Twelve

Martine stared at me. There was no mistaking the thickness of the envelope: much more money than I'd received previously. "What is that?" she asked, but clearly she knew.

"He's ordered me to come four days a week."

They were quiet, as if they'd expected it; maybe they were a little numb after all that had happened today. We went back to work as best we could, but not long after, the baker rode up to the curb with his bicycle and bread basket. I closed my eyes, thinking he must have heard the gossip and had come to shame us.

"What's he doing here?" Martine asked. "I can't take more bad news."

Simone stood up. "I asked him to make a delivery, and he wrote back that he would."

We both looked at Simone. Nobody delivered anything without collecting a fee, and Simone didn't have any extra money. And she wouldn't dare give him one of Aunt Blanche's spoons without asking, not like Martine.

He took a sack of bread from his basket, and walked toward our shop, looking confident. If I trusted my ears, he might have been whistling.

"He's up to something. I don't want his bread," Martine said, watching him through the glass, and Simone gagged when she said the word "bread." I ordered her into the back before Martine noticed her pale and pasty face—the look of someone about to vomit—but Martine just thought I didn't want her conversing with the baker.

Martine swiftly folded her arms when the door opened. "Jacques the baker," she said as the bells clanged and clanged. "What are you doing here? Bakers don't make home deliveries."

"Is Simone here?" He peeked over my shoulder to the back room where I imagined Simone was vomiting.

"She's not making herself beautiful for you, if that's what you're thinking," Martine said.

"She isn't?" he asked, and I sensed sarcasm in his voice.

"No," Martine said. "She isn't."

Martine leaned against the wall with her arms still folded, watching him as he stood waiting for Simone. A stare that would make anyone uncomfortable.

"I'll get our ration coupon." I went into the back room, hoping Martine wouldn't run him off by the time I'd come back, because everyone knew how much power the baker had with his bread.

I found Simone cowering over the toilet. "Oh no…" I held her hair back as she tried to stand and make her way to the front.

"Don't leave him alone with Martine," she said. "He'll never come back!"

I wiped her mouth with a piece of cloth. "That's the least of your problems."

"No, Gaby," she said. "You don't understand. He likes me. Does it hurt for the neighbors to know the good French baker visits? Especially now with that ribbon left on our door. He must not know yet, and his visits will give the neighbors something to talk about once I'm unable to hide my condition." She pulled her coat over her stomach before leaving.

In her own way, Simone was making plans. I should have been relieved she'd taken this step, but instead, I was worried she'd chosen the baker, who appeared to have more than friendly eyes for her.

When I walked out with the coupon, Martine gave me a look, something that made me think she was glad I'd come back.

"Thank you very much, Jacques." Simone smiled, looking grateful and beautiful despite heaving her guts out just seconds ago. She brushed a blonde curl from her face and lowered her eyes.

"The bombing didn't scare you, did it?" he asked, and Martine shook her head, though it was blatantly clear he was only talking to Simone. "Lots of smoke, but no real damage."

"What are you talking about?" Martine asked.

"They missed," he said.

"They missed?" I couldn't believe my ears.

Martine put her hands on her hips. "I don't believe it," she said. "There was so much smoke. They must have hit something. I also heard the oil facility was struck."

"Well, I heard a pen was damaged, but the U-boat made it out unscathed. Didn't hear about an oil facility." He turned to me. "The coupon?"

"Germans spreading lies and rumors, it sounds like," Martine mumbled.

"Here you are," I said, handing it over along with some coins for payment. "Thank you again for coming."

He turned to Simone. "I'll make another delivery when I can." He lifted his hand to adjust his cap, but I thought he was about to brush a lock of hair from her eyes, and by the horrified look on Martine's face, she thought it too.

"Time to go, Baker." Martine stepped in between them as Simone held the bread tightly in her arms.

"Goodbye," Simone managed to say, then puckered her lips and set the bread down. I thought she might vomit again.

"I don't like him," Martine said as soon as he was out of earshot and the door had closed behind him. "He's obviously got his eyes on you, and what are you going to do about that?"

"He's nice," Simone said.

"He's a liar. We overheard the neighbor telling Antoinette all about the bombing."

"Why would he lie? Even if it was just the pen that was destroyed, that's something, isn't it? It's a setback for the Germans. Nobody can take that away," Simone said.

"If so, then it wasn't enough." Martine pulled her hair back with both hands. "If only you'd agree and let me look for a missing bird, send more music to London. I'm sure we could dig up something valuable to tell them. We just have to look, because there's a pigeon out there waiting for us, and I'm good at finding things."

"Music to London," I repeated, gazing out the window.

"Just have to look…" For the first time since she'd mentioned the missing birds, I thought we could actually find one. Why wait for a drop? I'd bit my lip about what I heard at the commandant's house because of the risks. Then I imagined how I'd feel if I continued to keep quiet, and I felt a little sick.

I spun around, looking at Martine, who perked up. The back of my neck felt warm from the anticipation, the excitement, of having another pigeon in our hands— something I never thought I'd feel.

"Gaby?"

I kneaded my hands. "I heard something during Lauren's lesson," I blurted. "The commandant—he spoke in English and he doesn't know I heard him through the floor."

Martine's eyes grew wide. So wide, I didn't think she could blink without hurting herself. "What are you saying, Gaby?" She held back a smile.

"It's almost unbelievable, but I heard it with my own ears." I told them about the performance at the Monsigny, which didn't get much of a reaction until I told them who would be in attendance. "And Adolf Hitler is the special guest."

Martine sucked in a mouthful of air. "We have to find another bird now! We must go in search!"

Simone stamped her foot. "No! It's too risky. I never agreed that you could go in search of a pigeon, only that I wouldn't stand in your way if one dropped from the sky and into your hands like the first one. Those are different things." She folded her arms.

"What's the matter with you?" Martine asked. "This is extraordinary information."

Simone shook her head.

Martine threw her hands in the air and walked away. I bit at my thumbnail.

"You know, nobody can arrest us for taking a walk," I said, and Martine turned around with a smile taking up most of her face. "Lauren said she overheard something about a spy too, and maybe I can find out more about that—and by the time there's another drop, we'll be the only ones they mention on Radio Londres with all the information we'll send. The Heroines and their messages!"

"My goodness, Gaby, how you've changed," Simone said. "It's like you're a different person than you were a few days ago. You're emboldened."

She waited for me to say something, but I couldn't deny it. I did feel emboldened—I'd felt it after I heard The Heroines called out over the airwaves, and I felt it again deep in my bones when I played my piano after avoiding it for so long.

"We're only taking a walk, Simone," Martine said. "Nobody can arrest us for being near the cliffs. It's not illegal. If we find one, then it was meant to be. And don't you think the information about the Monsigny is worth a walk?"

I stepped forward. "Please, Simone," I said. "We won't talk to anyone."

She closed her eyes. I could tell our pleading had gotten to her once she started tapping her foot. "Fine. But you promise you'll be careful? And just a walk!"

I ran for my coat and Martine did too.

"Wait! You're going now?" Simone asked.

I turned sharply to kiss her cheek. "Yes!"

"Gaby—" Simone said, but we were already out the door.

We walked away from the village toward the sea, conscious of every eye on us, locking our arms and staying close. "Keep your head down," I whispered, and Martine looked at her shoes. I didn't want to make eye contact with any of the shopkeepers, not after the look Madame Roche had given me.

Rémy's sister appeared before us, startling Martine and standing in our way. "Martine."

"Hallo, Hélène," she said, her lip stiff.

Hélène didn't look angry or concerned about what people might think of her talking to us in the middle of the pavement. She looked sad.

"I heard what they're saying about you," Hélène said to us.

Martine rolled her shoulders back, trying to look confident, but to me she seemed nervous. "Do you believe it?"

"Do you care if Rémy believes it?" she asked, but Martine wouldn't give anything up about her feelings.

She hooked my arm a little tighter.

"He's left for forced labor, you know this?" Hélène's eyes shifted to the passersby on each side of us.

Martine nodded. "Was he sent to Poland?"

"He will be. In the interim, he's working at the munitions depot on the Belgium border. You can write him, you know this too?"

Martine pulled on my arm to walk around her into the chilly breeze, leaving Hélène with her mouth open. "Martine, wait," I said as she dragged me, holding her collar closed with her free hand and her hair flittering over her shoulders. "Martine—"

She stopped, eyes closed tightly, before glancing back over her shoulder. Hélène had continued on with her business.

"Don't ask me about it, Gaby," she said. "I don't want... I can't..."

"I won't." I didn't want to upset her further with questions about Rémy, because I knew it tore at her heart that he'd left, even if she denied it to my face. We hooked arms again. "Come on."

The clouds had rolled in, covering us in endless gray, and I thought we'd walked for an hour, though Martine said it was exactly twenty-eight minutes. "There's a farm near the cliffs. That's where we need to walk. Maybe they found a bird or two, and put him in their coop? Or maybe there's one in the grass where he landed and still in the box?"

"But we're not to talk to anyone," I said. "We promised Simone."

"I know."

We followed a windswept trail from the main road toward the cliffs where the wind whistled mercilessly in my ears. No pigeon would roost in that wind, and we agreed our best chance was to continue to the farm. She'd assured me there were no German guns on this stretch of the beach, and she was right. It was strange to see the coastline natural and how it was before the occupation.

"The wind is too vicious up here for the Germans," Martine said. "But up that way"—she pointed—"there are patrols and bunkers. As long as we stay on this dirt trail nobody can see us unless they break their neck to do it."

The wind stopped howling once we made it to the edge of the cliff and stood in a strange pocket of dead air. The sea appeared peaceful, and razor-thin clouds allowed a stream of sunlight to break through, illuminating the faintest white cliffs across the sea in England. A narrow footpath, with charming flower-lined bends and twists, led down to the beach and to Martine's favorite cave.

Now I understood why Martine met Rémy at the cliffs. It was beautiful, and private.

"I know about Simone," she said out of the blue, and I turned toward her. "You're surprised? Don't look at me like that or try to deny it."

I tried to find words, but they'd escaped me.

"Do you deny it?" she asked, and I shook my head.

Martine nodded once, as if she needed me to confirm what she already knew, and we carried on. "The farm's this way." She pointed, and we walked away from the cliff, the breeze picking up again. I stuffed my hands in my coat pockets.

"Simone asked you not to tell me, didn't she?"

I hesitated before answering, knowing she was going to get upset when I told her the truth. "Yes," I said, and she puffed, tossing her hands up. "I told her if you asked me outright, I wouldn't lie. But, Martine, do you blame her? She must be scared, and the father… who knows if he'll ever come near her again. She says they're in love, that they have plans." Martine rolled her eyes. "I don't know what we're going to do…"

"She probably thinks he'll send for her," Martine said, shaking her head, then turning to me. "Don't you go and tell her I know, Gaby."

My mouth hung open. "Martine… I…"

"I mean it," she said. "You kept her secret, now you can keep mine." She stopped abruptly. "There's the farm."

In the distance, down a lone gravelly road, was indeed a farm with a fence and animal pens, but no animals. It was close to where Martine had found her pigeon, and it struck me as an obvious place for the Abwehr to visit.

"Don't you think the Germans would have gone there looking?" I asked.

"Probably, but there were Germans at our home and they didn't find our pigeon. Let's go," she said, pulling me along with her, looking over her shoulder toward the main road, as we made our way to the farm. We entered through a section of fence that had been pushed over, probably by a storm.

"Wait," I said, stopping in the weeds. "We need a plan."

"We don't have time for a plan," she said, pointing at the clouds. All the light that had graced us a few moments ago at the cliffs was gone, and the smell of rain now coated the air like heavy smoke.

"We always have time for a plan," I said.

"If they're anywhere outside, they're in one of those animal pens. That one looks like it could be a coop!" She pointed. "Let's start there. They'd have to be secured so they wouldn't fly away."

We walked a few feet more toward a chicken coop, and a pasture that looked like it had once been the home to a few cows. We ducked down behind the coop while I surveyed the pasture. Normally, I'd think it would smell awful on a farm, but instead, it smelled delicious—something carried in the wind with the smell of rain. Something being cooked.

"Oh no," I said. "He's cooking meat. What if he's cooking the pigeons?" The coop was in fact a shed with windows. I'd peeped through the glass to the other side where the farmland spread out beyond the house and saw smoke coming from a spit.

Martine popped up, trying to get a look. "Bastards," she gritted, and I elbowed her.

"Not so loud," I hissed.

We clung to the side of the shed, thinking, wondering what to do. But what could we do? The farmer was close enough to see us if he walked a few feet around the shed. I was about to tell Martine we needed to go, turn around before we were seen, when a pigeon flew up inside the shed through the window.

I gasped, hand to my mouth, before sinking to the ground and taking Martine with me.

"Thank God," I said. "He didn't cook it." I took another look into the shed. "There's two!"

I pushed the door open and crawled inside on my hands and knees with Martine right behind, but the hinge had creaked like a splitting tree and we both froze in the half-open doorway, listening to see if the farmer heard; it appeared he hadn't because he'd started talking to someone about the weather. Maybe it was his wife.

"Don't let them fly away," Martine whispered, just before two pigeons flew off a shelf, disturbing the tilling tools hanging from hooks and making a break for the outside. I shut the door, blocking their escape, and they landed on the ground in a puff of feathers, cooing in distress and flapping their wings like chickens with their heads chopped off.

Martine swiftly took one by the head and the other by the feet, and stuffed them down her coat sleeves.

"Let's go!" she said, and we scrambled for the door just as the farmer appeared at the window, trying to get a good look into the shed. We ducked, hands pressed to our mouths.

He shouted to his wife, "Did you hear that?"

My heart hammered in my chest, then nearly exploded when the farmer headed around the side of the shed with his shovel. I reached for Martine, pulling her in close behind the door, and scooting as flush as we could against the wall.

"Who's in here?" He threw the door open, almost hitting our noses. The butt of his shovel hit the floor—*thud*—followed by the scuff of footsteps. Tilling tools swayed, metal skimming on metal, when a third bird flew out from behind a fallen beam, startling the farmer with a yelp.

"What's going on in there?" his wife yelled from outside.

I squeezed my eyes shut, waiting for him to see there was nobody in the shed, before he finally answered.

"Nothing. Just the birds," he said, closing the door, and my eyes popped open.

I pressed my hands to my chest, relieved that he'd left, but soon we realized he wasn't gone, with the constant murmur of voices filtering through every crack and crevice of the shed.

"Why isn't he leaving?" Martine whispered.

"Shh," I whispered back.

We went from stiff and frozen to taking guarded peeks out the window where the smoke was still thick and strong coming off the spit. "We'll have to wait," I said, but waiting turned from a few minutes into hours. When the shed turned darker from the setting sun, I started to worry.

"What if we're here all night?" Martine squirmed in her coat, holding the birds in place. "I don't smell the meat anymore. Do you?"

I popped up for another look out the window, this time holding onto the window ledge. All seemed peaceful, except for the occasional creak from the floorboards. I gasped when I saw a light flicker in the house. "He's gone inside!"

Martine scratched at her arms over the bird mounds. "Are you sure?"

It was my best guess. "I think so." The other bird wouldn't come out from under the beam. I wanted to reach for him, but knew I'd be risking our lives. "Run once we clear the fence."

I took Martine's hand and we snuck out, slow at first, tiptoeing through the grass then flat out running once we'd reached the fence, both of us huffing and puffing.

We hugged once we were safe on the main road and out of sight.

"I thought we'd never get out of there!" Martine said.

I felt my head and heart. "It's over," I said. "We got the birds. We did it. Are they hurting you at all?"

"A little." She winced from some scratching and clawing. "That was too close, Gaby."

I helped her button up her coat. "Come on, let's go."

We started the walk home. I hated that we had to leave that other bird, but at least we'd grabbed two. I tried to think of a good place to let them go.

"Where'd you let the last pigeon go? Out your bedroom window?"

"Out Simone's."

I shot her a look, knowing Simone wouldn't be happy about that.

"What?" Martine said. "She was asleep."

Once we reached our road, rain started to spit on the pavement, but I didn't mind since we were almost home. Our pace quickened.

"Remember what I said about—"

"I remember, but I don't like keeping secrets," I said.

"You kept her secret," Martine reminded me.

"That's not fair," I said. "I already told you why I did that."

"Is the father…"

I shook my head. He wasn't German, but the truth didn't matter in occupied France with so many of our men away or dead. And this was something we'd need to address very soon.

"Come on, let's hurry." I was anxious to show Simone what we found. "Almost home," I said, but lurched to a stop in front of Antoinette's house where it was dark. A car was parked outside our home. A nice car. "Oh, no..."

"Is that..."

My heart stopped. "The commandant's car."

Chapter Thirteen

W e hid between our home and Antoinette's, under her window and out of sight. "What's he doing here?" Martine asked, then rasped the rest of her words. "And what are we going to do?"

I bit my nails as the rain spit down upon us.

"He's here to see you," she said.

"I know, I know," I said, but I was still wondering what to do.

She yanked on my arm. "Gaby!"

"I'll go inside. You stay here." I scooted Martine over, positioning her in the darkest space under Antoinette's window. "Don't move."

"But what's he doing in there alone," she whispered, "with our sister?"

I gasped, dashing across the wet patches of grass and reaching the door without even taking a second to shake the rain off myself.

I burst in. "Hallo—" I froze as the collage photos fluttered up from the wall with the breeze I'd let in.

It wasn't the commandant, but Lauren and her mistress, Irma.

Simone stood by the cellar door, hands twisting and eyes shifting. "You have visitors, sister." She managed a smile and it was the flakiest I'd ever seen. She pointed into the main salon, but my eyes were already there.

"Lauren…" I said, and she swung around on my piano bench where she sat, the lid flipped up and Irma looking on contently, leaning against my piano as if waiting for a song.

"Teacher!" She beamed.

I was out of breath from the run and trying to make sense of things, looking at Irma, then Lauren, then at my piano, with rain dripping from the ends of my hair. "What brings you here?"

Lauren's smile faded when she heard my voice, which might have come across as unwelcoming rather than worried.

"She wanted to see where you lived," Irma piped.

"No. I didn't say that." She glared at Irma. "I said I wished I could visit. And *you* said we should take a drive."

Irma mumbled with no clear words to explain herself. I didn't want Lauren to think she was unwelcome, but at the same time, I was angry at Irma for driving the commandant's personal car to our home. I caught a glimpse of Martine's dark shape outside the window as she stood in the rain against Antoinette's house.

"Well…" I walked over to Lauren. "This is where I live." I motioned with my hand to the dim salon and the kitchen, then my piano.

Lauren ran her fingers up and down the keys, which jolted Irma away from the piano to cover her ears. Lauren snickered, and I patted her shoulders, making her stop, then to my horror, Antoinette's house lights flicked on through the window. Martine ducked, but all Irma had to do was turn around and she'd see her, and all Antoinette had to do was look out her window.

"Ah…" I smiled, though my heart was racing. I was afraid to move when the lights were switched on. "It's been a long day."

Antoinette's lights flicked off.

"A long day?" Irma questioned.

"Yes!" I hurriedly reached for Irma's shoulders, guiding her toward the door, which caught her by surprise, but I wanted to move her away from the window in case the lights turned back on. "I don't mean to be abrupt, but I'm not in a position to receive company right now."

"You're asking us to leave?"

"The commandant's personal vehicle is parked outside our home," I said low enough for Lauren not to hear. "Yes. I'm asking you to leave."

She looked shocked at first, but then her face changed. "It doesn't sound like you're asking." She turned to Lauren. "Time to go."

Lauren reluctantly reached for her coat and then waved me down to her level where she whispered. "Are you mad?" Her breath smelled of cake and tea.

I petted her head, running my hand down her soft hair until it curled near her shoulders. She was innocent in her visit, and I wasn't mad at her. "I'm not mad at you. I'm tired."

Irma ran out to the car, covering her head amidst the patter of rain with Lauren following behind her. Simone and I watched from the doorstep as she started the engine, as if she was used to driving his personal car. "She drove the commandant's car," Simone breathed. "Everyone must know now."

"I know," I said through my teeth. I just wanted them to drive away now so that Martine could come inside. Lauren waved through the rain-streaked car window.

"Did she do it on purpose?" Simone asked.

"I'm not sure," I said. "But I have no doubt *he* knew what he was doing by allowing it."

I waited for them to drive away, then when it was safe, I motioned for Martine to come in from the shadows, but she was already making her way over, rain dripping off her hair and face too.

Simone closed the door, and Martine ducked into the cellar, disappearing between the jackets.

"Did you…" Simone whispered.

I nodded, finger to my lips, afraid the captain was listening through our shared wall, but before I could whisper back that we'd found two pigeons, a knock sounded on the front door.

"Who's that?" she mouthed, but I hadn't a clue. Martine emerged from the cellar asking the same thing.

I lifted the curtains to have a look just as I heard, "It's Antoinette!" from the other side of the door.

"Don't answer it," Martine said, scratching her arms profusely where the birds had been, but I felt I had to.

"And let her knock all night?"

Martine's mouth pinched. "Then tell her not to come here anymore. She's not welcome."

I opened the door, but refused to invite her in, even while

she was being pelted by a burst of hard-falling rain. She held her coat over her head.

"What do you want?"

Martine stood on her tiptoes, shouting over my shoulder. "Go home! It's raining." She crossed her arms after giving them another scratch.

"Well, I think my hens finally calmed down after the bombing today," Antoinette said, when I expected her to ask questions about the commandant's car. "Mildred, she was a wreck earlier! Eleanor too."

"You gave your chickens people names?" Martine asked, and her voice was so thick and low and condescending, but Antoinette pretended she didn't notice and looked confused.

"Of course!" she said.

"Yes, well, it's late," I said, moving to close the door. "Goodnight, Antoinette."

"Wait!"

I stopped short of closing the door all the way and spoke through the crack. "What is it, Antoinette?" My patience had peaked.

"I know I mentioned it earlier, but that really was a beautiful duet you played with the captain."

She grinned, and my stomach sank.

"What?" Martine uncrossed her arms. "A duet?"

Simone walked up from behind, looking at me as if she'd seen a ghost.

"I wasn't playing a duet," I said.

"Oh, it was so lovely," Antoinette said. "Especially after the fright of the explosions. All the neighborhood heard—"

I slammed the door shut, and the wall jittered and shook.

Her smile was etched in my mind, so gentle and friendly, yet biting and sinister at the same time.

"Gaby..." Simone said, and I turned to face my sisters, hands twisting.

"It's true. I played." By the new looks drawn upon my sisters' faces, I wasn't sure if they were surprised I'd played, or that I'd been accused of playing with the captain. "I felt the urge to play again—I can't explain it," I said, though I could explain that part. I swallowed dryly, judging their frozen and emotionless expressions. "But I played for myself," I added, turning toward the wall where I was sure he must be listening. "Just me. Only when I was done he began to play, and the same selection. There was nothing I could do."

"Did you talk to him?" Martine asked, and after I didn't answer, her eyes bulged from their sockets. "My God, Gaby, did you go next door?" She pointed angrily to the shared wall, and I shook my head. "Germans are soulless, they'll trick you!"

"Of course I didn't go next door."

"I think you better tell us everything. Step by step," Martine said, so I started at the beginning, right after we'd said goodbye in the road, and as I retold the story, I realized our reputations had been sealed. It didn't matter about the lessons anymore, the commandant's car, or even the black ribbon. All of them together, added with the duet, made us absolutely, one hundred percent, bad French, and there wasn't anything we could do to change that. Both my sisters nodded; they understood now, but damn that Antoinette for making it seem as if our duet was on purpose and by agreement.

"I'm going upstairs," Simone said, exhausted, and she left, walking up to her bedroom without making a sound on the creaky old staircase, leaving me and Martine watching her from the foyer.

"I'm sorry, Martine," I said. "I'll only play when I know he isn't home." I didn't bother lowering my voice, because I wanted the captain to hear.

Martine nodded. The conversation about our duet was resolved. Now we had to talk about the pigeon, and tell Simone our good news, because I refused to let our miserable neighbor Antoinette spoil our entire evening.

Martine and I walked upstairs together, and not at all quietly like Simone had done. After changing into our night clothes, we found Simone sitting on her bed with a blanket over her belly hiding the bump. She looked over her shoulder.

Martine closed the door so we could talk freely without the captain hearing.

"Forget about the commandant's car, and forget about Antoinette and the captain," I said, sitting next to her. "We have something else to tell you."

"What is it?"

"We didn't catch one pigeon, we caught two," I said. "It was meant to be! And when the war is over, we'll tell everyone what we've done."

"Two pigeons?" Simone's eyes popped. "How'd you get two?"

Martine and I relived the story but left out the part about almost getting caught. "Then Martine grabbed both birds and stuffed them down her sleeves like she'd been doing it her whole life," I said, which drew a smile from them both. "It happened so fast, and there's still one left, the last of the missing four, but we had to leave it."

"And nobody saw you? You didn't talk to anyone?"

"Nobody saw us. And we didn't talk to anyone," I said.

Martine brought in her alarm clock, setting it for a three in the morning wake-up. "We're letting one go in the middle of the night."

I put my hand out. "All three of us will," I said. Martine put her hand on top of mine, then we waited for Simone. "You said that if we got the pigeons—"

"I won't stop you," Simone said, finally adding her hand. "But I don't want to be involved. Don't ask me to help." She lay down in bed and pulled the blankets up to her chin to cover herself.

I motioned with my head for Martine to say something, but instead, she lay down too, snuggling up against Simone like she used to do when they were little; though this time she reached around and placed her hand on Simone's bulging stomach, which caused Simone to gasp and make a defensive move of her arm.

After a quiet moment, Simone spoke. "Gaby told you?"

"No. She kept your secret. I figured it out myself a few days ago. You turned and I saw your belly when your coat flaps opened."

Simone sighed, rubbing her eyes. "For so many months it was easy to hide. I didn't seem to show at all, and my coat provided just the right amount of cover when my dresses started to fit too snugly, but I'm getting bigger now, and coat weather is going to end with it getting warmer."

"When is the baby due?" Martine asked.

"The end of June," Simone said. "Still many weeks away. Silly me, I thought I could hide the baby until the due date."

"Hide it?" Martine laughed in jest. "How can you hide a pregnancy?"

"I know one woman who did," Simone said. "She only looked fuller in the middle until the very last month and she's built like me, long and slender. And then you see a petite woman like Francine, when we saw her turning in her pigeon for the reward, and there was no mistaking her condition—she was all baby and no body."

"Is that what you're going to be like in a few weeks?" Martine asked, and Simone shrugged.

"What if you're showing like Francine in a few days?" I asked, but that question was met with silence.

I lit a candle after throwing a blanket over both of them, casting strange shapes all over the room. I crawled in next to Martine and lay closest to the wall.

"Who is he?" Martine asked.

Simone stared up at the candlelit shapes dancing on the ceiling. "His name's Christian. He's a résistant," she said. "Handsome. Daring."

"Oh good," Martine said. "I worried you might say he had warts and a hunched back."

"Martine!" Simone yelped, then she had a giggle. "Not at all. I would never. Not in a million years."

"A billion," Martine said, laughing.

"I expect him to be as gorgeous as you," I said. "Only the best for my sister. When will we get to meet him?"

"I don't know. It's dangerous for him to come out during the day. I only see him on occasion at the dances, when he thinks it's safe." She turned her head on her pillow, catching a glimpse of us both. "I won't go anymore," she said before Martine could. "Things are different now with the captain here, like you said, Gaby, and now that everyone thinks we are bad French, I'm not sure I'd be welcome anyway."

"Does he know about the baby?" Martine asked carefully, knowing I'd already told her they'd had plans, but I supposed she wanted to hear it from Simone.

"Yes," Simone said. I could hear the joy in her voice with just that one word. "He's making arrangements, then he'll come for me." She used a tissue from her bedside table to wipe her eyes, which gushed just from thinking of him. "We're going to be a family..."

Martine squeezed my hand under the covers. I knew she had little hope Christian would come for Simone, and I was glad she kept her words to herself. Simone was in a delicate state. Part of me shared Martine's doubt, while another part of me believed what Simone said, which brought buried feelings to the surface.

"Why didn't you tell us about him earlier?" I asked.

"Because..." she said, then it was quiet with only an occasional creak from the settling house. She didn't have to say anything more. She didn't tell us because Martine and I were miserable, each hiding our grief and feelings for the men we had loved and lost, albeit in different ways.

"Gaby?"

A painful lump bulged in my throat. "Yes?"

"Don't do that to yourself," she said.

"Do what?"

"You didn't kill Beau, so stop blaming yourself. You had every right to want to wait on marriage so you could pursue your studies. If you had married him when he asked, you would have never finished The Heroines—and that was important to you. You shouldn't have had to choose," she said. "And you too, Martine."

Martine put a hand to her chest. "What do you mean, me too?"

Simone gave her a look, the kind that said she didn't have to pretend anymore, but Martine had made an art of hiding her feelings by acting tough when her heart was as fragile as a glass egg.

"Don't blame yourself for pushing Rémy away when I know you're in love with him. It was probably better for him." Martine threw the covers over her head. "And Gaby, there's a man out there right now dreaming of a woman with your talent. Someone who'll be stirred by your music, deep in his heart, with equal parts forgiveness and hope—someone who'll wait for you, until the end of time if he has to, while you chase your dreams."

Tears spilled over my cheeks, and I slid under the covers where I could hardly catch my breath. We were talking about Simone and the baby, and somehow it turned into a talk about me and Martine, leaving me feeling exposed. Though there was also a strange sense of relief too, at least for me, to talk about what I'd kept hidden in my heart for so long.

Simone blew out the candle, and Martine sank into the saggy middle between us, reaching out only for the alarm clock, and pulling it in close.

The alarm startled all three of us out of our dreams, scrambling to find the clock in the sheets as it rang and rang, worried it would wake up the captain because it was loud enough to penetrate the walls, and also wake up Antoinette next door. "Where is it?" I asked.

"Got it!" Martine clutched the clock close to her chest after turning it off.

My heart thumped like a rabbit's foot on wood, and my ears were still ringing from the alarm long after Martine had turned it off. I flopped backward in the covers, trying to recover with a hand over my eyes.

A dog barked somewhere far away, and Simone reached over, touching us both as Martine disentangled herself from the electrical cord. "Shh…"

We stayed quiet for some time, then, when it sounded safe, Martine got up to light a candle. She'd closed Simone's curtains so that nobody could see the glow from the road. "You get the sheet music, I'll get the bird," she said, after rubbing her eyes, and I finally got out of bed.

Simone had laid back down, hand to her forehead, but Martine came rushing back before I'd made it out the door, scaring us both. "I can't do it."

"Why?" I asked.

"Because of the stairs. They creak!"

Simone yawned, and we both looked at her, realizing who had the talent to sneak down the creaking staircase unnoticed. "Why are you looking at me?"

I rubbed my face, trying to figure out an easy way to tell Simone she had to be the one to go into the cellar and into the bureau to get my sheet music, but there wasn't an easy way to tell her, other than to tell her. "You have to go," I said.

She threw a hand to her chest. "Me? I told you I'm not going to help."

"But you're the only one who can make it downstairs without a peep. What if the captain's listening? He might wonder what we're walking around for, especially if he heard the alarm." Martine and I waited for Simone to say she'd go, but she was taking her time. "Simone…"

She groaned. "Fine, I'll go just this once, but it's only so I can go back to sleep." She tossed back the sheets and found her robe, tying the belt with a sloppy bow while I apologized for having to make her go. She took a deep breath in the doorway. "How do I grab the bird? By the legs?"

Martine had been nibbling on her fingernails. "Any way you like," she said. Simone nodded. "Wait!" Martine handed her a pillowcase. "Put him in this. We only need one. Leave the other in the coal chute."

"I'll be back."

Martine and I waited in Simone's bedroom, listening, but we couldn't hear a sound. Simone was an expert walker, stealthy and quiet. "It's unbelievable," I whispered.

"What?" Martine whispered back.

"Her walk," I said, but then I heard something that wasn't at all reminiscent of a woman walking creaky old stairs, and more like the howling and squealing of two people in bed. Martine lifted the curtain to look at Antoinette's bedroom window where it was dark.

"It's three in the morning," she whispered, putting her ear to the glass. "I can hear him grunting."

Simone emerged with a lumpy pillowcase clenched in her fist, and a sheet of my music, which she handed to Martine.

"Thank you, Simone," I said, but she wasn't interested in my thanks and climbed back into bed as if she hadn't slept in a hundred years, throwing the sheets over her head and telling us not to wake her again until the sun had risen.

"My heart is racing," I said.

"So is mine," Martine said.

After cutting my music to fit into the capsule, I drew a map of the village with all the major locations noted and how to find the theatre. There would be no mistaking the location.

On 29 May. Confirmed Adolf Hitler and other notable German command will be at the evening performance at the Theatre Monsigny in Boulogne-sur-Mer.

I had rolled the music up tightly when Martine suggested we draw a rose in the corner and ask them to mention it, so we'd know which messages they received, and when, because we were sending two. Martine held the bird steady, helping me stuff the note into the capsule around his leg.

"Where are you going to let him go?" Simone whispered, pulling her sheet down below her eyes, and I realized she still had no idea that Martine had let the first pigeon leave from *her* window.

"Out your window," Martine whispered, "like last time."

"My window?" Simone asked, but when Martine didn't explain, she pulled the sheet back up.

Martine blew out the candle and I opened the window, listening to make sure the moaning from Antoinette's hadn't stopped—she was up, but she was occupied and wouldn't see.

A salty sea breeze blew through the open window, while the pigeon squirmed in Martine's hands. "Go," I said.

Martine kissed the top of the pigeon's head. "Fly fast," she whispered, and he flapped off into the night, over Antoinette's house with the squeals of her German lover rattling her windowpanes.

Chapter Fourteen

London

Guy Burton couldn't believe his ears when Arthur Ripley telephoned with news of another pigeon. He thought about traveling out to Ipswich himself to get it, but then decided to wait because of policy, driving his colleague, Clive, absolutely mad.

"Take a seat." Clive pushed tacks into a wall map of France, and with each new tack he looked at Guy. "You're distracting me, and I have an appointment today about my promotion. You don't want to bungle my chances with the brass, do you?"

Guy shook his hands in front of him after rubbing his neck. "I can't sit," he said, then looked up. "What are you doing with that map?"

"The Abwehr are closing in on the north," he said. "The brass want a report."

Guy briefly examined the map before pacing again, and by the time the messenger arrived, he'd gone through the gamut of emotions: from nervousness, through moments of excitement, to dread at the prospect that the message might be a stinker—a poem or some information the War Office couldn't use, like good tidings from the Germans or jokes about pigeon dinners.

But as soon as Guy unraveled the scroll from the bird's messenger capsule and saw Gaby's sheet music, he leapt out of his chair and ran up the stairs to the second floor with the pigeon stuffed under his arm.

Smith's secretary, Daisy, tried to stop him, but Guy ran past her for the door, catching Smith by surprise. "They sent another one!"

The door banged against the wall as Smith leaped to his feet behind his desk, staring at a panting and sweaty Guy Burton in his doorway. "Bring it in, bring it in..." Smith waved him forward, telling his secretary that it was all right and to close the door.

"Goodness me, Mr. Burton," Daisy said, holding her chest. "You about gave me a heart attack running past me just now."

"Sorry, Daisy," he said.

After she closed the door, Guy let go of the pigeon to flap around on the floor, and showed Smith the twisted scroll in his hand. "Look!"

Shortly after Guy met with Churchill in the War Rooms, he was told Operation Columba had been suspended. He pestered Smith for another meeting after he heard about the successful RAF bombing in Boulogne-sur-Mer, destroying the oil facility and the U-boat pen. Though something had changed in his supervisor, and for reasons unknown, Smith was now against sending more pigeons just like The Five.

The pigeon tried to fly out of Smith's closed window with

no luck, hitting the windowpane and flopping back to the floor. "Have you verified it?" Smith put his glasses on to have a look at the scroll. Guy assumed he was asking if he'd taken it to Professor Caron for verification, when in fact, he'd read Gaby's name in the notes.

Guy nodded—it was verified in his mind.

"Let's have a look, then," Smith said, turning on his desk lamp even though there was plenty of light in his office already.

Both men leaned in, only to back away in shock after reading about the Monsigny performance and their special guest of honor.

Smith took his glasses off. "Date and time of Hitler's whereabouts."

"My God, sir. This is proof we can't stop now!" Guy smiled broadly. "We have to call the Air Ministry, get a flight in the diary."

Smith shook his head. "Afraid not." He put his glasses back on and sat down.

Guy's mouth hung open, then it nearly hit the floor when Smith opened his ledger and recorded a translated version of the message and assigned it a number, as was policy before sending it to Churchill, which meant Smith believed the information to be true. Guy was severely confused, because surely there was value in the Secret Pigeon Program if Smith was sending the message on.

"The Heroines need pigeons, sir."

"Looks like they're doing fine on their own locating pigeons from the original drop, now, aren't they?" Smith folded his arms.

After a pause, Guy clenched his fists out of frustration. If this new message didn't convince Smith about sending more, then what would?

"Sir?" he questioned, but when Smith refused to continue the conversation, Guy left, afraid he'd say something he'd regret, and walked back downstairs to his basement office, where he hoped he'd cool off.

"Everything all right?" Clive asked from his desk.

"Yeah," he said, but Guy didn't want to face him while his cheeks were hot, and held onto his file cabinet, looking at the wall, thinking.

"Was the message a good one?" Clive asked, then quickly followed up with, "I know, I know. You can't tell me."

"That doesn't keep you from asking, now does it?" he snapped.

Guy felt Clive studying him even with his back turned. "Maybe you should bunk off early," Clive said, which he thought was a good idea.

Guy filed the newest message away in his cabinet, slammed the drawer shut, and took a deep breath. "Yeah." He reached for his bag, slinging it over his shoulder, then remembered Clive had his important appointment with the brass while he was out.

"What's the news from the top? Are you moving up a floor?"

"I am," he said, giving his jacket lapels a tug. "Can you believe it? I just got off the phone with my wife and told her the good news. You'll have your office back to yourself, and I won't be pestering you with questions you aren't allowed to answer." He laughed, and Guy felt bad he'd snapped at him.

"Congratulations." Guy shook Clive's hand, telling him he deserved the promotion, though really, he thought it had happened a little too fast. Guy worked his tail off and had never been promoted.

Other agents from down the corridor came to congratulate Clive too. Suddenly Guy's office was crowded with well-wishers, which allowed him to sneak out in the middle of the afternoon without any questions.

He barely remembered the drive home because his mind was on one thing—three things, actually—and they began and ended with Gaby and her sisters.

Guy walked upstairs to his flat, barging through his own door, but found his sis writing him a note at the table, and nearly scared poor Madge into the rafters.

"Guy!" She took a few deep breaths. "I didn't expect you. You're never home at this time."

"Sorry." After kissing her cheek, Guy sat down at the table for two by the window, holding his head in his hands and feeling exhausted. "What are you doing here?"

"I brought you a Woolton pie, figured you could pick at it for a few days," she said, pointing a finger behind her to the kitchen counter, where the warm smell of cooked vegetables and pastry was strong, "but after checking the icebox, looks like you haven't eaten anything I've brought you this whole week. I thought all you did was work and eat, but it appears you only work."

"How am I any different from your husband?" Madge's husband, Roger, was in the RAF and always away. When he was home, his mind was on his aircraft and the next mission.

"Because your job is killing you, Guy." She lifted his head up by the chin as he sat slumped over at the table, possibly seeing something Guy didn't want her to see, when she looked deeply into his eyes. "I worry about you."

"Today was a bad day, that's all." He tried to brush her off, but she was the only woman besides Jennie that he couldn't fool.

"No, that's not all, Guy," she said. "I don't have to be a secret agent to see you're completely knackered every second of the day. You used to wear pressed suits, now you look like you pulled your clothes from the hamper." She paused. "I hear you in the night, you know? Thumping footsteps on my ceiling. You sound like an elephant, carrying the weight of the world on your shoulders."

"The war doesn't stop on the weekends. Wouldn't it be nice if it did?" he said as if that was an excuse, but the truth was he had poured himself into his work since his wife died. It was how he dealt with the loss. "But even if it did stop, I guess I wouldn't know what else to do, now would I?"

Madge had sat down, studying him as he hung his head, before reaching over and touching his hand for comfort.

"Have you thought about taking your ring off? It might help."

He pulled his hand out from under hers. "It's more than that, sis."

"Is it?" Madge asked. "I feel like I lost my brother that night and not just my sister-in-law, and it's breaking my heart." She held her chest, and Guy sat up, now feeling more irritated than sad—he didn't expect to have this conversation when he came home. Far from it. But in the same breath, he knew she was just looking out for him, and he decided to tell her some of what was bothering him, because keeping it bottled up was starting to rip at his insides. Guy also wanted her to understand.

"All right, sis. I'm going to tell you something."

Madge sat up tall, looking very attentive.

"You know the pigeon service I'm in charge of? Well, one was sent back recently. One with good, solid intelligence. Two actually, as of today."

"That's great news!" she said.

"Yes, but apparently it isn't enough to keep the service going. They aren't sending more pigeons, and now the program is dead, just as it was starting to pay off." He looked out his window and over the rooftops, shaking his head. "I don't understand, and now I'm worried about my agents in France."

Madge rambled on about how sorry she was that work was so dismal, but also that he needed to pull his head out of the sand. "Your focus on work is distracting you from what matters, from being happy and living your life. Let me introduce you to someone. You're an attractive man, Guy. Wavy, sandy-blond hair, dark eyelashes, strong jaw, a heart of gold. I know quite a few ladies..."

"Ah, Madge, not now," he said, standing, but she continued, while his thoughts bounced back to Smith, the pigeons, and Churchill.

They'd both said something that didn't make sense. Churchill seemed encouraged that his heroine agents would still collect intelligence even without the pigeons, and then Smith said they were doing just fine on their own. It was as if the War Office wanted the sisters to bring attention to themselves and scramble for a means to deliver messages after that boost from Radio Londres. *Emboldened agents with nowhere to go.* His last thought was of the map Clive was working on. All those Abwehr officers closing in on northern France when they had the whole country to monitor.

"And that's what I think," Madge ended. "Your work is a red herring, brother. Keeping you from focusing on your life."

Guy turned sharply away from the window, which startled Madge in her chair. "What did you say?"

She unfolded her arms. "It's keeping you from focusing on your life," she repeated, but Guy shook his head.

"No," he said, eyes clenched. "Before that…"

"Red herring?" she questioned, and with that Guy's heart thumped in his chest. "It's a distraction, you must know—"

"My God!" He gulped two mouthfuls of air before grabbing his sister by her shoulders. "Thank you, Madge!" He kissed her hard on the cheek. "That's it!" He reached for his messenger bag and flew out his door for the War Office, leaving her in his kitchen.

———————

Guy ran up the stairs to the second floor because he didn't have time for the lift, and threw open Smith's door, again bypassing his secretary Daisy, who came running in after him, unable to stop him.

"The Heroines are decoys, aren't they?"

Smith had stood up from his desk, looking stunned at first by his question, then motioned for Daisy to leave them alone.

"I'm right, aren't I?" Guy asked after Daisy left them.

Smith's lips pinched. "Guy Burton, you're a persistent fellow, I'll have you know." He pointed to a chair with his eyes. "You better sit for this," he said, but Guy remained standing. "Go on. Sit."

Guy finally sat down, but he wasn't sure for how long he

would stay seated. Smith owed him an explanation and he owed it now. "Sir, I deserve to know."

"I think so too, dammit. I'll tell you, and then deal with the consequences later if I have to." He looked briefly at the floor. "The first drop was a mistake. The pilot was off course. Those pigeons were supposed to go to Belgium, you know this. Now the Germans are clued into the location of Boulogne-sur-Mer and The Heroines are on their list. We have our own intelligence that the Abwehr are searching for them in that vicinity."

Guy moved to the edge of his seat.

"You're right, Guy. The Heroines are our decoys," he said, and Guy stood up and paced the carpet. "It was weighed which strategy had more value, whether to send more pigeons to that area, or let your heroines *think* we were sending them and hope they become emboldened. Your agents are ordinary people, as you admitted. They will make thoughtless mistakes. They will cause suspicion and be noticed, and the War Office is counting on it."

"They'll get caught," Guy said.

"It is, I'm afraid, a risk they are willing to take."

Guy swallowed. "Who ordered this, sir?"

"Who do you think?" Smith asked, and Guy's eyes grew wide.

Churchill. Once Guy thought about it, he felt lightheaded and took his seat again. He was responsible for the pigeon service and his agents—he was the one who drafted the Radio Londres announcement. He was the one who led Gaby and her sisters into the fire.

"I feel sick," Guy said, holding his stomach.

"Well, you look it too," Smith said. "Sorry, Guy. This plan

was presented to me. I wasn't given a say. The War Office keeps their invasion plans close to their chests, as they should, but what I do know is that the build-up of Abwehr around Boulogne-sur-Mer is a good sign their plans are working, and the decoys fit nicely into this arrangement. They were an unforeseen surprise. An added distraction for the Germans."

Guy got up to walk to the window, gazing at the people walking the pavement below.

"This is war," Smith said. "And there's nothing we can do about it." He went back to his desk and shuffled his papers, as if it was just another day and he hadn't delivered the blow of all blows to Guy Burton, but then he added one more. "Keep this under your hat, Guy. I've been approached that there could be a leak."

"In MI6?"

"Somewhere in the War Office. You can never be too careful. Understand?"

"I understand."

With nothing left to say, Guy left, apologizing to Daisy for running past her, then down to his office in the basement. He was glad to see Clive wasn't there because he wanted to be alone. He sat at his desk with his head in his hands, having a moan to himself about what he'd just learned, when out of the corner of his eye he noticed his cabinet padlock had been disengaged.

His heart beat a little faster.

It was very slight—in fact, you'd have to be at the right angle to see it wasn't locked—and he thought he must not have pushed the prong in hard enough. To be safe, he reached into the cabinet, making sure the sheet music was still there—both pages—and to his relief it was.

After a moment with Gaby's sheet music in the uneasy silence of his office, Guy came to believe that he was just a little paranoid after the conversation with Smith. Wasn't he?

He went to file the music away again but caught himself looking at the photo of Gaby instead.

He sat down, swiveling around in his chair to face the wall, and studied her expression, which was neither sad nor happy, but somewhere in between. He wondered what she had been thinking of when the photo was taken. Her hair looked brown, and he thought maybe her dress was blue. But it was her eyes he was drawn to most, as if she was looking at him specifically, and even though they'd never met, he felt a little part of him knew her—maybe through her music, or maybe through her acts of bravery—and he felt guilty and helpless for not knowing what to do.

He'd felt helpless before.

Guy had woken up to the sound of German bombers swarming overhead. Jennie threw back the curtains. Guy had heard his fair share of rumbling engines when he was in the RAF, but the terrifying sound of German aircraft in the night was unlike anything else.

The whistling, the whirring, and the screams shook his bones and his body in places he didn't think he could shake. Guy felt it coming up from the floor through his feet, and coming down from the ceiling through his head, prickling all his senses, with only one place to escape.

"The shelter!" he yelled, though he could barely hear his own voice over the wailing sirens and the exploding bombs.

He took Jennie's hand and they ran out of their flat, down the backstairs like they'd practiced so many times before, and toward the basement with the rest of the building's tenants; but her hand slipped from his somewhere between the ground floor and the shelter, amidst the chaos of people screaming, pushing and hurrying, carrying him inside without her.

He immediately tried to go back out and look for her even after all the tenants had packed themselves inside. "But my wife!" he said, and someone said she was in the back, and in that half-minute when he called for her in the shelter instead of trying to find her on the stairs, a bomb struck the next street along, sending a shudder under their feet and shaking the walls. Guy remembered the sound of the brick, mostly, when the building caved in on top of them, then the smell of ash and fire, before waking up in the hospital to his sister sitting by his bedside.

"Madge?" His head pounded. "Where's Jennie?"

Madge had been crying, he could tell by the pink splotches on her cheeks and her puffy eyes. He tried sitting up.

"Madge?" he asked again, and she wiped her eyes with a soggy tissue, telling him the bad news.

"I'm sorry, brother. She passed so bravely too."

He didn't register what Madge had said. "Where is she?" Guy yanked off the sheets to go in search of his wife, but when his cold feet met the even colder floor, his legs gave out underneath him. "Jennie!" he called, as if she was lying in another bed, which made Madge near inconsolable.

"I'm sorry, Guy," she said, embracing him as he lay on the floor. "She's gone."

Guy clutched at his heart where he felt a pulsating pain, and looked up, expecting to see the heavens, but all he saw was the ceiling, and all he smelled was the festering wounds of those who'd survived and the antiseptic the nurses used to help keep them alive.

Guy rubbed his face with that memory, then reached up to file Gaby's photo away and leave for good that day, but something held him back. He pulled the sheet music out again, running his finger over the notes, but his eyes were drawn to his wedding band.

Before the bombing that took his wife from him, Jennie and Guy talked about what-ifs and what they would do if one of them didn't make it to the end of the war. He only indulged Jennie because she'd heard about the widows from the Marble Arch station bombing and was worried about him; she hoped he wouldn't let life pass him by if she was gone. "Live your life," she'd said. "Promise me, promise me."

He couldn't say what it was exactly that gave him pause, or why he chose that moment to take his band off when he'd had three years of opportunity to do it, but he did. Slipped it clean off, right there in his basement office. He felt the bareness of his finger against Gaby's sheet music, and realized it was long overdue.

He jumped into his car, but instead of leaving for home, he headed for the Royal College of Music. Professor Caron didn't look surprised to see him for the third time; in fact, she looked as if, once again, she had expected it.

"Hallo, Mr. Burton." She smiled, holding out her hand. "Let me guess, she sent you another sheet of The Heroines?"

Guy pulled Gaby's music from his book, and she began to play.

Chapter Fifteen

We sat at our kitchen table the next morning drinking lukewarm tarragon tea with sprigs that had been soaked the previous day. None of us said a word to each other after letting that pigeon go, even though we decided it was safe to talk freely in the kitchen without the captain hearing.

Simone stirred her tea, looking up at me and Martine every so often as if she had something to say. She reached for the loaf of bread the baker had brought and smeared a glob of lard roughly over her slice. "I'm scared," she finally said, dropping her knife on her plate. "I have someone else to think about now." Her hands went to her stomach, and I instantly felt guilty. It wasn't just the three of us anymore, and I wasn't sure why I hadn't seen it before—it was why she'd been hesitant about the pigeons in the first place. "And what if the captain is spying on us? Taking notes to report to the Abwehr later?"

"Don't be scared. Nobody saw us. And we haven't said anything illegal or suspicious within earshot of the captain. Right now, I'm more worried about you, the baby, and how we're going to keep it from the neighbors. We'll need to figure out a story."

Simone took a shaky breath. "Eventually they'll find out."

"But every day they don't, it's better for us," I said.

"You mean every day they don't call me a whore?"

"Anyone calls you a whore, you tell me," Martine said. "They'll wish they never heard of Boulogne-sur-Mer or the Cotillard sisters." She clenched a fist as if she was going to punch someone on the street.

"Please, don't fight anyone," Simone said.

"Martine, don't," I said, shaking my head, and she hid her fist under the table.

Simone got up from her chair, patting Martine on the back, then walked to the sink to wash out her cup.

Antoinette had come out to her garden to gather her eggs, calling her chickens to her like kittens. "Why don't you give them cake, *Marie Antoinette*," Martine mumbled, peeking out the window.

I covered my ears briefly at the sound of Antoinette's voice so early in the morning, especially after experiencing her visit last night. "What is it about her voice?" I asked.

"It's because she's a miserable person," Martine said. "She's gathering her eggs to sell for triple the cost and it's outlawed, but you tell me why the Reich lets her do it."

I joined her at the window. "She has a German lover, that's why."

"She's the whore, Simone," Martine said over her shoulder. "Not you."

Simone reached for her coat on the hook, yawning and looking quite tired. "Let's get to the shop." She wrapped a scarf around her neck to protect herself against the wind and waited for Martine by the door.

Martine slurped the last drop of her tea. "I'll listen to the radio before we open, see if there's any news, though there probably won't be anything until tonight during their program. It feels good to have another bird, doesn't it?"

"Maybe I'll hear something at the commandant's today." My heart sped up at the thought of listening with a purpose.

"We can let him go when Antoinette's busy with her lover, as a cover. She sounds like a dying animal in bed, doesn't she?"

Tea spurted from my lips, and Martine cupped her hand over her mouth, giggling at herself.

"I'm leaving!" Simone called from the door.

"You better go." I pushed Martine toward the door, but she came back for a hug. Then both my sisters were gone, leaving me with the remaining cups to wash, and Antoinette still calling to her hens out the window.

"Damn you, Antoinette," I said to myself.

The captain had turned on his tap, which always, and for some reason, rumbled the pipes under our cabinet. I put the cups on one side to dry, following his footsteps upstairs until they disappeared into what used to be my aunt's bedroom. Moments later he walked back downstairs, every step creaking.

This was our life now. Both of us listening to each other go about our lives.

I pulled the hatbox of photos from the bureau and shuffled through them, finding one of Martine when she was about ten, and one of Simone wearing her favorite dress. Two photos for finding two pigeons.

I went to the wall to add them to the collage, straightening the photos just so with pins, when I thought I heard the door to his private entrance open and close. I listened for something more, thinking he'd left, and was overjoyed at the possibility of being alone—truly alone without his German ears or fingers meddling with my morning.

I raced to the window to flip up the curtain and saw a coated figure walking away from the house and down the road, then raced with equal passion over to the bureau for something to play, but I didn't have time to be choosy and picked the first one I saw.

I lifted the lid after placing the music on the stand. Chopin. Aunt Blanche's favorite.

As I played, the melody filled every crevice of the house with such warmth and so many memories it was hard to keep count, then I stopped trying and just let myself relax into the music. I thought of flowers blooming in the spring and blue sky—sky without the stain of bomb haze—and beach days with children running and laughing and trying to sail paper boats against the surf.

I don't know how long I played, long enough to flip over a few sheets, when piano music erupted between the shared wall.

I stood up, robbed of all my breath, feeling for my chest.

He had left. I could have sworn he'd left!

Confusion grew into anger, warmly creeping up my neck and face. Playing a duet without asking felt like an unwanted kiss, a touch on bare skin. *How dare he.*

I walked briskly toward the wall, about to shout for him to stop, only to change my mind and head out my back door to his private entrance to confront him. I rapped forcefully on the doorframe, scaring the birds in the trees.

"Hallo!" *Bang! Bang! Bang!* "I do not give you permission to play with me!" I said, and he stopped. Dear God, he stopped. A spring blossom fell from a tree limb where a bird had flown back to perch again. I let out a huff, turning on my heel to leave, when his door cracked open.

"Fraulein?"

I couldn't move, with my heart pounding and holding my breath, and I wondered if he'd paralyzed me. I didn't expect him to answer the door.

"Gabriella, is it?" he asked, and with that, I was able to turn around and face him.

I lifted my head high, listening to that bird sing directly over my head, getting my first look at our German *guest*. He had a soft appearance and round nose, not German-like at all, and had gray hair that needed a cut. I still didn't know if I was breathing.

"Yes?" I was about to tell him he could die. That if he dropped dead in my aunt's apartment there was nothing I'd like more, but I struggled to find the courage to speak such words to a German captain, a retired one nonetheless, but one that still had some power in the Reich if the Abwehr was willing to fall all over themselves to accommodate him.

"I'm sorry about your aunt."

"What?" I didn't think I heard him right, and just before I cupped my ear to understand him better, he opened the door a little wider.

"Please," he said. "Come inside." He motioned for me to enter but I hesitated on the back step, unsure, folding my arms as he held the door open, all his heat escaping to the wind. I checked for neighbors, but their view was blocked by the trees, and Antoinette would only be able to see me if she stood on top of her chicken coop.

"Very well." I pursed my lips and walked inside, partly because I wanted him to know I wasn't scared of him, but also because I wanted to see what he'd done to my aunt's apartment *and* what he'd ruined. About halfway down the long hallway, I regretted my decision and thought he'd tricked me somehow even though I'd walked in on my own accord.

How was I going to explain this to my sisters? Martine especially.

I kept my head up, hands clasped in front of me, breathing in the rich scents of cinnamon and clove. Aunt Blanche detested cinnamon, which was just another reminder of how different the space was without her.

"I don't give you permission to play with me." A blazing hot electric heater plugged into the wall lit up my legs.

"You don't?" He looked genuinely hurt, tilting his head slightly.

I should have left on the spot—I should have turned on my heel and walked wildly back down the hall, clicking my shoes against my aunt's wood floor—which she hated, but I was sure she'd give me permission to do so in this case—and slammed the back door.

"Why not?" he asked.

I scoffed. "Why not?"

"Yes, that's right. Why not?" He walked to my aunt's old kitchen table, which I hardly recognized with the embroidered linen of sailing boats and ships, and poured me a cup of tea from the teapot we'd given my aunt for Christmas.

"Well, for starters," I said, "you're German."

"And you are French."

My mouth hung open, and he pushed the cup of tea at me. I searched for a place to set the cup down without having to walk across the room.

"What of my reputation?" He moved to the beige divan pushed against our shared wall, sitting down with his own cup and taking a sip. When I continued to stand, he moved a pillow so I could sit next to him, but still not be close enough to touch. "Please, sit. Tell me… What about *my* reputation caught playing with you? Do you think I'm not risking something, too?"

I sat down stiffly, barely resting my bottom on the cushion as the electric heater blazed against my knees. I imagined that my aunt was standing nearby, telling him to get his soiled fingers off her pillows. I took a sip of the tea, and God it was good—dark and flavorful black tea, which was nearly impossible to find, much less buy—a far cry from the diluted tarragon tea I'd had that morning. It was even better than the herbal tea at Lauren's and that was quite good.

After I'd swallowed, I realized I had gone too far by accepting his drink. I set the cup down on the end table and stood. "Are you saying the risks are the same?" I moved to leave. "Good day, monsieur."

"It wasn't my choice to be here," he said, which stopped me. "I was called out of retirement to perform at the theater after someone heard I was a pianist."

"You're playing at the theater?" There was only one theater that would accommodate a pianist with his skill, and that was the Monsigny.

"Yes. So, I'm here. In France, far away from my ancestral home where I lived with my wife of forty-five years. I heard you playing Rachmaninoff the first time and Chopin just now, and I couldn't resist. Both were my wife's favorites, after me, of course. Every morning she'd ask me to play something I'd composed. And I did. She said that when she heard me play, she felt something stirring inside of her." He tapped his heart. "She said she felt it in here, and that gave me comfort and I vowed never to stop playing, even after she was gone."

"Where is she?"

His eyes drifted to the floor. "She died while I was at sea." He'd walked to the kitchen table to set his cup down. "She was… alone." Instead of hanging his head, he looked toward the ceiling as if it was the sky. "I wish I was with her now. I'd do anything to make it so."

I wasn't sure what to say, listening to him struggle to even say the word "alone" and then look upward as if she was waiting for him.

"Now, do you see? I wasn't trying to cause you stress." He rubbed his hands, paying special attention to his knuckles where they were beginning to show signs of arthritis. "I'm sorry it upset you."

"You're sorry?" I didn't think a German could be sorry about anything.

"Clearly, playing gives you joy, and I don't want to spoil it for you. I'll stop so you can play without the worry of me joining in." He walked over to his big black piano, shiny from having been recently dusted, and pulled the lid over the keys.

I was stunned. There was no other word to explain it, and I left as fast as I could before I said something nice—something I'd regret—and ducked into my side of the house.

I stood in the quiet coldness of my home. Not a step, creak, or thud came from his side of the house, and I wondered if he was sitting on the divan. Or, was he still at his piano bench with the lid closed and thinking I'd ripped his heart out by accepting his offer to not play?

I wondered if we'd been wrong about him, then chastised myself for entertaining such thoughts. He was a German, and he must have been trying to trick me, play on my kindness after his sad story, because what German would be so considerate to a French woman?

But who would make up a story like that, and in such raw detail? No, she must have died like he said, passed away alone and without music, while her husband waited for his own death just to be with her, which seemed utterly sad and hopeless.

I clutched at my heart.

His story made me think of my own. I didn't want to end up like the captain. I found myself walking upstairs as fast as I could and into my bedroom, thinking about how many months I'd had Beau's jacket and his note when I needed to let them go, but had been too scared to.

I threw back the bed covers, staring at Beau's jacket.

When you're ready, Aunt Blanche had said, *and not a moment sooner*.

Instead of slipping on his jacket like I'd done so many times, I reached into the pocket before I could talk myself out of it, and pulled out the crumpled note Beau had left me. I stared at it in my palm near the window where the sun was warm. The strength of what I'd done in the last few days was what propelled me to unravel it, but it was sheer courage that brought me to read it.

I held my breath.

Be your own heroine.

I slumped forward, but not because I was sad. It was because for the first time in so long, I felt free. In a way, Beau had given me permission to stop punishing myself for what happened to him, and for what happened to us.

I hung the jacket in the closet with the others we used for sewing scraps, and briefly closed my eyes in goodbye.

Chapter Sixteen

I walked up to the commandant's house at exactly nine in the morning as instructed. I was standing there, checking my watch and waiting for the housekeeper to answer the door, when I heard the swift patter of feet running up behind it.

"Good morning!" It was Lauren, and she'd swung the door wide open.

"Where's the housekeeper?"

She shrugged, then frantically waved me inside.

The air was warm and thick with the smell of sugary biscuits cooking in the kitchen. "How are you this morning?" After I took off my gloves, I tucked a lock of hair behind her ear that had come loose from her braid.

"Better," she said. "Now that you're here." She flung her arms around my waist, squeezing tightly, and I gave her a pat after I regained my balance.

"Easy," I said, almost laughing. I glanced at the commandant's study and he appeared to be out; no light was showing under his closed door. I'd have to wait to listen, and

ANDIE NEWTON

then also pray he'd have something worthy to dispatch with a pigeon—maybe more about that spy Lauren overheard something about.

She tugged on my hand to follow her upstairs and into her music room, but once the door was closed her face changed. "I'm sorry about our visit. I only wanted to—"

"I know," I said, reassuring her.

I didn't want to tell her how showing up in the commandant's private vehicle was the last thing my sisters and I needed. Lauren was a child. She didn't know. I blamed Irma because it was her idea, and then the commandant for allowing it.

"Where's your mistress?"

Lauren went to her doll shelves. "I don't care…" She stood on her tiptoes to pull a Bavarian doll down by her leg. "Her name's Gretel." She shoved the doll at me to take a look. Its once polished face was dull and chipped from being thrashed against the piano keys.

"She's lovely," I said, trying to give it back, but Lauren refused.

"No," she said, pointing to the skirt. "Look under there." She put her finger to her lips. "And shh, don't tell anyone."

I lifted the dress, and tucked under the doll's tiny white undergarment was a gold coin. "Where did this come from?" I rasped. The only time I'd seen a gold coin was in the commandant's hand. Despite all his gifts, I was certain he'd never give her a coin like that, so she must have taken it.

"Why?" She looked frightened by my voice.

I didn't want to accuse her outright of stealing from the commandant, but I knew exactly what she'd done and I was scared for her. "Because it's a gold coin and you're a child."

She took the doll away from me, flipping down the skirt and smoothing it flat. "I thought you'd like to see it. I've stolen the cook's biscuits too." She pulled a crumbly biscuit bite from her pocket.

"That isn't the same."

"I shouldn't have shown you." Lauren whipped around, her braids flinging over her shoulders. "Don't say anything."

"Lauren, I—"

"I'll tell my mistress I don't want you here anymore." She gave her doll a few pats on her head before racing to the shelves to put her back. "If you say something."

I walked toward her as gingerly as I could. "I would never say anything," I said, and she spun around, throwing her arms around my waist again, but this time she cried into my skirt.

"It's so we can escape," she said between weeping hiccups. "I can get more. Will you come?"

"Where?"

"Anywhere but here," she said.

I kneeled down, taking one of her little hands and holding it close. "And what about your mother? Don't you want her to come too?" I said, but Lauren cried and cried and cried. "Shh…" I said because she was getting quite loud. "Shh—"

The door opened again and I turned, expecting to see Irma, but it was the housekeeper. "Gabriella Cotillard," she announced.

She'd never said my full name before. "Yes?"

"No lesson today," she said. Lauren wiped her eyes, and I think we were both equally shocked. "Get your coat."

I reached for my coat as directed. "Did something happen I'm not aware of?"

She pointed out the door. "Leave."

Lauren's face fell even more than it had. "I'll see you tomorrow," I said, but now I wondered if there would be a tomorrow with this strange turn of events. I noticed Irma down the hall, talking to someone I couldn't see inside Danielle's bedroom.

The housekeeper pointed again for me to leave.

"I'm going." I left down the backstairs, out the servant's entrance, only to find the commandant waiting for me near the kitchen like before, though this time he was wearing his Abwehr uniform.

My heart pounded.

The cook iced biscuits nearby on a tray, watching us with a stern side-eye. "Irma informs me you made our little girl cry." He casually pulled a cigarette from his pocket, flicking his lighter open.

"I made her cry?" He exhaled a mouthful of smoke after lighting up his cigarette. "There must be some kind of misunderstanding. Lauren was crying over her doll," I said to cover up the cry she had over escaping.

"I'm talking about last night," he said. "You threw her and her mistress out of your home, did you not? The stress it caused her mistress, but more importantly the stress it caused my wife when word got back that you'd refused Lauren, embarrassed her..." He shook his head, clicking his tongue. "As a result, my wife was useless to me last night because she had to tend to Lauren and her distraught mistress."

"But Lauren's all right," I said. "She was disappointed just now when I had to leave. Please, let me stay and teach."

"Now you want to teach? After begging me to let you off the hook more than once?" he asked, and I felt my body tense, knowing how suspicious it seemed. "You should just be glad it's for one day, and you have my wife to thank for that. As horrendous as your actions were, she pushed for a warning. I wanted to dismiss you, and you know what that would mean. How does it feel to be thrown out of someone's home?"

He turned on his heel to leave, tossing his lit cigarette in the sink just before he walked away.

I burst out the back door without further delay and collected myself, taking a few deep breaths and feeling for my chest where my heart was thrashing. Then I felt eyes on my back.

I carefully looked up, and was surprised to find it was Danielle, watching me from her bedroom with her red and shadowy curtains drawn to the side, and one hand pressed to the windowpane.

I went home, instead of to the shop, to have a rest after what happened, but the relentless birdsong coming from the back step made me dizzy. I grasped the side table, waiting for the bird to stop and fly off, but it grated on my nerves as much as my thoughts and showed no signs of ending.

Chirp, chirp, chirp, chirp...

I let out a huff, stomping all the way down the hall and throwing open the back door, ready to eat that bird if I had to, but the tree was bare, only the dew glistening in the morning sun.

My head throbbed, and my cheeks felt clammy. I needed to relax. It was a warning from the commandant, that was all. Tomorrow, everything with Lauren and the commandant would be smoothed over. The Lerouxs were still safe, after all.

Nothing had happened to them. I took a breath of the outside air through my nose.

The captain's back door popped open from a light breeze, and I caught a glimpse of him sitting alone at his piano, hunched over. His silhouette was dark gray, still. I swallowed dryly, watching him struggle with not being able to play in the morning, lifting his hands and then dropping them gently into his lap.

I hung my head, reminding myself that I'd already dispatched the news of the performance at the Monsigny where he played, and he'd be dead soon, once our pigeon reached Britain. I let out a shrill little cry because I knew what I had to do—what was right, what all musicians would do. I heard Martine's voice in my head telling me to ignore him, that he'd tricked me, but in fact, I believed the story about his wife. It was too wrought with detail and emotion to not believe it.

And I understood, most of all, how important it was to possess that rare skill of stirring something unseen in another's heart.

I put my hand up, poised to knock.

"Aunt Blanche, don't be angry at me for what I'm about to do," I said, glancing at the sky.

I rapped three times on the doorframe, and the captain turned around, trying to glimpse who I was. I cleared my throat.

"It's Gaby, from next door. Can I come in?"

"This is a surprise." He waved me in, and I walked down the hallway to stand near the wall, letting the heater's element radiate against the back of my knees, searching for the right words—something that wouldn't sound suspicious.

I twisted my hands, and he adjusted his glasses.

"It's me that will stop playing."

He blinked and blinked and I thought he was at a loss for words.

I took a step to leave.

"Why?" he asked, once my back was to him, and I shut my eyes at having to explain when I didn't want to—that it was a last wish before he died, confirmation that I had a heart and that I wasn't as callous as I thought?

"I'm sure you know I work for the commandant. I can play there in the mornings, with my pupil, Lauren." I turned around, expecting to find him still standing behind me, but he'd sat down on the divan between two pillows, his gaze locked on the ground in disbelief, looking a little tired.

"I know you are giving lessons," he said. "But even so, are you sure? Playing on your own piano isn't the same as giving lessons."

"Playing in the morning in memory of your wife is important. I don't want to be the one responsible for taking that away."

There. I had said it, and he knew I believed his story. He had to understand now, and I didn't have to go into specifics about how his story had stirred something inside of me, too. He was lucky enough to have had the love of his life request him to play, sit side-by-side on the piano bench, and he should be able to hold on to it, even after she'd passed on.

It was a small gesture from one musician to another, since I knew of his fate, but I also knew Martine would have my hide over this. She'd wonder if I'd gone mad. Simone too.

"That is all," I said, and I tried to leave again after staring at him, but he stood up from the divan and asked me to finish that cup of tea he'd given me earlier, only he'd pour me a fresh cup. My tongue felt dry and fat and thick, listening to that black tea glug from the teapot and into a teacup meant for me.

"Here you go," he said, smiling politely, and the next thing I knew I was sitting at my aunt's old kitchen table having a proper cup of tea with our German guest, drinking from my aunt's favorite set, no less, with its whimsical pink and yellow flowers—the teacups she only used on Sundays.

The house was quiet, all but for my stomach noises from having missed the biscuits at Lauren's. The electric heater cranked up with a buzz. "These are my aunt's teacups," I said. "Her teapot..." I studied the room, from the kitchen cabinets to the salon. "This is where she lived, and it was given to me when she died. And she never would have had a heater on in May."

"Did you play for your aunt? I never get to talk about music anymore. Not with anyone." He took a deep breath and looked more relaxed than a dog on a warm day, which made my brow furrow. "Who are your favorite pianists?"

I wasn't prepared for chit-chat that felt personal and intrusive. Talking about my aunt's apartment was different than talking about who I was. "I shouldn't stay. I shouldn't even be talking to you. In fact, I was ordered not to bother you at all, and look what I've done." I started to get up and he put his hand out to stop me.

"I know you think of me as part of the Reich, but do you know my full name?"

"Should I?" The question caught me off guard, and I sat back down, trying to place his face as if I'd seen him at the Conservatory.

"Before I was Captain Walter Weber, I was just Walter, a pianist from Germany who studied in America before I gave up playing professionally and joined the naval academy in Kiel. Known then as the Imperial Navy."

"You studied in America?" I added up how many years ago that would have been and who he must have studied with.

"I played in New York once. Carnegie Hall," he said.

I was stunned, and I'm sure it showed on my face because he had smiled.

"I have a thought." He pointed in the air. "If a German can discuss methods in music with Sergei in the lounge of an American hotel, perhaps a French woman and a retired German naval captain could set aside the war for a moment and just be pianists? At least in the privacy of this house when nobody can see or hear."

Sergei. I'd picked up my teacup only to set it back down, then laughed thinking it was impossible. "Sergei Rachmaninoff?" I said as a joke, and I knew it sounded as if I was mocking him, and maybe I was, but he nodded and chuckled without trying to hide it in the least, which had me sitting up straight in my chair.

"More tea?" He topped off my cup, then added a sugar cube, which dissolved into a creamy fizz. He began to prepare another pot of hot water. "Thank you for coming here. I will accept your offer and play in the mornings," he said. "Will you accept my offer to talk about music? At least until you finish your tea, perhaps?"

I took another sip of my tea, now thinking, what could it hurt? "Yes."

"Will you be at the Monsigny performance at the end of the month?" he asked. "It will be quite the show. All the Abwehr will be there, and some special guests."

"Monsigny?" I wasn't even supposed to know about the

performance and was surprised he'd mentioned it as if I should. "No."

"Aren't you? I thought the commandant would have invited you." He turned away from the stove with a kettle full of hot water, but his watch distracted him. "Oh no," he said, just as a car drove up outside. "I'm afraid my car is here to take me to rehearsal. Please. Make yourself at home. Finish your tea. I trust you know the way out." He hurriedly set the kettle down to reach for his coat.

I stood up. "I shouldn't stay here alone."

"No, no…" he said. "I have nothing to hide. Make yourself at home." He vanished out the back door, leaving me alone in what used to be my aunt's kitchen, and on the wrong side of our shared wall.

My eyes roved over the apartment, getting a much better look at the place without him there. My aunt's clock still hung above the kitchen table, the one Martine had broken when she was twelve, and the tall bookcase that had once been filled with children's books from when she ran the boarding school sat strangely empty and in the wrong place. He'd moved it from the back of the house to the front near the door, and that made no sense since there was nothing in it. Not even a vase or a book of his own. No photographs of his wife, from what I could see from my seat. Yet I remembered how many boxes had been brought in, the morning he moved in.

The thought of sneaking up to his bedroom entered my mind, to see what he had in there, maybe even have a peek in his wardrobe, as if I was that bold. My aunt would tell me to get out, she'd warn me that it wasn't her apartment anymore or mine. He could be testing me, I thought, when suddenly the captain came back inside, throwing open the door and racing down the hallway straight toward me. I held my chest.

He apologized while reaching for his hat. "Sorry for the fright."

I took a gulp of tea.

"And about the Monsigny," he said, fitting his hat on his head. "I'm sure it's an oversight. I'll make sure you get an invite."

"Why would I be invited?" I asked, then wondered how much I should say—how much I should admit knowing about it. I set my cup down.

"Don't you want to be there to hear your pupil play?" Now it was me giving him a strange look. "The commandant has arranged for his daughter to introduce me—Lauren. She's who you are teaching, no?"

I felt myself go pale. "What?"

"I heard she has quite improved." The car engine revved outside, and he apologized for rushing off again, but I was breathless and near choking on the tea bubbling up my throat.

"Lauren!" I leapt to my feet after a few heaving breaths, thinking about her dying in a fiery blaze and how it was all my fault. I had to get a message to Britain, and I had to get it there now!

I tore out of his apartment and into my own, ripping off a strip from my sheet music to make it fit, but then froze with my pencil to the paper, my heart thrashing with urgency in my chest. *What do I say?*

Saying the venue had been changed or that it was canceled could be verified through channels, and maybe they'd bomb it anyway. I decided to tell them exactly what I knew, and prayed it was enough.

*Monsigny Theatre information is incorrect. It's a civil performance
with children and families 29 May. Repeat. Theatre information is
incorrect. It's a civil performance with children! Please reply. The
Heroines.*

I raced downstairs for the pigeon, but he slipped from my
hands when I pulled him from the coal chute and flapped
wildly around on the ground in the cellar. "Get back here!" I
commanded, huffing and puffing, until I finally managed to
shoo him upstairs and into the salon, where I threw my shawl
over him. "Got you!" I grabbed his stomach where he was
squishy and stuck my message in the capsule.

I threw aside the window curtains, spying Antoinette in the
road talking to the neighbors. "Damn her!" She'd see me if I let
the bird go from Simone's window.

The back garden!

I ran out the back, offering the bird to the sky as a gift.
"Go!" I said, giving him a toss, but instead of flying off like his
friend had last night, he flew awkwardly into the tree to perch,
cooing and tilting his head.

"I said, go!" I flung my arms angrily in the air, and he
finally took off, flapping over Antoinette's rooftop.

I dashed down my hallway to the salon to see more and
threw open my front door, only to yelp at the sight of
Antoinette standing in my way, about to knock.

Chapter Seventeen

A black speck soared above the trees toward the sea behind Antoinette's bobbing head. I held my chest, watching that pigeon fly away and feeling my heart thump. Martine would be angry I'd let the bird go without her, and Simone would be angry I let it go in the daylight. But I had no choice, and nobody could have seen me from the back garden. I thanked God our guest had left, but more so that he'd told me about Lauren.

Antoinette cleared her throat, and my eyes moved to hers. I dropped my hand.

"What are you doing here?" I asked.

Her face fell. "Well, good morning to you too, Gaby." She pointed to the neighbor she'd been talking to across the road. "I was talking with—" She cleared her throat again. "There's been some burglaries in the area. Wanted to let you know."

I'd had it with Antoinette coming to our home, spreading gossip and collecting information from us that she could use later. I reached for my coat, and, without a word back, I closed the front door, pushing her off the step and leaving her with her mouth hanging open.

I was quite certain Antoinette's burglar story was a ruse to talk about the captain or the commandant, but when I arrived at the shop, I found our front door had been smashed—the jamb split and broken as if a crowbar had been thrust into it several times.

Martine pulled me inside after I examined the damage, and I was surprised to find Simone talking to Madame Roche near the counter. "Can you believe it?" Martine asked. "Someone tried to break in last night. Bastards."

"Tried?" I questioned, looking for evidence that our radio was stolen without alerting Madame Roche.

"Doesn't look like they made it inside," she said. "Though we need a new lock."

"But why?" I asked. "We've made no secret our scraps come from old clothes, and thread too, aside from a few spools."

"People think you're a black ribbon shop, Gaby," Madame Roche said. "Which means you must have money. Now, don't worry. Your secret is safe with me. In return, I told your sisters one of my secrets as a sign of trust." She grabbed my hand and put a heavy new lock in it, giving me a wink. "If anyone asks, I made you pay triple the cost."

She walked away under a clattering of bells, blustering across the street as if she was angry and giving the neighboring business owners a sight to see. I turned and faced Martine since I knew Simone wouldn't have been the one to tell Madame our secret.

"You told her?"

"I had to," Martine said. "There's no other lock shop that would sell to traitors like us. No matter how many years they've known us."

"What secret did she tell you in return?" I asked, thinking maybe she was part of the resistance, which wasn't a stretch since she hated the Germans, but what if she was The She Wolf? Madame was angry enough to be her.

"She paints in private," Simone said. "That's her big secret."

I sat down holding my head. It wasn't the secret I thought she'd say, but I didn't have time to dwell on it. So much had happened and it wasn't even midday yet. I still had to tell my sisters about the pigeon.

"What's wrong?" Martine stepped forward, realizing there was more to my mood than our broken lock. "Is it the commandant?"

I sat up. There was no easy way to tell them. "I let the other pigeon go," I blurted.

"In the daylight?" Simone asked.

"Without me?" Martine raised her voice and I winced. "Gaby, how could you do that? After all the talk about plans and doing this together and—"

"Lauren's performing at the Monsigny," I said. "She's a child, and she's innocent. Can you see the urgency? I sent a message to counteract the first, said it was a civilian performance for families and children, so there'd be no incentive to bomb it. I let him go in the back garden where nobody could see."

"But what if someone did?" Simone asked. "How could you be so reckless?"

"Nobody saw," I said. "I'm sure of it. I was alone." I pulled at my hands after checking my watch. We still had several hours before we could listen to the broadcast. "Do you think we'll hear something tonight, find out if our first bird made it safely? It's been roughly nine hours since we let him go."

Martine looked exhausted and beaten from my news and sat heavily down near the window. "It took days to hear last time."

Simone finally took her hand away from her mouth, but then reached for her coat. "I don't like this," she said. "I don't like Madame Roche knowing our secret, and I don't like knowing you let the pigeon fly away in the daylight."

"Where are you going?" I asked.

"It's too late for Jacques to deliver now and if I don't get our ration, we'll have no fresh bread for today." She paused. "Will you come with me, Gaby? I'd feel safer if you came." She looked out the window. "I'm a stranger now. An unwanted stranger in my home village."

Staying at the shop and watching the hours tick toward five o'clock would only make me anxious. "Yes, of course, I'll go." I turned to Martine, who had stood up because normally she would have been the one to walk with Simone. "Don't close up while we are gone, not even to leave for lunch. I don't want the shop unattended. We won't be long."

She nodded, reaching for my hands when she noticed them shaking. "It'll be fine, Gaby," she said. "Maybe the first bird got shot down? Don't worry." She smiled, but I could tell she was as uncertain as I was. "And I'm sorry about before—raising my voice at you. You did what you felt you had to." She kissed both my cheeks.

"Strange to wish our bird got shot down," I said, "but that's exactly what I'm wishing for. And why haven't they sent more pigeons?"

"I don't know," Martine said.

I left with Simone, walking into the street and into the flow of foot traffic. I hooked her arm at the same time as she lifted her other, crossing it over her stomach to hide her roundness. "Is there a reason you didn't want Martine to go with you?" We weaved in and out of people, when one knocked my shoulder, sending me back a step.

"Collaborator," he hissed, and I closed my eyes.

"Because of people like that man right there," she said. "I'm too afraid of what Martine would do. Walking to the shop in the morning is stressful enough with her."

We stopped at the curb, waiting for a convoy of German military trucks to pass, packed like sardines with Wehrmacht.

"There's so many…" I was surprised by how young they were, as if they'd never seen a war, with clean uniforms and helmets.

"And in the village too," Simone said. "Are they preparing for a battle?"

"It must be because of the bombing," I said, though I'd started to wonder when I saw more military vehicles, ones with heavy equipment and long guns, and they weren't driving toward the harbor, but north to the cliffs. The thought crossed my mind they were preparing for the invasion we'd been waiting for—for the Allies to save us—but in Boulogne-sur-Mer? There'd be nothing left of us if it was here.

By the time we'd made it to the bakery, the long morning

lines of hungry customers had shrunk into something more manageable. Simone tapped my arm when she spotted Jacques in the distance, behind his near-empty counter. "There he is." She waved. "He must not have been able to get away for deliveries today."

We walked inside and in that split second when every eye turned to us, I regretted going to the bakery at all. The din of chatty customers hushed to a lull, then utterly and painfully dissipated into a cold quietness. Jacques stood behind the counter, staring at us. The faint scent from that morning's bread had been swept out the door—bread that had been bought, bread that was gone.

We took a step forward. Simone's coat had separated over her belly, and I reached over and tried my best to fasten the button. It was as if she had grown two sizes overnight.

"You should be ashamed of yourself," an old friend of my aunt's whispered to us, while another tightened her grip on her handbag as if we were about to snatch it from her.

"Head up," I said to Simone, and she lifted her chin. A swoosh of cool air brushed the back of my neck from the door opening, and I felt someone standing behind me.

"You turned me in," I heard someone whisper.

I spun around to see Mme. Leroux standing stoically behind me. She pulled on her son's hand, moving him closer to her, but he nearly tripped over his own feet. Although still weak-looking with gaunt eyes, he had a little more color in his cheeks, which I was glad to see.

"Pardon me?" I said.

"There was a German standing outside our home this morning for a half hour watching us." Her voice was curt and threatening. "Someone from the Reich. Uniform. Gun. Slick black boots. I asked him if he was lost, and he said to ask you."

"You think I had something to do with that?" My mouth gaped open, as if I couldn't imagine, but deep inside I did imagine, and it had everything to do with me throwing Irma and Lauren out of our home. The commandant was sending me a warning about my behavior. "After all that I have given you?"

"Shh!" Her eyes narrowed. "Don't speak to me again." She took a deep breath, collecting herself, and even smiled at a customer in front of us in line. "Understand?"

I turned back around, my heart racing and my cheeks warm, but I wasn't about to start an argument with her in front of her son. Simone seemed oblivious to the encounter and pulled me forward. "We're next," she said, and we stepped up to the counter, waiting for Jacques to hand us a fresh loaf.

"Hallo," Simone said, smiling, but Jacques didn't look the least bit receptive to Simone's pleasantness. "You didn't come by so I—"

Jacques grabbed a misshapen loaf of stale bread from a lot of six perfectly good loaves he had left and slapped it on the counter with a snarl.

"But there's..." Simone turned pale, looking even sicker than she did the morning she vomited in the toilet. "There's a fresh one on the counter."

Mme. Leroux scoffed behind us, followed by another woman who was walking out with her loaf. "Bad French," someone whispered, followed by a renewed quiet in the bakery that sent chills bumping up my arms.

"Don't talk to me," he said to Simone. "There's the door." He pointed. "Next!"

Simone's chin quivered, and she burst out of the bakery with her hand over her mouth. I handed Jacques our ration coupon and coins for the bread, but inside I'd reached a boiling point. I was upset about Mme. Leroux and even more upset over his treatment of my sister.

I gave him a stern eye. "You're a horrible baker, do you know that?" I said, even though it might cost us later. "We only come here because we have to. Not because the bread is good."

I walked away defiantly, finding Simone crying to herself in the alley outside. "He…" Simone wiped her eyes, but the sea-swept breeze whistling through the stones was doing an adequate job of drying them for her. "He…"

"He thinks we're bad French like everyone else." I put my arms around her. "Doesn't make it right though. You're the sweetest person alive, Simone, and that shouldn't have happened."

A piece of paper clung to her foot with the breeze. "I worried this might happen from the beginning," I said as I peeled the paper away. "When you told me your plan to be friendly with a man who had eyes for you. Martine and I are used to such behaviors, but you…"

"I didn't expect the coldness. I wasn't prepared, and now we're paying the price with our bread."

"We'd pay the price anyway," I said, taking a glance at the paper, then realized it was a German flyer, seeking information about The Heroines and offering a reward.

My stomach sank.

"What is it?" Simone asked, still teary-eyed and trying to reach for my hand, but I shoved the paper in my pocket to throw away later.

It must be a response to the Radio Londres announcement,

but what was especially alarming was that the Germans suspected The Heroines were, out of all the villages in France, in Boulogne-sur-Mer.

"Gaby?"

I threw my arms around her again, my heart pounding. "After the war, everyone will know the truth." A German truck rumbled by with more Wehrmacht headed toward the sea, shaking the ground. "Come on." I looked down both ends of the alley, to see if anyone saw me pick up the flyer, but all seemed clear. I needed to show Martine, and I needed to show her now. "Let's go."

We walked back to the shop with our measly bread ration, finding Martine exactly where we'd left her, behind the counter and watching the clock. I needed to get her alone, but with Simone in the same room, I didn't know how without looking suspicious. My heart was still racing.

Simone, tired from the short journey, set the pitiful loaf of bread on the table, breaking Martine's concentration.

"What is this?" Martine peeked hesitantly into the crinkly sack—something to touch carefully, something to fear. Her lips twisted. Then she took a sniff.

"It's our ration," I said.

"That's not a ration," Martine said, tapping the entire loaf on the counter. "It's hard as a rock, too."

"You won't have to worry about Jacques coming around anymore," I said.

"Oh?" Martine smiled, looking pleased, but after taking a long look at Simone, who had her head down and was still sniffling, she moved away from the counter to give her a hug. "He was mean to you?"

"Yes." She wiped her nose with a handkerchief. "I've never

been treated like that before. Even if he has the wrong idea about me, it still hurts because we've always been friendly."

"He's a pig," Martine said. "And I never trusted him, coming here with his deliveries. Jacques the baker, he's on my list. For after the war." She nodded as if to reassure Simone that he'd pay for his behavior, but she buried her face in her hands, and I saw my chance to pull Martine off to the side.

"I have something to show you," I rasped, reaching into my pocket for the flyer, but shoved it back in when Simone burst into tears over her sewing kit.

Martine rushed over to her. "Don't cry over the baker."

Simone shook her head. "It's not just that," she said. "I have so many feelings bubbling up inside of me, feelings I don't know what to do with. I'm happy, then sad, and always exhausted." She wiped her cheeks of tears. "When I used to think of what it would be like to have a baby, I never thought I'd go about it alone, feel every flutter, roll, and kick and want to share it, but be unable to."

"But you're not alone. You have us to share it with," Martine said, but it was obvious to me Simone wanted to share these things with Christian.

My heart broke for Simone. I couldn't imagine what she was going through on the inside when on the outside she had always looked unburdened.

"What do we do?" Martine mouthed, and I threw my hands up.

Martine handed Simone a dry handkerchief since she'd soaked the first one. "What if you bought some of that cheese she likes?" Martine asked me.

"She needs more than cheese."

"But what else can we do?" Martine asked. "Please, can you buy some? I'll stay here with her."

I closed my eyes briefly. "All right. I'll go." Our sister needed us, and the flyer would have to wait.

I bought a double portion of soft and creamy Camembert from a shop at the bottom of the hill that was willing to do business with me in exchange for sewing services.

We sat around the counter spreading the cheese on thick slices of hard bread, waiting for closing time. Simone had quieted, and I was back to thinking about the flyer in my pocket, and how I still needed to tell Martine.

"Pretend it's a cracker," Martine said. "Thick crackers." She took a bite, and even with the soft cheese, it was dry and hard to chew. She motioned for me to say something about the food, and I sat up to take a bite.

"So much texture," I said, but I could barely move my lips because the bread felt like a brick in my mouth, though that did get Simone to laugh.

"See, old ugly Jacques did us a favor," Martine said. "We have crackers for lunch."

"You don't have to call him names," Simone said.

"You're too nice, Simone," Martine said, licking the cheese from her knife. "He gave you stale and misshapen bread. It's all right to not like him for what he did."

Martine had set her knife and bread down. Pretending the bread was something to joke about and calling it a cracker took a lot of effort for her, and she did it all for Simone. Inside, I was sure Martine was cursing the Germans and making plans, moving Jacques up to the top of her list with every choking swallow.

Antoinette passed by on the pavement, not even taking a

glance into our shop windows, which surprised Martine. She had a fancy pink hat on and a warm-looking coat, too warm for May in the daytime, and too expensive for the good French to buy.

"She won't be bothering us anymore," I said.

"Why not?" Martine bit into her bread, crumbs sprinkling onto her shirt like dandruff.

"Because I told her not to."

"She won't stay away," Martine said. "She's too nosey, like a dirty rat sniffing the streets. We worry about the Abwehr knowing about us, but we should be worried about her." I shot her a look, and Martine frowned. "What?" she mouthed, but I shook my head—not now—because Simone was still too close for me to share the flyer with her.

"Later," I mouthed back.

We closed at exactly five o'clock and went into the back room to listen to the BBC broadcast. I gave Simone all the blankets we had to sit on for comfort. Martine tuned in the radio signal while huddled on the cold floor.

Bom, bom, bom, bom… Bom, bom, bom, bom…

I was surprised she'd found it so quickly. I inched closer, praying hard that they mention the second message. *Please, please, please.* I squeezed both my sisters' hands.

"This is London calling. Before we begin, please listen to some messages to our friends…" But instead of the usual coded messages to their agents, there was only a singular message to The She Wolf. "Thank you. Take courage. We will not forget you."

I blinked. "That's all—"

"And thank you Heroines for the rose," the announcer

burst in almost as an afterthought, followed by "Le Chant des Partisans" over and over.

"Oh no!" My hands flew to my mouth. "This is awful!" If they'd only received the second message, then it wouldn't matter what happened with the first, but now we knew exactly what had happened. The wrong pigeon made it across the sea, alive and well.

Martine moved to her knees, fine-tuning the station, but the broadcast had finished, and it didn't matter how delicately she tried turning the dial.

"What are we going to do now?" I asked. "Wait? See if the second pigeon made it? We're running out of time." I held my stomach where it ached.

"What else can you do but wait?" Simone asked, and I looked at Martine. There was one thing we could do.

"We can send another message," I said. "Just to be sure. Go back and get the other pigeon—the one we left behind." I bit at my nails, nodding incessantly, waiting for Martine to agree, but she scratched her head as if she wasn't sure.

"Right, Martine?"

"No, Gaby," Simone said instead, and I closed my eyes. "It's too dangerous. They must know they've been robbed of two pigeons already. There's always tomorrow and several days after that. You must be patient. No sense in risking your life now when the bird may not have even landed."

"But, but…" I got up and walked to the front. The farmer wouldn't keep that pigeon forever. He could be cooking that bird on a spit right now for all we knew, and we had no other way to reach London.

If I was unsure about Martine's feelings on the matter, she

made it clear to me moments later, walking to the front of the shop and reaching for her coat. "We should wait and see, Gaby. Simone is right. It is too dangerous to return to the farm so soon, especially when we have time." She glanced back at Simone, who hadn't made her way to the front yet. "What did you want to talk to me about?" she whispered. "You have something to show me?"

I felt the flyer in my pocket. *Wait and see?* She'd never go back with me if she knew that the Abwehr were looking for The Heroines in Boulogne-sur-Mer. I couldn't tell her. "It's nothing."

Simone walked up next, reaching for her coat. "Have hope, Gaby."

I nodded because I didn't have the heart to tell her that having hope felt even more dangerous.

Chapter Eighteen

I couldn't sleep that night and found myself alone at the breakfast table the next morning fully dressed before six o'clock, sipping diluted tarragon tea and listening to Antoinette call to her chickens out the window.

Martine emerged from her bedroom an hour later, pounding down the creaking old stairs. She paused at the shared wall, putting her ear to it to hear whether the captain was up, before walking into the kitchen. "How are you?"

I shrugged after swallowing a mouthful of cold tea. All I thought about was the farm and the pigeon we left under the fallen beam. "I want to go back," I blurted, reigniting the conversation from last night. "We need that bird. No sense in waiting."

"I know you want to go back, but we discussed this already. I think we should wait a little longer because of the danger."

"But, Martine—"

"Gaby, we can't," she said, and the way she said it, her

tone, made me rethink how I should approach her. I should tread lightly, maybe bring it up later at the shop, after a morning of doing business with the Germans, so she can be reminded of her hatred for them, and not after she'd just woken up.

I changed the subject. "Where's Simone?"

"She wants to sleep in. She says she's tired, but she's getting bigger, and I think that is the real reason."

"I noticed her coat kept opening yesterday, and maybe a man wouldn't notice, but a woman would. Antoinette would. It's probably best she stays in and misses the foot traffic." I held my head with a moan. "What am I going to do, Martine?"

"What about talking to Lauren?" she asked. "Maybe she wouldn't want to play for the Germans?"

I set my cup down, giving that some thought. Maybe Lauren didn't know the commandant had committed her to the performance, since she hadn't mentioned anything to me about it, and you'd think she would have.

Martine patted my hand, then fixed herself some breakfast. "I bet Antoinette is eating fresh warm eggs this morning." She had a bowl of clumpy plain oats that stuck to her spoon. "If I really think about it, I can smell them—fluffy and warm frying up in a pan." She closed her eyes, rolling her tongue around as if tasting them too, and my stomach growled.

"Talking about what we can't have makes the hunger worse," I said.

She pulled open the window curtain and pointed to one of Antoinette's chickens. "That one, right there. I bet she'd lay me a nice egg—a four-minute egg that's perfectly gooey in the middle."

As soon as she said the word "gooey," my mouth watered.

"With salt?" I asked, now unable to help myself from playing along. "And croissants with strawberry preserves and maybe even some baked figs?"

"I can get the figs and the preserves on the black market, but it will be expensive. German expensive. And I know you don't want me to sell the spoons."

I shook my head before she was done talking. "No, Martine. We can't spend the commandant's money."

"Well, why not? The village knows you work for him after that dimwit mistress drove his car here. Does it matter now?"

"It does matter," I said. "We'll just have to talk about a proper breakfast, rather than go out for one."

She grabbed my hand on the table, giving it a squeeze. "Remember that restaurant in Paris that served the flakiest croissants?"

I pulled my hand out from under hers. "Café Boul'Mich. Yes, I remember. It was me and Beau's favorite place."

She covered her mouth. "I'm sorry, Gaby. I wasn't thinking."

"It's all right," I said. "I told you to talk about breakfast. Besides, he's gone now. And Paris is in the past. We've moved on, haven't we?" I asked the question while at the same time thinking I should start acknowledging it.

Martine looked a little shocked by my revelation, and she didn't know what to say, preferring to kiss my cheek and get up to wash her cup and bowl. But when she gathered some of the old clothes from the closet to take to the shop for scrap, she noticed I'd added Beau's jacket. "Gaby?"

"Yes?"

She looked at his jacket once more in her arms. "Ah… Never mind," she said, then threw her voice so the captain could hear. "Goodbye!" she said, then mumbled, "Boche bastard, listening to us..." as she walked out the door.

I continued to sip my tea at the table after she left, occasionally peeping over the window ledge to watch Antoinette with her chickens through the curtain slit. She had a handful of seeds and wore what appeared to be a brand-new pink peignoir. New, because I could see it had bright white lace even in the dim morning light as if it had never been washed or hung on a clothesline—something she bought with her egg money no less, when the Reich should be fining her.

She threw her seed with a giggle, brushing off her hands and spying me through the window. "Oh, Antoinette," I breathed. She turned on her heel, walking swiftly inside with her peignoir furling behind her.

The captain played his piano on the other side of the wall, just like I told him he could do. It was a melody I swore I'd heard before, romantic and dreamy. I tucked my skirt under my legs and sat on the stairs to listen, trying to place it right up until he finished.

"Gaby," I heard through the plaster, and I sat up.

"Yes?" I answered, reservedly. I didn't want Simone to hear me talking to him, even though she was in her bedroom.

"Would you join me for some tea?" he asked.

I knew I shouldn't go, but I so desperately wanted to talk to someone about music, and not the way I talk about music with Lauren.

I put my hand on the wall, about to answer, when Simone walked up behind me and stood at the top of the stairs.

"You're up!" Her eyes flicked to the wall as if she'd heard the conversation, but I couldn't be sure. She tied her cloth robe loosely around her belly. "I didn't know you were still here," I said.

Simone yawned, then looked me over as I waited for her to ask me why the captain was playing when I'd told my sisters he wouldn't, but she walked back to her room as silently as she had walked to the stairs.

I pushed my ear flush against the wallpaper.

"Gaby? Are you there?" the captain called again, and I cupped my mouth. My sisters wouldn't understand, but I could separate the pianist from his German military title. I closed my eyes tightly.

"I'll be right there," I whispered back.

Seconds later I was at my aunt's old private entrance and walking into a warm room, and being given an even warmer cup of delicious tea, more delicious than the black tea he had served me before. *Lemon.* God, I looked forward to the day when we could get lemons again.

"I didn't think you'd come since you only agreed to one conversation," he said.

"I almost didn't."

"Why did you come?" he asked.

"I enjoyed your piece." This was true. I did enjoy the piece he played. "And I enjoyed our talk about Rachmaninoff. It's been so long since I've talked about music with someone who can play."

He offered me a place to sit at the kitchen table. "Please. Sit."

He moved the electric heater closer to where I sat, then topped up my cup with more tea from my aunt's teapot. "Does the heater bother you? May on the French coast feels unseasonably cold. I can turn it off…"

"The heater feels nice." I thought I should bring up something about his music since that was why I was there, but I couldn't take my eyes off my aunt's teapot. "My sisters and I gave this to my aunt for Christmas."

He studied my reaction to it, my finger tracing the hand-painted winter roses. "Take it home," he said, sliding it closer to me. "Please. It was your aunt's."

"The entire apartment was my aunt's."

He took his hands off the teapot and placed them in his lap.

"I'm sorry," I said because I didn't mean to sound bitter, even if I was. I knew now that it wasn't his choice to commandeer my aunt's apartment.

"No, I'm sorry," he said, and suddenly we were at a standoff, and I caught myself smiling at the irony.

"We can both be sorry," I said.

He nodded. "Very well."

The bookcase he'd moved was now filled with what looked like his own books and not my aunt's. It was hard not to gawk, and I found myself taking in every detail.

"Does it bother you that I moved the bookcase?" He sounded more interested than judgmental. "Or is it my choice of books?"

"It's just another reminder that things have changed," I said.

He got up to walk to the bookcase. "When I was in New York…" He searched his titles, pulling some books out and pushing others back in until he'd found what he was looking for. A white book. A big book. He thumbed through the pages, then opened to a chapter about crescendos. "See here. Sergei and I had a very interesting conversation about crescendos once."

He turned the book around. "It's in English," I said, then I noticed who the author was.

"You wrote this?" I asked, and he laughed.

"When I was younger. One of many pianists who contributed. I heard the Conservatory in Paris was teaching from it."

I gulped, now realizing where I'd heard that piece before. He gave me a strange look, a look that warranted an explanation.

"You're full of surprises," I said. "A famous pianist isn't what I expected when I was told a retired naval captain was moving in." I took another look at the chapter, which had examples, though I wasn't just looking, but reading the music and thinking about how it would sound.

"Would you…" He pointed to his piano. "Like to play?"

I pivoted in my chair, looking at his black piano, and its bright, shiny keys, and rubbing my fingers. The last Steinway I'd played was Professor Caron's.

"Please…" He swayed his hand in the air, offering me his piano, and I stood up, only half thinking I shouldn't do it, but the closer I stepped toward the piano bench and imagined myself playing, the less I could resist. Simone, she'd think the captain was playing again, and probably wouldn't even get out of bed to investigate because she was so tired.

I set my hands on the keys.

"Go on," he said.

He took off his glasses while I played, listening the way Professor Caron used to listen to her students, with his eyes closed to really immerse himself, and I lost track of time.

"Oh—" I pulled my hands from the keys. "I didn't realize how late it was," I said. "I'm so sorry, but I have to go."

"Yes, of course," he said. "I shouldn't have kept you." He smiled. "Another time?"

I nodded.

Back on my side of the wall, I paused at the staircase, listening for movement from Simone, but she must have fallen asleep.

I arrived at the commandant's promptly at nine o'clock. The housekeeper answered, and she looked surprised to see me.

"I'm here to teach Lauren," I said, which I thought was obvious, but her face remained frozen through the door crack. "Piano."

She suddenly came to life with a blink. "Oh," she said, opening the door. "Come in."

I walked straight upstairs with one thing on my mind and one thing only. Lauren and the performance. I needed to talk to her, but delicately.

Instead of waiting for me at the top of the stairs, I found Lauren sitting at the piano with one of her dolls as if she'd given the poor thing a bash over the keys. "Good morning," I said, trying to sound cheerful and as if the last time I was there I hadn't been thrown out. She bolted to her feet after I closed the door, running toward me with her arms open.

"Mademoiselle! Teacher!" She hugged me tightly around the waist. "They told me you might not come back."

"Who told you that?"

She blinked a few tears away. "My mistress and the housekeeper."

I heard Irma and the housekeeper talking to each other in

the hallway. "Why would—" I stopped short of asking her a question I knew she couldn't answer, smoothing a lock of hair away from her eyes. They either hoped the commandant had punished me more severely or hoped he would in the future. "They're mistaken," I said, giving her a pat and she ran off to her piano.

"Lauren…" I sat down, interrupting her as she played with another smooth of her hair. "Have you heard anything about playing in front of…" I took a breath. "An audience?"

My words hung in the air—words that felt out of the blue—something an adult would notice, but perhaps not her. I waited for a response as she sat, smiling with her little fingers frozen on keys.

"An audience?" she asked, scrunched-faced, and I patted my clammy forehead where I felt the beginnings of a throbbing headache. She didn't know, and now I had to find another way to bring up the performance, this time to warn her, and do it without sounding suspicious. I had to remember she was a child who liked to talk, with a mouth that ran like water. She might not even be aware of what she was saying around the wrong person, and any hint that I knew more than I should would be detrimental to my family.

Lauren went back to her selection, playing a few bars while I collected my words.

"Lauren, there's a—"

Irma burst through the door with her tray of biscuits and tea, and I held my chest where all the air had escaped, watching her set down the tray with my heart thumping under my palm. I expected Irma to mention how lovely it sounded—her usual statement—but instead, she smirked. Lauren ran for the biscuits.

"Oh, did I scare you?" Irma looked up as she was bent over, and it was then I saw something different in her eyes. Something disdainful.

My spine straightened.

"Irma," I said as she unfolded the linen and arranged the teacups. "Why would you tell Lauren I wasn't coming back?"

"I don't know what you're talking about, Fraulein."

That was the first time she'd called me Fraulein and not mademoiselle.

"Here." She spooned a stiff helping of sugar into my cup before offering it to me, but she let go of it too early and it flipped over, spilling tea all over my lap.

"Ack!" I jumped to my feet with tea dripping down my legs and into my shoes. Lauren's hands flew to her mouth, and Irma pranced around as if she didn't know what to do, crudely twisting a napkin in her hands instead of offering it to me. "Give that to me." I swiped it away from her to wipe my lap, but what I needed was some water. "I need a washroom."

Irma pointed to the floor and I took that to mean it was on the ground level. "I'll be right back," I said to Lauren, who immediately turned to Irma, giving her a stinky eye and then reached for one of her dolls to throw, which I prayed was just a threat.

I padded downstairs, looking for the washroom and trying not to look like I was snooping. I found a closet, a backdoor into the kitchen, and then finally a washroom in the hall near the stairs.

I cursed Irma's name under my breath as the water gushed from the tap. She hated me for asking her to leave our house and was going to make me pay. *I can't trust her*, I thought, as if

I ever could. I soaked a hand towel in water and wiped myself off, but still felt sticky with sugar.

"Yes, yes," I heard on the other side of the wall, and the wet rag fell from my hands. It was the commandant. I turned the tap off to hear better. He was speaking to someone about the security of his office at home and didn't seem pleased. I inched toward the wall, pressing my ear to it carefully. "I have Burg Stahlhart locks. No need to worry. And yes, The Heroines are being sought," he said, and I covered my mouth. "We believe they are dispatching via a messenger pigeon. Bastard Radio Londres." He slammed the receiver down, and I jumped away from the wall.

I stood still in the quiet space of the washroom, thinking he knew I'd been spying, but thankfully I heard him telephoning someone else.

I rushed out before anyone noticed I was there, tiptoeing down the hall and reaching for the handrail, but my head was turned and I ran right into Danielle. "Watch out!" She clutched her chest through her flowing red nightgown, before sinking to the stairs on her bottom with her gold bangles clinking around her wrists.

I panicked. "I'm sorry!" I said, reaching to help her up.

"I can stand on my own, thank you," she said, brushing her hair back and adjusting her peignoir over her silky nightgown. I smelt her thick perfume. "What are you doing down here?" She looked me over.

"I..." I had a reason to be in the washroom, but I didn't have a reason to loiter while the commandant was having a private conversation. "I had a spill." I managed a smile. The commandant opened his study doors behind me and a pocket of warm air flitted against my legs where they were still damp.

"What's going on here?" the commandant asked.

I resisted the urge to close my eyes with Danielle watching me. "Good morning, Commandant," I said, turning around, hoping he wouldn't notice the cold sweat beading on my brow, but he walked closer, heel to toe, throwing his hands behind his back and studying my face.

"Why do you look nervous?"

"Because I scared the poor girl, Streicher," Danielle said. "That's why."

My jaw dropped. Clearly, I had been the one who'd scared her.

"Is that so?" He turned to me, and Danielle dipped her eyes once from behind his shoulder as if telling me to agree.

"I'm afraid it is," I said. "Some tea was spilled and I was just coming back from washing up..." I pointed toward the kitchen as if that was where I'd been. "I wasn't looking where I was going." I smiled, lips pressed, with nothing more to offer, waiting for him to say something, but he held his gaze, blinking hard. "I must get back to my lesson. Pardon me." I walked up the stairs, hoping he wouldn't call me back, and was delighted when he didn't.

"I'm back," I announced to Lauren, feeling relief, but when I went to close the door, the commandant and Danielle were also in the doorway.

"I have a surprise for you, Lauren," he said.

She stood when her mother motioned for her to do so, looking at me, then at her mother, but I had nothing to add. The commandant snapped his fingers for me to come over to the piano and join them.

"You've improved a great deal these last days with your

new teacher," he said to Lauren. "Well done. How would you like to play in front of an audience?"

Lauren held her breath, eyes popping. "An audience?" she questioned, and when he nodded, she covered her mouth, jumping up and down. "Where? Where?"

"It's a formal affair at the Monsigny at the very end of May," he said, and my stomach sank, having missed my chance to get to her first. "You can play whatever you like as a budding pianist. The people will love it." The commandant turned to look at me, and although I did my best to straighten, I felt utterly sick and queasy. "Perhaps your teacher can help you learn something for the occasion—you seem to learn so fast, and you have several days to prepare."

"Oh, Streicher," Danielle said. "Is this true?"

He took Danielle in his arms, kissing her harshly on the lips, yet she looked genuinely pleased for her daughter. And who wouldn't? Lauren's eyes had lit up.

"Just like you said, teacher." Lauren grabbed both my hands. "Isn't it wonderful?"

"Like you said?" the commandant asked.

I let the question hang, not knowing what to do other than to hug Lauren, and while we hugged, I prayed he and Danielle would forget, get caught up in each other and leave us for their bedroom, but when I pulled away, they were both still looking at me, waiting for an answer.

He cleared his throat.

"Just this morning, she mentioned something about playing in front of an audience," Lauren said, answering for me.

"You did?" he asked.

"I mentioned she'd be perfect for it," I said, lying with a smile.

"Can you come? Please! Please! Please!" Lauren jumped up and down the longer I stayed quiet, tugging and tugging on my hands. Then she turned to the commandant. "My teacher's invited, isn't she?"

"Of course! Madame Leroux wouldn't want it any other way." He smiled.

"Who?" Lauren asked, but he was quick to pat her shoulders, which meant not to ask.

My head throbbed. Only a trained eye would have seen that I had fallen into a chair instead of sat.

"Something wrong, Fraulein?" he asked, and I took my hand off my forehead.

"Not at all. I'm only wondering what she'd play," I said.

"I'm sure whatever piece you choose, she'll play it expertly." He took his wife's hand, leaving ahead of Danielle's train of satin. When the door closed, it felt as if the lights had gone out and I wanted to curl up on the floor, but little Lauren wouldn't let me, taking my hand and leading me back to the piano bench for something to learn—something she could play for her performance.

She flipped through the sheet music. "How about this one?"

"Lauren, the performance…" I said as she flapped the music in my face, but what was I going to tell her? To take the opportunity away from her now would make me the villain. I needed to send another message—I needed to go back to the farmer's, despite the risks, and despite my sisters. And I needed to go now. It was the only way.

"I'm so excited!" She threw her arms around my neck, nearly choking me of all my breath.

Chapter Nineteen

London

Guy had gone to bed worrying about Gaby and her sisters, only to wake up the next morning with the same aching twist in his stomach. Things didn't fare much better at work, where he spent hours sitting at his desk, tapping the end of his pencil on a pad of paper and watching the phone. Though it was the first time since the start of Operation Columba that he didn't want the phone to ring—he didn't want Arthur Ripley to call with news that another of Gaby's pigeons had been received. In fact, he wanted Gaby and his sisters to stop.

Guy closed his eyes briefly to reset his thoughts, but when he did, he heard the professor playing Gaby's music—he heard it in his bones. It embodied every thought he believed about his program, about the fighting nature of the French people. To see it crushed, to know his agents were to be sacrificed, tore at his conscience and at his soul.

When Clive asked him to help carry the last of his things up to his new office on the ground floor, he was hopeful, at least for a few moments, that the change in scenery would take his mind off it.

Clive loaded the shelf full of photos of his wife into a box, then they both walked upstairs. "Welcome to the London Controlling Section," Clive said, walking into his office first. "Next week, I transfer up a few more floors to work with the Joint Planning Staff." He leaned in and whispered, "Working with The Five."

"You'll be assisting with invasion intelligence?"

"Can't wait. Rex Smith is going to be involved too is what I hear. I'll have to warn my wife that I'll be working late from now on."

It didn't surprise Guy that Smith was involved since their little MI14 two-man detachment had come to a halt.

Together, they looked over the cramped office, which consisted of a table and four agents writing reports. Two others were huddled over a radio, listening to The She Wolf's latest broadcast. "And nobody hates the Germans more than me," they both said proudly, mimicking The She Wolf's signing off.

"Get back to work," Clive said, and they abandoned her broadcast for their pencils and pads of paper, calling him "sir."

Clive turned to Guy. "I'll never get used to that," he said. "Sir…"

"Comes with being a supervisor. You deserve it." Guy set Clive's box down, but much to his dismay, his mind was still on Gaby, and what he could do to change The Five's minds. There had to be something—there had to be a way.

"You all right?" Clive asked.

"Yeah, yeah," Guy said, though he wasn't listening. Guy

knew that in order to get to The Five, he had to convince Rex Smith first. But that came with its own consequences. He risked demotion. Worse, he risked being made redundant.

"Clive, you ever get that feeling that you know more than the brass?"

He watched Clive pull the photos of his wife from the box and arrange them perfectly on the shelf, which only made him think of Gaby, and her photo, and his responsibility to her and her sisters.

"All the time. Why?"

Guy nodded. It was exactly what he needed to hear. For whatever reason, he needed to know that what he felt mattered, and possibly had merit. "Thanks, friend," he said, but instead of going back downstairs to his basement office, Guy bolted upstairs, bypassing the first floor for the second.

He realized that he couldn't live with himself if he didn't talk to his supervisor, demand a meeting with The Five to pitch his position, and make them believe.

Guy saw Smith's secretary from down the corridor, rising from her chair and shaking her head as he clipped down the tiles. "You can't go in," Daisy said, before putting her hands up as he got closer, as if that would stop him. "He's on an important call!"

Guy opened Smith's door, finding him on the phone just as Daisy had said. "I need a meeting with The Five, sir!"

Smith looked alarmed at first, then waved him in. Daisy stood in the doorway, patting her chest before quietly closing the door. Guy worked to smooth his wrinkled shirt flat, but it was no use since he'd slept in it.

Smith hung up the phone after finishing the last few words

of his conversation. "Guy, what's the meaning of this? I was on an important call."

"Sir, I—" Guy's gaze had traveled to Smith's desk where there were many papers laid out, and also sheets of music.

"What are these?" Guy picked one up, and Smith tried to stop him, but he took a step back. Guy noticed right away that this sheet hadn't been shorn of its last bar, and didn't have a message. It was intact and crisp, as if it had just been lifted from a piano stand. He followed the notes with his finger all the way to the end of the second bar, then had the shock of his life when he recognized Gaby's name hidden in the notes.

"Where'd you get this?" Guy asked, and it was in no way pleasant. He had shouted.

Smith looked like he was going to shout back, but then his shoulders dropped and he took off his glasses. "Have a seat."

Guy's stomach took a sour turn; whatever he had to say, Guy just knew it wasn't going to be good.

"I'd rather stand, sir," Guy said, though his legs felt like jelly and his fingers too.

"These were found in Paris months ago by one of our agents. There was a tussle for it. Germans were looking for résistants, and when they became interested in the music, our agents decided to transport them here to us for analysis."

"What?" Guy wondered why he wasn't called and found himself feeling for the chair behind him and having a seat after all.

"Guy, the brass want you to take a few days off. You're overworked. I can tell you haven't slept." Smith made mention of his clothes, how crumpled they were even for him, and his worn complexion. "When was the last time you had a holiday?"

Guy stood sharply. "I don't need a holiday."

"Don't you?" Smith sat back down at his desk, hands in a steeple position, and Guy realized that he wasn't asking, he was telling. "What happened to the old Guy Burton, the agent who wore pressed suits and was put together?" he asked, and Guy tugged on his jacket. "I know after Jennie—" He closed his eyes briefly. "Look, I gave you some slack to get your life in order, but you've gone full circle now. There is such a thing as working yourself to death."

Guy shook his head.

"If another pigeon comes in with a message and we think it has value, I'll ring you up."

"Has another pigeon come in?" Guy asked, thinking there had been one and they didn't tell him about that either, but Smith wouldn't answer.

Guy's spine straightened. "Sir, I humbly request a meeting with The Five. My agents are worthy of protection, not sacrifice. The map they sent, the successful bombing campaign from the RAF because of it, and what about the intelligence about Hitler? I might be able to convince them."

"There are dozens of agents worthy of protection, agent Burton," Smith said, which made Guy recoil because he'd never addressed him so formally. "You've become too close to the program, if you want my opinion. It's clouding your mind. There's a war going on, for God's sake, with thousands of lives on the line, not a select few." Smith picked up his phone. "Now, if you'll excuse me."

Guy watched Smith ring Daisy up just beyond the wall, asking her to connect him with his wife to tell her he'd be working late.

"See you in a few days," Smith said to Guy, his hand over

the receiver. "Oh, and I'll need the original messages brought up while you're away. Don't worry, I'll keep them safe. Daisy will lock them up here, as policy," he added, before going back to his phone call.

Guy's neck felt warm and he was a little breathless, looking over Smith's desk, over Gaby's music, and unable to do anything but walk away.

Daisy stood up from her chair. "Everything all right, Mr. Burton?"

"I'm…" He looked up. "I'm leaving for a few days."

"Oh, you mean I get a few days without a heart attack?" she joked, but must have realized something serious had just happened in Smith's office because she then tried to console him. "I'm sorry, Guy," she said as he walked past. "I can see you're having a bad day."

Guy motioned with his hand, a slight acknowledgment, and walked downstairs to his office just as the basement was emptying out for the night, thinking of all the things he wished he'd said while counting up all the things still left unanswered. A terrible knot twisted in his stomach.

"Watch it!" an agent said when Guy ran into him in the corridor.

Guy looked up, astonished to find so many people downstairs because he was completely unaware. He slipped into his office and closed the door. The place felt sterile and barren now that Clive had moved out, and it was just as well.

He pulled the original messages from his locked filing cabinet, but then froze with Gaby's photo in his hand, listening to the rest of the basement empty out for the night, which came in chatty pulses until he was alone and staring at her portrait.

He made the mistake of closing his eyes so he could hear

Gaby's music; it played in his heart as much as his mind until he ached all over.

What came next surprised him most of all as his hands curled into fists. "Dammit!" He kicked and punched his filing cabinet in an explosive burst of frustration and anger, the sound of clanging metal filling the room. Collapsing, he rested his forehead against the drawer.

The basement turned stone-cold quiet, and without much choice, he gathered the messages and threw them into his bag – when his phone rang.

Brrring! Brrring!

He whipped around from the door, his heart pounding.

All he kept thinking was, please don't be Ripley. "Dear God. Please..." He answered it carefully, bringing the receiver up to his ear. "Hello?"

"Mr. Burton?" It was Professor Caron and there was panic in her voice. "Guy, is that you? There's an emergency, come quickly!" she said, then all went quiet.

"Professor?" he asked. "Hello! Hello! Professor?" He slammed his phone down when he realized she'd hung up, and sped off to the Royal College of Music with his messenger bag, forgetting all about handing over the messages to Daisy, and double parking his car outside with a lurch.

He ran past the reception to her studio, shuffling down the stairs to find her nearly in tears by her piano, papers strewn across the floor, and the photos of her best students on the wall tossed about, some left half-hanging from tacks.

"What happened?" He stood in her doorway, hands bracing the sides.

She walked toward him, sniffling, then whispering. "There was a man here asking about Gaby. He said he was from the

War Office, but you told me not to talk to anyone but you. And then I knew he wasn't from the War Office when he wrecked my studio."

"What did he say?"

"He wanted Gaby's name, then said I'd better give him all the information on The Heroines, or else." She rested the back of her hand on her forehead. "He was beastly. A large man with a gray overcoat, and a hat that hid his face."

Guy stood in shock, covering his mouth, then took a seat. He didn't know of anyone at MI6 that could be described as beastly. "Or else what?"

"Well, I certainly didn't want to find out!" She shook like a leaf in a breeze, clutching her stomach.

Guy prayed she didn't tell the man Gaby's name. "What did you tell them?"

"A load of rubbish, of course. That The Heroines was a man, a famous composer."

"Ah, thank God," Guy breathed, but one thing was certain: the professor's identity was compromised, and she was at risk. "Professor, do you have someplace to go? A friend perhaps that you can call on?"

She shook her head. "And leave my studio? My post at the Academy?"

"Professor, a translated message with how to find you was given to a select number of people—the top brass—five people total besides my immediate supervisor. We don't include specifics on sources in reports. Nobody should have found you."

Guy worried he'd been followed, then wondered if his padlock had been pried open and not accidentally disengaged like he'd thought. He pressed his palm to his forehead where perspiration had collected, trying to think clearly, but a thousand thoughts bombarded his mind.

"Take me to your supervisor," she said. "Surely, he can provide a safe place for me."

"I can't," he said.

"Why?"

"I've been forced to take a few days off." Guy tightened his grip on his bag, glad he'd made it out of his office with the originals because now he didn't trust anyone.

The professor covered her mouth.

"Again, is there somewhere you can go?"

"I don't have anywhere to go," she said. "Can you help me?"

There was only one place Guy thought the professor would be safe. A place where nobody would find her, or if they did, they'd have a devil of a time getting to her—his sister Madge's house.

"Grab your things," Guy said. "I think I know a place—a place where you'll be safe."

The thud of footsteps traveled down the staircase, and they both froze, listening to whoever it was come closer. Guy scanned his surroundings for a weapon to use, but there was nothing but papers and a leathery briefcase, and those wouldn't do.

He inched closer to the door with clenched fists, breath held tight in his chest while the professor closed her eyes—another step closer, then another—fingers squeezing, only it was another professor just passing through, none the wiser.

They both exhaled, holding their chests.

"We need to get out of here," he said. "Now!"

"Where are you taking me?" The professor reached for her things, hurriedly stuffing them into her briefcase.

"I'll tell you on the way there." He guided her out the door, but in the corridor, she paused, looking solemnly up at him.

"You're worried about the girls, aren't you?"

He nodded.

"Me too, Mr. Burton," she said. "Me too."

Chapter Twenty

I threw open the front door to our shop. "We need to close." Simone and Martine stared at me from behind the counter as the bells thrashed and clanged. "Now!" I raced to pull the curtains, but Martine stopped me, running over and gripping my arm.

"We have a customer," Martine said through her teeth.

A German officer walked out from the back, buttoning his jacket, and my heart slammed in my chest—*boom, boom, boom*—but he was completely absorbed with the sight of his new buttons, looking in the mirror and paying Simone for the trouble. He fit his hat to his head before bidding us adieu. I felt my chest, waiting for the bells to stop clanging after he opened the door to leave.

"Sorry," I breathed. "Sorry…"

"What were you thinking?" Simone asked.

"I didn't expect a German to walk out from the back." I collapsed into the chair by the window.

Martine put her hands on her hips, examining me hunched

over with my coat still on and sweating from the dash over. "What happened?"

I dug my palms into my eyes. "Lauren didn't know anything about the Monsigny."

"That's good!" Martine said, kneeling next to me, but I shook my head.

"She didn't know anything until the commandant asked her to attend right in front of me. And as if that's not bad enough…" I pulled my hands away from my eyes, my nose running. "I'm going too," I said in a spitting cry.

Martine straightened up. "No," she said. "You can't go. You can't!" She turned to Simone, who looked like she didn't know what to say, before turning back to me, only this time pointing her finger. "You are not going, Gabriella Cotillard!"

Now it was me standing up. "If I don't go, he'll punish Mme. Leroux. He's already sent a German in uniform to her house as a warning." My hands twisted. "And you know he won't bother with another warning. I'm damned if I do go, and damned if I don't."

"To hell with Mme. Leroux!" Martine said. "She was glad to take those rations knowing the consequences, only to point her judging finger at us later."

"But what about her son?" I asked. "He doesn't deserve it."

"Our situation keeps getting worse," Simone said. "If it's not a pigeon problem, it's a commandant problem, or a neighbor problem, or us being bad French, whores and traitors—"

I took Martine by the shoulders, cutting Simone off. "Was there a broadcast from London? Did you listen this morning?" I asked, even though I thought she would have told me first thing if there was.

She hung her head. "I didn't hear anything."

I took my hands from her shoulders. The clock ticked. Waiting for five o'clock wasn't something I was willing to do. "We must go back to the farm—steal the other pigeon. I've already thought about it," I said.

"And we already talked about this. We still don't know the fate of the last pigeon you sent, and the performance is several days away at the end of the month," Simone said. "There could be another drop."

"But what if there isn't, and what if the farmer puts the last surviving pigeon in a pie? This is urgent, more urgent than ever." I stopped short of mentioning the flyer, and that I knew the Abwehr was looking for us locally.

"It's too dangerous. Not while we still have options," she said. "Hope they drop more pigeons. That's what we do. Hope."

"Hope?" I threw my hands up. "Hope isn't an option. Martine, grab your coat," I said, and she looked at Simone.

"But I don't agree," Simone said. "It's our pact. Our pact for a reason, Gaby."

"I'm going."

Simone gasped, and when she realized I wasn't changing my mind, she walked to the back of the shop and shut the door, and that was fine with me since she wasn't blocking the front door. She didn't need to be involved and the less she heard the better.

Martine bit her nails, alternating her look between me and the back of the shop, but Simone wasn't going to open that door.

"I need your help, Martine." I couldn't believe she was hesitating. Revenge was what Martine wished for the most, and with another pigeon, we could save Lauren and do so much more, still. "After all the schemes I let you involve me in."

"It feels wrong without Simone's blessing."

"When does something ever feel right in occupied France?" I asked. "Put your coat on. Because if you don't, I'll just go without you."

I waited for her to respond, folding my arms.

She looked back and forth between me and the back door where Simone was. "Fine," she said, shoving her arms into her coat sleeves. "But it's only because I don't want you to go alone."

The walk was a tense and silent one. I wanted to get there as fast as we could and wash away what had happened with my last message and get that bird, yet I resisted walking too fast to avoid suspicion. Martine walked a step behind me with her arms folded.

We entered through the down fencing like before, getting a good look at the farmhouse. The curtains were drawn and dark, and there were no signs of the farmer or his wife. "Nobody's home! This will be quick because nobody's here."

I pulled Martine by the coat sleeve through the weeds, but she dragged her feet. "What's wrong? Now's our chance!"

"We need to be careful. What if it's a trap?"

I scoffed. "But nobody's home."

"How do you know?"

I paused in the field grass, scanning the entire farm once more and looking for signs of life, but everything was just as quiet as it was a few minutes ago, which convinced her to keep walking. A shift in the clouds allowed for some sunlight.

"What's your plan if we're caught?" she asked. "What will we say?"

I turned, looking at her over my shoulder, slightly annoyed since Martine had never cared much about plans before. "We'll say we're hungry. Stealing the pigeon for meat."

I bolted ahead two paces, reaching for the door to the shed where they kept the pigeons, and Martine yanked me back, pulling my coat off one shoulder. Her eyes skirted over the farm and toward the cliffs. "Something's off, Gaby. I think we should turn around, leave."

"We're here." In my mind, the bird was already dispatching my message to London and halfway across the sea. All I had to do was get in there, snatch him up, and get him home. I reached for the door again, pushing with a light touch, and a slice of sunlight lit up the dark floor, enough light for me to see some hay sprinkled about on the ground, but all the rest was shadowed.

"Come on," I whispered, and Martine reluctantly followed me inside, the floorboards creaking and cobwebs brushing across my cheek. "Where is he?" We looked to the rafters where we heard noises, and a pigeon flew down from his perch, wildly flapping his wings. Feathers, dirt, and hay flew into the air as I scrambled to catch him.

"I got him!" Martine grabbed him by the middle and shoved him head first down her sleeve from the top of her coat. Then it was quiet, both of us panting and huffing.

I closed my eyes briefly, letting the relief sink in.

"He feels different," she said, motioning to the bulge under her coat. "Fatter."

"We'll walk closer to conceal him." I felt my chest where my heart was still thumping. "Let's go."

We ducked out of the shed only to hear bristling footsteps coming up fast from around the side. Martine took my hand. "Gaby—" The farmer burst out from behind the shed with his shovel, chasing after us.

"Hurry!" I said, and we ran for the fence through the thick grass, but Martine twisted her ankle and tripped, and before I could even stretch my hand out to help her, the farmer's wife appeared from nowhere and pointed a revolver at us.

"Hold it right there," she said.

My chest felt as if it was going to burst. I couldn't breathe. I couldn't move!

She walked briskly up to Martine and pulled the pigeon from her coat with one hand. "Thieves! Whores!"

"We were hungry," I said. "Please, you don't have to turn us in." The farmer lowered the shovel, only to look at us like prizes he'd won, his eyes wide and glistening. "Pigeons are outlawed," I exclaimed, thinking maybe he'd listen to reason. "You'll be punished too if you report us."

His wife gave a snaggle-tooth smile, holding the pigeon up by his feet. Only it wasn't a pigeon. It was a dove. "Who said anything about a pigeon?"

My stomach sank, and when I looked at Martine's drawn face, I felt I might vomit, because we were helpless, and worse, women were a valuable commodity on the black market.

The wife cocked her revolver. "Walk that way." She flicked her gun toward a barn where they had a car. We had no choice but to get in with her gun to our backs.

The farmer drove off, through the bumpy open field and onto the road, and, as I thought, instead of taking us to the police station in the village, drove us to a decrepit old prison on the outskirts run by Vichy collaborators who made up their own rules.

"I'm sorry," I mouthed to Martine, and she hung her head, which only made me feel worse.

The couple dragged us by the elbows up to the front entrance where a dirty guard with a scruffy, unkempt beard handed the wife a bag of coins for payment. He straightened his police cap over his greasy head, before pointing inside where it was dark and smelled of urine even from the front step.

"Do what they say," the farmer warned as he left with his wife, but when Martine and I stayed frozen on the front steps, the guard grabbed both of us and pulled us inside, stumbling feet over feet.

"Watch your hands." Martine sneered when he touched her, but he paid no attention. She hobbled forward, trying to look strong and unaffected, but I could tell her ankle hurt by the way she held her weight, leaning slightly to the side.

A woman's laugh carried down the dark corridor, followed by words about rotting in hell and how much money she'd make. High heels tapped against the stones as she made her way to the front. "Pleasure doing business with you," I heard her say to one of the guards, and there was something about her voice, something condescending and familiar.

I elbowed Martine. "That's Antoinette," I said, and though I wasn't surprised she was making deals with the collaborators, I was relieved that someone we knew was there.

She emerged confidently from the dark corridor wearing a pink hat and a beige woolen coat, confident as if she visited daily and might have some pull with the guards. She took a startled step backward when she saw us, then smiled slyly.

"Antoinette, thank God," I said. "Help us." I turned toward the guards. "How much to get out of here?" I asked, but he wouldn't say, alternating his look between Antoinette and Martine, who now had their eyes locked on each other. "I'll reimburse you whatever it is when we get home. I promise, Antoinette. I have the money..."

She fingered the top button of her coat. "Who are you?" she asked. "And how do you have money?"

My jaw dropped.

I know I'd treated her harshly over the last few days, being curt and leaving her on my step, but never did I think she'd leave us in prison and at the hands of unscrupulous men. She was just being tough because Martine was with me, that was all, I thought.

"Well, well, if it isn't Marie Antoinette," Martine said, and Antoinette's eyes narrowed.

"Look at you two. Dirty and ragged. What did you steal?"

"You can at least tell our sister where we are," I said. "Right? You'll do that..."

She dismissed me with a turn of her head. The guards laughed between swigs of alcohol they shared from a flask, watching and listening.

"I know you'll tell her, Antoinette," I said when she headed for the door. Martine scoffed. "I know you will!"

The guards tucked their flasks away after she left and shooed us into a cell of iron bars where the odor of urine not only wafted up from the floor, but seeped from the moist corridor walls.

"How much is the fine?" I asked. He unhooked a ring of keys from his belt and locked us up. "Won't you tell us?"

He spat from the side of his mouth through the bars. "Shut up," he said, before turning on his boot heel and walking away, the keys from his key ring jingling all the way back down the corridor.

I huddled in the corner with Martine.

"I'm..." I swallowed the lump in my throat, but then my eyes welled with tears and I cried into my hands. "I'm sorry."

She put her arm around me, petting my head.

"What's going to happen to us in here?" I wiped my eyes, and it struck me how calm she was when normally she'd be a ball of questions or trying to convince me of something.

"I've been here before."

"What?" I scooted up, trying to look at her face even though it was dark. "When?"

"A few months ago. Rémy paid my fine. I didn't want to worry you so I kept it to myself." She turned to me after pausing. "It was for stealing."

"Stealing what?" I asked, thinking it must have been one of her schemes, some devious plan of hers to get back at the Reich.

"Meat," she said. "I wanted you and Simone to wake up to the smell of meat sizzling over the cooktop with four-minute eggs for breakfast. I know that's something that you miss from before in Paris—a real breakfast. I still want it for you."

I felt even worse than I already had.

"We might be here for a while. It will take a few days for Simone to come up with the kind of money they'll want. That's if Antoinette even tells her."

"She will. She'll at least do that," I said, but Martine

couldn't bring herself to believe she would. "Antoinette will tell Simone, Martine. I know it. And she can use the money I received from Lauren's lessons."

Martine shook her head. "She'll need more, Gaby. A lot more."

"More?" I blinked, wondering how much more it could be than what was in all those envelopes. And who could afford such a thing? "How did Rémy afford your fine?"

"I don't know. I never asked." A few moments passed with Martine staring into nothingness. "You think he loves me?" she asked. "Simone said she thought he did."

"Don't you know the answer?" I asked. "Loves you more than the stars, is my guess."

"Maybe he did once." Martine wiped her nose with the back of her hand.

"Send for him. He said he'd come if you wrote."

She shook her head. "I can't."

"Why not?"

She dug her palms into her eyes, pausing. "Because it will hurt too much if he doesn't. The fear of disappointment—it's why I always pushed him away first."

It was what Simone and I knew all along, but never had she admitted it.

"*Mon Dieu*, Martine. What will life be like for us when this is over? Will we ever be happy—happy like Simone is happy with her talk of Christian? Or will we be alone?" I asked, but Martine didn't answer, and I thought she was thinking of what life would be like too. Would we be alone?

We held each other on the floor for what seemed like hours, listening to moans and screams and people begging to be let out. That's when the scale of what had happened hit me hard. We didn't have a pigeon, and there was still the matter of Lauren and the performance.

"What am I going to do, Martine?" I said, my head buried in her shoulder.

"I don't know. Hope they drop more birds, or that they receive your message. But if you ask me, hoping is a waste of time." She rubbed her eyes, pausing. "I'll go with you to the performance, Gaby, if we get out of here in time. We did this together. You shouldn't go alone."

"Get out in time?" I squeezed her arm. "But the performance is in a few days."

"I know," she breathed.

Hours had passed, and it already felt like years. I couldn't imagine what a few days or weeks would feel like. Just when I was about to cry out to the world, a guard came down the corridor with a torch.

"You there," the guard barked, shining the light in our faces. "Get up!" Martine and I struggled to stand with his torch in our eyes.

"Did our sister pay?" I clutched my chest. "Are we free?"

He opened our cell. "Well, I'm not here to feed you." He pointed down the corridor where we heard voices—a guard accepting payment and laughing about how women fetched the highest price.

"Antoinette told Simone!" I said. "I knew she would!"

Martine stumbled ahead of me the best she could with her swollen ankle. "Simone!" she yelped. "Simone, thank God…"

She stopped in the entryway, hands bracing the moist bricks when she realized it wasn't Simone, but a man paying our fine.

I stepped forward, getting a better look around Martine, when he turned, tipping his hat. "Captain Weber? How did you—"

Simone stepped into the prison next, arms out, and we fell into her embrace, leaving Walter to finish settling the debt, and pay what Lauren's lesson money couldn't cover. I was thankful the captain helped us, but wasn't sure what Martine would say, and just hoped she wouldn't say anything mean.

"You asked *him* for help?" Martine asked Simone, and she shrugged.

"I had no other choice. He had the money."

Simone looked at me briefly, as if she knew I'd been friendly with the captain, and I realized she'd probably heard us playing together, maybe even visiting.

"Oh, Simone," I said, throwing my arms around her again. "I'm sorry." I took a deep breath of her Chantilly-scented hair, which was the most welcome scent in all the world. "I should have listened. I broke our pact. Can you forgive me?" I asked, and she said she would. "I'll need to ask Antoinette to forgive me too. I'm so thankful she told you."

Simone pulled back. "Antoinette?" she questioned, and with that Martine's brow furrowed.

"Isn't that why you came?" Martine asked. "Antoinette told you where we were?"

"No, I asked Madame Roche for help after you didn't come home, and she found out where you were. Antoinette had nothing to do with it."

"That bitch!" Martine said, but I was just glad she didn't call her a Boche, since that would have brought on more fines to pay. Simone hustled us outside. We were free, and I never wanted to step foot in there again.

Walter had a car and asked us to get in. It was the same car I'd seen him take to rehearsals, but I didn't ask why he was the one driving because I didn't want to know.

Martine got in first, and Simone turned around and faced me just as Walter started the car, the robust engine muffling our voices.

"You can't see him anymore," she said, and I nodded. "Martine is furious at Antoinette, and she doesn't need to be furious with you too. He helped us, and I'm grateful, but it must end."

The drive was silent and short. I was too embarrassed to look at Walter and wondered if he knew what we'd done at the farmer's. He parked around the back of our house near his private entrance. Martine bolted out of the back seat, followed by Simone, but I remained seated. "I was hungry," I explained. "Me and my sisters."

He nodded and told me to wait when I got out of the car. Then he rushed into his side of the house and came back out with my aunt's teapot. "This is yours. I put a bag of that black tea you like inside for you and your sisters, and some of the lemon. Should last you a few days. I suspect you won't be visiting anymore. Your younger sister seems very upset with my presence." He went back inside before I could reject his gifts.

I expected Martine to barrage me with questions about the teapot and how I managed to get it back, but instead, I found her standing quietly by the window with the last of our gin, staring at the dark lump that was Antoinette's house. "Martine—"

She threw her hand in the air. "Not now."

I set the teapot down and took off my coat, looking to Simone for what to say, but she patted my shoulder. "Come on," she said, turning to go upstairs. "It's late."

"Martine?" I said one last time, but she tossed back a swig of gin and braced the window ledge in the dark with her eyes set on Antoinette's windows.

Chapter Twenty-One

E ven on the day of the performance, Simone continued to talk of hope, yet there hadn't been any news from London about the second message or a pigeon drop in the days since we'd come home from prison. I'd have to go to the performance with Lauren, just as I feared.

I woke to the smell of something warm cooking in the kitchen as the sun rose. I thought my mind was playing tricks on me, or that I dreamt it, but how could I smell in a dream?

I ran into the hallway with my robe on, following the warm scent down the stairs into the kitchen where I found Martine with a spatula in one hand and a frying pan full of eggs in the other.

She spun around. "Good morning!"

"Where'd you get all those eggs?" I asked as she heaped a spatula full of them onto plates. One for me, and one for her. "Martine?"

She sat down with zest, scooping a spoonful of eggs into her mouth. "Mmm..." Her eyes gleamed. "Salt?" She threw a pinch at my plate, sprinkling salt over my eggs like a dusting of frost. "I thought we deserved a proper breakfast today."

Antoinette's back door had swung open outside. Martine smiled slowly, cheeks bulging with eggs. "You didn't," I said, but her smile had taken over her face. "You did."

She reached over the table and grabbed our aunt's teapot. "Tea?" She poured me a cup just as Antoinette was finding out she'd been robbed in the middle of the night.

Martine laughed deviously into her cup of tea before setting it down and reaching under the table. "That's not all." She pulled up a stock pot, plopping it on the counter, with Milly's chicken feet sticking straight up, plucked of all her feathers and ready to boil.

My jaw hit the floor.

"We're having soup today. Soup with meat. And maybe a Milly pie if there's enough to spare," she said.

"Mildred..." Antoinette called from her garden. "Milly! Milly!"

We scrambled to the window, watching Antoinette search her garden and all its hiding places for her lost hen. "I told her she'd pay for leaving us at that prison," Martine said. "Pity she didn't believe me."

"It is a pity." I tried, but couldn't hold back a laugh.

Antoinette whipped around, spying us through the glass, and we ducked, hands over our mouths as we giggled.

"Are you angry with me?" Martine asked, and I shook my head.

"But how'd you do it?

"I bent back one of the fence posts and slipped into her garden. Can't even tell it's broken if she looks."

"I wish I'd thought of it myself." Antoinette continued to

call for Milly, louder and louder, and now dogs were barking and lights flicked on at the neighbor's. "Are you going to tell her or leave her to guess?"

Martine got up. "For God's sake, she should have figured it out." She opened the window. "You there," she shouted. "Marie Antoinette! You're waking up the neighbors."

Antoinette looked surprised Martine had yelled at her and stood on tiptoe, looking over the fence that divided our back gardens. "Have you seen my hen? It's not like her to fly over the fence."

Martine snapped for her plate. "If I did, I wouldn't tell you," she said, shoveling eggs into her mouth.

"What?" Antoinette said.

"I said I wouldn't tell you!" Martine opened her mouth, showing Antoinette the mushy yellowy yolks inside just before swallowing, hard.

Antoinette's eyes grew to the size of moons, and Martine let out a howl of laughter.

"Goodbye, Antoinette!" I said, reaching over and closing the window with Martine still chewing her eggs and laughing madly with a full mouth.

Simone stepped into the kitchen. "What's going on?" She took a deep breath through her nose, then looked out the window, seeing Antoinette storm back into her house with the clack of a slammed door. I closed the curtain.

"She deserved it, Simone. You know she did. And look!" Martine showed Simone the pot before pushing the lid down over Milly's feet. "We have ourselves a meal."

Simone sat heavily in her chair with the silky peignoir smoothed over her round belly. She didn't seem to care at all about breakfast or Milly, pushing her plate away after Martine gave her a scoop of eggs. "There's something I need to tell you." Simone's eyes flicked up once.

We both took our seats. "What is it?"

"People know about the baby," she said, and I instantly reached for her hand. "Madame heard customers talking yesterday in the lock shop. Someone noticed my belly when I had my coat off—it's too warm for a coat now and I was sweating, which looked even more suspicious."

"Do they think—" My stomach had knotted up.

"They think it's German," she said.

I tipped my head back.

"Who said this?" Martine's fists clenched and I had no doubt she'd pay them a visit, which I absolutely didn't want.

"It's everyone, Martine." Simone held her belly. "Now we have to decide if I'm going to reject the rumor, all the while we serve the Germans, talk to the Germans, find employment with the Germans, or..." She closed her eyes, exhaling from her mouth. "Embrace the rumor. I still have a month left before the baby's due."

"Reject the rumor, of course," I said.

"What if we don't win?" Simone got up from her chair to stand at the counter. "You work for them, and nobody can deny our black ribbon and the influx of German customers we've serviced. Captain Weber said I'd qualify for some extra food if the Reich thinks it's one of theirs."

Martine leapt out of her chair. "You had a conversation with him about your baby?"

"It was in the car ride to the prison," Simone said. "I couldn't hide it in his car. It was the one time."

"I don't trust him." Martine's eyes turned beady. "Even if he paid our fine."

"He rescued us, Martine," I said.

"And why'd he do that?" she rasped, placing one hand deliberately on our aunt's teapot. "And why aren't you whispering anymore when you're close to the wall? He could be listening."

"So what if he is listening?" I asked. "If he's been keeping notes about our neighbor and ration gripes, so be it. We have other things to worry about today."

"Have hope, sisters," Simone said, but Martine folded her arms. "There is so much that can still happen."

After our eggs, Martine set Milly to boil, then left to listen to the broadcast at the shop, one last listen in case they had received the message, but I refused to listen for a message that would never come. Simone had gone up to her bedroom to rest, leaving me alone and thinking about what lay ahead.

I knocked on our shared wall for Walter, shaking a few photographs loose from our collage. "Walter?" I pinned the photos back. "Are you there?"

I heard him press his ear to the wall before walking down the hall to the private entrance where he unlatched the door. I met him outside.

"This is a surprise," he said, and it was. I wasn't sure exactly what brought me to his side of the wall other than it was possibly our last day alive.

"Hallo."

"Won't your sisters be angry if we visit?"

It no longer mattered to me that I promised Simone I'd stay away from him. I shook my head.

He motioned for me to come inside and I took a seat at the kitchen table where he poured me a cup of tea. "Walter," I said.

He sat down too. "I..." My hands twisted in my lap. "I wanted to see how you are. Are you doing well?"

"Yes, of course." He took a sip of his tea. "Why?"

He'd hung paintings since the last time I was there. Small ones, large ones, some bright and modern, and some ugly as sin. And the bookcase was painted dark blue. My aunt detested the color blue, but she probably would have expected it since he loved the sea.

"Because the village must know by now that we're friends after you drove us home," I said. "A car motoring through the streets with all of us in it, it's a hard sight to ignore, even at night."

"The Reich believes you and your sisters are their friends, so I've received no backlash." He reached over and patted my hand. "I hope you and your sisters are benefiting. Business is good?"

I nodded while he sipped his tea—Germans paying for Simone's meticulous work had compensated for the work she'd lost from the good French, contrary to what we believed would happen. He topped up his teacup. "My wife and I used to have tea together in the afternoons," he said. "I'd work on my compositions and she'd write poetry..." He went on about his wife, how they spent their time, how they met, at the opera, he'd said. "It's a cherished part of my life, all lost to me now." He tapped his heart. "Except for what I carry in here, when I remember how my music made her feel."

My eyes welled with tears, and he patted my hand again, looking as caught off guard from my reaction as I was.

"Sorry," I said when the tears spilled over my cheeks. "I'm not sure what came over me." I searched for a tissue and ended up using my hands and wiping them on my hair. I wondered if he'd forgive me after he was reunited with his wife once the night was over. I liked to think he would, and that helped to wash my guilt away.

I took a few more sips of tea, and we sat quietly, two pianists, one German and the other French, just like he said we could do when we met. I asked about his early years, who taught him, and who his favorite composer was.

The clock was ticking down, faster and faster toward the evening hour, and I should have expected it—I should have foreseen the final chime coming, but when the kitchen clock announced the five o'clock hour, it sounded like a bellowing drum rather than a chime, shaking the teacup in my hand and making it jitter in the saucer.

God help me, I thought. It was time to get ready. I pushed the cup and saucer away from me on the table.

"I enjoyed our time together," I said, and he looked at me strangely. "I wish there had been more days like this." I nodded my goodbye, leaving before he had a chance to rise from his chair and see me out.

————————

Martine came home from the shop with her head down. I didn't have to ask her if there was a message because the news was written all over her face. She went ahead with the chicken dinner she had planned, without mentioning why—today of all days—she had decided to kill Milly.

"Can you smell that?" Martine used Aunt Blanche's oven mitts to take the pie out of the oven and set it on the counter. Cream bubbled up along the edges in spots where she didn't pinch the pastry enough, but by the time it was cool enough to eat, my stomach was in knots.

I watched them eat their portion.

"I'm sorry," I said, standing from the table. "I'm too nervous. Can we go?"

Martine seemed to understand and put on a dress that matched the blue one I was wearing, hanging up her trousers for the first time in months.

Simone saw us to the door where we hugged. "I refuse to say goodbye," she said after pulling away. "I have hope that everything will work out. I'll see you after the performance." She nodded once and then walked upstairs.

I hooked Martine's arm and we started off down the road.

"There's one thing I regret," Martine said as we passed Antoinette's windows.

"What's that?" I thought she'd mention something about Rémy.

"I wish I'd spit a feather from my mouth when Antoinette asked about Milly."

She almost got a laugh out of me with that one. "I'm sorry I couldn't eat your dinner."

"It's all right," Martine said.

We'd made it to the Monsigny, and much quicker than I expected. Fancy cars pulled up to the valet. Elegantly dressed women, taking advantage of the warming weather with exposed shoulders and backs, walked toward the entrance hooked on the arms of equally elegant men. No sign of Hitler, though I expected him to arrive at the last minute and make a grand entrance.

"Is there anything you regret?" she asked.

I shifted in my dress, taking one last look at the stars

speckling the clear night sky. I regretted we didn't do more. I was at the commandant's house often. I could have listened harder, looked harder, taken notes on his comings and goings. Though we still would have needed a pigeon. "I wish we'd found that missing pigeon."

"I wish I'd never brought one home."

"What?" I asked, stunned to hear this from Martine.

"Gaby…" She felt for my hand. "I don't want to die. I've been trying not to think about it, but now that we are on the front steps and the performance is here…" She'd closed her eyes, breathing heavily, and usually I'd follow suit, but there was one thing I noticed among the glitz and the sparkles— there were a great many civilians in attendance. More than I would expect for a Reich performance with Adolf Hitler as their special guest.

"Martine," I breathed. "What if I was wrong?"

She opened her eyes, looking cautiously over my shoulder. "What do you mean?"

"I thought the RAF would send bombers. But why would they do that when the chances of killing civilians would be so great? Maybe they'll do something more targeted. Bomb Hitler's car or…" Now it was me looking over the crowd. "What if they dispatch a sniper?" I whispered.

She gasped, evidently not having thought of the chances either. "Do you think it's possible?"

"Why not? Be on the lookout. Run if you hear gunfire."

She nodded repeatedly.

We entered the crowded foyer where patrons were making their way into the theatre and finding their seats. I searched for Lauren, though it wasn't long before I heard her calling my name.

"Teacher! Teacher!" She waved for me to follow her backstage where she pointed to the piano.

"Are you nervous?" I asked, but it was my heart that was racing.

She pulled on her dress collar where the lace was tight, fidgeting all over, and then played with the maroon bow in her hair, which kept slipping. "No," she said, but I could tell she was terrified. "I'm glad you're here."

"She had no choice," Martine blurted, and I glared at my sister. "It's true." She shrugged, looking over the backstage, where a few people roamed, and up to the ceiling and the long ropes that let the curtain down from above.

Lauren didn't understand, tilting her head. "You didn't want to come?"

"I had no choice because I wouldn't miss it for the world." I smoothed a curl behind her ear, and she smiled.

A stagehand told Lauren she should take her seat at the piano, and my racing heart moved into my throat and felt more like gripping hands. Hitler must have arrived if they were starting. I reached for Lauren before she could run off, hugging her tightly and talking into her ear, but I wasn't sure what to say.

"Teacher?" She pulled away.

"Good luck," was all I ended up saying, and when she trotted out on stage, Martine held onto me.

An assistant fixed Lauren's dark dress skirt on the bench, and all that white lace, before tightening her bow, while I watched anxiously in the shadows of the stage like a nervous mother, eyeing every door, every guard, and every exit, looking for movement and listening for anything suspicious.

"Is that her mother?" Martine pointed, and when I turned, I

saw Danielle had been watching me the entire time from behind a stage prop. "Where's the commandant?"

"I don't know."

Lauren had started to play, and it struck me that something was off. There weren't very many stagehands and now the guards had disappeared. The curtain rose to a lukewarm round of applause, and I was surprised to find half the seats empty.

"What's going on?" Martine whispered, noticing what I had noticed.

Not one uniform was in attendance, and there was no sign of Hitler. I squeezed Martine's hand.

Lauren played her selection. It was short and simple for a beginner, and she could have handled much more. She had the talent for it, but she wanted to play something she knew she could play flawlessly. The audience clapped when she was finished and she bowed before running off stage to her mother, who had a bouquet of flowers waiting for her.

Walter walked up from behind, and Martine squeezed my arm.

"She was excellent." He adjusted his cufflinks.

"Where is everyone?" I asked. "The audience…"

He blinked rapidly. "Whatever do you mean?" he asked, and now I could care less if he knew that I was aware of the particulars.

"I thought this was a performance for the Reich. Important people. Maybe even Hitler himself." I motioned to the thinned audience. "Hardly anyone is here."

He talked to a production assistant about the lighting and the sound before turning back to me. "The Führer?" he asked, but it wasn't a question. "Plans change suddenly in occupied

France. He was supposed to attend, but must have decided it wasn't safe, is my guess. I'm just here to play, and I'm paid either way. Führer or not."

He walked out on stage, taking his seat at the piano.

"Does this mean what I think it means?" Martine asked, and I clutched my chest, nodding.

"I think we're safe." Hitler wasn't coming, and perhaps the RAF knew he'd turned back too, because nothing had happened. My eyes searched the ceiling, where the sky beyond sounded peaceful.

Martine wanted to leave right then, but I knew we'd have to wait until Walter was finished to avoid suspicion. We listened like good patrons, though inside we were counting down the minutes, the seconds until his piece was finished, but just when the curtain fell heavily to the floor in velvety folds, the commandant burst onto the stage, storming past us both with papers scrunched in his hand, followed by a long line of Abwehr clipping at the back of his heels.

A commotion ensued, which made everyone look, sharp German words and a confused look from Walter as the commandant shouted, finger pointing at the papers, but this time he called them sheet music.

Martine pulled on my arm to leave. "Let's go!" she rasped, but I could barely move with my eyes locked on Walter.

The commandant demanded to know everything Walter knew about it. "Have you seen this work before? And who composed it? The Heroines," he said, and I put my hand over my mouth, but Martine didn't hear and pleaded for me to leave, pulling and pulling on my arm, leading me to the door.

Walter shuffled through the sheets, but the commandant had grown impatient, snapping his fingers at his men to do something, and then, in a total breach of etiquette, slapped his hand on the top of the piano after Walter took too much time studying the notes.

"You there!" The commandant motioned to me. "Gabriella Cotillard!"

Walter looked shockingly up from the sheet music and straight to me, as if he knew—as if he'd read my name in the notes.

"Don't go," Martine said, but I had to go. He had summoned me and if I tried running now the entirety of the Abwehr would chase me down.

"Stay here," I said, taking carefully placed steps toward the commandant and his men huddled around the piano. "Yes, Commandant Streicher?" I refused to look at Walter though I felt his gaze upon me. My hands trembled.

"Do you recognize this?" The commandant took some of the sheets from Walter to thrust into my hands.

I cleared my throat before taking a look, bracing myself for how my body would react, but nothing could prepare me for the moment when my stomach fell to the floor. I shook my head feverishly. "No," I said, though it was more of a guttural sound. "I haven't seen this work before." It was partially true. The first and second pages were copies of mine, almost note for note, but the rest of the sheets were reprised, as if someone had guessed the completed work.

"Well then, give them back!" The commandant snatched them from my hands, giving them to the captain again and demanding he play. I clung tightly to the piano, watching Walter sit down and arrange the sheet music, waiting for those first notes to thrum, and thinking I'd faint when they did.

"Can I leave?" I managed to squeak out, and the

commandant motioned dismissively with his hand, which I took as permission. I turned on my heel, beelining for Martine by the door. Her face was a mix of shock and confusion as Walter began to play the opening chords of The Heroines.

I yanked Martine outside, taking a ragged breath that hurt my lungs.

"Is that…" Martine pointed to the door as it closed, the piano music fading. "Did he…"

"Don't say it," I said. "Don't say anything."

I closed my eyes tightly. The RAF might not have bombed the Monsigny, but there had been an explosion, and I was struggling to breathe.

Chapter Twenty-Two

S imone came down the stairs after we walked inside, dressed in her pink peignoir and grappling for the handrail. "Sisters," she said. We met her halfway up where she threw her arms around us the best she could with her growing belly. "I knew you'd come back. See! I hoped and hoped and hoped and now it's over."

Martine and I exchanged looks. Nothing was all right and it was far from over, but we smiled back at her as if we agreed.

"Will you sleep with me tonight?" She cupped her belly. "Please."

We both nodded, and yet we still hadn't said a word since we left the performance.

We crawled into Simone's bed with her. After Simone positioned herself, stuffing pillows between her legs and one under her belly as she lay on her side, she reached back, touching Martine's leg and my arm with searching fingers as if making sure she wasn't dreaming, and that we were there.

"Goodnight," Simone said.

The captain's car crept slowly past our window, beams of light shining on the walls amidst the sputter of his engine. Martine tensed under the sheets when the captain's back door opened and closed, but it was me who shuddered.

"Goodnight," I said back after a delay, eyes open in the dark, searching the air for an answer, what to do. But there was little I could do. If Walter read my name, surely, he'd tell the Abwehr, wouldn't he? Maybe he was waiting until I'd left, unable to look me in the eye as he told the commandant what he'd read hidden in the notes. That was it. God, that was it. Maybe the Abwehr were on their way here right now.

I threw the covers over my head, closing my eyes, and hoping for a few winks before they hauled me off to prison— one last sleep with my sisters—but I tossed and turned all night, jerking awake with every single peep and scratch.

In the early morning hours, I rolled over to find Martine already up and looking at me with the blanket up to her neck.

"Did you sleep?" she asked, and I shook my head.

Simone moaned, repositioning herself and causing the mattress to ripple and wave before sitting up and swinging her feet over the bed.

"Me either," she whispered back.

Simone turned her head, looking surprised we were up. "What time is it? I want a cup of tea but I'm afraid that if I walk downstairs now, I'll never have the energy to walk back up," she said, rubbing the small of her back.

"Do we tell her now?" Martine mouthed.

"No!" I mouthed back, then motioned for her to help Simone with that tea.

Martine scooted off the bed to go downstairs. "I'll make breakfast."

Simone moaned again, taking a stretch, and I reached out for her, barely able to grasp her peignoir, thinking I only had a few morning minutes left with her before the Abwehr came. "What does it feel like?"

"The baby?" Her eyes lifted to mine over her shoulder.

"Yes, and being pregnant."

"Well..." She exhaled from her mouth. "At first it didn't feel like anything at all, but now it's different. I don't know how to explain it other than a heaviness—a load I must carry. I feel it in my feet and my back." She motioned with her hands over her belly. "And my entire insides feel connected and tight, but not all the time. It's been like this for two days." She sighed deeply as she felt her belly. "It was so strange how I managed to hide it for so long, then once I told you and Martine it feels as if the baby just popped out, and my body is making up for the lost time. How am I going to look at the end of June when I'm due? I don't know if I can last that long feeling like this."

"You don't have much of a choice, do you?"

She tucked a lock of hair behind her ear, smiling. "I suppose not. God help me if I have a girl like Martine," she said. "There's only room for one Martine in this family."

"Hell, in all of France!" I said, and she laughed.

She caught me staring at her belly, trying to imagine how a baby could fit inside all folded up, legs, arms, fingers, and toes, and whether she was having a boy or a girl.

"Do you want to feel it?"

She placed my hand onto the chilly folds of her silky peignoir. I waited and waited, and then was rewarded with a thump—a fine kick, and then two. I looked up, gasping. "Did you feel that?" I asked.

"I feel it every time," she said. "Must be a boy."

"A boy," I breathed.

"Christian will be elated," she said. "Though he'll be elated with a girl, too."

I glanced up with my hand still pressed to her belly. Hearing her say his name like that made it sound like she'd talked to him, which surprised me. "Has he made contact with you since…"

"No." She took my hand off her belly to place it on my lap. She knew what I was implying. "But he will. Christian's an honorable man. We've talked about living in the country near Chartres, his family's ancestral estate. You'll see. My child will grow up riding horses and picking wildflowers…"

Her faith in his return was unbreakable. I admired her for it, but in this instance, I pitied her. "I hope this for you," I said because I knew she needed to hear it, but I felt deeply that he was never coming back.

"Come here." She motioned to her trousseau chest. Inside were the linens and dishes she'd been saving, but she'd added nothing to help with the baby. She was prepared in the way a child was prepared for friends to come over. A few clean dresses but nothing practical, and no plan for when the baby comes. I touched the dishes, and felt the linen.

"Simone, what are we going to do about this baby?" I asked. "Who will deliver it?"

"You always need a plan, Gaby," she said, "but even the best-laid plans change. Everything will work out. We have weeks before we need to think of delivery and labor. Don't worry. I have hope it will all work out."

"We need more than hope for the delivery, Simone." I closed the lid on her chest. "We need to look for someone," I said. "No French midwife will help us now, not as long as there's a rumor the baby is German."

She placed a hand on my shoulder. "Trust me."

No matter what she said to try and convince me otherwise, I knew a plan was what we needed, and hanging her hopes on a phantom of a man wouldn't serve any of us.

"But what if I'm not here?" I asked. "What if..." I turned toward the wall, trying to find the right words to tell her about last night, because I thought that if she wouldn't prepare for the birth, at least she could prepare for my arrest. I turned around to find her looking strangely at me, and if ever I had the courage to tell her, it was then.

"Simone, I—"

"Tea is ready!" Martine shouted up the stairs. "Hurry before I eat all the toast."

I smiled. "After you," I said, motioning to the door, and we walked downstairs where Simone took a heavy seat at the table.

Martine was finishing up the toast, sprinkling tarragon over the thin layer of lard, when Simone brought Christian up, only instead of trying to convince us that he was going to call on her, she talked about their future again.

Martine turned around, apron a muss and a teapot in her hand. "Tea?"

Simone stopped talking mid-word.

I held my cup out and Martine poured, eyes shifting to me, first ignoring the awkwardness that had fallen between us, but then increasing it by asking about a birthing plan.

"I already asked her," I said.

Martine set the teapot down and took a seat. "Well, what is it?"

"We have weeks left to think of that," Simone said. "Don't worry. Everything will work out. Besides, since when have you asked for a plan?"

"I think plans are good," Martine said.

Simone laughed into her cup, which drew a sharp look from Martine.

"Are you saying you're becoming more like me?" I asked.

Martine shifted her shoulders. "Well, to tell you the truth, I think you're becoming more like me, Gaby." I sat up. "It's true." She turned to Simone. "And when it comes to birthing a baby and how we're going to do it, yes. I think plans are good."

Simone sighed.

"Let's enjoy the breakfast," Martine said, giving me a look, and I nodded once with a glance to the clock, wondering what time they'd come—what hour it would be when the Abwehr burst through our door.

The pipes rumbled and growled from Walter turning on his tap behind our shared wall.

Martine kicked my foot under the table, stressing with her eyes to tell Simone about last night, but I'd already decided she didn't need to know after trying upstairs. I could hear Walter's clip-clopping footsteps, then the plunk of his ear against the wall, right behind our collage. Martine kicked again, and I fanned from my neck from a flash of heat.

"It's warm in here," I said.

"It's not warm," Martine said.

"I'm warm!" Simone said, fanning herself, but I was sure that had to do with the baby inside her belly.

Walter walked away only to clip-clop back to the wall, followed by another plunk of his ear. I took a sip of my tea, closing my eyes, but now my heart was thumping because I thought he knew the Abwehr were on their way that very moment.

"Shh!" Simone said, looking toward the shared wall. "I think he's trying to listen to us."

I stood, my chair screeching across the kitchen floor.

"Tell her," Martine said, but I said I wouldn't. "Then I will."

Simone set her cup down. "Tell me what?"

My hands twisted. I was embarrassed and felt responsible since I had befriended Walter to begin with. It was my fault. Had I not talked to him, then maybe he wouldn't have known my skill as a pianist and read my name hidden in my work.

"Tell her, Gaby," Martine said.

"Give me a second," I hissed.

A rattling lorry drove up our road. Simone stood, followed by Martine. We each searched for the other's hands. Doors slammed closed and feet trampled up the walk.

"Three," I whispered, followed by Simone who thought there were four.

"Five," Martine said.

Five. That was it, and I was about to be arrested. I couldn't let them hurt Martine or Simone, so I broke away to stand near the door. Make it easy for the Abwehr to arrest me and spare my sisters, only I rushed back, throwing my arms around them and hugging tightly one last time.

"I'm not scared," I said, though I was trembling throughout my body. I inhaled to remember the Chantilly scent of Simone's hair, and the feel of Martine's bushy mane against my hand as I petted the back of her head. "Don't worry about me. Don't dwell on it."

"What is it, Gaby?" Simone was visibly concerned, but I

hadn't the breath to explain, and dashed to the door for good this time, waiting for it to burst open, but the only thing that burst was Martine's tears from her eyes.

Simone asked her over and over again what was happening, while I waited for our door to be kicked in, only it was Walter's. A shudder ran through the wall that separated us, followed by a trampling of jackboots thumping down Walter's hallway. Shouts and a scuffle played out in his main salon.

"It's the commandant," Martine rasped, and I told her to be quiet, don't move. The German words were muffled—I could only make out a few of them, until I heard the commandant speak, his voice cutting and direct, making everything crystal clear.

"Captain Walter Weber," the commandant announced. "You shall be stripped of your title and your position and charged with treason. What do you have to say for yourself?"

"It was beautiful, wasn't it?" was all Walter said.

I threw open the front door, watching in horror as they dragged Walter to the front of the house and to the lorry puttering in the road, watched by many who had come outside to see the spectacle. His head swung up to look at me just before they threw him in the back, and I expected him to reveal what he knew, shout out that it was me who'd written The Heroines, but instead, he gave me a parting smile.

I gasped, closing the door and throwing my body up against it. I couldn't breathe. I couldn't think. "He's…" I clawed at my face, eyes darting toward the window where I heard the lorry's rattling engine shift into gear. "He's…"

"Gaby…" Simone said, but my mind was spinning, and I felt sick. Martine took me by the shoulders.

"He's taking the blame?" Martine asked, and I nodded because it had to be true. "But why would he do that? He doesn't even know us."

I held my chest where it hurt. "He knows *me*. We've had a secret friendship for weeks. I didn't want you to know. He's different. He's not one of them. Clearly, because he knows I wrote that music." All those conversations we had about his wife came flooding back. He missed her, wanted to be with her. Of course, that was it. "He's taking the blame so he can be with his deceased wife once they execute him." And there was a part of him that did it for me, too, I thought. *"Mon Dieu…"*

"Gaby…" Simone called out, but Martine and I were still trying to make sense of what had happened, too frantic to pay attention.

"What if he tells them in prison?" Martine asked, tossing up the curtain and taking a peek outside, up and down the road.

"He already accepted the charge in Aunt Blanche's apartment," I said.

Martine latched onto me for a thankful embrace, but I wanted to cry.

"Gaby!" Simone shouted this time, and both Martine and I broke away to look, seeing her standing in a puddle of water that trickled down her leg.

"The baby's coming."

My hands flew to my mouth. Martine and I looked at each other for what to do. "Help!" Simone said, and we ran to her, each taking an arm. Martine tried to set her on the divan, while I tried to get her upstairs. She moaned at each option.

"Then where?" I asked.

She panted a bit before finally agreeing to go upstairs,

giving an exhausted nod when I pointed, which I was glad about if only because I thought that was where babies should be birthed, in a bedroom, and not a salon or on the piano, or in the kitchen for that matter.

We laid her in her bed, then both Martine and I took a step back. "Now what?" I asked Martine.

"Don't look at me!" she said.

Simone moaned again, shaking her head from side to side.

"*Merde*! This is why we needed a plan! You said the baby was coming at the end of June!" Martine said, but then I yelled at Martine for yelling at Simone. My head pounded, and I felt bad for showing Simone how worried and hysterical I'd become.

"Get someone," Simone said, gripping her sheets. "Madame Roche. She'll know what to do. Who to call."

I ran downstairs and out the door for Madame's lock shop just as Simone's laborious moan echoed from her bedroom window and curled down the road with a tumble of tree blossoms. Everything was happening so fast. I still hadn't reconciled what had just transpired with the captain, and my heart felt like it was about to explode.

I arrived at the lock shop out of breath and panting, but relieved to find Madame Roche inside after thinking she hadn't come in because the curtains were drawn. I lumbered through her store after closing the door, the bells clinging and clanging, when I heard her shout at me from behind the counter, someplace unseen.

"Madame Roche!" I called, and she emerged from behind a beaded curtain where she'd been painting in secret, a streak of blue paint in her hair. "What are you—" she started, before noticing my sweaty brow and my fraught face. "What is it?"

She took me by the shoulders, then held my hands where I was shaking the most.

"We need help," I said. "I wouldn't have come if it wasn't an emergency. Please, Madame. Please!"

My agitated state must have said it all because she didn't ask any questions and followed me home. I worried that if I told her Simone was in labor she wouldn't come, and if I could just get her in our home, in Simone's bedroom to hear her moan in pain, she'd have to help. She'd have to. But once she followed me upstairs and saw Simone panting with her legs up, she recoiled in fear.

"You're in labor?" She took a stumbling step back into the hallway.

"What do we do, Madame Roche?" Martine pleaded. "Help us, please!"

"How?" Madame questioned, hand fingering her collar, her eyes darting through the door at a laboring Simone. "I'm not a midwife!"

Madame was as old as Aunt Blanche would be if she was still alive. She had to know something about birthing babies, but the longer I absorbed her reaction the more painfully obvious it became that not only did Madame not know anything about birthing babies, she was also on the verge of running away.

Martine closed Simone's door so Madame couldn't hear, and I blocked the stairs so she couldn't escape. "You have to know someone," I said.

Madame bit her fingernails, mumbling to herself about every woman she thought would help. "I don't know anyone."

"You know everyone!" I said.

"Nobody who'd deliver a baby for girls like you," she said,

which felt like a gut punch. "Only…" Antoinette had come outside calling for her other hen, Eleanor. Her voice seemed to scrape against the glass. Even when she went back inside, the slam of her door could be felt way up in Simone's room. "You know who would know?"

"Who?" Martine crossed her arms, waiting for this mythical person we hadn't thought of, when Madame gestured toward Antoinette's house.

"Your neighbor."

Chapter Twenty-Three

Martine unfolded her arms, and for a second, I thought she was going to laugh. Madame Roche had to be joking, but the longer we stared at her unwavering face, the clearer it became that she was serious.

"No!" Martine shook her head. "Absolutely not."

"You can't spit on the pavement without Antoinette knowing about it or telling someone about it. If there's a midwife who will help you, she'll know who it is," Madame Roche said, and while Martine continued to shake her head, what she'd said actually started to make sense.

I took Martine by the shoulders. "She's right. Antoinette knows the good French and the bad, and she probably has over a hundred people who owe her favors."

Martine tapped her foot. Simone moaned. "Fine!" She pointed. "But you're coming with me, Gaby."

"Why do I have to come?"

"Because I don't trust myself with Antoinette alone, especially if she says no."

We rushed outside, but Martine's pace slowed tremendously once on the pavement, taking tiny mouse steps and guarded peeks at Antoinette's dark windows. "She's probably watching us right now."

"I'll take the blame for her chicken," I said.

"No," Martine said. "She'll never help us if we confess." Her eyes brightened. "The captain. That's who we'll blame. Say he's a traitor since the Abwehr took him away, and she might just believe."

I closed my eyes. "The captain," I said, feeling guilty and responsible, but she told me to forget about him because we needed to think about ourselves.

"All right?" she asked, and I nodded.

We walked up her front step and stood near her flower boxes where it smelled of jasmine. It felt strange to be at her house, a place I'd seen thousands of times but had never been so close to.

Martine rapped on the window, which sent a rattle through the neighborhood from knuckles on glass. Antoinette opened the door swiftly; she must have had her fingers curled around the knob and was waiting.

"Hallo." Her nose drew up and her mouth too.

I inhaled a lungful of air. "Good morning, Antoinette."

"Is it?" One eyebrow rose into her forehead.

We stood outside waiting for her to let us in, but she showed no signs of accommodating us. Neighbors watched unabashedly from their front steps and through their windows. I pulled my shoulders back.

"What do you want?" she asked.

I gulped, thinking the best way to ask was to blurt it out. "Simone's in labor and we don't have a midwife."

Antoinette looked horrified yet concerned. "She is?" She reached out to touch my hand, which shocked me enough to take a step backward.

"Can you get us a midwife?" I asked.

Antoinette grabbed her handbag then pushed past Martine on the front step and shut her door.

"Don't touch me," Martine said, hands flailing in the air.

"I'll meet you at your place," she said. Then she was gone, getting into her car and driving off into the village, leaving me and Martine dumbstruck and standing on her step.

"She didn't even bring up her chicken," Martine said.

"I'm confused also," I said, watching her drive away, "but if she's going to help us, I don't care." The neighbors were still watching, even more intently now that Antoinette had driven away. As we walked back, Martine told them to mind their own business.

"I mean it!" Martine warned, before slamming our door.

I tried my best to make Simone feel comfortable, but she looked miserable and was out of breath. "Antoinette's getting help." I held her hand.

"Antoinette?" Simone asked. "But she despises us and we ate Milly. How do you know for sure?"

Martine reached for Simone's other hand, giving it a squeeze. "If she doesn't bring help, if this is an act or some kind of cruel joke, that Boche will have more to cry about than a missing chicken in the morning."

Simone didn't mind Martine's threats this time, and nodded, almost as if it made things a little hopeful.

Madame Roche knew enough that we should get a bucket of warm water and clean rags ready, which we did. Then we waited. An hour passed, and I wondered if Martine would have to make good on her threat, with no sign of Antoinette. Sweat slicked Simone's hair and skin and she was moaning every five minutes, though sometimes it felt much closer to two.

"Christian," she called, near delirious. "Christian, where are you?"

Both Martine and Madame Roche sat in their chairs like twins, legs crossed and shaking their right foot.

"He's not here," I said, wiping a sticky lock of hair from her eyes.

"Send for him, Gaby. Send for him, please."

"How?" I took her hand again.

"I don't know…" She wept for her lover, which propelled Martine out of her chair.

"You have us," Martine said. "You don't need him. We're the ones that are here for you. Me and Gaby and Madame Roche, and even that bird-brain neighbor of ours if she's really bringing help. We're all you need." Martine folded her arms, but I grabbed her by the sleeve and dragged her into the corner.

"Stop," I hissed. "That's not helping."

"What else are we supposed to do? Let her keep talking about this invisible man? A man that left her a baby the village thinks is German? He should be ashamed of himself. He's never coming for her, but if I ever find him—if I ever see his face—he'll wish he'd never seen mine."

Simone had covered her eyes again and sobbed mercilessly. "Christian, I need you…"

Martine clenched her fists. "Hearing her call for him… It's unbearable. Her heart is breaking at the same time as she's giving birth." Martine's eyes welled with tears and before she could stop them, they fell effortlessly down her cheeks with one blink, and she had nowhere to hide or escape.

I reached for her and we embraced.

The sun had set, and with the dark rising, I started to face the inevitable situation that we'd have to birth the baby ourselves. I was about to announce that we were on our own, when a car drove up outside. We all looked toward the window, even Simone in a rare moment of lucidity.

Two car doors opened and then shut.

"Antoinette," I breathed, but before I could wonder who else it could be or how many, Martine bolted downstairs and threw open the door with me running up from behind. A stout woman with a black bag puffed inside.

"Where's the mother?" the woman asked, and we both pointed upstairs. Antoinette came in next, pulling her white gloves hastily from her fingers.

"We aren't too late?" Antoinette asked, nearly out of breath, and when I said no, she held her chest in relief. "Thank God!" She chased after the midwife upstairs.

Martine and I exchanged glances but didn't have time to ask questions and took Antoinette's good graces toward our sister with open arms. We stood in the doorway as Madame and Antoinette watched a laboring Simone, where the scent of Chantilly I so often smelled on her had been replaced with the warm scent of birth as she panted and huffed.

"Everyone out!" the midwife snapped as Simone spread her legs apart for her to take a look. "Only me and the mother."

"But—" I started to say.

"That's an order!" she barked before arguing with Antoinette about how it was her rules or no baby. Madame Roche ushered us both out into the hall. Antoinette followed, leaving only a stranger in Simone's bedroom with her, which didn't sit right with me. I reached for the knob after having second thoughts, but Antoinette caught me by the hand.

"Don't, Gaby," she said. "This midwife works in secret, and only by herself. She's serious, and will walk out if you don't obey her rules."

I recoiled to the wall with the others, waiting, listening. It crossed my mind that Antoinette had orchestrated the entire thing and that the midwife would kill Simone and maybe even the baby. But for what? Over a chicken? Simone cried out for Christian and I heard the midwife tell her to push. I reached for the knob again, only this time Antoinette threw her entire body in my way.

"Don't do it!" she said.

"I don't trust you," I said, and there was a standoff with Antoinette and her twitching eye.

"Tell her," Madame Roche said, but she wasn't talking to me, she was talking to Antoinette.

Antoinette's shoulders dropped, and I backed away, nearly stepping on Martine when I realized they had a secret. "Tell me what?"

"I'm in the resistance," she said. "Working as a secret agent for the British."

"What?" I held onto the wall and Martine did too.

"I've been watching you and your sisters for weeks, a request, a debt I owed someone important. It wasn't my choice. You and your sister..." She flicked her chin at Martine. "Haven't made it easy."

Martine's face looked like she'd fallen from a window, and I was sure mine didn't fare much better. So many thoughts ran through my head, trying to make sense of this information, but one question stood out among the rest.

"Who asked you to watch us?" I asked, then a baby wailed, and I busted open the door to see the midwife holding Simone's baby in her arms, which was coated in a white substance and streaky with blood.

Martine and I hugged. I didn't care who asked Antoinette, after seeing the baby, and neither did Martine.

"It's a boy!" the midwife said, clearing his nose. "He's early, but—" She laughed a robust laugh as he exercised his lungs. "He'll be just fine by the sound of these lungs."

Martine and I landed on our knees near Simone's bedside, holding her hands and telling her how beautiful he was. We were so caught up in the news that we didn't hear the door open in the main salon, but we did hear the rapid pound of footsteps coming up the stairs.

We stood up at the same time, guarding a helpless Simone with our lives, when Simone cried out with joy.

"Christian!"

He'd slid into the room, hands bracing the doorframe. "Out of the way," he said, pushing us to the side to cradle Simone in his arms. He had tears in his eyes when the midwife showed him his baby, a boy who was the perfect blend of both mother and father.

"How did you know to come?" Simone asked, and I don't think I could have been more shocked when Christian pointed to Antoinette.

"I asked my partner to watch over you," he said.

Martine and I stood back, flush against the wall, with our

mouths hanging open. It was so much to take in, but it was Christian's unmistakable affection for Simone that dominated the room. He coddled her, wiping her hair from her eyes and talking about all those plans Simone had mentioned—the country house with horses, a place for all three of them—it was all true!

"He came back for her," I breathed, and Martine nodded shakily, looking upon them as if it was the strangest sight—something she couldn't believe—a man of his word, a man who'd been taking care of her even from afar, and I saw it in Martine's eyes, she was thinking of Rémy and that promise he'd made her. "Martine," I said, reaching for her hand this time, but she covered her mouth and turned away in thought.

Christian stood to thank us for taking care of his two loves, but it was I who thanked everyone, starting with Madame Roche for staying with us, and then of course Antoinette, whom I thanked last over the midwife, mainly because I was embarrassed about how we'd treated her, and most importantly, that we'd eaten her chicken.

"I'm sorry for what we've done to you," I said. "I'm sure my sister Martine feels the same way." I looked for Martine, but she was nowhere around.

"Out there, Gaby!" Madame Roche pointed out the window where Martine was walking away from the house and up the road. "Where's she going?"

"Martine!" I called out the window, and she turned. It wasn't often Martine surprised me in a good way, and I smiled breathlessly before running downstairs, chasing after her.

We met in the middle of the road where I gave her a hug.

"I love him, Gaby. I'm not going to push him away anymore. I'm going to send for him, like he asked me to do.

He'll answer, won't he?" she asked, but deep down she knew the answer.

She pulled away to look at me.

"He will, Martine. He's always loved you."

"*Mon Dieu*, Gaby, I've wasted so much time rejecting him. Simone was right all along. Hope and love are the only things that matter."

She moved to leave and I pulled her back for one last embrace.

―――――――

I sat with Madame Roche and Antoinette at the kitchen table, while the midwife gave the new parents upstairs a basic education about how to take care of a baby.

"Madame, you knew about Antoinette?" I blinked.

"I didn't know until last night." She gave Antoinette a careful look before continuing. "I heard a noise in my shop and immediately reached for my gun hidden in my waistband. I know it's illegal but no German is going to come for me without getting a bullet in his chest first." She took a breath after getting a little heated with the thought of Germans breaking in. "Only it wasn't a German. It was Antoinette."

"I broke into her lock shop because I needed to know everything about a certain lock. Madame Roche was nice enough to let me plead for my life first, thankfully. And she believed me, but only after I proved it."

"How did you prove it?" I asked.

Antoinette raised her eyebrows. "I told her what I knew about you."

"Oh?" I sat up, and Antoinette took a sip of her tea.

"Firstly, I should tell you I'm the one who broke into your sewing shop. My intent wasn't to steal from you. I was protecting you. In my own way."

My mouth drew open for a second or two, but we probably should have suspected her from the beginning, especially when she was just our miserable neighbor.

"My entire persona as a bad Frenchwoman, a collaborator, was manufactured."

"The men?" I asked.

"Men I used for intelligence. Nothing more," she said. "Oh, I've done so many things. Befriended almost every dubious black-market seller in northern France, every double agent... I even befriended your employer."

"Commandant Streicher?"

"Speaking of him..." Antoinette leaned over the table and whispered even though we were the only ones there. "I need your help." She cleared her throat. "I need you to get me something in his file cabinet."

The words struck me like a lightning bolt, making my heart race. "File cabinet?" I asked, though it wasn't a question.

"You've seen it?" Antoinette asked.

I nodded. "In his study. There's a heavy lock on it."

"A Burg Stahlhart," Madame piped. "It's German. We know, and I can teach you how to pick it."

I stood up, my chair screeching across the floor, thinking about what it would be like sneaking into the commandant's study. Even if I was able to get into it, there was still one problem. "But we're out of pigeons."

"Did she taste good?" Antoinette asked, out of the blue. "Milly. You had a nice meal? My chickens were decoys for the pigeon I've been keeping," she said, and my jaw dropped. "I needed an excuse for the Germans to give me bird seed. I wasn't crying over a chicken. I was worried someone stole my pigeon. She was hiding as it turned out." She smiled at having outwitted the Germans, and of all the things Antoinette had told me, that was the most surprising. "So, you see, I have the tools to make this a success. If you'll help."

I covered my mouth, remembering that night Martine came home with the pigeon. Nobody saw her, just like she said; the Abwehr had the right house all along when they arrived at Antoinette's.

"Well?" Antoinette asked.

I took my seat again. "I don't want to get caught. I don't want to get arrested or end up dead."

"Don't think about the risks," Antoinette said. "If you don't think about it, you won't be nervous." She leaned over the table again. "Gaby, you should know what's at stake."

"The less she knows the better. For her protection," Madame countered, but Antoinette continued.

"There's an invasion planned. Germany knows the Allies are planning an attack, they've been preparing for it, they just don't know where it will be. Only there's a German spy embedded with the British who could tip them off. We think in the MI6."

"MI6? I've heard of this before. What is it?" I asked.

"The United Kingdom's Secret Intelligence Service," she said, and I closed my eyes, remembering what Lauren had overheard the morning of the bombing. That must be how the Abwehr knew about my music.

"The name of that spy is in Streicher's file cabinet," she

said, which seemed quite plausible; he didn't like me standing next to it when I first met him and didn't want his staff touching it either.

"Even with twenty-four hours' notice of the location, the war could tip in Germany's favor and we'd never recover. If we can flush the traitor out, perhaps, just perhaps, we can win this war."

"Do you have a plan?" I asked.

"Oh, it's a grand scheme!" Antoinette pulled a pack of cigarettes from her pocket and told me her plan as she smoked. She knew of a meeting the commandant had scheduled in a few days, away from his home. I'd be in the house with Lauren and the rest of the staff would also be away collecting their rations. I could slip into his study, find what Antoinette wanted, and slip back out without anyone knowing.

"Are you sure all of them are leaving for rations at the same time?"

"Only you, Lauren, and Danielle will be in the house," she said. "I have spies at the bakery, the butcher, and at the markets throughout the village. His staff have made special appointments to receive the best picks on that day."

I bit my lip. I had to talk to Martine and Simone before I could agree.

"Isn't there another way? There's a risk a pigeon won't make it across the sea, and for something so urgent…"

"I have reliable channels that can get the name to London, but there's a delay that could take days, or even weeks. A pigeon can deliver in a matter of hours."

"What about a transmitter?" Madame Roche asked.

"I lost my Paraset operator. Releasing a pigeon is our best

option, regardless of the risk. I have thought about this extensively."

We ended our chat after she told me how she'd been covering for us in secret after Christian reached out to her about Simone—she'd seen the pigeon I'd let go from my garden, and the first one Martine had let out of Simone's window. "I have a strong network of people—bad French and Germans—who believe me because I've built a reputation for turning in troublemakers. I'm a trusted traitor to them."

They both got up to leave. "Madame Roche will have to teach you how to pick the lock. You will let me know soon?"

I looked to the ceiling where I heard Simone and Christian upstairs talking about their plans to leave as soon as she was able.

I nodded.

Madame Roche left along with Antoinette and the midwife, leaving me to think about what they'd proposed. By the time Martine came home, I was nearly jumping out of my skin at the thought of doing it.

I rushed to the door, startling her. "Martine, you won't believe what—"

Her face was conflicted.

"What's wrong?" I worried something had happened to Rémy and my heart sank.

"The post can take more than a week, so I arranged a transport to the border. I wrote a note that his mother died, like he said to do. I have to trust that the Germans will grant him a funeral waiver like they give out in Poland—I have to try."

I put a hand to my chest, caught off guard by her news that she was leaving too. "But how will you pay? Transports are expensive."

She reached for the vase Rémy had gifted her. "He'll understand I had to sell it, and I simply can't wait. Will you be all right, if I go?"

I wanted her to go after Rémy, but I also didn't want her to leave, though I knew it was wrong for me to hold her back. I nodded.

She exhaled with relief. "Thank you, Gaby." Her eyes sparkled. "Now," she said, "what was it you were saying?"

"Oh…" I turned to wipe my eyes where they'd welled with tears. "It was nothing."

"Come on then," she said, "I want to see Simone and our new nephew before I go."

I followed her up the creaky old stairs into Simone's room where we held our nephew for the first time. That's when Simone officially broke the news of their plans. She and Christian were leaving in the middle of the night to a place where they would be safe from the villagers wanting revenge, thinking the baby was German, a place where they could spend some time together; they were just waiting for the car to arrive. This didn't surprise me as much as Martine's news.

"I wouldn't be leaving if the captain hadn't been arrested," Martine said. "You have nothing to worry about now, and I'll be back in a few days."

"Have hope, Gaby," Simone said. "Have hope."

Hope. There was that word again, the word she always used when faced with a test of the heart.

"Who knows, maybe you'll enjoy the quiet with us gone," Martine said.

I reached for their hands. In the days to come, I'd be learning how to pick a German lock, then I'd be sneaking into the commandant's file cabinet, without their help, knowledge, or blessing. And if I was caught, there wouldn't be a box left behind with my things, and the commandant would make sure my sisters never knew what happened to me.

A painful lump formed in my throat.

"Yes, that's it." I smiled. "I'll enjoy the quiet."

Chapter Twenty-Four

June

Madame Roche came over the morning of the meeting. Since my sisters had left, all I'd focused on was the lock—it was all that mattered, and I'd gone over it a hundred times and become quite good.

Pick-click-unlock. Pick-click-unlock.

She handed me a hairpin as we sat at the table. "Don't you want some eggs?" I asked, offering what eggs Antoinette had given me, but she shook her head.

"I haven't shared breakfast with someone since my husband died." She must have seen my face change hearing that familiar echo, because hers sank. "But don't feel sorry for me. I have my paintings to keep me company. I still look at them, reminders of what my life has been."

I swallowed dryly.

"You'll get used to it." She patted my hand.

"Used to what?"

"Being alone."

She motioned with her chin to keep on with the lock after I'd paused, and I picked again.

"That's right," she said, eyes lifting as I twisted the pin. "Be gentle…" She winced when I turned the pin sharply, as if I wasn't careful enough, but the lock clicked over. She sat back in her chair, letting out a noisy breath of air.

"I know how to do it," I said. "I've been practicing day and night."

"Yes, but I worry you are not doing it with enough finesse. All locks are different. Some are sticky. What if his lock is a sticky one? You must go slower. You've never picked a lock while under duress, have you?"

"Have you?" I asked.

She looked offended at first. "Well, a woman never tells," she said, then blurted, "Yes."

"I picked this lock a thousand times since you gave it to me to practice with. I've also thought about the file cabinet more times than I care to admit. I have finesse." I picked the lock successfully again.

"But if you find the lock not clicking over, if you find…"

I looked up, a little annoyed, but if I was caught, the Abwehr would seek out the lock shop first, and find who'd helped me. She had a right to be invested in my success.

"Blow into the mechanism. There might be dust in there."

"All right."

"Try the lock again." She flicked her fingers for me to continue, but there was a knock on my door.

"Hide the lock," Madame rasped, and I shoved it into my apron pocket, peeking through the curtains while Madame chewed her fingernails behind me. "It's Antoinette."

I answered the door, concerned. "What are you doing here?" I asked, looking over her shoulder to the neighbors.

"Fold your arms," she said, so I did. "And look angry."

I tapped my foot for the neighbors. "You don't have to worry," I said, assuming she felt the need to check up on me. "I have the picking down. Madame is even here to go through some last things."

"I have some distressing news. I just got word that the staff are leaving ahead of time."

"What?" I reached for my chest. That closed the gap between when the staff would be out of the house and the commandant too, giving me a limited window of opportunity if I hurried. "I'll be late if I don't leave now, and I'll have to run!"

I turned to Madame Roche, who walked up close enough to hear.

"They're leaving early!" I said, and Madame's eyes bulged.

"That gives you less time," Madame said. "You must hurry!" She pushed me to leave, and Antoinette put her hands up.

"Calm down," Antoinette snipped. "Your time has changed. Don't let it ruin your focus. I'll meet you here after the sun sets. And remember, it's the gold folder."

She'd told me the color many times. "I know." The neighbor across the road came out to water her flowers but they'd been dead since winter and now it was spring. "Now leave," I said. "People are watching." I pointed in the air as if I was throwing her off my front step. "Go!"

Once the door was closed, I ran about the house, slipping my shoes on and reaching for my handbag, telling Madame to let herself out through the back door. Then I was gone, run-walking up the road toward the commandant's house, looking at my watch and praying I'd make it in time. I arrived a little out of breath.

I brushed back my hair before knocking, but the door opened, before my knuckles met the wood, to a satin-draped Danielle with a yellowy drink gripped tightly in her hand.

"Madame Streicher."

She shook the ice in her glass. "Danielle," she corrected, breath reeking of booze. "I told you to call me Danielle." She motioned for me to enter and I walked in like I normally would, looking at the commandant's dark study first.

"The staff have appointments today." Danielle pointed upstairs with her glass. "Lauren's waiting." She turned on her heel for the kitchen, her satin robe trailing behind her like a pink wave.

I wanted to go into his study right then, but I had to see about Lauren first. If I didn't, she'd come looking for me. I felt the hairpin in my hair, just above my ear. "Teacher! Teacher!" Lauren appeared at the top of the staircase, jumping up and down.

I went upstairs. "How are you?" I swept the hair from her eyes, and she smiled.

"The staff are gone. Would you like me to play something complicated for you?"

I nodded, keeping my smile, though that meant more time wasted since I'd have to listen to her. Lauren sat at her piano, stretching her hands out and giving her fingers a good crack before placing her palms over the keys. "You'll love this one."

While she played, I stood by the window, nervously watching passersby and the road, looking for the commandant and any sign of the staff walking back from the village center.

Lauren stopped abruptly, turning around on her bench. "Do you love it?" She beamed, and I didn't have the heart to tell her I hadn't listened, even though I had heard.

"Yes," I said. A door closed in the hallway, and Lauren's eyes darted toward the noise, which must have been Danielle.

"I saw your mother at the performance the other night," I said. "She was proud."

Lauren spun back around and placed her hands on the keys. "Mmm." Her fingers plunked along, another piece she'd written and fairly complicated. "Did you hear about the captain?" she asked, and I put my hands on hers to stop playing.

I wondered what exactly she knew. "Have you?" I asked.

"I overheard the commandant on the phone. Is it true that he was arrested?"

"Yes."

She nodded, staring at her still hands, and I realized she was sad about his arrest. He was a professional who had encouraged her. And even if she didn't know him very well, she was aware of his reputation and he was the most famous pianist she'd known.

"I liked him too," I said. "Even if he was a German. It is important to acknowledge the kind ones."

She smiled; I had let her know it was all right to like him, and to be sad.

I caught a glimpse of the clock hanging near her doll shelves, and my heart beat a little faster with the passing of time, more time than I expected. "I'll go get us some tea since your mistress is away. Play while I'm gone."

"Bring me a biscuit," she said.

I nodded while slipping out, then paused in the hallway.

Danielle's bedroom door was closed, and the house was quiet except for the muffled sound of Lauren's playing.

I raced quietly down the stairs and ducked into the commandant's study, instantly smelling his past visitors' brandy and cigar smoke emanating from the fabric walls. I pulled the pin from my hair, and it was then my heart took on another tone, one of thrashing and wailing in my ears with the thought I was really doing it.

I began to pick, moving the pin just like I'd done in my kitchen a hundred times and expecting it to click over, but this lock wouldn't budge. Sweat beaded on my neck and forehead. My head pounded.

I moved to blow into the mechanism as Madame had advised when I heard voices outside—Irma and the cook, smoking just outside the study's window. I pushed my lips flush to the metal, blowing away the dust. *Whew, whew, whew.*

"I don't trust that piano teacher," I heard the cook say, followed by Irma, who said I was a whore for asking her to leave my house.

I jammed the pin into the lock.

Click! The relief I felt was only slight until I'd gotten out of that study. I flipped through the file folders, pulling the one piece of paper from the gold folder, before closing it back up and leaving as I had entered, slipping through the study's double French doors back into the hallway, and tiptoeing toward the stairs.

I did it. I really—

The paper slipped from my hands. Danielle was watching me from the stairs, looking sharply down at me with hooded eyes.

"Danielle!"

My mouth hung open, not sure what else to say because I was speechless. The women were at the door, unlocking the bolt. I tried snatching the paper from the floor but Danielle got to it first just as the front door opened and Irma walked in with the cook.

They chatted and giggled about their bundle of rations and the extra pack of cigarettes they'd received from the black ribbon merchants while my heart was on the verge of exploding, thumping and thumping as Danielle stared at me. I waited to see what she was going to do.

Then the most incredible thing happened. She moved her arm nonchalantly behind her body, hiding the paper in the folds of her pink peignoir.

"Good morning," they said to her.

Danielle reprimanded them for smoking, reminding them that the commandant didn't approve of his staff smoking while at work. "Finish those in your rooms."

They apologized, but it was Irma whose evil little eye flicked once in my direction while I held my chest, as if I had something to do with them getting caught.

Danielle handed me the paper once the pair were out of sight, which I swiftly folded and stuffed down my brassiere.

"This isn't the first time you've helped me. Why?" I asked.

"Don't you know?" she asked. "But why are you doing this, Gaby? You must know he could have you arrested and hanged."

It was the one question I hadn't been asked by Madame, or Antoinette after I'd agreed. It would be easy to say it was because I was a patriot and that I hated the Germans, but all the good French hated the Boche. "The Reich destroyed my dreams. I have one page of sheet music left to my name and it's not to be wasted—not if it can help."

Her eyes narrowed as if she didn't quite understand, and that was all right. She didn't have to.

She sent me upstairs to see Lauren as Irma's laugh carried down the hallway. I found Lauren holding a doll she'd pulled from her shelf, examining the stolen gold coin she'd hidden under its dress.

"Teacher!" She ran over carrying her doll, eyeing my hands where I should have been carrying a tray of biscuits. I didn't expect the gush of tears to spill over my cheeks when she approached, wide-eyed and listening. She'd read me. She'd always been able to read me, just like Martine, even though we'd known each other only a short time.

"You're leaving, aren't you?"

"Yes," I said, wiping my eyes. "Promise me something," I said, and she nodded. "There will be a time when you'll have to run away—away from this house, the Germans, and the war. Take every piece of gold you've stashed away and flee with your mother. Insist on it." She shook her head when I mentioned her mother. "Lauren, listen to me."

I looked into her eyes, wondering if she would understand the message I was about to tell her at only nine years old. Her mother wouldn't want me to tell her. But she had a right to know, and I feared I'd never see her again. I wanted her to know she had someone. She'd always had her.

"Children in this village, they aren't fed like you are. Their bones are brittle and breaking and most are orphaned, or will be someday with their parents displaced, arrested, or sent to a factory. Mothers make difficult decisions. Your mother did what she had to do to keep you alive."

A tear snuck down her cheek, and I thought she did understand. The door opened, sending a cool whoosh of air into the room. Danielle stood in the doorway, twisting her hands and looking a little angry as if she knew what I'd done, but then turned complacent. "Lauren?"

Lauren hesitated.

"Would I lie to you?" I asked, and with that, her face changed and she shook her head. I smoothed her hair away from her eyes. "Remember when I said I'd keep your secret about knowing how to play the piano? Now, it is you that must keep a secret about your mother."

I gave her a pat and she bolted to the door for Danielle, who suddenly seemed relieved her secret was out, kissing her daughter over and over, telling her not to tell anyone.

Danielle waved me forward while holding onto Lauren. "Out the back," she whispered. "You should be safe that way while Irma and the cook are in their rooms."

Lauren reached for me with grabby hands, moaning the way a child does when their teddy is taken. "Is this goodbye forever?" she asked, though she was smart enough to know it just might be.

"Look for me in your music," I said. "I'll always be there." I smoothed her hair back and kissed her cheek goodbye before she buried her face in the folds of Danielle's satiny peignoir.

I padded down the stairs and out the service entrance as Irma and the cook finished their cigarettes. My heart broke in two once I'd made it outside, but not because I felt sorry for Lauren. I felt sorry for myself—I was going to miss her.

"Be safe," I whispered, before dashing away.

Chapter Twenty-Five

London

W hat was supposed to be a short holiday away from the Columba program lasted several days, with Guy ringing up Rex Smith's office every morning, asking when he could return to work. Then at the beginning of June, Guy got his answer. Smith sent a formal message to Guy's flat requesting his appearance at the War Office the following morning.

He'd waited for this day, and he thought he'd feel relieved, get back to his paperwork, and monitor Gaby's safety from afar, but then it crossed his mind that something terrible must had happened for him to be allowed back to work after so many days of stonewalling.

At first, he was angry, but then he felt something else. Something he'd felt stirring in his heart for so long, yet it was only just now that he allowed himself to believe. He had feelings for Gabriella Cotillard; in fact, he'd had feelings for her since he first heard her music—there was no other way to explain it—and now, in the eleventh hour, it might be too late.

Guy needed to talk to his sister. He needed her advice. He also needed the professor's advice, since the two had become close friends since he first arrived at her studio, and especially since she'd been staying with Madge.

Guy took his work summons with him downstairs where they were having breakfast. Madge only knew that the professor was from France and that she needed their protection, which was enough for her at the time. But now, Guy needed to talk to her about Gaby, and that meant telling Madge more than she probably should know, or what was legal for him to tell her.

Guy paced the carpets while Madge and the professor drank their morning tea. "Smith said I could come back."

"That's great news," Madge said, but Guy shook his head.

"It sounds like it, yes. But I have a terrible feeling, and now I don't know what to do."

"What do you mean, you don't know what to do?" she asked. "You wanted to go back to work and now you've got your wish."

"No, sis. You don't understand. There's something I never told you."

He paced the carpets again with his hands rubbing the back of his neck, searching for the right words to explain how he felt about a woman he'd never met. "She's all I think about. And now… Now it might be too late."

"Who?" Madge stood up.

"Are you talking about Gaby?" the professor asked.

"Who's Gaby?" Madge put her hands on her hips when the

professor and Guy looked at each other. "Somebody better tell me what is going on."

Guy's hands twisted. "Is it possible to have feelings for someone you don't know?"

Now it was Professor Caron who'd stood. "You know her, Mr. Burton, through her music. I know you feel it in here." She tapped her heart. "You can't tell me you don't."

"Will someone please tell me—"

"Sis, you better have a seat."

Madge sat back down, folding her hands in her lap. "I'm waiting."

Guy exhaled through his mouth because he wasn't sure where to start. "You know Professor Caron needed a place to stay, but what you don't know is why," he said, then proceeded to tell Madge more than he would ever tell a civilian—he talked about the messages, the secrets, and the lies coming from the brass, but what he spent the most time talking about was Gaby's music and how it made him feel. "I think about her day and night, only now…" He showed her the crumpled message Smith sent him. "With this notice to promptly return to work, I think Gaby and her sisters are on the brink of being caught, or maybe they were already."

The professor's hand went to her chest, while Madge's mouth hung open.

"Guy Michael Burton," Madge said. Only his mum called him by his full name when she was alive, and only when he was in trouble, which got him to tense up. "Is this why you finally took off your wedding band? Don't think I didn't notice…"

"Madge, did you hear what I said?"

321

She talked to herself in mumbles, before looking up and scolding him once more.

"Sis…"

Madge crossed her chest, talking to Jennie like a spirit watching over her brother. "Help them find each other," she said.

A knock sounded from Guy's front door, and all three of them looked toward the ceiling.

"Who's that?" Madge whispered.

"I don't know." Guy peeked out the window to see if Smith's car was parked outside. There was another knock, but much more forceful. "I'm going upstairs to find out."

"What if it's that beastly man who threatened me?" Professor Caron asked, hand to her mouth.

Madge grabbed the mallet from her kitchen drawer and thrust it into his hands. "Be careful!"

Guy snuck out his sister's front door and around the side to his private staircase, creeping up the stairs as the knocking continued, but it was hard to see with a shadow casting over them in the dim stairwell. He raised the mallet once he saw the hem of a woman's trench coat, stepping closer, and closer, then the person turned around and screamed.

"Daisy?"

"Guy!" Daisy grappled for the handrail, taking a few frantic breaths. "Why'd you have to do that? You're always nearly giving me a heart attack!" she said, but that didn't explain why she was at his front door.

Guy had dropped the mallet. "What are you doing here?"

"Well…" She reached into her coat pocket, pulling out an envelope. "You never came back with those papers you promised, lucky for you Smith hasn't asked for them, but I noticed and I had to wonder why you'd keep them. What nobody knows below the ground floor is that I'm not just a secretary. I'm an MI6 agent too, with agents of my own in occupied countries. I've always known you to be a good agent, Guy, a sound person at heart. Someone to trust." She shoved the envelope at him. "I think there's something you should know."

Guy took the envelope.

"There's a German spy among our ranks—someone we believe is intent on compromising the location of the invasion."

"What does that have to do with me?"

"Our agent in northern France... Your Heroines were her decoys, only now they've teamed up to infiltrate the Abwehr and unmask the name of the spy together. Though I'm afraid the situation is dire. We have reason to believe the spy has passed on information to the Germans regarding at least one of their identities, and we don't know who will come out of this alive."

Guy's knees buckled. He was right. They were on the brink of being caught.

"Maybe we should go inside so you can sit?"

He agreed, and after unlocking his door, he immediately took a seat at his table, but Daisy remained standing with her trench coat buttoned and gloves still on.

"Why are you telling me this?" he asked.

"You don't know?" she asked. "Smith thought you had gotten too close to the pigeon service, too protective, but the man can't see the forest for the trees. I've read the reports and if you think I can't hear everything that's talked about in Smith's office, then you don't understand what kind of power a secretary has. I'm at work late too, Guy. I knew it wasn't just the program because I've also become close to my agents. It was your Heroines—or heroine, to be more precise. It's Gabriella Cotillard, isn't it?"

He imagined Madge and the professor listening with their eyes to the ceiling and nodding. Guy motioned to the envelope. "What's in here?"

"Call me a romantic, but if your heroine survives, I thought you'd want to meet her. It's a close enough address to where she lives. My job is changing now, and I don't expect to see you again. I wanted you to have it." She turned for the door. "If only we could hop on a boat or a plane and cross the sea and save them all."

Plane?

Guy's heart pounded.

It appeared Daisy had no idea what she'd sparked with her last words before she left because she never turned back around.

He threw open the curtains and looked off to the horizon over all those smokestacks and then to the sky. He knew where Gaby lived now, beyond the generality of Boulogne-sur-Mer, and he was familiar with the cliffs and the topography near the sea. As a pigeon flies it wouldn't take him very long to land and find her, then get back in the sky before the Germans spotted him, not with the details he knew from his endless research. He closed his eyes; he knew exactly what to do now.

He rang up the Air Ministry because there was only one place he knew he could catch a clandestine flight to Boulogne-sur-Mer.

"Yeah, Newmarket," a voice answered.

"This is Guy Burton from the office of Rex Smith. I've been authorized to put a flight in the diary." The clerk at the airfield questioned him, but it was hard to hear because the connection was bad and his voice was crackling. "On my way now. Have a flight ready!" he added, before replacing the receiver.

Guy reached for his messenger bag and book where he kept Gaby's music, taking one last look at her photo before stuffing it all inside. He'd lied to the Air Ministry, and it was only a matter of time before they figured out this flight hadn't been authorized. He had to hurry.

He rushed down the stairs where Madge had come out of her front door. "Love you, sis," he said, giving her a quick peck on the cheek.

"Where are you off to?" she asked, hands on her hips. "Will you be back for dinner?"

"I wouldn't count on it!" was all he said.

Guy drove to Newmarket, but it wasn't an easy drive or a short one with bottlenecked roads getting out of the city and finding just enough petrol to coast into the parking lot. He parked his car outside the hangar, thinking it looked mighty quiet for a busy RAF airfield with plenty of planes but none in the air.

He threw his bag over his shoulder and went inside the hangar, announcing who he was at the front desk to a man who looked like a mechanic with greasy overalls and a wrench in his pocket.

"Where is everyone?" Guy asked, remarking about the grounded planes and the lack of pilots.

"I tried to tell you on the phone," the mechanic said. "There's only one here at the moment." He hiked his thumb in a general area. "Bob Watson. But I don't think—"

Guy left for the tarmac as the mechanic talked, walking up to Bob Watson, who was the only man in sight, and, thank

God, had a flight suit on. He was attending to his RAF Whitley just as he ordered.

"I'm Guy Burton. I called about the emergency flight."

Bob stepped off his small ladder, sticking a cigarette in his mouth. "No flight today."

"I called, ordered one for the diary," Guy said.

Bob pulled a metal lighter from his pocket to light a cigarette. "I don't care what you ordered. I'm not putting wings in the air," he said, pointing at Guy who was wincing. "What did you say your name was?"

"Guy Burton. I'm from the War Office."

"I know you!" he said, a little accusatory, then looking deadly serious. "You're that pigeon fellow—yeah, I know who you are. I almost got shot down last time transporting those stupid birds for you over France. My crew too. Look!" He pulled his cigarette from his lips to point at the bullet holes along his fuselage.

Guy adjusted his messenger bag, unsure how to respond because Bob was clearly angry and he was also his only option. "I have orders." Guy reached into his bag and pulled out a sheet of Gaby's music, flapping it in the air as if it were his orders, then showing Bob the map on the other side, hoping he wouldn't become suspicious of the small writing, but would focus on the drawing.

"These are the emplacements. This is where you were shot at, most likely. Can you avoid it, land over here?" Guy pointed to a blank area he knew was flat and hidden from the Germans, according to the drawing and his extensive research, which he had no reason to doubt. "Here, take it." He pushed the map at Bob, hoping he'd take a closer look, but he refused.

"I don't care what you got." Bob walked away with his cockpit hatch in the belly of the plane hanging open.

Guy chased after him, pleading with him to just look at the map. When Bob did turn around, Guy thought it was merely out of annoyance because he was following him.

"Look," Bob said, taking his cigarette from his mouth for the second time and pointing at his plane. "I couldn't take you up even if I wanted to. There's a no-fly order, just got passed down."

"For the entire Air Ministry? But why?"

"I don't ask questions, but my guess is the invasion is coming real soon. The only question is where." He walked off, leaving Guy on the tarmac.

"The invasion," he said to himself. Goddamn. He looked back up at Bob's plane with its hatch hanging open. It appeared to be completely fueled, with a ready-stand-by tag on the wheel.

His heart pounded in his chest. Guy hadn't flown since before the war, since before he and Jennie got married and he joined MI6. But flying a RAF Whitley was like riding a bike, he had always thought. He swore he heard Jennie's voice in his ear, urging him to do it. Take the chance.

Bob stopped short of the hangar, and Guy looked back up at the plane.

"Hey!" Bob yelled, and Guy took a step backward, then another, before turning and bolting for the aircraft, but Bob had caught up to him and tackled him on the tarmac a foot from the plane.

"Get off me! My agent's in jeopardy!"

Bob stood up, breathing heavily and swiping back his hair after struggling with Guy. "Well, you certainly can't steal a

RAF plane." He tugged his ruffled flight suit back into place, then waved the mechanic over and told Guy he'd have some answering to do with the brass if he didn't watch himself.

"You don't understand," Guy said. "I have to get to Boulogne-sur-Mer."

"You can't get into France today." Bob and the mechanic had escorted Guy into the hangar and thrown him into a chair. "You can only escape." Bob shouted to another pilot who looked worse for wear with a tattered flight suit, "This bloke thinks he can fly into France. What do you say about that?"

"Good luck!" The pilot rubbed the back of his neck. "I barely got out of there alive after dropping a team of six last night, German fortifications all up and down the northern coast of France hurling artillery at anything that flies."

"Team of six?" Guy questioned, and it was as if a light had turned on inside Guy's brain. If the Secret Intelligence Service was still parachuting agents into northern France to work with the resistance, the brass would have an escape route planned, a clandestine transport to safety. They'd make sure of it. He only needed the code word for the meeting point, then maybe he could send a message over Radio Londres to Gaby.

Bob and the pilot started walking away.

"Can I use your telephone?" Guy asked.

Bob looked over. "Find your own phone."

"It's for official war business," he said, trying to get them to understand, but everyone was on official war business. "A woman's life depends on it!"

"A woman?" Bob asked with a laugh, then swatted the air. "Now it all makes sense."

"No," Guy said, but Bob and the other pilot were all laughs

as they joked and smoked their way out of the hangar. "You don't understand!"

Guy groaned, thinking how long it would take to find Rex at the War Office, then drive to the BBC radio room and find Bertie for the broadcast. But he also needed petrol since he'd basically coasted into Newmarket on fumes.

"A woman, huh?" the mechanic piped up.

"Yeah," Guy said, because he wasn't going to engage after the way Bob and the pilot had reacted, but then the mechanic pulled out a telephone from under the desk.

"Just make it quick, all right?"

Guy raced to the phone after thanking him and rang up his supervisor at the War Office. Smith answered on the first ring.

"This is Guy Burton, sir."

"You're still on holiday," Smith said.

Guy closed his eyes. He didn't want to spend precious time arguing about if he should be working or not.

"Sir, would Daisy's agent know the escape code?" he asked, meaning, was Daisy's agent briefed on the code word, and would she understand where to go if ordered to flee?

But what followed was a lingering silence, and Guy wasn't sure if that was a good sign or a bad sign. Smith was probably trying to figure out how Guy knew about Daisy's job as an agent in the first place.

"Why do you want to know?" Smith finally answered.

"Because, sir. There's a way to save my agents. I know they've been compromised—"

"Shh," he said. "Not over the telephone!"

"You know they don't have to be expendable now," Guy said, trusting that Smith understood this since the invasion was about to commence; he certainly wasn't going to blurt that over the phone because he'd said enough already. "Sir…"

"What do you plan to do with it?" Smith asked.

Guy felt a twinge of relief; Smith was entertaining the idea of telling him the code.

"Bertie, sir," he said, knowing Smith would understand he meant Bertie at Radio Londres. "That's what I plan to do with it."

"You're too late, Guy. Don't you know the time?" he asked, and Guy looked at the clock. It was indeed past time to make the broadcast for tonight.

"He owes me a favor," Guy said. "He's done it once already. He'll do it again. The code, sir, will you tell me?"

There was an even longer pause than before. A car drove up to the hangar and parked next to Guy's. He watched carefully as the driver got out, brought his keys inside and placed them in a basket near the front counter, telling the mechanic that he'd be back in an hour to drive back to London.

Guy turned, hiding his conversation from the mechanic and anyone else who could hear, yet eyeing those keys in the basket. "Sir, are you still there? Sir—"

"I'll meet you at Bertie's," Smith said, and Guy nearly jumped for joy.

"Thank you, sir, thank you! I'm leaving now."

"Where are you?" Smith asked.

"I'm at the airfield in Newmarket. Long story, I'll tell you when I see you," he said, slamming down the receiver.

Guy nicked the keys from the basket.

Now, he just had to hurry.

Chapter Twenty-Six

I raced home from Lauren's house and unfolded the paper where nobody could see. It was a memo sent from Berlin to the commandant with the spy's real name and where he worked.

"Clive Cox," I said out loud because it was the most ridiculous name I'd ever heard. "You dirty bastard."

I pulled my last sheet of music from the bureau and wrote out the message. Then I waited, and hours passed. It was nighttime before Antoinette knocked on my back door, and by then I was agitated and restless from having such important information in my possession.

"Where have you been?"

A storm had rolled in with the night, blowing her hair straight up on end as she stood on my back step.

"I thought I was followed." Antoinette walked in with the bird between her hands. "I had to take the long way home." She unfastened the capsule from the pigeon's leg, and I reached down my dress for the message. A lorry drove by, rumbling the windowpanes, but it was going too fast to stop and didn't worry me.

The bird tried to flap away in the dark as she held him. "Light a candle," she hissed.

"No," I hissed back, "someone will see." I tucked the note into the messenger capsule when another lorry drove down my road, only this one made my bones shake—a heavy lorry, one with two people inside, maybe even three. *Four*, I thought when the lorry lurched to a stop outside.

I felt the color drain from my face.

Doors opened and closed, and I stole a peek out the window. "They're at your house!"

"Antoinette Gagnon!" they announced, a second before the Abwehr broke down her front door.

"Out the back!" she said.

I tucked the bird under my arm and ran out the back, but was met by a gust of wind that nearly blew me away, cracking the tree limbs above us and blowing spring blossoms over the garden like snow in the night. I tossed the bird up with a heave, but instead of flying away, he landed heavily on the ground and made a run for the fence. I caught him by the wing.

"Get down!" Torches shone through Antoinette's windows onto her garden, scanning her coop. The wind howled. "What are we going to do?"

"I don't know!"

The Abwehr's torches retreated back into her house, and then back outside toward their lorry. "Fly!" I said, chucking the bird into space, but he again landed a few feet away on the ground and ran for the fence.

"Why isn't he flying away?" I cried.

"He must think this is his home."

I heard the lorry drive off through the roar of the wind, giving us more time to come up with a plan. "They're gone," I said, but then a new set of headlamps shone softly on the side of Antoinette's house, which meant they were parking in front of mine.

"Oh no!"

"Come with me!" I took her by the hand, running inside and rounding the hallway for the cellar, when a stiff wind blew my front door open. I clutched the bird tightly against the incoming gust that ripped my photos from the wall.

"In the cellar," I said, throwing open the door and pointing to the secret stairs behind the jackets. We hunkered down in the dark in the musty secret room with my front door flapping back and forth against the wall with intermittent bangs.

"Shh!" I shut my eyes when footsteps clunked across the floor from the salon to the kitchen and back again. The front door closed with a bang, and we squeezed each other. My heart pounded, my pulse thumping in my ears, my fingers tingling.

"Gaby?" I heard, and my eyes sprang open at the sound of Martine's voice. "Are you here?"

I gasped, oh so relieved, just as she opened the cellar door, shining a candle on me and Antoinette squinting behind the jackets. I almost collapsed after trying to stand.

"What are you doing in there?" she asked. "And Antoinette?" Rémy peered over Martine's shoulder, getting a look at us. I pulled Antoinette into the salon with me, scuttling against the wall. "Well?" Martine crossed her arms.

I felt my knotted hair, tangled from the wind, and gave it a swipe from my eyes. "I thought… I thought you'd left," I said.

"I told you I was coming back."

I was still shaking and fumbling my words when Martine gasped from seeing the bird tucked under my arm.

"Don't get mad," I said, but instead of looking at me, she'd settled her bulging eyes on Antoinette. "It's not Antoinette's fault. It was me. It's my scheme. I agreed."

"What scheme?"

"I broke into the commandant's file cabinet," I said.

She clamped both hands over her mouth. "I didn't agree to this."

I reached for her when she tried to walk away. "Martine, you should know I found out something—it's bigger than the U-boat pen and the Reich's oil facility."

"What is it?"

"I've uncovered the name of a German spy embedded within the British—in MI6—their secret services," I said.

Rémy had to help her into a chair.

"It's true," Antoinette said before Martine could question. "Both sides would kill for this information—one side to have it, the other to keep it buried. Only we have no way to dispatch it."

"What about the pigeon?" Martine asked.

"He won't fly," I said. "He runs back to the coop every chance he gets."

Rémy stepped into the light, searching the brim of his hat in his roughened hands. "I know a way."

We all three looked at Rémy. A sweet boy, a young man now, with the barest of evidence in his eyes of what forced labor had done to him.

"How?" I asked.

Antoinette edged forward. "Haven't you been working for

the Germans, someplace up north? How can we trust you?" she asked.

"Leave him alone," Martine said.

Antoinette squinted. "I'm not talking to you."

"You're talking to him, and that's talking to me," Martine said, and with that, I got between them even though Martine was still sitting. It was like no time had passed between her and Antoinette, and my sister forgot whose side our neighbor was on. I worried she was on the verge of calling her Marie Antoinette like she'd done so many other times.

"Settle down, Martine," I said. "She's right to ask about Rémy. She doesn't know him."

Martine pressed her lips together, giving in, which I was thankful for.

"Well?" Antoinette said to Rémy.

"I'm a good Frenchman who worked for the Germans because I was made to," Rémy said, eyes lifting. "A good Frenchman whose sister has a transmitter."

Martine threw her chair back when she stood. "What?"

"My sister, Hélène, has a transmitter," he repeated. "At least she did before I left for forced labor. I'll get in trouble for telling you, but I'm sure she'll understand after she hears what you have."

Martine wouldn't blink—I wasn't sure if she could blink—but stood staring at him, brow furrowed and trying to make sense of what he'd said. He'd mentioned it so casually, yet my pulse was racing. I took him by the shoulders. "Can you take us there now?" I asked, and he nodded.

I tossed the poor bird down the cellar after pulling the message from the capsule, and we left under the cover of the darkest night I could remember, not even a light from the harbor, just the blasted wind.

Hélène couldn't have been more surprised to see her beloved brother burst through her door. "Rémy!" They embraced near her table where she'd been listening to the radio on low and taking notes by candlelight. Her eyes drifted over his shoulder to Martine. "What's she doing here?" She pulled away. "All of you. What's going on?"

Rémy explained that Martine rescued him, which made Martine blush, and then told her what Antoinette and I had, which brought an excited smile to her face. "Is it true? You have the name of a spy?"

"Yes, we have it. Will you help us get a message to London?" Antoinette asked. "If you want the Germans out of France as much as we do…"

She straightened with her head held high. "Nobody hates the Germans more than me."

"What did you say?" Martine nudged her way to the front. "It's not just your voice… Your words. It's familiar. But also—"

"Nobody hates the Germans more than me," she repeated.

Martine's eyes widened. "You're the… the…" Martine's hand flew to her mouth. "The She Wolf!"

Hélène shrugged and gave a sly smirk. I expected nothing less from The She Wolf.

We shook her hand, but Martine was a little overzealous with her shake and Hélène had to pull her hand away. A moment of silence followed with only the faint scratch of music playing from Radio Londres. It didn't escape me that she hadn't answered Antoinette, because even for someone like Hélène, this was a dangerous request. "*Will* you help us?" I asked.

"I can't broadcast over the radio anymore, not since the Germans found my antenna. I'll have to code and transmit the message over a Paraset, and I can only allow thirty seconds."

"Thirty seconds?" I asked. That couldn't be enough time to get all the information sent. I reached for Antoinette's hand.

"I'm afraid so. The Germans can detect our location in a matter of minutes."

"All right. Thirty seconds. It will have to do."

We followed Hélène into a tiny dark room with a door that had been wallpapered to match the surrounding wall for concealment. She set her flickering candle down next to a metal case. "Now," she said, taking a chair, "what do you want me to say?" She broke the case open like a valise, exposing its wires and dials and switches.

I slid my music to her on the table. She checked the message over, making notes with her pencil before slipping on a pair of headphones. "Pray a lorry doesn't pull up or the message gets jammed." She handed Antoinette a watch, then switched the transmitter on, but it was my heart that was buzzing.

"Start the time," she said to Antoinette, and she began to tap out the message. There was so much to worry about. The Germans, the spy, if our message would be received or if we'd run out of time.

"Ten seconds," Antoinette announced, holding up the watch while Hélène tapped, tapped, tapped. I pulled my collar away from my neck, my heart slamming against my chest. "Five…"

"Done!" Hélène jumped up and turned the receiver off with a breathy gasp just as Antoinette belted out that time was up.

I held my chest, which was moist and warm. All of us took a restless sigh, realizing it had taken twenty-nine seconds.

"The Germans are deciphering your message right now, Gaby," Antoinette said. "And at the same time, so are the British."

"Now what do we do?" I asked.

"Sis, come quick!" Rémy said from the front room. "There's a broadcast."

He turned the volume up just slightly as we leaned in, hearing that all too familiar introduction to Beethoven's Fifth.

Bom, bom, bom, bom… Bom, bom, bom, bom…

"Maybe it's about the invasion," I said.

"Maybe it's too late," Antoinette said.

My stomach took a plunge.

"I interrupt your evening for a special message to our friends," the announcer said. Right away I could tell his voice wasn't the same.

"It's someone different," Martine whispered.

"Shh!"

"This message is to my heroine across the sea. You don't know my name, but I know yours." Martine looked at me when I covered my mouth. "A person will forget a melody, but they'll never forget how it made them feel in their heart," he said, and I was near breathless. "I will never forget. Hugh says hello. Take courage."

I stood in shock, my eyes fixed on the speaker, feeling my chest where I felt a stir.

"Who is Hugh?" Hélène asked.

"My God," Antoinette breathed. "It's a code—a code I was given to escape! They must know the Abwehr are searching for me."

"You must run! All of you," Hélène said, but I still couldn't move.

Hélène gave Antoinette what money she could spare, and half of the coins ended up on the floor, clinking and clanging around our feet as she scrambled to shove them into her pockets.

"But I just rescued Rémy," Martine said, shaking her head. "I don't want to leave!"

Rémy reached for her, kissing her madly and telling him he'd wait for her, but that she had to flee.

"Let's go!" Antoinette pulled me awkwardly out the door by the sleeve then reached for Martine too, but my gaze was still set on the radio, playing back that man's voice in my mind —what he said about me, my music, and feeling the thrum of his words, deeply.

We snuck away with Antoinette, hugging the outer edge of the village and avoiding German encampments by traveling a clandestine pathway she'd been briefed on—a network of sympathetic homes—often walking through their front doors and slipping out the back with the owners still asleep in their beds.

"Wait!" Martine said in the middle of nowhere. "Antoinette. Why did you turn me in?"

I closed my eyes. I'd been waiting for this question.

"You accused me of being a man, just so I had to prove it to disgusting collaborators."

Antoinette took a deep breath. "You have a right to know. It wasn't me."

"What? Who was it?" Even in the night, I could see Martine's mouth hanging open.

"Mme. Leroux," Antoinette confessed, and my hand went to my mouth. "I knew it was better for you to think it was me. It lent well to the reputation I was building."

"Mme. Leroux," Martine said through her teeth, turning to me. "After the war…"

"I'll go with you," I said.

Never in my life did I think I'd harbor a grudge, not like Martine could—she was an artist when it came to grudges in the same way a pianist experiments with tone and articulation —but knowing the truth about Mme Leroux, and that she'd turned Martine in while we were giving her illegal rations, deserved a visit so I could at least say my piece.

I nudged Martine to keep walking, but she resisted with a fold of her arms. She wasn't done.

"Something else you want to ask? Now's your chance," Antoinette said. "I have nothing to hide."

"Why did you leave us to rot in that jail? You didn't even have the decency to tell Simone where we were. She had to hear about it from Madame Roche, and thank God she did because we could have been in there for—"

"Who do you think told Madame Roche?" she asked, and now it was my mouth that hung open. "I knew she was a friend of yours, and she'd waste no time getting the news to Simone when I couldn't. It would have looked suspicious if I told Simone directly, and my cover would have been blown for helping you without a payment or favor in return. Spreading it to Madame as gossip was the best choice."

Martine uncrossed her arms, and what came from her mouth was a surprise, even after learning all we had about

Antoinette. "Well then, in that case, I'm sorry for eating your chicken. And for calling you several names, most you don't know about, but I'll leave you to guess what they were."

She smiled, and they shook hands. The feud between Martine and Antoinette was finally over, and we were able to walk on, and while Martine thought about Rémy, and Antoinette thought about the escape, I was still thinking about the announcer on the radio who'd listened to my music... Called me his heroine.

"He was talking to me, wasn't he?" I asked, as if not sure, or perhaps I just needed validation. "On the radio—what he said about my music and feelings and never forgetting?"

Martine wrapped her arm over my shoulders. "I heard it."

"I heard it too," Antoinette said.

"He must have been the one who received the messages, and Professor Caron must have played my music for him." He'd listened to my work, and I felt oddly connected to this stranger in a way I couldn't explain.

"But Gaby, you're in the resistance now that you're with me," Antoinette said, as if she knew I was thinking much more into it, and into him. "It's probably best you put all thoughts of him aside. He's a world away, across the sea, and we are still occupied by the Germans."

I nodded, though a little part of me would carry his words and the sound of his voice in my heart where nobody would know.

The sun had started to rise, turning the sky shadowy blue instead of dead black. Antoinette stopped abruptly, making us duck in the bushes. "Don't say anything. Don't react. Do you trust me?"

I peeked over the hedges to see where we were. "We're at that prison!"

"Oh no," Martine said, trying to retreat, but Antoinette pulled her back.

"We must," Antoinette said. "It was the message dispatched over Radio Londres. Hugh is the code to flee to this prison, a place of safety. You'll have to trust me. A transport will come for us there."

Antoinette pulled me up by the sleeve to walk, and I pulled Martine's. The prison was as I remembered, damp and dim and smelling of urine. Antoinette slipped the guard the money Hélène had given us. They both nodded after whispering a secret conversation. Shortly after, he led us down the corridor to the last cell, where it was even darker and smellier with bodily fluids. I gagged, holding my arm to my mouth and nose, and trying not to vomit.

"Now what do we do?" Martine asked.

"We wait," Antoinette said.

———

A couple days had passed then we were finally escorted out of the cell and into a line of raggedly dressed agents like us, also fleeing. We climbed into a lorry, squashing in together like cockles in a jar before taking off, but to where I didn't know; into the country was my guess. I rested my head on Martine's shoulder as we jostled and swayed on an uneven road, only to sit bolt upright when I heard a downshift of gears.

My heart sped up.

I worried we were being stopped, then was sure of it when I saw the others' strained faces.

"Be brave," someone whispered a moment before the engine cut off.

Martine clenched my hand. Voices could be heard, the driver arguing with a German about prisoners for exchange, a rougher prison, and on official orders.

"Open it up!" we heard, and every agent in the back stiffened.

The back hatch sprang open to a burst of headlamps shining on us, and a German officer in uniform demanding a look at our faces. He climbed up, and I held my breath.

Antoinette instinctively folded like a piece of wet laundry and lay limp near his jackboots, which drew a disdainful gasp.

"She's sick," I said, followed by Martine who said she might have tuberculosis, which got him to step away, and everyone else too. He locked the hatch back up and the engine roared with life.

Nobody said a word.

We moved Antoinette back into her seat, where she gave us a wink, and I finally took a breath.

We drove for what felt like another hour or so.

"When the lorry stops," Antoinette said suddenly, holding onto my hand, "whatever you do, don't let go."

"Why?" I asked. "Where are we going?" Martine reached for my other hand, holding on tight.

"Just don't let go. Don't lose me." Antoinette sat up, then some of the others stood. The guard held onto the latch, telling us to get ready to run, then everyone was standing, even Martine and I.

The lorry slowed down. "Go!" The guard pressed down on the latch and the doors opened up to torrential rain. People spilled out the back and vanished into the shadows. Antoinette jumped out almost last, taking me with her onto a sloshy muddy road, but Martine had lost her grip and stood at the back of the hatch refusing to jump, with the lorry moving slowly away from us.

"Jump!" I pleaded, but she shook her head, too afraid to take the leap.

Antoinette ran after the lorry and pulled Martine out of it by the hand. They landed in the mud together and lay there with the red taillights glimmering off puddles in the road, before they sat up and hugged each other.

"Where are we?" I said to Antoinette, but she'd scrambled to her feet and pointed off into the dark countryside.

"We head this way," she said, leading us into a field that felt exposed and eerie, especially in the rain, since it was hard to hear anything other than thunder and the sharp spat of the rain on soggy wheat.

Then I saw a light, a single candle in a glass windowpane flickering dimly. We followed a fence, one for horses it looked like, but I didn't see any horses. I didn't even see the house, just the light against the glass, until I got closer. Antoinette opened the front door and I saw the other agents who'd made it, then I heard a familiar voice and my heart jumped.

"Gaby? Martine?" It was Simone and she came rushing toward us.

We collapsed into her arms, sobbing.

The man who knew my name, who'd heard my music, had given Antoinette the codeword that delivered us to a safe house, but not any safe house. The one where Christian had brought my sister and their baby.

I took a deep breath of Simone's Chantilly-scented hair, and it was soft. So very soft against my face.

"I was so worried about you when I heard about the invasion," she said, "but I had hope in my heart, and now you're here!"

We pulled away. "An invasion?" I held my chest.

"The Americans landed this morning. Took the Germans by surprise. Normandy."

"Surprise?" My legs felt like jelly when she said it was a surprise. I turned to Antoinette at the same time Martine did and we congratulated each other on a job well done.

Simone looked at us strangely. "Are you involved in another scheme?"

"We gave up schemes. Didn't we, Martine?" I elbowed Martine.

Martine wiped her eyes of tears. "No more schemes. It's over."

We hugged again, this time squeezing each other as we'd never squeezed before.

Chapter Twenty-Seven

Hitler declared Boulogne-sur-Mer a fortress after D-Day and encircled it with kilometers and kilometers of military emplacements. Guy scoured reports looking for any scrap of news regarding The Heroines' escape and fate, but despite the French people's best efforts, very little information was getting in or out of the heavily defended area.

Yet, still, Guy was hopeful.

Hope was all he had left.

Guy sat in his car with Professor Caron outside Latchmere House in Ham, where the most dangerous and secretive spies were held for interrogation, a place so secret the Secret Intelligence Service often denied that the former Victorian home was even the property of the War Office. He gazed out of his windshield and up to the high windows where he thought he saw shadows moving through the glass, thinking only of Clive Cox—that dirty double-crosser.

He was in one of those rooms, somewhere, and after weeks of being told Clive wasn't a guest at Latchmere House, Guy and Professor Caron were granted permission to visit after the brass pulled some strings.

Maybe Guy would talk to him, or maybe he wouldn't say anything at all. One thing was for sure, his visit would end with a slug to Clive's nose. Guy felt he needed that, and so did Professor Caron.

"Ready?" he asked.

The professor nodded sternly. "Ready, Mr. Burton."

As Guy walked up to the front doors with the professor, he noted a soldier with a rifle pacing the ramparts, giving him the eye. He gathered not many people walked through the front doors of Latchmere and lived to tell about it, and the thought of never walking back out gave him a shiver.

Guy and Professor Caron checked in with the guards, passing through the gated reception of the former private estate, before being brought into a special room where they'd finally get the chance to tell Clive what they thought of him. The ornately carved furniture had been replaced by basic wood chairs, but the botanical wallpaper remained, sun-bleached in areas, with the faintest outline of a potted fern that had once grown in the corner.

"He'll be in soon." The guard waited with them.

Guy smelled dust coming from the fabric curtains, made worse when the guard closed them, blocking most of the light.

The professor gripped her handbag fiercely in anticipation while the guard watched Guy.

"You worked with this traitor?" he asked, and Guy nodded. "At MI6?"

Guy nodded again. Nobody wanted to be known as the

agent who'd been had, and he waited for the guard to insult him for sharing an office with a traitor, but instead, he offered something Guy hadn't heard about prison number thirty-six.

"He's the most dubious person we've ever met," he said. "He'll lie straight to your face, and it could be about anything, about what he ate for breakfast, and you'd swear he was telling the truth, but nothing that comes out of his mouth is the truth. He's a master liar. Thank God your agents found out who he was before it was too late. He'd fooled everyone at the War Office, even the top brass."

"Was his wife at home when he was arrested?" Guy asked, thinking of all the times Clive mentioned his wife, her dinners, and those photos of her around his desk. He was a double-crosser, but Guy hoped his wife had been spared.

"That was another of his lies. Didn't have a wife."

Guy's mouth hung open, then his lips pursed when he heard the thud of footsteps and the jingle of chains coming down the hallway.

The guard opened the door to a downtrodden Clive, shuffling into the room with his head down and bringing with him the odor of iron and sweat. He looked worse than Guy expected, with slicks of hair dangling over his eyes, and beard stubble months in the making, though he shouldn't have been surprised, given the rumors about Latchmere House and their interrogations.

"That's the man who wrecked my studio," the professor said, jaw clenched.

Clive looked up, giving the professor a snarky smile, and with that, he unleashed a beast.

The professor came at Clive ready for a gun battle, when Clive only had what was left of his wits. "You!" she bellowed, finger pointing, followed by a tirade of French words that nobody could understand even if they spoke French. Clive took a stumbling step back that ended with him falling to the floor in a twist of shackles as she loomed over him like a giant, despite her tiny size.

The professor held onto the wall once she was done, taking an empowered deep breath.

"You want to say something?" The guard asked Guy.

Guy watched Clive struggle on the floor, a shred of a man and nearly dead. He thought about the danger Clive had imposed on his country, the world, and how he tried to expose Gaby and her sisters. Instead of feeling angry, as he'd expected, Guy felt deeply satisfied at seeing a chained Clive Cox on his back and not able to get up, and any slug to the nose would have cheapened the moment.

Guy shook his head. "Turns out, I got what I came for," he said, and Clive's eyes lifted, straining to see Guy as he turned to the professor. "Shall we, Professor Caron? The sun is out, and it's such a nice day for a cup of tea in the shade. Would you like one?" He stepped over Clive like a squashed bug and offered the professor his arm.

The professor lifted her chin. "Oh yes, that sounds lovely, Mr. Burton," she said, locking arms with Guy and walking out of the interrogation room as if they owned Latchmere, and the guards, and also knowing that while they walked out, Clive Cox never would.

Outside, Rex Smith drove up in a flurry, shooting pebbles out from under the tires and lurching to a stop just next to Guy's car before they could leave.

"Guy!" He ran around the side of his car to a shocked Guy

Burton and took him by the shoulders. "Boulogne-sur-Mer has been liberated."

Guy was speechless, and part of him wondered if he heard him right.

"Does this mean—" Professor Caron started to ask.

"They escaped," Smith said, "before the Germans made the village a fortress. And…"

"And what, sir?" Guy held his breath.

"We have reason to believe Gaby will be making her way home soon."

With a hand to his mouth, Guy slumped onto his car bonnet. Part of him couldn't believe it. "How do you know?" he asked, because Smith sounded like he'd talked to someone who'd talked to Gaby, or at least someone who knew her well.

"The Cotillard sisters have connections to a résistant our agents in the region have been working with. We have every reason to trust him. He called Gaby his sister-in-law, so he must be married to one of her sisters."

Skipping the handshake, both Professor Caron and Guy hugged each other.

Guy had already requested a transfer to France, just as soon as Boulogne-sur-Mer was liberated, in order to collect data and take reports from agents formerly under siege. Now he had even more reason to celebrate.

He turned to Smith, but before he could get his question out, Smith blurted, "I've set up a flight for you this afternoon."

Guy packed his rucksack for France and went downstairs to tell Madge and the professor goodbye, but this time his sister was the one pacing the carpets.

"I don't understand," she said. "You didn't slug that traitor in the nose?"

Guy placed his hands on her shoulders. "I love you, sis."

She broke away to pace some more, only now she was twisting her hands. "And now you're leaving for France, but the war isn't over. What if you're shot down?" She placed the back of her hand on her forehead.

"The war isn't over, but the battle for Boulogne-sur-Mer is. I know a safe route. Trust me," he said.

She threw her hands up.

"Sis, this is what you prayed for. Isn't it?"

Madge stopped pacing and took a deep breath before nodding. "You're right." She gave him a warm embrace, and he went back to his rucksack, tightening the buckles.

"But what are you going to *do*?" she asked, and Guy looked up.

He knew what his sister meant, and by the look on the professor's face, she was wondering the same question. What was he planning to say to Gabriella Cotillard? Walk up to her home and confess his love for her? She'd be smart to run away if he did that. No, he wasn't that kind of man. He was, however, the kind that made sure his agents were safe, and that they were thanked.

"I'm going to thank her for her courage, what she did for the world, and what she did for me. That's all I can ask for—to meet her and thank her. These are my hopes," he said, though deep in his heart he hoped for more.

"Hope," Madge said. "That's a word you don't hear much anymore."

"Well, Mr. Burton," Professor Caron said. "Those are wonderful things to hope for."

After giving his sis another hug goodbye, and promising the professor to give her regards to Gaby, he left for the airfield at Newmarket for his flight to northern France, though this time the flight was legally in the diary and they were expecting him.

The airfield was abuzz with activity, quite different from the last time he was there, just before D-Day. He walked up to the hangar with his rucksack slung over one shoulder, and the mechanic looked up from the front desk, wrench in his hand.

"I'm here for the flight to Boulogne-sur-Mer," Guy said.

After looking in the logbook, the mechanic pointed with his chin to the Whitley getting ready on the tarmac. Guy made his way toward the plane.

"Hey, aren't you that bloke…" the mechanic started to say, but a plane roared by on the tarmac heading for takeoff, allowing Guy to pretend he didn't hear.

"What's that?" Guy asked, cupping his ear, because he had no intention of admitting he was the one who'd stolen the car from the parking lot.

"Never mind," he said.

Guy was glad to keep walking, but was met with another unwelcome surprise when his pilot turned around.

Bob.

"You!" Bob said, and Guy smiled because he wasn't sure what else to do. "I should have known. No pigeons this time, I see."

"No pigeons." Guy handed him the flight plans and Bob gave them a brief look before lighting up his cigarette.

"You know there's still a war going on."

"I know," Guy said. "But Boulogne-sur-Mer has been liberated. You won't be shot at this time."

"You're on official war business, right?"

Bob didn't have the right to question him, since his flight was legally in the diary, but Guy still felt he owed him an explanation, considering what happened last time. Guy decided to tell him the truth.

"I think I'm in love with my agent in the field—a woman I've never met—and now's my chance to meet her. Might be my only chance." Guy smiled, and Bob laughed from his belly.

"Son, you better come up with a better story because if we do get shot down and the Germans question you—we don't have a chance." He tossed his cigarette. "Get in."

Guy climbed up into the Whitley and took a seat. Bob started the plane and began his takeoff just as another pilot burst from the hangar along with the mechanic, waving and yelling. Neither Bob nor Guy could hear what they were saying, though Guy had a pretty good idea.

"You know him?" Bob shouted over his shoulder to Guy.

"I think I stole his car," he said.

Bob laughed again. "Hold on!"

Chapter Twenty-Eight

The day the Americans came, we said our goodbyes to our hosts, filled with gratitude, but also angst at what we might find at home—who'd survived and who had not. Christian came and went, but promised he'd meet Simone and their baby in Boulogne-sur-Mer once the Germans were pushed out. They'd been married in the garden at night just after the invasion, when it was safe for them, and it was beautiful.

Antoinette and Martine stole us a car with a full tank of petrol from a German who'd left it behind. We crept back home along with thousands of others, across burning fields littered with dead cattle and bodies of servicemen who'd fought and died for the nameless good French who would never be able to thank them. American soldiers marched along with us, not going much faster than we drove. The British came next, followed by the Canadians.

I thought I'd never forget the smell of our little village near the sea, where lilac and sea mist moistened the air, but once we crested the harbor, the smells of war, the cinder and bomb haze from weeks past, replaced my memories. Church roofs toppled inward, and entire streets and neighborhoods where homes once stood were reduced to rubble, which of course made us worry about Madame Roche's fate, and Rémy's, if they'd stayed in the village.

"I'm scared," Martine would say, and Simone would remind her to have hope, which Martine now took to heart after all that had happened.

We drove as close as we could to the center of the village, then had to walk the rest of the way, since we were following the pack, and the pack had turned into a parade through the center of Boulogne-sur-Mer.

Word that we'd come home spread like wildfire when the four of us walked up the street to the sewing shop, Simone carrying her baby proudly in her arms, and Martine, Antoinette, and myself walking with locked arms behind her. We didn't know if we'd be punished or revered, hearing some of the bad French women were being dragged from their homes and humiliated in the streets, but the humbling thanks we received from the first group of shopkeepers let us know they knew what we had done, and that we weren't traitors.

"I'm sorry," we heard from some of those who passed us. "I never believed." But these Frenchmen, with French flags draped over their shoulders and toasting the Canadian troops marching through the village, were the same Frenchmen who'd had black ribbons tied to their doorknobs without protest and spread vicious lies and gossip. The baker was the first to bring us a loaf of bread. Martine didn't want Simone to take it, but she did, and she did it with grace.

"Thank you," she simply said, before turning her back.

Martine pointed to our sewing shop, and I gasped, but I wasn't surprised.

The windows were broken, and what sewing supplies and machinery had survived the raids and robberies since we'd been gone were now scattered to the ocean breezes, but Madame Roche's lock shop survived intact, and we were relieved to see her outside and standing guard by her door. "Not one of those Boche-bastards bothered to question me," Madame said, as if almost offended. "I had a hand in the deception too!"

I gave her a hug. "Of course you did."

"Simone!" Christian came out of nowhere, and just like he'd said he would, he'd met her by the sea. He ushered her into a safe spot on the pavement where they could reunite properly with a full-mouth kiss and a pet of his son's head.

Simone told him that although she loved the idea of living in the country, she couldn't bear the thought of being separated from her sisters again. He kissed her over and over again, telling her that they'd settle in Boulogne-sur-Mer if that's what she wanted.

Antoinette gave me and Martine each a kiss on our cheek as if she was leaving.

"Where are you going?" I asked.

"I have something—someone—to take care of," she said, which drew a raised eyebrow from Martine. "It won't be pleasant for them." Antoinette smiled, and I thought Martine would remind me that I'd promised to see Mme. Leroux with her, but she was too busy looking over the crowds for Rémy. "I'll see you later." Then Antoinette was off, disappearing into the mob of people before us.

Madame Roche had no news for me about my house,

saying the bombing was an incredible sight—everyone had taken cover. She still didn't know why her building, out of all the ones in the shopping district, had survived such blasts. "Wait!" She grabbed my arm. "Maybe it's because of my good heart," she said.

"That's it," I said. "Your good heart." I winked at Martine, who winked back.

Through the crowd and far away we heard someone yelling for Martine. It was alarming at first with the chaos of the crowd, with most people yelling for someone to punish, but this one was a man's voice. A sweet man's voice.

Martine latched onto me, weighing me down. "It's Rémy!" Her mouth hung open as if she didn't believe it really was him. "It's him! I had hope, just like Simone said. And look!" She pointed.

"What are you waiting for?" I asked. "Go to him!"

She smiled breathlessly before running toward him into the crowd as he jostled his way through, until they met in the middle with a crashing force, kissing madly.

Madame Roche and I watched. "Well, that's odd," Madame said. "I thought Martine would stay single. End up like me one day." She shrugged. "I suppose war has a way of changing people."

They walked over to me, smiling gleefully and clutching each other like a life preserver. Rémy handed me a piece of paper he pulled from his pocket, which I recognized right away as my last surviving piece of sheet music—the last of The Heroines—which I'd left next to his sister's transmitter because it was too dangerous to take with me. "My sister wanted you to have this."

I was thankful she'd saved it, and at great cost to her if it had been found before the liberation. I felt the folds, the sharp creases. It would have to be a souvenir now since the rest of the work was lost—some in Paris, some in England, and one sheet lost in the sea, I presumed. A lone sheet was just a reminder of all the other sheets still missing.

"Please tell your sister thank you. She is well, I assume, since she gave this to you?"

Martine tugged on Rémy's arm from behind; she was not letting go, and she also wanted him to herself. "Yes, she is well." He turned back for Martine and they kissed and kissed and kissed.

Though not everyone was getting a kiss. Some of the bad French had been rounded up in the street and put on display like we'd heard about, heckled and stripped of their clothing even in front of their children.

Madame saw me grimacing. "Don't look, if it bothers you."

"Do you know what happened to Commandant Streicher's wife and her child, Lauren?"

"I haven't heard, but he was captured a few days ago dressed as a French peasant and trying to board a boat to Britain. Wasn't hard to point him out. Cried like a baby when they dragged him away," she said, then laughed to herself. "I hope he rots in hell."

I was glad he'd been caught but was a little disappointed she didn't know about Danielle and Lauren.

Madame Roche wished me luck with what I'd find at home, and when I walked away, I started to prepare myself to find nothing at all. I'd survived and that was all that mattered, I thought, though deep down it wasn't all that mattered, and when I saw the shell of the home that used to stand so grand, my stomach sank.

"*Mon Dieu*," I breathed.

I stepped through the front door carefully, feet crunching on glass, wiping away the tears that had welled in my eyes.

The windows were shattered and the roof had caved in, and hardly anything was left of my aunt's private apartment but that awful blue bookcase the captain had painted, which for some reason made me smile. The creaking old stairs Martine used to pound up and down were still half attached, and Simone's coat was still hanging on a hook as if she'd never left and didn't have someone of her own to love, but she had, and Martine had too, and now I was the only one left.

Brick had tumbled out from behind plaster, and the photos of me and my sisters were scattered about, bent and creased and rained on.

My eyes lifted to my piano.

Strangely untouched, it stood glossy and black against the rubble with a lone flower and a letter folded nicely on top, only it wasn't just a letter. It was a piece of music from Lauren, something she'd composed, with a note on the back.

I covered my mouth, oh so glad she was all right.

Mademoiselle, I hope this note finds you well. Do you remember what you told me the day you left? I have 44 coins in my pocket, and my mama has a place for us to go. Sorry I missed you, but we must rush away.

P.S. These biscuits were not made by the cook. I stole them from someone else.

Next to the note, she'd also left two biscuits wrapped in a lace doily, which warmed my heart. I laughed out loud. It was just like Lauren to leave me a biscuit breakfast.

I dusted off the bench and sat down, cracking my knuckles and stretching out my hands, and just before I laid my fingers on the keys, I wished I had The Heroines back and in one piece. It was part of me in a way I'd never realized before. And like this house, and this life, I would have to find a way to rebuild it, brick by brick.

"Hallo?" A man walked in, scaring me half to death and causing me to leap to my feet, which he promptly apologized for.

"Yes?" He was attractive with wavy, sandy-blond hair, and didn't sound French even though he had a believable accent. He must be lost, I thought. "Can I help you?"

He smoothed a wavy lock away from his eyes before clearing his throat. "I'm looking for..." he said in French. "Are you..." He stepped closer, examining me while I stood, and it was then I noticed his eyes. Blue with dark lashes. "Gaby?"

I placed a hand on my chest. "Yes. That's me. Who are you?" I asked, but I could have sworn I'd heard his voice before.

"I'm Guy Burton. Sorry to intrude," he said, stepping over the glass, and glancing at his feet as if he was ashamed he even had to do it, but the glass was everywhere. "However, I've traveled quite a distance to come here and meet you." He pulled a wad of papers from his brown bag, and I thought he might be a messenger. Something else from Lauren, or maybe her mother, because who else would know where I was?

I motioned for the papers, only they weren't just papers or letters, they were sheets.

I gasped, looking up, the breath shocked out of me, when I found myself holding my composition—though now yellowy and pasted back together where the pages had been torn—

even the sheets I'd left behind in Paris. "Where did you get these?" I asked, flipping through them.

"I'm from British Intelligence. Professor Caron sends her regards and plans to visit once it's safe. We've become good friends." He cleared his throat again, but this time he looked a little nervous.

"It was you." I gulped. "You were the person who received my messages—you were the one I heard on the radio, weren't you?" But what was in my heart, what was on my mind, was when he'd said he'd listened to my music, and that he'd never forget how it made him feel.

"I tried to do better. I attempted to steal a plane on the eve of the invasion, fly over here and rescue you from the Abwehr, but I was stopped by one angry pilot." He laughed to himself, then straightened. "What you did was very brave. Exposing Clive Cox, and sending the pigeons."

"You tried to rescue me?" I asked.

"You're my agent." He smiled. "I'd do anything to protect you, but I can see now that you made it to the safe house in good condition and are well," he said, which made me blush, and I reached up to tuck a lock of hair behind my ear.

My eyes trailed to Lauren's biscuit breakfast, and for a split second, I thought, how silly. France was in the throes of being liberated and the Germans were retreating. Surely, a secret British agent had other pressing matters to attend to in France than to share a plate of biscuits in the morning and listen to me play, but looking at him as he stood in a twist of light shining through the exposed roof, I wondered, what did I have to lose?

My palms had turned a little sweaty. "Would you like me to play it for you? I mean, you came all this way." I was prepared for him to say no, but then he sat down next to me on the bench.

"I thought you'd never ask."

"You don't have somewhere pressing to go? Back to Britain or—"

"No," he said. "In fact, I took a transfer here so I could stay and help with the intelligence gathering in Europe."

"Oh?" I smiled, and even with the tumbled bricks that used to be my home largely at our feet, the strangest thing had happened—it was what Simone had talked about and Martine already knew.

My heart fluttered, and what came with it was a feeling, something I could only describe as…

Hope.

And I began to play.

Author's Note

The story of Gaby, Simone, and Martine was inspired by the real-life story of the Debaillie family of Lichtervelde, Belgium, who were given one of Columba's pigeons, and then had to decide what to do with it. As with Gaby, Simone, and Martine, there were different opinions on what it meant to be a patriot; some of the family members wanted to use the pigeon and send intelligence, while others did not. It wasn't an easy decision for various reasons, but in the end, they decided to use the pigeon rather than destroy or eat it.

I found the Debaillies' story by complete accident while writing *A Child for the Reich*. What intrigued me the most about Columba and the Debaillies' story, and other families that used the messenger pigeons dropped by parachute, was that these were regular people. They had no formal spy training or much support. They were citizens of an occupied land, doing their best with what they had, and when presented with an opportunity, they acted; sometimes they acted rashly and made mistakes, but their hearts were always in the right place.

The dual narrative with Guy and the pushback from the brass regarding his pigeon program was also inspired by the real MI14 agents who faced difficulties with Columba. As with The Heroines, there were hiccups along the way, delays, and mishaps, all exacerbated by the impending invasion, the need for secrecy and deception, and the intricacies of the Debaillie family operating in secret among the watchful Germans.

This is a work of fiction, and I took certain liberties when necessary to craft a compelling story. However, Gaby, Simone, and Martine's living conditions and what they endured were inspired by interviews, reports, articles, and diaries of those who lived through the occupation, specifically those who lived in the northern and coastal areas of France. I was particularly drawn to the stories involving village gossip, rumors, and the behavior between "good French" and the "bad French." Family members kept secrets from each other, and in most cases, even secrets with good intentions had disastrous outcomes. The sister who wanted to be honest with her siblings struggled with the part of herself that wanted to remain guarded, for various reasons, most of which were personal.

I was inspired to make Gaby a pianist after reading about Le Six, which was a group of musicians in Paris—five men and one woman—who were scattered to the wind during the war. I wondered what it would have been like for a woman, who was on the cusp of making a name for herself at the beginning of her career, to then be put in a position where she'd have to destroy her life's work for the greater good, without guarantee of success. I don't think it would have been an easy choice.

Years after my grandfather passed away, my grandmother (who was in her eighties at the time) decided to remarry. She told me that one of the things she missed about being married was sharing breakfast with the person she loved; it was where they connected before the day had begun. This conversation, and how she described the simplest joys of companionship, stayed with me. I wanted to show this through Guy and Gaby, especially since both had been through so much with their past relationships and in the war.

Thank you for choosing to read *The Secret Pianist*. If you enjoyed this story about my heroine sisters, Gaby, Simone, and Martine, please consider leaving a review. I also invite you to check out my other books, *A Child for the Reich*, *The Girls from the Beach*, *The Girl from Vichy*, and *The Girl I Left Behind*.

Thank you!

Acknowledgments

I'd like to thank Charlotte Ledger at HarperCollins UK and the amazing team at One More Chapter. Thank you to the staff at The Kate Nash Literary Agency and in particular my stellar agent Kate Nash, who has suffered through countless emails from me; I am a girl with questions! I have an amazing writing tribe whose support has been invaluable, and I can't thank them enough: authors Aimee Brown, Sandy Barker, Fiona Leitch, Nina Kaye, Paula Butterfield (who reads all my first drafts), Casey King, and Terry Lynn Thomas. Fiona, especially, who read through Guy's chapters and answered all my questions about being British—I had a lot! Thank you to the talented Annastasia Workman, a musician who thankfully didn't run away after receiving a printed copy of my book in the mail (if you've ever seen a novel printed out, you know what I'm talking about), and read through all my musical elements. Thank you to my family, and especially my husband, Matt, and my two kids, Zane, and Drew, for their endless support. Last but not least, thank you to the readers out there who have bought and enjoyed my books.

The author and One More Chapter would like to thank everyone
who contributed to the publication of this story...

Analytics
Abigail Fryer
Maria Osa

Audio
Fionnuala Barrett
Ciara Briggs

Contracts
Georgina Hoffman
Florence Shepherd

Design
Lucy Bennett
Fiona Greenway
Holly Macdonald
Liane Payne
Dean Russell

Digital Sales
Lydia Grainge
Emily Scorer
Georgina Ugen

Editorial
Arsalan Isa
Charlotte Ledger
Bonnie Macleod
Jennie Rothwell
Tony Russell
Caroline Scott-
Bowden
Emily Thomas
Kimberley Young

International Sales
Bethan Moore

Marketing & Publicity
Chloe Cummings
Emma Petfield

Operations
Melissa Okusanya
Hannah Stamp

Production
Emily Chan
Denis Manson
Francesca Tuzzeo

Rights
Lana Beckwith
Rachel McCarron
Agnes Rigou
Hany Sheikh
Mohamed
Zoe Shine
Aisling Smyth

**The HarperCollins
Distribution Team**

**The HarperCollins
Finance & Royalties
Team**

**The HarperCollins
Legal Team**

**The HarperCollins
Technology Team**

Trade Marketing
Ben Hurd
Eleanor Slater

UK Sales
Laura Carpenter
Isabel Coburn
Jay Cochrane
Tom Dunstan
Sabina Lewis
Erin White
Harriet Williams
Leah Woods

**And every other
essential link in the
chain from delivery
drivers to booksellers
to librarians and
beyond!**